DELIVERANCE

SAIMA MIR

A POINT BLANK BOOK

First published in Great Britain, the Republic of Ireland and Australia
by Point Blank, an imprint of Oneworld Publications Ltd, 2026

Copyright © Saima Mir, 2026

The moral right of Saima Mir to be identified as the
Author of this work has been asserted by her in accordance
with the Copyright, Designs and Patents Act 1988

ISBN 978-1-83643-189-3
eISBN 978-1-83643-188-6

Typeset by Geethik Technologies
Printed and bound in Great Britain by Clays Ltd, Elcograf S.p.A.

This book is a work of fiction. Names, characters, businesses,
organisations, places and events are either the product of the author's
imagination or are used fictitiously. Any resemblance to actual
persons, living or dead, events or locales is entirely coincidental.

The authorised representative in the EEA is eucomply OÜ,
Pärnu mnt 139b–14, 11317 Tallinn, Estonia
(email: hello@eucompliancepartner.com / phone: +33757690241)

Oneworld Publications Ltd
10 Bloomsbury Street
London WC1B 3SR
England

Stay up to date with the latest books,
special offers, and exclusive content from
Oneworld with our newsletter

Sign up on our website
oneworld.co.uk

'I'm just speechless and spellbound by Saima Mir's brilliant follow up to *The Khan*. It is an incredibly rare occurrence for a sequel to be as good as or better than the original. Saima Mir's *Vengeance* not only lives up to its predecessor's reputation but equals it.'

Surjit Reads and Recommends

'A tight and tense thriller set in the heart of a British Pakistani crime network… You can't not get drawn in.'

Bookbag

Praise for *The Khan*

A *Times* Bestseller
A *Times* & *Sunday Times* Best Crime Books of 2021
A Waterstones Thriller of the Month

'A fascinating glimpse into a world rarely portrayed in fiction.'

Guardian, best crime and thrillers

'Bold, addictive and brilliant.'

Stylist, Best Fiction 2021

'Compelling and gritty.'

Cosmopolitan

'A Bradford take on *The Godfather*.'

Mail on Sunday, best new fiction

To twenty-one-year-old me. You were always enough.

PROLOGUE

'You were just a fucking whore,' he said. 'You would have died on the streets if it weren't for me.'

The words brought with them the rancid taste of days she'd rather forget.

They scuttled out of his mouth, into her ears and down her throat, but she swallowed and held her nerve.

'You've been accused of skimming from the take,' she said, her arms folded across her black blazer. 'The Khan has asked me to look into the matter.' Her composure was faultless. You didn't rise through the ranks of Jia Khan's organisation unless you were strong, your emotions locked, your mind sharp.

He spat on the mottled concrete in front of her, his eyes boring holes into her asbestos eyes, resistant to all forms of degradation. 'You remember this place?' he said.

She did. This was the multistorey where she'd turned her first trick.

Sakina knew her enemies and their swords well. She understood that a secret was a grenade, and this was why she had none.

That she had exchanged her warm body for cold cash was known throughout the city, so Khalid's insult fell flat at her feet. She rolled it back and forth, considering what to do with it.

Khalid had been there with her, had held her hand as she'd cried after the first punter had taken her in the back seat of his car. He'd wiped her tears, spoken kind words and then readied her for the next john.

'You're bringing trouble to my door, accusing me of stealing. Shit. I ain't done nothing!' he raged at her when she failed to react.

Sakina knew men, knew their fragile egos – and the structures that held them up – well enough not to be surprised by his words. She knew he was lying. She'd seen the books, spoken to the girls and done the mathematics that paid his salary.

She saw him for what he was, a weak and sad man, and her only regret was that she'd relied on him when she'd been working these streets.

His face slithered as he looked from her to his friend, who was leaning against a grey Volkswagen Golf. Surrounded by pimped rides, from the red Audi RS3 to the black AMG Mercedes and white M4 BMW, the man clearly thought himself a lesson in aura farming. 'Cars are to this city what shoes are to Carrie Bradshaw,' Khalid had said to Sakina back in the days when she had mistaken him for a friend.

Those days were in the past.

'You know what?' Khalid said. 'I'm sick of the shit that you women have been pulling since Jia Khan took you on. I'm done with it. Even my wife's been giving it backchat.' He'd had enough of the complaining and the constant demands. The arguments rang in his ears like tinnitus, day and night, and they were getting louder.

He looked at Sakina. She might be dressed in a black Dior suit, her hair tied back, her shirt pristine, but she was still a prostitute. He leaned in towards her, the scent of Frédéric Malle softening his senses the way money does a hard life. 'Once a whore, always a whore,' he said.

Sakina wiped the words from her shoulder and looked him in the eye. Men like Khalid didn't frighten her. They had once, but those days had clambered off with her innocence.

He knew that, and that was why he was flailing. Every move and every look she made was a siren, bursting his eardrums with the cry that she didn't need him. And if a woman like her didn't need his help and had no fear of him, what woman would?

Khalid was incensed.

'She's Punjabi, she ain't no Pathan,' he said to his mate, whose face was a multitude of unreadable emotions. 'Ain't no one coming for her.'

The anger coloured his vision, took over his senses, and he hit her. It wasn't a slap. It was a clenched fist full of rage and power, the kind men usually reserved for men, their equals in this world, in life and work. And she deserved it. By the time his fist made contact with her face, though, an inkling of what he'd done began to trickle through. But it was too late.

He was about to punch Sakina again, when she blocked him, grabbing and twisting his hand so swiftly that he didn't have time to react, and when she bent his wrist back, the pain that spread along his nerve all the way to his shoulder was unlike anything he'd ever felt.

'You moron! Don't you know whose bird she is?' said his friend, coming between them. He'd been watching from the sidelines, aware that to get involved was to invoke death. 'You absolute idiot. You're dead. And I ain't havin' no part of it.' He backed away fast.

By this time, Sakina had shoved Khalid hard. He hit the bonnet of the blue BMW behind him, sliding down and on to the floor, the car alarm beeping loudly, its orange lights flashing as if signalling the danger to come.

'Once an arsehole, always an arsehole,' she said. She'd hoped to avoid this. She'd hoped that their history and her position in the Jirga would have given him some clarity. But good men didn't sell women. Khalid had always been a small-time pimp. If he'd been a bigger man, he'd have moved through the ranks of the organisation and sought forgiveness for his sins.

Khalid's friend was shaking now, clambering into his car. 'Ain't no way Idris is gonna let this pass.'

'Idris?' the name clung to Khalid's lips, a sign of the slow realisation of whose woman he'd hit.

His friend was in his car now, engine roaring, window wound down. 'You're on your own!' he shouted from the window. 'Sakina, I'm so sorry! It weren't me. I promise, I din't know!'

The screech of his tyres echoed around the car park as Sakina kept her eyes on Khalid, a myriad of emotions running through her, none of them controlling her. She picked her way through them, examining each one and pushing it aside.

He'd caught her off guard. It had been so long since someone had hit her that she was still startled by it. She wondered if she was going soft, but she had known Khalid for a long time, worked for him, and he'd always been good to her. As good as a pimp can be.

This was the first time she'd seen him since taking a role in Jia Khan's Jirga. She'd been asked to talk to him about complaints some of the women had raised about him. Jia had trusted her to handle it.

Sakina knew Jia Khan was conflicted about the buying and selling of women's bodies. Each woman was free to make her own choice, and who was any other woman to dictate the righteousness of her decision? As long as women asked for her protection, she would continue to offer it. The money was fed back to them through salaries, savings and pension schemes. None of it powered the Khan family business. The street economy stayed, but only because they minimised its impact on wider society. 'It is not my place to tell a woman what she should and shouldn't do to make money. We've been told what to do for long enough,' Jia Khan had said.

'What did you wanna do that for?' Sakina said to Khalid, offering him her hand and steadying him as he tried to stand.

'I'm sorry,' he said as she touched her cheekbone, feeling the blood pulsing to control the damage. 'I've got an ice pack in my car.'

It was going to bruise and there was no way she would be able to hide it from Idris, not that she had any intention of keeping secrets from him. She knew what his reaction would be, and it was the hurt in his eyes that she wouldn't be able to bear.

'But you accused me of misbehavin',' said Khalid, speaking the word as if it were a woman's name, Miss B. Avin. 'I ain't skimming and I ain't taking 'vantage of the girls, alright?' He had taken the ice pack from his glove compartment and was offering it to her.

'You smacked me in the face,' she said.

'I got a wife at home and she's been wanting a baby for years. We're going for IVF, that's how serious I am. I am wanking into pots in a hospital for this woman. I ain't got nowt to give anyone else.'

'You smacked me in the face,' she said, repeating the words. 'I know you've been having a hard time. I heard all about it. But that does not give you an excuse to raise your hand.' She shook her head, saddened by what she knew she was going to have to do to rectify the situation.

He knew it too. She could tell from the way his breathing accelerated, the muscles in his neck tensed and his pupils dilated that he understood he was taking his last breaths. He'd fucked up. Idris was going to kill him. You couldn't mess with a Pashtun's woman and get away with it.

'I din't know you were with Idris jaan. Honest, I din't.' He was sorry, she could tell from his face, but it was too late.

She looked at his thick, meaty hands, his dark hair cropped short, his Turkish beard freshly trimmed, and she wondered why he was more afraid of Idris than he was of her. For so long she'd been unprotected, and now the addition of a man's name to her was enough to make others think twice about how they treated her.

'You think it's OK to go around hitting women?' she said, straightening the lapel of her Dior jacket. 'And now you know I have an important boyfriend, you realise it was a mistake? You're a cocksucking cunt.' None of those words were derogatory in Sakina's book, not the cocksucking nor the cunt, but she knew that the world Khalid lived in was different.

She walked to her car, a shiny black Range Rover, a gift she'd bought and paid for herself. The insurance on it alone was more than the average Englishman's rent. This thought reassured her about what she was going to do. She picked up her Saint Laurent from the passenger seat, the handbag she'd chosen for today's job, slipping open the quilted leather. She took out her metal nail file and began filing her nails, leaning against the car.

'I wanted to give you an out,' she said. 'You have a wife, she wants a family – I know a little something about that.' Maybe if he'd confessed, she would have been able to allow him to make amends, she could have spoken to Jia, but he was insisting on his innocence. 'I can't let this go, Khalid, you understand. If you'd just listened instead of using your fists, things could have worked out differently. But now…'

Khalid nodded at her. He looked smaller somehow, like a little boy hoping his mum would forget he'd messed up and hand him a lolly and give him a hug. But in the world that Sakina and Khalid lived in, you couldn't expect a hug every time someone stepped on your balls.

She sighed. 'If I don't handle this, he will. You understand that, right? Because your mate, the guy who left here, is probably already on the phone to him, telling him what happened. And Idris, he really loves me. He's probably on his way over right now. Bless him.'

Something about the way she was pointing the nail file made Khalid fear for his life. 'Sakina, sister, listen, I made a mistake. I did. I'm sorry.'

He was running through options in his head, but he knew that stories travelled faster than high-speed broadband in this city, and she was right – his mate would have been on the blower as soon as he got in the car, covering his back and spreading the news.

Idris would have been told, and he'd be on his way over. There was no way out. The Jirga drew lines in indelible ink, and those who crossed them were embedded in legends – Jia Khan's foot soldiers were mythical. Khalid knew death was fast approaching. It was just a question of at whose hands.

Silence descended between them, the air now thick, congealing with fear and anticipation against the low hum of traffic coming from the streets below. The moment was unending, Sakina leaning into the quiet, Khalid desperate for her to speak, to bring an end to his fear.

Eventually the buzzing of her phone brought with it a decision. Sakina glanced at the caller and then looked at Khalid.

'Time to choose,' she said, her eyes on him calm and cold, the adrenaline lowering all demands and answering all questions, giving her focus on the job at hand.

Khalid was a pillowy man. Despite his size, he was more teddy bear than polar bear. He controlled circumstances by comedy, and the occasional threat of fear. He harboured old misconceptions, one of which was that the woman would deal him a better hand than Idris.

She knew she had to make an example of him. She'd known when Jia Khan had given her the job. They'd discussed it at length, how the men were finding it hard to accept the new order, the arrival of women among their ranks. They were used to hard words, testosterone-filled rage, death. Patience, words that coached boys to men, life – these were alien to them.

'They will remember that they were raised in a religion that protects women and children, those in need and groups who others seek to oppress,' Jia had said. 'Until they learn that, fear will have to do.'

They'd sat in her office the night before, in oversized leather chairs, the only light coming from the lamp on Jia's desk. They were two women taking tea and putting the world to rights, as women often did, but these were no ordinary women. They wielded a power that could burn the world down if they chose. Society had shunned them, derided their decisions, called on others to take them apart. Despite all this, their language was tempered, and their plans, although illicit, illegal and immoral, were built on an idea of love and empathy for those around them.

That said, they knew many were reluctant to accept that they knew best. 'I did not take this decision lightly,' Jia had told her. 'It was always going to take time for them to accept change. Power is never given. It is always taken. If needed, you must make an example of him, Sakina. You will not be the same after, but, my sister, if someone pushes you to the brink, then the decision is made.'

Sakina put the phone to her ear. Jia Khan's voice was soft. 'I heard what he did,' she said. 'I'm so sorry.' Then something shifted. 'Now, kill him.'

Sakina hung up the phone and took off her blazer, folding it neatly and placing it on the back seat. She leaned into the front of the car. Khalid's eyes widened as she pulled a machete from under the passenger seat and began moving towards him, her resolve strengthened by the words of her Khan.

Khalid shrank backwards, trying to disappear into the cold, dank walls of the car park. He turned and ran towards a grimy yellow door, desperately trying to open it. A chain rattled, a sign that someone had locked and barred the exit from the other side.

'You'll find they're all locked, and the entrances are blocked off.' Sakina looked at the machete in her hand, then added, more to herself than anyone else, 'I bet every woman who's walked through this place at night on her own has carried her car keys in her hand.'

She looked back up at Khalid.

'You know there's nowhere the Khan and her Jirga won't find you anyway. Plane, train or automobile, land and sea, haven't you heard? Our access is greater than any governmental organisation because we are blind to borders.'

He cowered in a corner as she inched towards him, the roar of the traffic now louder than before, his arms covering his face. An ambulance siren rang out somewhere close by as she struck the first blow. She was glad she'd removed her Dior jacket.

When she'd done what was needed, she sat covered in his blood, machete in one hand, nail file in the other.

The pool of blood had washed away her trauma. Each hack of the machete had been powered by a memory of the times she'd wished she'd not lived – her father's funeral, the knock of the debt collectors, her mother's worries bearing down on her, the first time a greasy punter ran his finger up her arm, along the inside of her thigh, the urge to vomit after each john or junaid she serviced, the shame that would not wash away in the shower. Her anger had spilled out with every blow – but then something had changed, and slowly, like a glassblower's instrument held in fire, making something new from old, the rage had transformed, eventually resting as grief. She sat with a deep sadness of all the things that had happened, all the lives she would never live, and all the loss she'd accumulated at each step of her life.

People thought she was tough, hard and sharp as nails, but the truth was that she was scared, afraid of everything. She just never had any option other than to move forward. She had been unprotected and unchosen by love for so long that she knew she had built her life with the sticks and stones that had been thrown at her.

When Khalid had called her a whore, he had reached inside her deepest wound. He'd touched a nerve that, despite being covered in flesh, blood, skin and body armour, was raw.

His body would prove beyond doubt the lie that women are more merciful than men. That a woman as petite as Sakina could inflict such damage was testament to the rage that lay deep within her.

Sakina had assumed that killing Khalid would exorcise her demons, but now she wasn't so sure. It had unleashed something within her.

When Idris found her, she was numb, sitting in the middle of the floor, Khalid's contorted body beside her, blood splattered on her face and hair. She had been keeping it together for so long, she had assumed she was fine. She was far from it.

Idris had brought her hope, and although she had stayed at his house, slept in his bed, she hadn't been able to allow him to touch her that way. She could not strip herself to that emotional level. When he'd proposed, she'd said yes, because that was what she wanted. A life. A real life, with a family of her own, with children, and a future. But she could not see into his mind or understand why he'd chosen her, and that frightened her.

Idris helped her up, putting a blanket and his arms around her. He led her to his car. The clean-up crew waited patiently behind his green Range Rover. As he drove off into the night, they descended like scurrying ants, wrapping Khalid in plastic, lifting him into the back of a van, pouring chemicals on to the ground and scrubbing away all signs of what had happened.

At home, Idris wiped the face of the woman he loved, standing her in the shower, the water pouring over her face, the blood running down the plughole and away from her. She stood, catatonic, letting him wash her hair with shampoo, run conditioner gently through her tresses, his clothes soaked through as he stayed with her. It was only when he wrapped her in a soft towel and slowly wiped the water from her face that she cracked. Her eyes met his, and there was an affection so honest and deep in them that the dam she had built broke.

She cried that night in a way she not done in a lifetime. The salty tears she cried flavoured her life, and he was glad she had chosen him.

He kissed her eyes, and she let him. Any pretence there may have been between them was gone. He had seen her at her most awful, and he had responded with kindness.

She allowed herself to be loved that night, touched in ways that only the men who had paid for her services had touched her before. Idris had seen her in her entirety and not turned away.

Afterwards she lay in his arms, chosen, protected, and having killed a man. The world was not what she had imagined it to be. Love was not an equation to be solved. But if it was, Idris was the other side of hers.

CHAPTER 1

On the other side of the world, six girls huddled together in the back of a Bedford truck, afraid of what was to come.

The men had driven the heavily painted vehicle like a Trojan horse into the dusty college campus, the blue gates swinging open to let them through. Once in the grounds, their AK47s held aloft, their faces covered, they had jumped out and sprinted towards the library. They knew their way around the college campus – they were led by Mukhtar Ghulam, a former student expelled for plagiarism a week earlier. These men knew exactly what they were doing.

Amatus Sami had been looking through her notes when the men arrived, her head bowed as she squinted her way through the heart, its chambers, veins and arteries. She and twelve of her fellow students, six of them women, were preparing for their final biology exam. They were medics, diligent, the hope of their families.

As the eldest of five sisters, the responsibility to succeed weighed heavily on Sami's shoulders. So when the men arrived, she knew she would not let even that deter her from her goal.

'Be careful,' her father had said that morning, looking up from his copy of the *Daily Jang* newspaper. 'Don't argue with any of them, my love. Even though you are right and are smarter than they are.' He'd been reading about the scores of young men who were falling in with right-wing extremists, their arguing against the Islamic rights of women.

She'd kissed his head as she'd left. 'They think this dupatta makes me stupid,' she said.

'Maybe, but inside they know how powerful women are.'

'Many of these boys are from our neighbourhoods,' said her mother. 'That's the most disturbing thing.'

She thought of her words when the men burst in and the scarf fell from the face of one of them. It was her neighbour's son. She had known him since they were children.

'Akeel, what are you doing here?' she said.

He was just sixteen, and for a moment she thought he was going to cry. But then he pulled the cotton cloth up, covering his mouth and nose, and grabbed Sami. 'Stop talking,' he said. He dragged her and pushed her towards the five other women who had been separated from their colleagues.

'Don't say anything more,' he said, and he pointed the gun at her stomach, his eyes darkening, his face set.

The message was loud and clear. It was telling her to know her place and stay in it. She'd seen it before in the eyes of shopkeepers, teachers, butchers and bakers. She knew the truth of men, because her father had revealed it to her: 'Weak men fear you.' She stepped back and put her arm around another of the female students, waiting for what was to come next.

They bundled the women into the back of the truck, slamming the doors of the vehicle, leaving them in darkness, amid the smell of fear and petrol. It would have overwhelmed them if it wasn't for Sami. She wrapped her chador around her body and steadied herself. 'Now is the time for prayer, my sisters.'

Now was the time she had been preparing for.

CHAPTER 2

Jia Khan swept along the promenade, flanked by towering graves. She stepped through the forest of obelisks, urns and crosses, each one of them working to outdo the other in their attempts to touch the sky, in search of salvation.

The turned-up collar of her Italian tailored coat was pulled high to keep what little warmth there was in and the icy November wind that whipped through the undergrowth out. She pressed her lips together, and they deepened to match the colour of her cheeks and the red scarf that she'd wrapped around her slender neck, her dark hair tucked inside.

Her soft leather boots were laced all the way up, protecting her from the ice and the gnarled roots that covered the ground. Surely it had only been yesterday that she'd carelessly stumbled and tripped over the moss-covered graves as a child. Her father would bring her and her brother Zan to get them out from under their mother's feet and give her time with the younger two.

'You want to know who is buried here?' Akbar Khan would whisper, and they would nod their heads in readiness for a story. 'Now listen carefully,' he'd say, and they would take his arms as he talked of lives lived, of work completed, of the hopes and dreams of men and women long since dead and now buried in the magnificent acreage through which they strolled. There was always snow in Jia Khan's memories, deep, crisp and clean, mountains of it. The fire was always lit at home, awaiting their return.

Zan and Jia would run to the car in boots and woollen coats, hats and scarves, knowing that hot chocolate was soon to be sipped at Café Lahore, and a plate of hot, crispy pakoras eaten along with blood-red ketchup, the sauce of choice for South Asians.

She missed the days of them collecting deep fried puris, crispy and golden, from the Sweet Centre, along with soft, sweet halva. Jia would pick out the green pistachios from the orange semolina and pop them in her father's mouth. Sundays were sacred. None of her father's men came knocking on that day. His study door remained open, and music from his cassette or record player, or tracks from *Movie Mahal* on Channel 4, filled their home.

In the afternoon, Bazigh Khan and his wife would come over with their sons, Idris and Nadeem. They would play Ludo and carrom, and tell ghost stories that frightened Jia. Zan would put his arm around her, reassuring her that there was nothing to fear.

As she looked out across the morning mist, Jia wished for those days again, because now there were worse things to fear than ghosts, spectres and spooks, many of them inflicted by family as well as outsiders who wished to do them harm.

She gazed across the Pennines, taking a moment to let the clean air fill her lungs. The last few months had been arduous, and she'd found herself holding her breath, wondering whether it had all been worth it, the taking of lives, the creating of a new order, the dispensing of justice. Maybe it would have been better to let her father's criminal enterprise crumble.

She took a sip from the travel cup in her hand, tasting the doodh patti the housekeeper had prepared for her. Filled with pistachios and fragrant cardamom, the frothy milky tea was rich, and she preferred it in the mornings, much like the Italians and their lattes.

She considered how alike her people were to those from the Alps, Apennines and Dolomites. Their ideas around family and loyalty, their love of good food and, in the case of Pashtuns, their olive skin and dark hair.

Jia Khan's people came from the mountainous regions of South Asia, but she was born and raised in the north of England, among the hills and valleys of Yorkshire. Mountains watch empires and their people come and go, and even Allah spoke of them in the Quran: 'He created the heavens without pillars and placed firm mountains upon the earth, so it does not tremble.'

She'd read these verses this morning. Rising early, washing her face, passing her wet hands over her feet the way her mother had taught her, before standing on the soft prayer mat that had once belonged to her father, Akbar Khan. She was the head of the family now and she needed guidance. Even the earth needed gravity to steady it.

The love and loyalty of her family were what held Jia Khan's life in place. Her faith in herself was strong. It came from having built and rebuilt a life. Jia Khan needed no one. She chose this life, and her empire would soon be the world's biggest crime syndicate.

She ran her hand over the name of a long-forgotten merchant carved into a stone monument. As a child she'd brought paper and charcoal and done rubbings of the mini mausoleum, wondering why the grave of a Yorkshireman was watched over by a pair of small sphinxes. Superstition was found in all parts of the world, it seemed, and even dry-witted and stoic men hedged their bets when it came to the afterlife.

She thought of Elyas, the father of her two children, as she played with her wedding ring. It felt tight around her once slender fingers. The privileges that came with wealth and power had not brought a carefree life; in fact, they had doubled her responsibilities.

Jia Khan stood alone against the backdrop of stone monuments, each one a representation of Christian knowledge, strength and compassion. She'd take whatever help she could from whatever god there was at this point. She inhaled deeply.

'The world takes your breath away, doesn't it?' said a voice from beside her, and she smiled at the sound of her father. She turned around and found Akbar Khan young again. He ran his kid-leather gloves through his hair. It was as thick and dark as it had been when she was a child. His white shirt, waistcoat and sharply tailored suit, which was visible under his open overcoat, was just as beautifully pressed. He cut a striking figure among the dead, of which he was one. She knew this because she had been responsible for his death. She'd stood at the side of the grave as they'd lowered him into it, and she had heard the thud of soil as it hit his coffin.

Yet here he was. He'd stayed with her since she survived a shooting three years ago, an incident that almost took her life.

Jia Khan knew that no one would understand her conversing with the dead, and that if she mentioned it to Elyas or Idris, they would think she'd lost her mind. Maybe she had, but what was sanity in an insane world? She was a complicated woman, with a complicated life.

She had tried to simplify that life by leaving everything behind, by moving to London and hiding herself away from the contradictions that came with being a barrister and the daughter of a criminal kingpin. Things had not turned out how she'd planned.

'After every tragedy, one must invent a new world,' her father had replied when she'd once asked him how he was still in the graveyard when the afterlife waited. 'The world is never given to our people – that is why you and I are, so that we can take it and hand it out to those in need, the deserving.'

She knew he was right, and that he had always been right – it was Jia Khan who had not understood. She'd missed him after his death, when there was no longer anyone to turn to for guidance. When it came to family and the criminal enterprises, there were few voices she could trust.

So when she first started hearing her dead father's voice, she'd stayed silent. She began to come to the cemetery, returning week after week to talk to him out in the open and uncomplicated grave-yard. Here there was death, and death was the only certainty.

She no longer questioned why she could see him, preferring to believe that the veil between worlds had been torn the day she'd been pulled back from the brink of death.

'We're caught in a trap,' he said.

She smiled as he walked her back to their childhood game of speaking in lyrics.

'I can't walk out,' she whispered under her breath. It was a thing they used to do, exchange lyrics in English and Urdu, Hindi and Pashto. It was a relic from an easier time, when Akbar Khan had been alive, and she had believed that people were good or they were bad, when light vanquished the dark and sent monsters scurrying away. Nowadays, she believed that people were just people, and she was the monster. She inhabited a grey area, its shades stretching all the way to midnight black, much like the clothes in her wardrobe.

'Are we the abyss, Baba?' she said. He didn't answer. 'I am pulled in all dimensions and directions.'

'You have survived where others could not,' he said. 'We appear in the world for a moment and then disappear forever. All that is left are the lives we save, the ones we change and the trees we plant.'

'Have we saved lives? Is the tally in our favour, Baba? The only time I ever feel alive is when I work or when I fight.'

'This is not true,' he said. 'I've heard you laugh with the boys some days.'

'You've been spying on me,' she said, and smiled. She ached for her father's arms, the arms that had held her in childhood, but she knew they could not hold her now. The girl she had been would not have been able to build the business he had left into an empire.

It sprawled across the country, traversed oceans and had roots and branches in multiple countries.

'I have. You have rattled cages. The five crime families? The message you sent them was clear, and their women now work for you. You've taken them out at the knees. You should be proud of that.'

'Of what? More death? We have been at war for three years.'

'You've shaken up the order of men, my daughter. This is no small thing. And they are making their way to peace, I hear.'

'I never wanted this. I wanted a legitimate business for our people and our family. But now…'

'But now what?'

'The higher I go, the more corruption I see. The more money we make, the billions we have in our accounts in Switzerland and various offshore banks, the more messy things become.'

'It's the camel, the poor man and the eye of the needle, Jia jaan. The world, it stands between men and heaven. Allah told Jesus and Moses and Mohammed and all the other men that came, but we don't listen.'

She sat down on the sphinx and leaned back against the headstone. She was tired, exhausted to the bone, her shoulders aching, her head heavy.

'I had a call from a man at the Foreign Office. He said he knew you.'

'Beta, be wary of men in politics. Their allegiance is only ever to themselves. Did you look into Balochistan?'

Jia stood up and walked to the edge of the hill, staring across at the mill chimneys that scored the horizon. Lines of golden stone terraces step-climbed the hills in neat, slanting rows. She thought of the men and women whose lives had been changed, the millworkers and their families. The wealth of this city had always been shared.

'I'm working on it,' she said. 'Bazigh Khan says it's the largest reserve of gold and copper in the world.'

'It may be the answer,' he said.

She turned back to the cemetery's crosses and slabs, to its veiled urns carved in stone and the weeping willows that lived on, surrounded by the dead. All around her, names and graves were disappearing under thick, bright green grass, with vines wrapping themselves around the needles of obelisks.

A pair of school children in uniform were leaning against a great stone edifice, bunking off between pillars and pediments decorated with prancing horses and clasping hands, all with well-worn lettering, cracked text and pieces sheared away.

'They are too far removed from this place to consider it anything other than a good place to hide,' Akbar Khan observed. 'Very few contemplate their own death. If they did, the world would be a different place.'

'Did you?'

'A little, not when I was their age, but after your brother was born and then until the end.'

'Did it change anything?'

'Choice is not for men like me,' said Akbar Khan. 'It is a privilege I wished for you and your brothers and sister, though.' He looked tired, and Jia realised that he'd aged in the time they'd been talking. She looked up at the statues close by.

'Armless angels and headless saints,' she said. 'If that isn't a comment on the impotence of society, I don't know what is.'

'Rich and poor are equal in the afterlife, but not in worldly memoriam,' said Akbar Khan, gesturing to the ostentatious graves.

'I didn't think you'd want a chunk of marble to mark your grave,' she said.

'You are my marble statue,' he said. 'My legacy.'

'Do you consider me made of stone?'

'So much is lost in translation between children and their parents.'

Jia looked down at the lines on her hands. She missed her father, she missed being the child who slipped her hands into his, and as she looked at her own, she could see them changing, as if bringing his hands back to her.

'Was that why you didn't tell me about her? About my sister? I would have liked to have known, to have had someone older than me after Zan died… Baba?' she said.

But he was gone.

CHAPTER 3

He waited until he heard her come out of her dressing room and paused before dropping the crystal vase on to the tiled floor. It was expensive, irreplaceable, and he knew how much his wife loved it. Tiny pieces shattered across the mosaic floor that had been painstakingly put together in the hallway of Yanik Kaplan's house.

Hearing the crash, she rushed in, ignoring the broken vase and heading straight to her husband. 'Did you hurt yourself, my love?' she said, checking his hands and face for cuts and marks. He shook his head and enjoyed the fuss she was making, soaking up the concern she was lavishing upon him. She shooed him into the bedroom, calling the maid to come and attend to the mess.

It gave him great pleasure to know she valued him above the expensive ornaments they'd filled the house with. It was his way of making sure she still loved him.

He admired himself in the mirror: tall, lean and golden. He had lived in many places, been schooled in England and the US, and home was wherever he decided. He'd chosen the island for tax reasons. His children were away at boarding school, his wife, Sarauniya, loved the beach, and his private plane allowed them access to much of the world.

Yanick Kaplan had lost weight since Jia Khan had left a bloody message in his bed. Like the heads of the four other targeted families, he had been unable to establish how she had delivered it, and so how he could protect himself remained unclear. They had cleaned the house and replaced the staff, but the fear was still real and he had no trust for the new staff either. If it wasn't for his wife, he would have moved to a bunker and stayed there until the war was done.

He stepped through the floating white voile curtains and on to the beach. The sky was cloudless, and the sea temptingly blue. Palm trees stood like sentinels, the leaves taking in the sun and enriching themselves. Some days he missed the old compound. Today wasn't that day.

Today was a good day to plan revenge.

He was a rich man from a poor country, not self-made but inherited. He had had a complex relationship with his family's wealth in his youth, but boarding school and university had soon knocked that out of him.

'Darling, I'm going to a meeting of the Charity Commission,' his wife said, as she finished putting her earrings on, their colour matching the golden glow within her dark skin. She adjusted the waist of her white linen trousers; her legs were graceful and strong.

His had been the opposite when they first met. Now, though, running along the beach every morning, he had started to feel worthy of her. He still didn't understand what she saw in him, but he never wanted to know what it felt like not to be under her gaze. She must never know the lies he told.

Yanick Kaplan was that rare thing, a crime boss who was committed to his wife. His money gave him access to every bright young thing the island had to offer, but his eyes were not ones to stray. He could not lose her.

He heard the door close. He headed towards the huge custom-built closet whose design and build Sarauniya had overseen. He found what he was looking for at the back of the bottom shelf, underneath a pile of folded cotton shirts. He pulled out the wooden box and opened it carefully, taking out the contents: a burner phone and a packet of cigarettes.

He scrolled through the phone and saw that he had voicemail.

He took the cigarette packet outside and lit up as he listened to the message, enjoying the nicotine hit as it filtered through his mouth and into his body.

'His name is Afzal Khan – we have enough on him, but there are things we must set in motion. We need to move fast. The investors in the mine are not going to wait. We understand she is one of the interested parties. Our plans must be bulletproof.'

The phone was on speaker, and the maid faltered at the sight of her boss, dropping the towels she'd been carrying.

She'd been told never to enter a room when Kaplan was in it. The housekeeper had warned her that the domestic staff were not to be seen, but to work stealthily.

'Sorry, sir. I'm so sorry, I thought you had gone with madam.'

Rage flashed across his face, and the maid stepped back in fear. 'Leave it,' he said. 'Get out!'

She stumbled out of the room and into the hallway, her pristine white pumps slipping on the polished wooden floor as she ran down the glass atrium that connected the main house to the kitchen, an annexe only the staff ventured into. She ran straight into the house-keeper, who read the fear on her face.

'But I don't know what I did,' she said to the housekeeper.

'It doesn't matter what you did. If you want to live, you have to leave.'

'But I didn't hear anything.'

'It's not what you heard. It's what you saw. Mr Kaplan is not like other men. I'm telling you to go now. Take your kids and get off the island,' she said. She unlocked a weathered green cupboard, pulling out a wad of cash, and pressed it into the maid's hands.

'But the money!'

'I'll handle it. You have to go.' The housekeeper had worked for Sarauniya's family and had come with her when she'd married Yanick: this gave her a kind of immunity. That and the fact that she had no living relatives.

She pushed the maid out of the house and bundled her into her car, watched her drive away.

But the maid was far from Yanick's mind. He was fixated on revenge. He had found his way into Jia Khan's empire. He sat back in his chair, relishing his cigar.

He was coming for Jia Khan and her Jirga, and he was going to blow them wide open.

CHAPTER 4

Ishy 'Two Spoons' Iman took another draw on her vape. She enjoyed these early mornings, looking down at the uncut meadows and fields of green and yellow, turning to red and golden with the seasons. The fog wrapped around the hills like gauze, hiding them from the world beyond.

This much maligned and misunderstood city was so much like the boyfriend whose bed she'd left that morning.

She still hadn't found the courage to tell him she was getting married; nor had she told her mother where she'd been spending the nights. Each secret was a side of the coin you paid for being British, Pakistani and female.

She'd been waiting for the right moment, but it hadn't arrived. With her mother, she skirted the issue over daal chaval, placing spoonful after hot spoonful of the softened lentils, along with rice, in her mouth to stop the truth falling out.

With her boyfriend, she filled his mouth with kisses whenever the subject arose, her hands travelling over his torso, making their way to the buttons on his jeans and then inside. Sex silenced difficult emotions, while making her feel alive. She felt as though she'd died so many times, in so many ways, yet when she was with him, none of that mattered.

She'd never lied to him. 'This is fun and all, but I can't marry a white guy. I can't let my mum down.'

What she hadn't counted on was falling in love.

She leaned against the Bentley and sucked at her vape, wondering if there was any way she could speak to her mum and get her to break off the engagement, her mind working it out like a mathematical problem…plus, minus, carry the one. She never was good at numbers, and life hadn't added up for a long time.

She'd left Steve's bed early, looking into his sleeping face and promising herself that she would at least try. He was the one who had pieced her back together after she'd left her ex-husband, a man she'd been so in love with that she had broken her parents' hearts to marry him. They'd hidden their tears and stood between her and the biraderi, and when he'd proven all their fears true, they'd helped her leave him and taken her back into their home without judgement. She didn't want to hurt them again.

She touched her ribs and remembered the bruises her ex had left on them. The emotional bruises were harder to heal, but she was free of him, had been for a year, and now she was loved by someone who touched her face with kindness. A touch she'd once shrunk from for fear it would turn into a punch.

She'd met Steve at a café in the city centre. He'd been behind her in the queue as she ordered.

'One regular dirty chai for Dishy,' called the barista, placing her cup on the counter.

Steve had leaned forward and whispered: 'Does he really think your mother named you that?'

She'd turned to see who had spoken, and he'd shrugged in a 'wtaf' kind of way. He wasn't conventionally good-looking, but his eyes burned with flecks of gold and joy and, like fishing rods, reeled her in. She'd laughed, her shoulders dropping tension she didn't even know she'd been carrying.

'Can I have your number?' he'd said.

She'd taken his phone and entered her details before handing it back.

'Aw, you're breakin' me heart. It's not in 'ere,' he'd said, scrolling through the contacts.

'It's under D,' she'd said. 'For Dishy.'

They'd spent that night talking about movies, and every Saturday since then, they'd spent together.

Her ex-husband had promised her heaven and delivered hell, but her boyfriend made her laugh. He brought her cheese-and-onion crisps and chocolate bars when she was blue. He held her hand when the days were hard and wiped her tears. No one else would fill his shoes, and she was too tired to get to know someone new. She couldn't leave him. She would have to speak to her mother. She just needed to find the courage – or borrow some from her boss, she thought, watching Jia Khan walk across the cemetery, her scarf wrapped around her neck and her face almost buried.

Ishy drove her here every morning before training. Walking between the graves and headstones, Jia Khan seemed to talk to the air, but Ishy had no judgement. For people like them, life was a choice between a funeral pyre and a cold grave, and rarely anything in between. It disfigured them and left them for dead, and when they rose again, it asked how they dared to survive.

If Jia Khan wanted to lay her face to her father's grave, if she'd found a way to be acknowledged by his once warm touch, Ishy understood what that desire for healing was like.

They were not broken things that lay in the dark waiting for rescue. They were birds that repeatedly grew new wings, learning to fly again because they had no option. Because it was rare that anyone would come for them. Jia Khan had rescued herself and then taught countless others the ways of her world.

And they were indebted to her. Ishy didn't know how many were under Jia's protection, but she had heard rumours. The numbers had risen steadily, and now they extended across the country and over water to faraway places. That was the thing about real power: it was steeped in myth and far from the realm of statistics.

Jia Khan was smart and rich in the kind of beauty that comes with compassion. Every man and woman who lived in the city wanted to be in her orbit.

Ishy knew what Jia would say about her predicament: 'Don't let the scars get in the way of life. You deserve to be happy.' She was right, and as Jia Khan swept back to the car, Ishy resolved to speak to her mother and come clean to her boyfriend. Some people made you feel braver just by being near them.

***

Jia paused and looked at Ishy's shoes. She climbed into the red leather interior of the black car and clicked her seatbelt into place.

'Nice trainers,' said Jia. They were blue leather with a bright red, yellow and orange eagle on them, and Ishy wore them with a black trouser suit. 'They're great for here, but don't wear them to the meeting. I'm afraid not everyone is as sartorially savvy as you are. Stick with black leather and charge them to me. Sakina can tell you where to buy them.'

Ishy nodded. She valued Jia's advice. It was delivered with kindness, and her orders with clarity.

'Can you get the security plan to me asap?' said Jia.

'Idris Khan has asked for it.'

'Idris is handling the Guild, but I want to make sure everything is in place before they come to the table.'

Ishy nodded. 'Is the war over?'

'Not yet,' said Jia. 'But it will be.'

Ishy put the car into drive, and the Bentley purred into action. Jia glanced out through the darkened glass of her window. The sky was turning shades of red, reminding her of the old adage about the shepherd's warning. She considered the flock she was responsible for and surveyed the decayed ruins of the cemetery as the car moved away.

The dead had once been powerful, and all that remained of them now were large stones and mounds of soil. The truth of how they had acquired their wealth had long since been whitewashed by generations of storytelling. The sins of rich men became respectable with time.

The car slipped through the streets of the city as, all around, a new day dawned.

CHAPTER 5

'This isn't 1920s New York,' said Adam Diaz. 'You can't burn and loot and expect to win this war. She has exceptional methods of targeting your money, your property, and shutting down your shit.'

'You understand she came into our homes?' said Yanick Kaplan. 'What are we supposed to do, knit booties and wait by the fire for the next time?'

It was a few months earlier, still summer, and the heads of the Guild were at the Diaz family orchard on Martha's Vineyard. It was a place of beautiful beaches, scenic landscapes, celebrities, politicians and other rich and powerful people. The Diaz family owned land here. It had been part of their long-term strategy to legitimise their business and make sure their future was untarnished by their past. They had succeeded, and now Adam had become a kind of broker for the promised land of legitimate business, an example of what could be.

They had walked through groves of apple, pear, persimmon and cherry trees, all of them in full bloom, and come to sit at the family dinner table. Many a peace had been brokered here between men, but it was rare for talk to turn to a powerful woman.

The table had been set with cream-coloured crockery, pale green linen napkins and silverware that was polished to a high shine. Their wine glasses had been filled, the pork and chicken carnitas served, along with pickled red cabbage, vibrant guacamole, soft tortillas and sour cream. The flecks of green coriander leaf in the red rice were a different hue from the sliced jalapenos. The pico de gallo and hot sauces had been passed around by the guests.

And Adam had watched them, wondering what Jia Khan had planned next and how he felt about it. He had known her for many years, long before she became the Khan. He respected her, and at one point he'd considered how things might be if they were together. They had shared an understanding of the kind of criminal enterprise that encompasses entire families, having both been raised by powerful men who were considered godfathers to their communities.

Both Adam and Jia had loved their fathers and had struggled with their line of work. Educated in systems that did not understand the immigrant dream and struggle, they had discussed bringing an end to their inherited criminal enterprises. But while Adam held on to that ideal, Jia had taken the other road.

The Guild members and their cities had been on edge since Jia Khan's bloody message had been left in their beds. It was a brazen an act of war. And that is what followed. Two and a half years of loss.

These were dangerous people, the crime kings that pinned the underworld in place. They were men who had kidnapped, killed and maimed countless people. Their pockets were deep, their memories long. They held grudges for generations, searing them into their bodies and the souls of their descendants. Their relationships with each other had been based on necessity, mutual respect and an equal measure of fear. They had counted Akbar Khan as one of them.

Jia's intervention brought an end to that, and the men had retaliated by attacking the heart of her operation in the old ways, trying to take out her button men and steal her countless shipments.

'It's time to try something new,' said Adam. 'It's madness to keep fighting fire with sticks.'

Jia Khan had chipped away at the empires of the men whose cages she had rattled. The women of her Jirga, and the ones who worked for them, had been sowing the seeds of discord between the families by exchanging information and secrets long before she sent her blood message. The information had been fed to the Khan's tech team, who had created their own AI tools to populate the internet with news, both fake and real, about the Guild. The men and their businesses had been bombarded by AI-generated videos, their social media had been hacked and information about their financial accounts obtained. The intention was to create chaos. And it had worked.

The men had fought hard, but in the last six months they had started making signals that they wanted peace. Unable to cope with the new ways of the criminal enterprise, they had called on the services of Adam Diaz, the son of one of their own, and close friend of Jia Khan.

'Many of us are committed to going clean,' he'd said to the heads of the Guild in an emergency video call before the orchard meeting. 'Don't let this war ruin all our plans. I know Jia Khan. She's a smart, savvy woman, and we could do worse than have her on our side. Let's listen to what she has to say.'

The mortar that held a truce between them had worn thin, and Adam was eager to repair it before they turned on one another. He had worked hard to bring each of the men to this table.

'Adam,' said Arjun Singh. 'We had great respect for your father and for you. This is why we are here. In our line of work, trust and loyalty are all we have.'

'Good,' said Adam. 'Then let's start there. Let's be honest. The body count has been high, and the losses have left you weak and vulnerable while Jia Khan's power has grown. You are no match for her invisible army of women, and for the brothers who have joined the ranks, or the technology empire that she has created. Her army is everywhere.'

The men knew he was right. They couldn't trust anyone anymore, from the coffee shop barista to the barrister who represented them in court. Jia Khan's tentacles had spread far and wide.

'And now I have it on good authority that Interpol is closing in on us.'

Yanick Kaplan, the most vocal of the Guild, had made a lot of money. He had been successful for decades, as had the others, but like the others, he had failed to spot and capitalise on the opportunities Jia Khan had. The arrival of the dark web, crypto and mobile burner networks had transformed the sale of illegal goods as well as the laundering of money. The members of the Guild had been too slow to board the tech train, and meanwhile others had stepped up, making allegiances with Jia Khan. The sun was about to set on their empires, and they were finally ready to negotiate with the Khan.

Except for Kaplan. He was here under duress, having been outvoted by the others. From the corner of the table, he watched. He had no intention of making peace with Jia Khan. He was here only to confirm his suspicions about the other members of the Guild: that they had gone soft and had already pledged their loyalty to her.

'I want that mine,' he said to Rajo Rani after the others had left the table. 'I know your uncle can help me get it.'

Rajo was the niece of Arjun Singh, and the only woman who had been present at the meeting. Her uncle was one of the founding members of the Guild, and she was part of his succession plan. 'What makes you think we can help?' she said.

'You're Indian, aren't you?'

'The mine is in Pakistan, Yanick.'

Rajo thought about Kaplan and the designs he had. He had reason to be interested in the Reko Diq mine: it was worth more than any other gold and copper mine in the world. But she was tired of being underestimated by men, especially ones with zero knowledge of geography.

She would have to consider her options wisely, and for that she would need her uncle's sage counsel.

CHAPTER 6

Jia was still in the car when her phone buzzed. She pulled it from her coat and held it at a distance, trying to focus. Her eyesight was changing. Time hardened the lenses and softened the soul.

'Idris jaan, salaams,' she said.

'Walaikumsalaam, cousin.'

'It's good to hear your voice,' she said. 'How's Sakina, and how was the Golden Triangle?'

Sakina's handling of Khalid had quelled any ideas of rebellion, and Jia had urged her to take a break before the real work began again. She'd arranged for tickets as a gift and had had Idris pack her bag and passport as a surprise.

'She's better. The week away helped her relax, and the Algarve is beautiful. Except, of course, for the old money judgement that comes with it.'

'I bet that changed when they realised how much money the new money has.'

'Better new money than no money.'

Jia smiled. 'Good,' she said. 'Are you both ready to get back to the task at hand?'

'That's why I'm calling. Adam says the Guild want to meet.'

'These years of war have taken their toll on everyone. I'm glad they're ready. And the other matter?'

'They want us to meet them at the Foreign Office.'

'That's interesting. They know what we do, right?'

'They do. They know everything.'

'What did you say the guy's name was?'

'James Singleton.'

'Do the usual due diligence on him. Get Haines to dig up everything. I'm not going anywhere near the Foreign Office until I'm armed to the hilt. I've met some crooks, but in my experience, there are few more crooked than politicians and their associates.'

'Where are you?' said Idris. 'I didn't see you at the gym this morning.'

'I was out walking,' said Jia. 'I couldn't handle the smell of sweat today.'

The truth was that she was tired, but she couldn't admit that to Idris. She was part of the generation of women who'd been told they could have everything. She'd given birth twice and had worked in the world of men, where no one talked about the trauma of giving birth, the impact of it on the body and the mind, especially for women in their forties. But Jia was feeling the consequences of it.

'Jia, one last thing, we'll need a secure location for the Guild meeting. Somewhere open enough for them to feel safe, and closed enough for us to case the place.'

Jia Khan gazed out across the city, watching the vast edifice that was the city's largest mill, and once home to the global silk empire.

'I'll have a think about it,' she said as she put her hand into her pocket and felt the silk handkerchief her sister had given her as a 'Monday morning present'. She pulled on the square, unfolding it and smiling at the red and black playing cards printed on it. Maria knew her so well.

CHAPTER 7

Jia sat in the back of the car, the silk square in her hand. It smelt of roses, dark and woody, like the Frédéric Malle perfume Elyas had bought her for her last birthday.

Silk had once been the city's biggest export. It had paid and built the buildings that the council had listed and was now scrambling to save. Small squares of fabric like this one created the fortunes of some of the most powerful men in the country.

They had built mills as monuments to the precious commodity, their floors filled with bustling workers, turning the wheels of the huge iron machinery, spinning bright and burnished thread into fabrics.

These empires had been built on the work of the silkworm. If it weren't for the cocoons made by the larvae of the silk moth, none of these mills would exist. All that finery that had travelled the globe, favoured by the wealthy and the elegant, the forefathers of political and business empires, was built on the back of a tiny worm.

Fortunes had been made, property amassed and hierarchies established, much like the Khan family business. Instead of silk, they now sold drugs, guns, information and influence, all with a side order of sex.

Western journalists pushed the notion that France, with its haute couture, was now the global silk capital, but the market, like so many others, was owned by two countries that were poised to run the world, China and India.

With the industry at an end in this northern city, its redundant mills had become a symbol of all that was wrong with a dying empire, of the squandered potential of people and places. Jia Khan's return and renewed interest in her hometown had changed that. She had brought prosperity back, albeit through means some would consider problematic.

The racing-green Bentley swept through the streets of the waking city. Shutters were being rolled up, bakers were delivering fresh bread to their customers, and coffee shops were doing a roaring trade as people made their way to offices.

'Stop at Afzal's gelato place, please,' said Jia as they drove through the city.

Ishy nodded at her boss in the rear-view mirror. 'I promised the boys,' said Jia, as if sensing her surprise. Jia Khan did not have a sweet tooth, and it was rare for her to make such a request. But she'd been craving sweet things for a few weeks and was starting to wonder if the South Asian curse of diabetes was about to make itself known.

Ishy pulled up outside the glass-fronted ice-cream parlour across the road from the Penny Arcade building. Housed in one of the old mills, the Sweet Spot was filled in the evenings with second and third generation British Asians, young and beautiful, with money to burn and nowhere to go. But during the day, as those people made their way to school, college and work, it was deserted. It was known for its high-end flavours: real saffron and authentic truffle sat alongside salted caramels, rich mangoes and salted pistachio.

'How much would you like?' said Ishy.

'Buy two boxes, please. See if they have the truffle oil. Afzal was saying he's perfected the recipe and that I should try it.'

'Is that the flavour everyone's calling Black Gold?'

'Yes, it's the bougiest ice cream but he says it's excellent, so I'd like to find out what all the fuss is about. Also, get something for your mum.'

Jia was known for her generosity, sending gifts to the families of the people who worked for her. Ishy's mother was one of them, but they were never received in the spirit they were sent. Her mother made her dislike of the Khan plain.

'Why can't you get a job in a bank?' she would say as she added daal roti to her daughter's plate after a long day's work. 'Why work for this woman? Her father was a criminal and I'm sure she is no better.'

Ishy would smile, nod and eat her homecooked meal. She had long since stopped explaining to her mother that not only were well paid jobs like this hard to find, but that, knowingly or unknowingly, everyone worked for the Khan. The family's business interests extended to every aspect of the city.

Jia waited for Ishy in the car and scrolled through the day's news on her phone. She found an article about the kidnapping of female students in Peshawar – some had relatives in the UK petitioning for the government's help to get the hostages released. Jia made a mental note to check with Idris in case some of the families they supported were involved.

She rubbed her hand over her lower back to relieve the ache she felt. She needed to ask the GP about it during the appointment she had scheduled. Her breasts felt tender, and although she knew it was probably due to having overexerted herself during last night's fight club, at her age she could not afford to disregard it. She leaned back into the soft leather of the Bentley and closed her eyes, letting go of what was and what was to be. Whatever was to come, she would handle it.

The sound of sirens interrupted her moment of peace and took her by surprise. It was rare to hear them in this part of the city since the Jirga had cleaned up, wiping away the overt signs of crime. She leaned forward and looked into the rear-view mirror, catching sight of the police car as it closed in. It drove past her and braked hard. It was closely followed by two other vehicles, one of them a van. Jia watched as the van door pulled open. Armed officers wearing bulletproof vests jumped out, guns at their side, their gaze focused. They surrounded the car.

She leaned back in her seat and closed her eyes. 'And so it begins,' she said.

CHAPTER 8

A week earlier, Afzal Khan had walked up the sandstone steps of the factory he had inherited from his father. The old man had bought it for a song when the textile industry abandoned the city for places overseas.

The steps were worn down in their centre, a sign of the thousands of people who had walked up and down them at the start and end of each shift. Each level of the lofty five-floor building had once been full of the sound of whirring and clunking machines. Today, it was crammed with art supplies, books and paintings, and the chatter and laughter of art enthusiasts and creatives. A little girl in a pink tutu and trainers was running the length of the hall as Afzal Khan stepped through the great iron-and-wood door.

The exhibition had been a success, with visitors arriving from across the county, thanks to an article in the *Guardian* about the North's rising art scene.

He glanced at the artwork, wondering what the fuss was about, but his dealer had suggested the purchase and promised that profits would rise, and that art was a respectable investment, a great way to go clean, to find a way into the hearts and homes of respectable people. 'I don't know, Laila,' he'd said to his wife. 'It all looks strange to me. As if it's been done by small children and students from the local college.'

She was the one who'd urged him to trust the London art dealer. 'We need this,' she'd said. 'We need to get out of this business. And this may be the only way they'll accept us.' Then she'd kissed him and looked into his eyes. 'You know I don't care – I take you as you are – but Alia, she's just a child.'

He'd nodded with understanding.

Their daughter had come home from school crying. When her mother had finally coaxed the reason from her, she'd discovered that other kids weren't inviting her to their birthday parties. 'We're scum to them, Afzal jaan. I've tried arranging playdates, attendings their coffee mornings. I've even been to their wine o'clock events and sat there holding a glass, pretending to be one of them, but they think they're better than we are. It's because they all go to the same tennis clubs, and go skiing, and then spend weekends in Center Parcs.'

'Center Parcs? What's the point of a British passport if we can't travel to Dubai, Singapore, Mauritius! I spend more on a single flight than they do on their entire holiday.'

'It's not the colour of your passport, it's the colour of our skin. We'll never be good enough for them. So let's be even better. Art is the answer,' she'd said.

He walked around the mill, the smell of oil now replaced by the fragrance of oversized lilies that graced the centre of the floor. He glanced at the artwork the agent had purchased and displayed at his request. He looked at the price tag of a painting of a tiny black square in a sea of blue.

'I'm robbing these people blind and they're happily handing over their cash,' he messaged his wife and then put his phone away.

He watched the visitors milling around, stopping and studiously staring at various pictures and paintings, whispering in hushed tones, fingers on the side of their faces. He wondered what the fuck they could see that he couldn't.

He considered if he'd agreed to too much, had sold his soul for whiteness. He'd been to a perfectly acceptable university and was well-read enough to know he wasn't stupid. But at moments like this, he wondered if all the other people in the world knew things that he didn't.

He had once been a major link in the drugs import chain, but his power had waned. Much had changed since Jia Khan had taken over the Jirga. She had offered him an alternative role, with larger profits, and the promise of pound signs had prompted him to accept.

But lately he'd found himself questioning her motives, having come to understand that by exchanging his existing business for a share in one of the tech companies owned by the Khans, he had lost any leverage he'd had over the Jirga. He was vulnerable, and he didn't like it. The action Jia Khan had taken against the international crime bosses had been brutal, sudden, and had shaken him. 'What if her loyalties change and she comes for me?' he'd said to his wife.

She'd shaken her head and told him to stop being so dramatic. Their life was going well. They were putting their criminal pasts behind them. 'Don't worry so much,' she'd said, kissing his cheek as she ushered their children out of the door to football practice.

But he did worry. His mother had treated him like a rare and precious thing. His feet were kissed from babyhood to manhood, and although times had changed, those old habits were hard to break. Despite being the father of daughters himself, he struggled in this world of equality, and he understood why Andrew Tate and his cronies were catching on.

Ever since Jia Khan had broadened the Jirga and brought on the women, he had felt their judgement on him. In their eyes he saw their self-esteem, and it made him feel reduced, as if they knew what he looked like naked, as if they were laughing at him. He felt he needed sharper elbows to get himself seen.

When Yanick's people had reached out to him, he'd hesitated momentarily before agreeing.

'It was a stupid move of hers,' he'd conceded to Kaplan. 'Men don't act like this, bringing war to another's door. I know, I know, it was a move only an emotional woman would make.'

He'd recently met with Yanick in a bar in Dubai. 'You should speak to Jia before agreeing to anything,' his wife had advised him beforehand, then the advice had been lost in between the things that men bonded over, down the crevices of conversation about cigars, fast cars and who had the larger swimming pool.

'Try this one, it's a Montecristo 520,' Yanick had said the next day, offering Afzal Khan the cigar as they ate lunch together by the hotel pool.

'After the peace is made, you should bring the kids and come and stay with us,' Afzal Khan said.

Yanick had smiled at him, his eyes sly and steely. 'And what if I don't want to make peace?'

Afzal Khan's interest was piqued. War was what he was good at. Conflict his comfort zone. 'Tell me more,' he said.

'There is a mine in the heart of Balochistan that can set us both free,' he said.

The men had laughed together and made plans. Kaplan had eased Khan into forgetting his fealty to Jia Khan, how she was leading the family out of the crooked pastures and on to clearer paths, where the only thing laundered was linen and where they could live an honest life, at least on the surface, without fear of judges, juries and officers of the law.

Yanick Kaplan understood ego and the insecurities of men, how they worried that women were manipulative and cunning and using men to further their plans, harnessing them the way a farmer does a bullock to till the land and turn a profit.

'Help me, and once Jia Khan is gone, you will be the head of the Jirga,' he'd said.

He'd drawn secrets from Afzal Khan, offered protection and money. 'With your help,' he told him, 'we can send Jia Khan a message she won't ever forget.'

And Afzal Khan had smiled at the prospect.

If only he had remembered that, under Jia Khan's auspices, the criminal fraternity was no longer a man's world.

<h1 style="text-align:center">CHAPTER 9</h1>

The ice-cream parlour had been empty when Ishy entered, except for a solitary customer waiting on his order in a booth at the back.

He nodded at Ishy as she walked through the great glass doors, and she reciprocated his greeting. She stood by the counter, staring up at the huge pale-pink menus that ran from the floor, past the mezzanine balcony and right up to the ornate Victorian ceiling. They detailed ice creams that ran from the purist to the artisanal, from vanilla to chilli, mango and mangosteen. She placed her order.

'One large tub of black truffle oil, and one of the salted pistachio,' she said.

'I'll have to get the black truffle one from the freezer in the back,' said the server, who was dressed in a pistachio green shirt and had a white hat pinned jauntily to the side of her head. It reminded Ishy of the paper boats her dad used to make. They'd take them to the park when she was a girl and watch them float down the river. 'It'll be a minute,' said the server. 'Is that OK?'

'Yeah, sure, I'll wait,' she said, and paused before adding, 'It's for Jia Khan.' The two young girls behind the counter straightened up at the name, as if Jia herself had walked in, and out of the corner of her eye, Ishy could see the man in the booth lean forward.

'Yes, of course. I'll have it packed and ready to go!'

'Thanks,' said Ishy. 'Where are the toilets? Out back?' The server directed her to the ladies' room, and she walked through the pink and green establishment, thinking of the Hello Kitty dolls she'd had as a kid. The man in the booth watched her walk by.

As she was coming back, she heard the staff whispering her name, so she lingered by the back door, out of view. 'Did you see her trainers? So cool.'

'Why do they call her "Two Spoons"?'

'You not 'eard the story? Well, you know my mate Rifaat? Someone nicked her dog. It were a right expensive breed, like the ones you see at Crufts. The police said they couldn't do owt. RSPCA said it weren't anything to do with them, and no one was helping. Then Rifaat called Ishy. They were at Colton Grammar together, see, and she knew she worked for Jia Khan. Ishy said she'd find out who nicked it and see if they'd agree to return it.'

'Did she get the dog back?'

'Oh yeah.'

'And then what 'appened?'

'They gave it back alright, along with all the other dogs they'd taken. Turns out they'd been stealing puppies to order since Covid days and hadn't stopped. But then something else happened.'

'What?'

'They left town.'

'What do you mean?'

'I mean, a week later they were gone. Up and shipped out to God knows where. Left everything behind, the house, all their gear.'

'What did she do?'

'No one really knows but…'

'But what?'

'There are stories. Rumours. You know she's skilled in Panantukan?'

'What's that?'

'Dirty boxing, Filipino style.'

'So's our Jack, in martial arts, I mean, but don't mean owt.'

'It were more than that. It was after that people started calling her Two Spoons. They said Ishy had gone round there in the middle of the night and bashed the door in, like proper off the fucking hinges. He'd been in bed, the guy. She dragged him into the street, broke his arm, like, gnarled up his left side badly, and then…' The girl took up two ice-cream scoops and dug them violently into the raspberry ripple tray. 'She took his eye out with two spoons.'

The gelato slurped as she moved the scoops around, carving out balls of ice cream, the red syrup running through them like veins. She grimaced as she put the ice cream into a glass serving dish and nodded at the silent customer who was still in the corner of the room. Her colleague took the dish over to him.

'Did you want to order some ice cream to take away?' she asked, looking at the cooler on the table. The man shook his head, and she walked back to the counter.

'What happened to the dog?' she said.

'Rifaat's got him. She walks him by the lake every morning. Right big fuck-off thing it is.'

Ishy decided it was time to make a reappearance. She winked at the serving girls as she made her way back to the counter and was about to speak when the sound of sirens forced her attention.

Everyone looked up, except for the man in the booth, who just kept eating his ice cream, spoonful after spoonful.

'Shit!' said Ishy under her breath.

She scrambled for her phone, dialling Sakina's number. 'I'm in the Sweet Spot,' she said. 'I don't know what's going on, but there's cops outside with Jia.'

'Stay calm,' said Sakina on the other end of the line. 'I'll send Idris – he's just round the corner from you. It's probably nothing.'

The girls working the counter placed two white tubs of gelato on the serving area, shifting nervously. 'What the fuck d'you think's goin' on out there?' one whispered to the other.

'I don't know – but is that Jia Khan?'

They'd heard countless stories about her and the women who worked for her, sharing them and helping them spread, the myth of the Khan taking root faster than the tales of men ever could. People needed something to believe in. They needed more than the truth; they needed fantasy.

They looked out as the officers led Jia towards their patrol car. From a distance, she appeared compliant, nodding at their words. 'You think they're about to take her in?'

'On what grounds? They can't pin nowt on her. She's as clean as my mum's conscience.'

'Knowing your mum, that don't mean owt! And I don't know. Tax fraud maybe, like Al Capone?'

Ishy kept her eyes on her boss as she gathered the ice-cream tubs and napkins from the counter into her arms. The officers were looking across at the Sweet Spot now. They had set up a perimeter, and traffic was being directed away from the building.

Ishy paused at the exit. 'You know that story? It's not true,' she said. The girls looked blankly at each other. 'I mean about Rifaat's dog.'

'It's not?' whispered one of the girls.

'You need to be careful of the stories you tell about people. They can hurt.'

'We're sorry. I heard about the spoons and your name —'

'It was forks,' said Ishy as she walked out of the glass doors.

'Excuse me, madam,' said one of the officers who was heading towards her, his arm on his weapon. 'Would you come with me, please?'

'What's happening?'

The officer didn't answer but navigated her away from the building and towards Jia, who was standing beside Idris under the stone arch of the Penny Arcade, deep in conversation.

'What's going on?' said Ishy, joining them.

'We don't know,' said Idris. 'We're waiting for one of these guys to tell us. But it's not about us. I've called Afzal to find out what he's been doing, but he's not answering his phone. I can handle things here if you want to go home? You don't look too well.'

He addressed this question to Jia, and when Ishy turned to her, she realised how drained Jia looked. She wondered how she'd missed it.

'I'm staying,' said Jia. 'I'm fine, just a little tired.' If Afzal Khan was in trouble, she needed to stay. Loyalty to the Jirga was important. They needed to see her, to know she was with them.

She watched as the officers surrounded the building.

'The "two spoons" story is still making the rounds,' Ishy told them.

Jia placed her hand on Ishy's shoulder. 'Congratulations,' she said. 'Society gives every smart woman a name for her perceived villainy, and now you have yours. They are going to talk no matter what you do, so do what you want.'

'What name did you get given?' said Ishy.

'Jia Khan,' said Idris.

Across the road, the police were escorting the two serving girls away from the ice-cream parlour.

Jia clocked the man in the booth. Unaffected by the activity outside, he was still eating ice cream, having made no attempt to move. The blue and white cooler was beside him on the table.

'It's him they're after,' said Jia slowly. 'Idris, brother, this is bad. There's something in that cooler, and I don't think it's ice cream.' Her voice was a hush now, her mind racing. 'Have you heard from Afzal Khan?'

Idris shook his head.

'Call Maria and tell her to go to Afzal's house.'

'I'll send one of the guys. Afzal isn't going to respond well to Maria.'

'Send her,' Jia said. 'And Sakina too. It's not for Afzal. It's for his wife.'

CHAPTER 10

The door was slightly ajar when Sakina arrived home. She pushed it open slowly, careful not to make a sound, and glanced around. She took her shoes off, leaving them on the white marble floor, under the walnut and maple sideboard she'd inherited from her mother's house. She slipped past the black and white photographs of her parents and her favourite snap of Idris, dressed in a black suit, and moved towards the kitchen. She pulled her phone from her back pocket, quickly typing a message to Idris: 'Someone has been in the house.'

She crossed to the other side of the hall, checking each room carefully before moving on to the next. They all appeared undisturbed. She headed to the bedroom, taking a quick inventory of her jewellery, keys, shoes – they were all there. But then something caught her eye: there were magazines spread across the bed.

Her phone rang. It was Idris. 'You OK?' he said.

'Yeah. Someone's been in the house, and they've left bridal magazines here.'

'It must have been your mother.'

'Yes, maybe,' she said.

'How was Afzal's wife?'

'Bad. I left soon after the police arrived. Maria was comforting her. Did that guy really have his head in the cooler?'

'Yes. He'd been sitting there, calmly eating ice cream for half an hour.'

'And the police? How'd they find out?'

'Someone emailed them footage of him being killed. They're looking into it. You must be tired. I'm five minutes away. I'll make you dinner and we can just sit.'

'Don't worry about cooking. Mum will have left something in the fridge – that's what she always does. I'll see you soon.'

She headed to the kitchen, dialling her mother's number as she did so.

'*Assalamualaikum, Ammi. Tussi khana fridge vich rakh diya?*' she said, slipping easily into Punjabi as she opened the fridge to take out one of the foil-covered food parcels her mum usually left when she visited. 'You left the front door wide open,' she said, staring at the empty fridge.

'I couldn't come today,' her mum replied in Punjabi. 'I had a flat tyre and was waiting on your brother to call the AA.'

'Never mind.'

Sakina closed the fridge, and looked around the kitchen, moving slowly. She silently pulled a knife from the block on the worktop and told her mum she'd call her back, before ending the call.

Someone had been here, and it wasn't her mother.

No one else knew about the engagement. Her mother was such a believer in nazar that she'd urged Sakina to keep it secret. Fear of the evil eye was better than a non-disclosure agreement in a desi household. Her mother would be whispering prayers and burning chillis in all corners of the world, if only she could, to protect her children. And yet, whoever had been here knew about Idris's proposal.

Her fingers wrapped around the black handle of the knife. She let her hand acclimatise to its weight. The blade glinting, she pointed it downwards, its steel against her thigh, and slipped towards the door.

There was a man standing in the hallway. He was slight of build, dressed in black, his face covered by a balaclava, only his eyes visible, staring at her, judging her next move.

'Get out while you still can,' she said slowly. Her voice was calm; she'd been here before. The adrenaline cooled her nerves, gave her focus. Death was her comfort zone, delivering it, waiting for it. If it was coming for her, she was ready.

He didn't answer; instead, he took a step closer. Her eyes and brain did a quick assessment of her exits, a way out that didn't involve a fight. It was a gift she'd developed while working the streets: the ability to read violence before it arrived, and the calculations that came with avoiding it.

He was blocking her path to the front door. She could turn and run into the living room, open the glass doors that led into the garden, but what would be the point? The garden was completely enclosed, the house detached. And, besides, she'd had a long day. She didn't need this shit.

'I killed a man last month,' she said, opening the drawer of the credenza without taking her eyes off him. 'Don't make me do it again.' She put the knife she was holding inside and closed the drawer. 'See,' she said. 'I don't want to fight you.'

Confusion flickered across his eyes and his shoulder dropped a fraction. He'd probably never known someone to willingly put away their weapon when facing him. It didn't stop him though. He edged closer and she saw the blade in his hand. It was small, hidden in his palm almost. She clicked her neck, one way and then the next. 'It took me ages to get the smell of blood out of my hair,' she said. 'But it's a small price to pay to attend my own wedding, don't you think?'

He lunged at her, but she sidestepped, curving her core away from the knife. She slipped the palm of her left hand along his strike arm and pulled it towards her, grabbing his fist with her other hand and thrusting it, with the knife, back at him. She pushed hard and he screamed in pain as the knife entered his torso. As he staggered backwards, she pulled the knife out of his hand and attempted to stab him again, but he managed to twist away and ran into the living room.

She turned to follow him, when there was a clatter in the hallway. Heart racing, the knife held out in front of her, she edged back into the hall, wondering how many of them there were. She saw a man on his knees. He looked up, his eyes annoyed.

'Why do you leave your shoes in the bloody hallway instead of in the cloakroom?'

It was Idris. His face paled when he saw the knife in her hand.

Without saying anything, she rushed into the living room. The door to the garden was wide open; bloodstains ran along the path and were smudged along the stone wall at the back that led into open fields beyond.

'He's gone,' she said, returning to the hallway and Idris. 'How did you manage to slip over a pair of flats?' she said, offering her hand to help him up.

'It's the Italian leather soles on these shoes. I haven't scratched them up yet and this floor doesn't help.'

'You OK?' she asked, as he rose unsteadily.

'I'll live,' he said.

'That's good, because I don't want a dead man for a groom.'

'It's you I'm worried about,' he said. His eyes were dark now, filled with concern 'Let's get you cleaned up,' he said. 'And pack your bags,' he said. 'You're not staying here alone.'

She looked at him, irked by his tone. 'Like I'm a child who needs to be told what to do?'

'No, like you're a person who needs another person,' he said. 'If I were a woman, I'd say the same thing.'

She looked at the stains on her hands. 'I hate blood,' she said. 'The smell of copper coins makes me sick.'

'I'll clean up out here,' he said. She went to the bathroom and stripped herself of the suit she'd been wearing, dropping everything on the floor, too tired to pick it up. She washed herself, swapping the smell of blood for mandarin-rind scented soap. She dried herself with the soft towel that hung on the rail and thought back to the last time she'd washed someone else's blood down the plughole. This was becoming a habit, one she didn't want.

When she returned to the bedroom, she found Idris flicking through the bridal magazines page by page, studying each one as if picking out designs for her wedding. 'There's a cup of tea for you on the table,' he said, without glancing up.

'What are you looking for?' she said, watching him as she dried her hair.

'Afzal Khan's killer left a message,' he said. 'I want to make sure one's not been left for you.' He stopped abruptly.

'What is it?' she said.

He lay the magazine on the table and flattened it, cracking its spine. There was a playing card in the centre, and he pulled it out, holding it between his thumb and forefinger. He looked at Sakina. 'I don't know what it means, do you?'

He handed her the card, and he watched her as she inhaled slowly.

'The ace of spades,' she said, turning it over in her fingers. 'They call it the "card of death".' She handed it back to him. He knew better than to ask her how she knew something that he didn't, so he waited. 'My grandfather and his brother were in the 25th Infantry Division of the Indian Army. They were called the Ace of Spades – it was their insignia, black on green. They inflicted more misery and hardship on the battlefield in their first spell of fighting than any other Indian division during World War Two.'

'The red thumbprint along the edge,' said Idris. 'There was one in the cooler with Afzal Khan's head.'

Sakina sat down, the adrenaline draining from her body, leaving her feeling heavy, her insides rattling. She needed to be held tight, encased by strong arms, to stop her shaking. Instead, she reached for the TV remote control. The sound of the news channel filled the room, and on the screen, local news was live from the ice-cream parlour, a reporter standing on the street outside the mill.

'We're told the severed head, which was found inside a cool box at this ice-cream shop, belonged to philanthropist, entrepreneur and local businessman Afzal Khan. Khan was responsible for the rejuvenation of several of the textile mills in the area and has been a member of the local council for some time. Police have charged a thirty-two-year-old in connection with the murder.'

She flicked the TV off and turned to Idris. 'The card means they won't stop until it's over. It's the equivalent of badal in your people. The act of vengeance and justice.'

'This one was in my car,' he said, taking something from his pocket and placing it in front of her. She put the two cards side by side on the table. They were identical.

'This has got the Guild written all over it. The blood is a nod to the old ways,' said Idris, 'when people would sign their names in blood to seal a contract. Those who couldn't write used their thumb-print.'

'Who else has had one?' said Sakina.

'I don't know,' he said. He looked at her, concern in his face. 'I know you won't stay at my house until we're married, but can you stay somewhere else? Please,' he said, pressing the word into her bones. He was afraid – she could see it all over his face, and it made her uncomfortable. Taking care of a man was not something that she'd ever wanted to do, and yet here she was. 'OK,' she said.

She went to her room, pulling out her suitcase and adding random clothes to it. She couldn't think straight. She took her toothbrush and nightclothes and decided she'd come back for other things if she needed them.

She heard his voice in the other room, speaking to Jia. He had her on speaker.

'I'm with Sakina,' he said. 'They've left a card here.' He looked at Sakina. 'Jia, Adam said they were ready to broker a peace.'

'Looks like he was wrong,' she said.

'I don't understand how they got to Afzal.'

'Greed,' she said. 'He was weak. I should have cut him from the Jirga long ago.'

'He was loyal to Akbar Khan.'

'Men like that are only loyal to men,' she said. 'I made a mistake, keeping someone from my father's people, and now Afzal Khan will have told the Guild things, information that means we are no longer safe.'

'We're human, Jia Khan,' said Idris. 'Sometimes we have to trust.'

'You're getting soft in your old age, cousin,' said Jia. 'For people like us, trust is what gets you killed.'

***

Jia ended the call and looked at her sons. They were curled up on the sofa, snoring gently to the sound of *Numberblocks* on the TV as the fire burned brightly in the hearth. Despite their age difference, they were close, and Jia was proud of Ahad for making time for his little brother. He understood family.

She flipped the playing card she'd found in her fight kit across the backs of her fingers, then back again, and she felt a chill run through her spine.

CHAPTER 11

'It's intense in there,' said Benyamin, catching his sister as she walked up the stone steps to the funeral home. The sun was rising, its rays beginning to light the dark streets and draw the economies of the night to a close. With it rose those who worked by day, walking down the paved paths between gardens, opening up the golden Yorkshire-stone buildings. The trees were skeletal, having lost their leaves. Their branches offered no protection from the elements and would not do so for months to come.

'You're leaving?' Jia said to Ben, glancing at the rows of parked Bentleys, BMWs and Range Rovers that lined the streets on the other side of the low sand-coloured wall that surrounded the funeral parlour. Men in dark suits and overcoats were huddled by their cars, their faces downcast, their conversations minimal. There was little left to say. This was the fourth comrade they had buried in as many months. They were his friends, his family by blood, marriage or the age-old Asian custom of calling someone 'uncle' and 'brother' as a mark of respect.

They had been losing pieces of themselves each time they put another of Akbar Khan's men – old allies who held the wisdom of their people – into the soil. They were men hardened by time and experience, but repeatedly standing at the grave of a member of their clan made even the least introspective of them consider his mortality and the life he was living.

Each loss extracted a brick from the wall that they had built around themselves to keep the world at bay.

The work they did came with cost and risk, but this many men in the ground had not happened since the early days of the Jirga. The losses left them pummelled, and their faces betrayed them.

'You'll understand when you go in,' said Benyamin. He looked tired, his eyes sunken, his face pale, making his hair appear darker. He was heading down the stone steps when he stopped and turned back, called out to her. 'Jia,' he said. 'I'm proud of you.'

She waited for him to continue, and he wanted to say more, to tell her that he saw what she was handling, and how well she carried it. That he knew what she'd given, that she was more than all of this… But he didn't. He stopped short of words that could have set them both free. He hadn't been given the tools for deliverance. Their wounds were deep, too cavernous to be healed in this life.

He stayed silent, knowing that any kind of response from her would trigger him. The emotions bubbling up in him were a reminder of all the funerals they had attended in the last few months. There were more to come, there was only loss left, and maybe that was what this blood-soaked life had gifted them. It was choking him.

'Where are you going?' she asked him.

'To pick up the cousins from the airport.'

'Why can't someone else do it?'

'I need the distraction,' he said.

She watched him leave, knowing he was drowning in emotion, just like every man she would find beyond these doors, none of them taught to name their pain, let alone kill it.

'Benyamin is a good man,' said Iram, as Jia joined her and the other women gathered at the top of the steps to the funeral parlour.

'They all are, but the bar is low,' whispered Iram's sister. 'I often wonder what life would be like if they valued us. If they were told our work was important – the food we cook, the babies we grow inside us – that none of this is easy.'

'They believe the money they make is worth more than our work, but their gold coins are forged in our flames. They get to do what they do because we keep the homes running,' said Iram.

'We are only worth fucking, and fucking with,' said one of the other women. 'We are not their equals, we are lesser beings, but without us they can't function. Whatever happens, they land on their feet.'

Jia glanced at the women, the seething anger and grief like flecks of fire in their brown eyes.

'Then we keep sweeping the leg,' said Jia. 'We already took out their systems. They will understand soon enough. But all that is not for now.'

Iram pushed the door and held it open as Jia walked through. The great marble hall felt cold and impersonal, and a chill ran through her body. She had walked this hall too many times.

The women covered their heads as they crossed into the room where Afzal Khan's body was. His torso had been recovered from a car outside the police station. The killer had told the police the location quickly and without duress. It made Jia question his motives, if that had been his plan all along, to take the fall.

Afzal Khan lay on the table, covered in a shroud, the men from his family standing close by, their faces stoic, their heads bowed at the sound of the recitation of the holy Quran.

The words of Allah did little to quell the overwhelming feeling in the pit of Jia's stomach that God was absent from this place.

She looked at her men and then the wireless speaker in the corner of the room. 'Whose phone is playing the Tilawat?' she said slowly.

One of the men pulled his smartphone from his pocket and handed it over.

'Unlock it,' she said, handing it back and watching as he tapped in the six-digit pin.

She flicked through and turned off the recitation of the Quran. 'Haven't any of you memorised verses? What about the words your mothers prayed over you?'

The men remained silent at the reprimand, their eyes downcast. Jia turned to her cousin.

'Nadeem, you knew every verse when we were kids. Recite what you know. Allah doesn't need our hollow attempts to send Afzal Khan to heaven. We all know what we are. You can't bribe your way in with some Spotify recording.'

The men flinched.

She slipped out of the room, her eyes signalling Idris to follow. They stood in the corridor, Idris with his hands in his pocket like a small boy.

'What the fuck's going on?' said Jia.

'What do you mean?'

'These guys look like they're losing their shit.'

'They knew him for a long time, Jia. We have to give them time to grieve.'

'And they say women are emotional,' she said. 'Idris, we can't do this right now. They need to get their shit together because they're coming for us. Make no mistake, the Guild will come for more of us.'

She pushed the door to the funeral home open and walked out into the cold air. She was beginning to tire of the company of men. 'Get Adam Diaz on the line,' she said. 'I want to know what he's found out, and what they're doing next.'

Afzal Khan was laid to rest as soon as his body was found. 'The speed at which we bury our dead makes my head spin,' Benyamin Khan had said to Jia when the funeral was announced. Processing the loss happened later.

Jia stood at the graveside, watching as they lowered her father's cousin into his final resting place. All around her, her men looked broken and weak, exhaustion written across their faces. Afzal Khan had not been her favourite cousin by any measure, but he had been the toughest among them, riddled with the old ways and hardened by experience. 'They don't make men like him anymore,' someone said as the thud of earth hit the coffin.

Thank God, thought Jia, keeping her feelings to herself.

'The old world must end before the new begins,' she said.

She left the proceedings early, leaving the immediate family to mourn in privacy. She had enquiries to make.

'Did you hear from Mark Briscoe?' she said to Idris as he walked her to her car.

He shook his head. 'The CPS say the man the police have charged acted alone, and that they aren't pursuing any further leads. Briscoe isn't taking my calls.'

'That's not like him. Someone's got to him. Remind him of our work during the riot, and also, of course, the things we know about his son,' said Jia. Data was king, but information was better. Her company mined data, then interpreted, organised and harnessed its power, using it as leverage. Knowledge was always power, and she knew that the man Chief Constable Briscoe had in custody may have killed Afzal Khan, but he had done it under orders from someone within the Guild. Adam had confirmed that, along with the fact that the death has divided them.

'Does Adam know who's behind it?' Idris asked.

'Apparently they are sworn to each other, and their loyalty means they cannot give him up without his consent,' she said. 'But my money's on Kaplan.'

'Are you alright?' Idris asked. 'You look tired.'

She looked at him, measuring how he would take the news, and then said: 'No, I'm not.'

'What is it? You been to the doctor?'

She nodded. 'Yesterday.'

'And?'

'I don't want you to overreact the way Elyas did.'

'Jesus Christ, Jia, what is it? Just tell me!'

'I told you to calm down.'

'If you're sick, you must tell me. I need to know so I can handle what needs to be done.'

'I'm not sick,' she said. 'I'm pregnant.'

His eyes widened. 'Again?'

'Yes, again.'

'But how?'

'Well, it turns out straight sex will do that.'

'Christ, Jia! Mubarak! But I thought that factory was closed.'

'Apparently not. Someone has managed to sneak in under the wire.'

Idris surveyed his cousin.

'Don't do that,' she said.

'Do what?'

'Figure out all the things that you need to do ahead of the day. Elyas is in overdrive and I'm ready to kill him.'

'I can help with that,' he said. 'I know some people who can sort him right out.'

She laughed. 'So do I.'

'Jia,' he said, turning back to the work at hand. 'Do you trust Adam Diaz?'

'I've known him a long time,' she said. 'I trust him as much as I trust anyone. Did you hear any more from the Foreign Office?'

'Yes, they're still pressing for a meeting,' he said. 'It sounds complicated, but from what I can figure out, they want two jobs doing. One is domestic, and the other is related to the abduction of the students in Pakistan that's been all over the news these past few weeks. I've asked them to send more details.'

'Keep me updated. I need to go home and sleep. I don't think I can handle any more funerals,' she said.

She climbed into the waiting car, Ishy holding the door open. 'We need to shut the Guild down,' she said, and gestured to Ishy to close the door, leaving Idris standing alone in the road, running through everything she'd just said. Jia Khan only revealed what she wanted people to know, and he wondered what she might be keeping to herself.

Ishy slipped the car into drive, her eyes on the road as she took her boss home to Pukhtun House.

In the back seat, Jia slipped off her shoes and fell silent as Noor Jehan sang about betrayal and lost love, the crackle of old vinyl recreated on Spotify. She knew the lyrics and the playlist, and every bump in the road, every missing brick from the walls they passed. The rhythm of the city and its people was etched upon her mind, and it was beginning to itch. She had spent too much time being driven from one place to the next. She needed to stop.

The roads were getting busy. Traffic was starting to queue as children flooded out of school gates.

Jia watched as children stepped on to the black and white stripes of the pelican crossing, their little blue and grey uniforms washed and ironed neatly. She wondered about each one of them walking the line, being made to conform to an imposed standard of what was today considered the right way.

She'd been driven to school along these streets by her father, and seeing primary school children in the city where she'd grown up brought with it a wave of nostalgia. Her father had been chattiest in the mornings, pleased to see his children enjoying a life that hadn't been granted to him. He'd taken the opportunity to plant the seeds of success on these drives, reminding them that they were capable of whatever they set their hearts on.

Her brother Zan would sometimes press him about his own childhood, but he revealed little. Family trips to Akbar Khan's homeland were never nostalgic. He was not the kind of man to entertain the past, choosing always to focus on the road that lay ahead. He'd brush questions aside, offering an alternative story that wove fact with fiction, and he'd continue with it until they arrived at school.

The route home took in the large Victorian buildings and black railings that had been her first school, and she thought of all the ways her father had tried to protect his children from his past, and all the ways he had failed.

She wondered whether she was destined to fail in the same way. She hadn't managed to keep Ahad away from the family business, despite having tried from the time he was born. He'd survived, and even though he'd been raised miles away from her, somehow he carried more of her traits than his father's.

'Parenthood is a headfuck,' Elyas would often say, and she wanted to tell her father this, assure him that he'd done his best and that she knew this.

Equally, she knew that the relationship she'd had with her parents was very different from the one her children had with her and Elyas. A single glance from her mother was all it took for her to fall silent in those days.

She was feared by those who knew her, but she was loved by her sons. It was the love she gave them that had made them fearless in her presence.

Her father had done the same, steeping her in a sense of self-respect that no one could take from her. She had assumed it was because she was his first daughter, but since finding his old papers, she had learned that that was not the case. She had a sister in the world, one whose cheek her father had kissed before hers.

Her feelings around Amal were mixed, and she needed to find out more, to follow the thread she'd found to its end. But there was so much to unpick before she did this.

The package that held the start of the process was waiting for her when she got home.

'What is it?' asked Elyas.

'It's a genetic heritage kit.'

'You're sure you want to do this?' he said.

She'd told him about her father's letter, but only because she'd decided it was easier to confide in him than to her siblings: he was interested but not emotionally invested. She had needed someone to talk to about her father and his relationship with Mary.

She took the letter opener from her desk and slit the tape along the seal. Inside the box was a plastic tube, a funnel and a plastic bag. She looked at the instructions, trying to make sense of them. She read them once, and then she read them again, but the information wouldn't register in her brain. She put them back in the box.

'Have you considered how you will tell your mum?'

She shook her head. 'One step at a time,' she said.

Elyas understood what was going through her mind. 'Here, let me help,' he said. 'I've used these for a story where we looked at the ethical implications of holding someone's genetic data.'

He looked up and caught the look on her face. 'Probably not the right thing to bring up now,' he said. 'This is the best way to rule things out, and you might find nothing, but you might get a hit. Let's try it.' He handed her the tube. 'You have to spit into the funnel, to the line.'

'Nice,' she said, taking the tube. She turned away from him to put her saliva into the testing kit.

'I've seen a baby come out of you, but saliva you have a problem with,' he said. Her contradictions are part of what made her attractive to him. 'You're like an equation I will never solve.'

'Maths never was your strong suit,' she said, as she took the small, clear plastic bag he was holding out. 'It says it will take three to four weeks.' She placed the tube inside, sealing it up and putting it in the box.

'Do you know anyone else who's taken this test?'

'Only white friends, and their results came back granular, with detailed analysis. Oh, and Amal. But I don't know what her results were because I left London before they arrived, and so we didn't get to discuss it.'

'Maybe you should give her a call?'

Jia nodded. There was a part of her that was afraid to call Amal, because she already knew the truth. The DNA test was a ruse, a way to confirm what she already knew, that her friend Amal was her sister, and that her friend may have known all along that they were siblings. That she had kept this information from Jia was what troubled her. She was emotionally mature enough to know that there were many sides to every story, that the mind had a way of making up what it needed or wanted to be true. In this case, Jia did not know what she wanted that truth to be.

That her trusted friend could be duplicitous was a heavy burden to bear, but the coincidence of finding and becoming close to one's half-sister in a city like London was huge.

Jia Khan already knew what the truth must be, that Amal had known who she was, that she'd sought her out, befriended her and spent time getting to know her because she was Akbar Khan's child.

She needed to figure out what this meant. The test results would give her time.

She sealed the box with tape, making sure every corner was covered. 'Yes,' she said. 'I'll call her, but let's see what the test result says first.'

CHAPTER 13

'You should not have killed him,' said Arjun Singh.

The Guild were gathered in the fading palace. They were old men now and nostalgia had overcome them as they stepped inside the lift that took them to the roof of the once beautiful building. Each one remembered the glamorous parties and obscene displays of wealth they'd encountered when the man who built the place had extended them their much-coveted invite.

Seated in the rooftop garden, where beautiful women had once served them cocktails, fine wines, white powders and pills on polished silver trays, they were now acutely aware of the contraindications of mixing alcohol with statins, diabetes medications and the opioids that eased their arthritis.

They were just glad to still be above ground, knowing that the man whose palace they were currently eating and drinking in was six feet under it.

'To Roman,' said one of them, interrupting to raise his glass. 'He was a great man.'

'He was a ruthless man,' said another.

'Aren't all of us? How else could we move from poverty to riches swifter than birds of prey?' said Yanick Kaplan. He traced his finger over his glass, drawing circle after circle, as if agitated.

'He would have continued to billionaire if it hadn't been for the hit and run,' said Moses Peterson. He looked to Yanick Kaplan as he spoke. 'You were his driver in those days. You know better than all of us.'

Yanick listened, a wrinkle of his brow his only response. Men of power did not rise to the bait. Their response to disrespect was never delivered in the moment. It was noted, considered and left to rise like yeast in bread.

They called it a hit and run, but it wasn't a fatal car accident. In circles like these, where it was known that death for men like them was often violent, they coated their pills in sugar and took them with their morning coffee.

'At least when Roman was killed, we knew something. Not much, but something. We knew the weapon, that the shooter was left-handed, that Roman was buying flowers from the market for his granddaughter,' said Arjun Singh. 'Those were the days. Remember, Yanick? Nowadays we don't see them coming. How do we fight an enemy we can't see?'

Yanick Kaplan looked up from his drink. The ice in the glass clinked as he placed it on the monochrome mother-of-pearl table beside him. It was the only thing that was black and white on the terrace; everything else was whatever colour you wanted it to be, including the truth. Money could do that.

Roman had not been shot by a stranger. Kaplan had put the bullet in his brain under orders from Arjun Singh, and together they had ripped his empire apart. Like bankers at a tech company, they'd stripped and acquired his assets.

But their friendship had started to wear thin recently. Arjun was ill – lymphoma, the doctors said – and it had made him consider life from a different angle.

'She thinks she holds all the cards,' said Kaplan, looking around at the others. 'We have to show her that she doesn't.'

Kaplan's naivety, along with the belief that minimal effort would bring maximum rewards, had begun to grate on Arjun Singh.

'You should not have killed her man without our agreement. We need to make peace,' he said firmly. He was an intelligent man, a gatherer of intel, distancing himself from rash decisions. 'I can't take any more losses. Half of my warehouses are gone, she's taken the drug routes, and I understand the tech she employs means that anyone with a mobile phone, laptop or tablet is a target. I am looking to retire, my children have no interest in the family business, and I want to make peace with my God before I leave this world.'

The other men nodded in agreement. They respected Arjun Singh. He'd been an astute don, he'd run a smart operation, and he was a man of reason and intellect. He'd done what they all aspired to do: he'd raised his children to be successful, respectable and clean of the sins of the father.

He placed the Padron cigar he'd been puffing on down on the ashtray beside him and watched the room carefully, waiting for dissent. He'd known these men for the better part of fifty years and understood their drives, desires and their rhythms. They'd made their global bones sparring against each other and were internationally renowned gangsters. Loss had been experienced on all sides, and eventually they'd settled into a respectful rivalry.

The internet had connected crime kingdoms as much as it had the rest of society.

They'd seen enough of life to know that money brought ease but not contentment, and their children had made plain their mistakes. In the old days, children were taught silence, and that silence was construed as respect.

But they'd raised their sons and daughters to speak their mind, and that had paid off in the ambitious professions they'd chosen. It would not serve in the family business, where secrecy, loyalty and respect protected criminal enterprises.

Arjun was a proud Canadian. The garbage business was where his family officially made its money. Their recycling trucks trundled across Canada and the US through winter, summer, spring and the season they called fall.

Unofficially, drugs, guns and women were the procurement of choice. There wasn't anything that the Singh family couldn't get for the right sum. Arjun Singh lived in Toronto, from where he operated his multimillion-dollar empire. Federal prosecutors estimated his gross earnings were over US $900 million last year alone but had never managed to prove it.

He was smart, and the family in Punjab that he'd sent money to for school fees had flourished, swept along with India's tech success. In the early days, they'd listened into police scanners and used voice scramblers to evade capture. Then they moved on to hacking, and now they could access every government record in the country if they chose. It was rumoured that, for this reason, the CIA sponsored Singh in exchange for what they called 'access'.

'Soft power is my future,' he said to Yanick. 'I have no quarrel with you, and I want an end to the quarrel with her.'

The country where they were currently discussing Jia Khan was a tax haven, and a place where these men could live the life they had dreamed of without questions, prying eyes or raised eyebrows. But time and age meant many of them had started wishing for their homelands. At his age, Singh did not miss the snow, but he did wish for real fires, hot chocolate and playing in the garden with his grandchildren.

Places like Dubai made perfect business sense, but until recently many of them had been devoid of the cultural pursuits his mother had inspired in him. He was a proud Punjabi man, and despite having spent most of his life in Canada, India ran through his veins like a hot toddy on a cold night. The sound of the dholak, the smell of the fragrant green saag and golden makhan-soaked makki di roti, were enough to bring tears to his eyes and sepia-toned memories of his mother to his mind. She'd fed him the leafy greens and chapatti, made from corn and dipped in butter, with her own hands.

Circumstance had hardened Arjun Singh into survival, and it had brought money, marriage and respect. The love of his children had softened him and as he moved towards the final quarter of his life, he wanted ease. 'After hardship comes ease,' his Muslim compatriots often told him, and he was ready to meet his maker. He had heard a lot about Jia Khan and was eager to meet her.

She'd dragged him into a battle that he would not voluntarily have engaged in. He'd hoped that a peace could be brokered swiftly. Now that looked in jeopardy.

He knew these proud men were tired, and that their children were less interested in taking over. Arjun was handing the illegal side of the business over to his niece, Rajo Rani. His sister's daughter, she was the first woman in her family to go to university and had made them proud. She would be queen after he took his leave. She had accompanied him to this gathering of the Guild, and the plan had been for her to fly to the UK with them for a meeting with Jia Khan. He hoped she would have more smarts than the men he was currently sitting with.

For now, she sat silently, taking the measure of everyone. Afterwards, he would ask her opinion and take great pleasure in noting that his mother's intelligence had been passed on to her.

'In the midst of life we are in death,' he said to her later that evening. 'These men don't know that. They think death sits far away, in another room, another country, some other place. But, in truth, it sits on the seat beside us, in the row behind, on the bench across the park. Always here.'

'Chachu,' she said, 'tell me more about the mine Yanick Kaplan is so keen to get his hands on.'

She was peeling pine nuts and pistachios the way they used to do back in Punjab when she was little.

'Reko, puttar?' he said, taking the pine nut she was offering and admiring her patience and skill at removing the shell and leaving the tiny sliver of seed intact. 'It's the largest undeveloped copper-gold project in the world. The Pakistani government doesn't have the resources to mine it and have sold half of it to a US company to start the process. Twenty-five per cent belongs to a federal state-owned enterprise, and the other quarter belongs to a British company. Kaplan wants to take over the entire project.'

'There must be other mines like this that governments are putting out to tender?'

'Not at this level. But that's beside the point. Mr Kaplan has made it personal. He's heard Jia Khan and her Jirga are interested in it.'

'What do you think? Of the plan?'

'Reko is in a district of Balochistan – that is close to Afghanistan and Iran. It's dangerous land, arid terrain with vast deserts and mountain ranges. The population is small because it's hard to survive there. The majority of the inhabitants are Baloch, with a mix of other ethnic groups, some Sikhs even.'

'Sikhs? In Pakistan?'

'Yes, puttar, of course. Your mother had a masi who was left behind during Partition. There are a few families in Quetta, and a gurdwara which is two centuries old.'

Rajo fell into deep thought.

'The area is underdeveloped,' said her uncle, 'and from what I know of Jia Khan, she will put education, healthcare and clean water on her agenda if she gets her way.'

'And Yanick?'

'You have seen what Yanick is like,' he said. 'But we have allegiances to the Guild, and we need each other, like the countries of NATO need each other. We must be strategic.'

Rajo listened to her uncle. He'd built up wisdom over many decades, and she had great respect for him. But she couldn't help wondering what an allegiance with a man like Yanick was worth.

'Chachu, we must make plans. We cannot be seen to be weak.'

'Puttar, we are warriors. But let us be warriors in fields of mustard. There has been enough bloodshed.' He took his niece's hand in his and pressed it gently, as his mother used to press his, as if pressing good sense into him. She hadn't succeeded and he knew he would fail here too.

Her brown eyes flickered with fire, her golden skin was soaked in the pride of the young and beautiful, and she had her mother's cheekbones, the bones of her ancestors, the countless women who had fought for their place in society while running homes and raising boys to manhood.

'There are people with so much ease in the world,' she said, thinking of the men and women of the inheritocracy, the ones with whom she now shared space at high-end restaurants thanks to her uncle's generosity. She contemplated their confidence when they walked into rooms, their nervous systems calm, unlike hers, which was frazzled.

'Let me tell you a story of a man to whom everything came with ease. Whatever he asked for, it would be done. He wondered why it was that his life was this way, why he had so much ease when all around him there was hardship. His guru took him by the hand and led him to a room filled with bones, skull piled on skull, femurs, tibias, ribs. He looked at his guru and asked, "What is this place?" And the guru answered, "These are all the lives you've lived and died and suffered in."'

Arjun Singh paused and looked at his niece. 'I want to reach mukti. I live my life with Waheguru in mind. I do not want to come here again, to this place. I want to break the cycle. You – you are young and must make your own choices. But if you learn one thing, remember – never trust a man.'

CHAPTER 14

'The therapist said my trauma has served me well!' said Elyas to his best friend, John, as they sat at a table in Café de Khan.

'He was right,' said John. 'You've got enough journalistic silverware for both of us. Personally, I would've stopped after the first Pulitz Surprise.'

Elyas shook his head at the joke. 'It was definitely a surprise, I'll give you that.'

'But you worked hard for it.'

'Hard work doesn't always pay off.'

'You ever speak to that reporter who was chasing you?'

'Yeah. I'm seeing him next week.'

'What's he after?'

'He's looking into a local story. I'll make some introductions.'

Elyas didn't have to make introductions. He didn't need to share contacts. But he understood the long game, how trust, generosity and connection built bridges. It's what made him good at what he did.

'Does all this AI talk worry you?' John asked.

Elyas shook his head again. 'Not really. Remember that sub who used to circle our copy in red when we started at the paper? He once told me, "You can teach a monkey to write copy, but you can't teach them to build contacts – and that's what makes a great reporter." AI's not going to steal your job, but someone who knows how to use it might.'

A waiter appeared and placed a plate of fresh, crispy poppadoms on the table. Elyas cracked one in half, dipped it into mango chutney, then scooped up some diced onions in red sauce.

'Steady on, mate,' said John. 'Anyone'd think you've never had one of these beauties before.'

'I don't make these at home! Remember all those NIBs we wrote about people burning down their kitchens with deep-fat fryers after a night out?'

'I do. Now it's all about phones left charging overnight.' John rolled his eyes. 'Did you hear about that machete attack? Five women. I've stopped reading the news. Sexual violence in Sudan, Gaza… the small boats talk again and that fucking PM of ours, Oliver Blundell, wants to ship refugees to Rwanda. And every time trans rights are brought up, someone starts wailing about toilets. The world is on fucking fire.'

'The world's always been on fire,' Elyas said. 'You're just more aware of it now.'

'You calling me woke?' John said, cracking a smile. 'Because I'll take that as a badge of honour.'

The waiter returned with a sizzling platter of chargrilled meats on a bed of soft onions. The smoke curled upwards, fragrant with spice and charcoal. Beside it stood the naan tree, pillowy bread draped like fabric from metal branches.

They didn't wait for one another. They never had. Their friendship was decades old, built in newsrooms and shared flats, over deadline panics and breakups and bereavements. Courtesies like 'you first' had never really applied.

'You ever interview Blundell?' John asked, tearing a strip of naan.

'No, but I met him a few times at the British Asian Trust dinners, back when I was a trustee.' Elyas spooned some meat on to his plate. 'The events were full of interesting people. Blundell stood out in the worst way. Eton, Oxbridge PPE, Dad's money, Mum's looks. Cookie-cutter politician.'

'What was he doing there?'

'He's got a Pakistani wife, posh Pakistani, not like me. They kept mentioning it, like that somehow made everything OK.'

'You think he'll win the election again?'

'No. Not a cat in hell's chance. That's why everything's burning.'

'What do you mean?'

'I mean, John, we've won. Men like Blundell are being seen for what they really are – mediocre, failing forward, clinging to Daddy's wallet and their mum's social capital. They know it too. That's why they're panicking. The racism's louder, the backlash stronger, the denial deeper – because they've looked in the mirror and seen their own cowardice. And they're terrified. And scared people fight dirty.'

John looked at him, not saying anything for a moment. He'd always admired how Elyas could take the same fragmented headlines everyone else saw and build a clear, terrifying and honest picture of what was coming next. Over the years, Elyas had been right more often than not, and John had learned to trust him.

'You know next week's lottery numbers too?' he said finally. 'I could use a win.'

Elyas smirked as John packed up the leftover chicken karahi he'd insisted on over-ordering. Not a drop of sauce was left behind. He'd even made sure they had extra naan to go.

'I'm cracking it open when I get home,' John said, stashing the foil container in a tote bag he pulled from his backpack.

Jia Khan lay in bed, considering the long day of negotiations. 'The more money we demand, the more they value us,' she'd told Idris. 'Stay humble, stay poor.'

The shift from black cash to a legit income was becoming more important now that her sons were growing. The mine in Reko Diq was a way for them to make enough money to launder their business and scrub the past away. She was making inroads with the government in Pakistan and just needed a little more time.

Beside her lay one of the few people whose opinion she cared about. He wasn't quite a man yet, but he would be one day, and until the world finally levelled the fields of power, she knew Lirian would, like all men, be seen as one of the masters of the universe. She wanted those eyes to look at him with respect and not judgement.

She was hoping to be awake when Elyas returned from his dinner with John, but she closed her eyes for just a moment and, before she knew it, had drifted off.

***

Elyas stood at the doorway and watched his wife and son sleep, the long brown hair she always kept tied back spilling on to the white of the pillow, her arm curled protectively around the boy, a book on her chest and her reading glasses still on her nose.

There'd been a distance between them lately, a quiet frost settling between their exchanges. He couldn't remember what he'd done to trigger it – said something careless probably.

'You were in your fortress of solitude,' he would tell her when their cold war ended. 'The place where Superman went to find himself and understand his purpose.' She used to laugh when he said it. He hoped she would again.

Marriage, he thought, required a kind of bravery even war zones hadn't demanded. It meant staying when you didn't understand what was being asked of you, and offering peace when you were the one wounded.

He wondered what she was dreaming of, where she went to in the recesses of her mind, the places that others could not access. Their marriage navigated the light and the dark of life. They withheld secrets from others and from each other, but at night they lay spine to spine.

There were days when, bored with life, they ended up hurting each other through throwaway words and conflicts that were not of the other's making. And then there were days when he wanted to hold on to Jia Khan and never let her go. Elyas understood that life was a long game.

He watched her breathing, the curve of her brow, her lips slightly parted as she slept, and he noticed that she looked older – another truth he could never share with her and live to tell the tale.

Elyas knew that he could survive without Jia, that time continued, the sun rose and children grew, but he was more alive when he was with her, his senses heightened, his dreams brighter. That was why he stayed despite his knowledge of her sins. He still believed that the young woman he had fallen in love with existed, and if he could just reach her, maybe he could save her.

He carefully climbed into the other side of the oversized bed, placing his head on the pillow beside his son's. He moved the little boy's fringe from his eyes. Lirian stirred, giving Elyas cause to regret.

A waking child meant a barrage of demands and conversation that he was too tired to have.

It felt as if Jia had only just told him she was pregnant and here they were five years on, lying side by side in bed, the baby a child between them. An ocean of fatherly love and responsibility crashed over him, and with it came a plan of packing him up and taking him away from the contradictions and complexities of this life. They would convince Jia to come. They would move to Karachi; he could get a job as a correspondent. They would live an ordinary life. His heart raced, his mind swam, and then he remembered who he was. He was not built for ordinary, and neither was she.

He glanced from his son to his wife. They shared both colouring and temperament, their large eyes closed. They looked as innocent as each other.

Jia stirred slightly and he adjusted himself to not wake her. Despite the size of the bed, Lirian had pushed himself into the small of his mother's back, nudging her to the edge. Her patience with the boy undid him every time, and he fell in love with her all over again.

He remembered raising Ahad alone, wondering, back then, if things would be better if his mother had been with them. The balancing act of the universe was now showing him what that parallel life would have been like, and he wasn't sure if it was any better.

He knew that it would have been a very different Jia Khan who would have raised their firstborn to the one who was with him now. This one was hardened to life but was softer on her sons. Still, her tolerance for bullshit was low, and he wondered how that would play out when Lirian became a teenager and began calling her out on the things no one else could.

Life had been a rollercoaster since she'd left lawyering to run her father's business. With Jia at the helm, the company had flourished, but as it grew, demands on her had increased. So she'd hired more women, and the success had continued, and eventually found an even keel that allowed family life to fall into a steady pace.

In spite of recent tensions, things were generally good between him and Jia. Ahad had graduated and was working now. He and his mother had grown close in ways that surprised even Elyas, playing chess and backgammon in the evenings, hiking on the weekends. There were moments Elyas had felt himself envious of their relationship, but he'd checked himself. Mother and son were alike: their heads together, you could not tell them apart, an echo chamber for each other.

As he lay in bed, he was hit by the fear that Ahad's life would become something he'd not planned for, but it was fleeting and he brushed it aside, under the rug where he placed many of things he wasn't ready to handle. What was there to worry about? He had everything he had ever dreamed of.

He had delivered on his latest book, edits were complete, and the publication date was still a few months away. This should have been that sweet spot where he could take things easy, but he wasn't built for that. He'd had enough therapy to know that he needed to stop searching for more, but the question of 'How much is enough?' plagued him.

He glanced at his sleeping wife, and lifted the spectacles from her nose, turning over the book on her chest, pausing to read the words she'd underlined.

Her red pen was prolific, and a secret known only to him, the man she shared a house and library with. She would do this to his books when they were first married, and it had annoyed him. 'You're defacing my collection,' he had said. Years later, he'd found himself opening books to run his fingers over the same red ink lines, a reminder that she had been an intimate part of his life, that she'd sat at his desk and touched the pages of his favourite novels, pored over them and been unafraid to leave a part of her on the pages. Where faces became lined, and bodies soft, and bones brittle, the memory of shared love and words remained untarnished.

He ran his thumb along the quote she had inked. '*The old is collapsing and the new cannot take shape; in this interregnum, all kinds of monsters arise.*' It was a loose translation, the original Italian by Antonio Gramsci above it. He placed the closed book beside her bed and kissed her forehead. She stirred a little and he moved back. She smelt like florals, sweet shampoo and the rich night cream that she kept in a black glass jar beside her bed.

He watched her sleep, her face serene, as if she slept the sleep of the righteous. She was a woman who knew herself, and so did he, but still he stayed.

He had known what she was long before he found the letter she'd written to her father, telling him how she felt and implying what she was going to do to him. Elyas often worried what that said about himself, that he had known and still stayed. He was a good man, an honest man, one who held the world to account through his works and his words, and yet he shared his life with a woman who crossed many of the lines he investigated as a journalist. How long before he would have to wrestle with this hypocrisy? His discomfort was growing day by day.

Jia Khan made no bones about her way of life. She carried the mantle of the Khan. She was the protector of her people, the one they came to when their world needed rearranging, when their children needed naming, their university fees paid for, when their husbands behaved badly, when their sons and daughters wanted to marry someone they considered unsuitable. Her businesses involved tech companies, consultancies, accountancy firms, and that was just the legal aspect.

They'd started building hospitals and schools in various parts of the world. He'd accompanied her to corporate and political events, watching her work the room calmly and confidently, never fawning, always measured. She was a woman who was fast becoming the most powerful person in the country.

But Elyas knew what else she did; he knew there was a reason Idris and Sakina had taken over responsibility for a large proportion of her business interests. He knew that whenever a body turned up, the news reports only told half a story. He couldn't help but gather the information he had. It was instinctive. But also, deep down, he feared that one day he might need protection, and his notes were that. He'd always kept a diary, but since moving in with Jia, he had started to keep more detailed records of who she met and when. The lines and squiggles of his Teeline shorthand meant that he was able to leave his notebooks lying around without fear.

He looked at his wife, her brown hair framing her face. She was what the writer of her book had described. She was the harbinger of death for the old world, the bridge to the new world. Now was the time of monsters.

He kissed her head again, lay down and turned off the light.

CHAPTER 16

Yanick Kaplan knew why Arjun Singh wanted out. He was an old man who had already made his money, and although he had not told his associates, Kaplan's sources had brought word that he was riddled with cancer.

'A man like that is weak in the world,' Kaplan told Ignacio Cervantes Perez, the head of the Valencia cartel, when they met the following day at the boutique hotel. They were sitting in the jacuzzi, bubbles forming and bursting around them thanks to the hot-water jets that lined the side of the pool. The sun shone down on them, warming the shoulders that had carried so much. Ordinarily the spa would have been filled with the men and women able to afford the luxury fees and escape the boredom that came with wealth, but Kaplan had seen to it that it was empty.

His associates had been offered a deep tissue massage before being taken to the spa rooms. The woman who had spent sixty minutes massaging Perez with hot stones and scented oils had led him through the corridor and up a flight of steps to a door marked 'The Cotton Mill'. She'd stopped and entered a pin code into the keypad. It had beeped red. She'd tried it again and again.

'What is wrong, my dear?' Perez had asked.

'The code seems to have changed.'

'It's OK, Magdalena,' a voice had come from behind. 'I'll escort Mr Perez to the spa.' It was Yanick. Then he'd entered the pin code and pushed the door open. 'My man here will escort the other guests.' He'd held the door open and Perez had stepped through.

'Where are the employees? The women who normally work here? You have heard something?' Perez had asked.

Kaplan did not know for sure, but he had his suspicions about who was passing information to Jia Khan. He had come to understand that women were building networks akin to the brotherhood that men had long enjoyed as a side effect of patriarchy.

After the jacuzzi, the men moved to the steam room. Wrapped in white towels, condensation trickling down the marble walls, they continued their talks, along with a few of the men Kaplan considered friends.

'Singh no longer cares for the ways of our world, obsessing instead with the afterlife. We are in full health and still have many years left.'

Perez nodded at Kaplan's words. His predicament was similar, but he moved between yay and nay. It would be nice to quit and live an ordinary life, but that wasn't on the cards for men like him.

But Yanick Kaplan wasn't looking for approval. He had set plans in motion long before the Guild had met to discuss a truce.

CHAPTER 17

A large consignment of bananas was due to arrive in Glasgow at two o'clock.

They had departed from Ecuador weeks earlier, but the number of days, like the quality of the fruit, was irrelevant. What mattered were the contents buried deep within the ripened crates: one-kilogram blocks of cocaine, seventy-three per cent pure, nestled into the yellow bounty like pearls hidden in an oyster.

Each crate was a message. Each kilogram, a line in a letter of war.

Yanick Kaplan had orchestrated the operation with clinical precision. His network, spanning Guayaquil in Ecuador, the Valencia cartel in Spain, smugglers in Abu Dhabi, East London brokers and trusted men in Glasgow, was global and loyal, and now, it was mobilised.

His goal wasn't just profit. It was revenge.

Jia Khan had humiliated him, and he wanted to return the favour.

The fury hadn't faded since he'd woken up soaked in blood that wasn't his. She had continued pushing him, dismantling one of his money-laundering streams, cutting ties with his supplier in Istanbul and leaving three of his men dangling in a warehouse in Bratislava.

He was going to take from her what she had taken from him.

The plan relied on a man named Bill Davidson, a sixty-eight-year-old Glaswegian market trader whose best days were behind him. His hands were rough from years of labour, his mind dulled by the quiet erosion of hope. Once, long ago, he'd spent six months in prison for theft. Since then he'd kept his head down, sold fruit and vegetables, and lived for a beer down at his local pub and his granddaughter's visits.

It was through her that Kaplan's people had reached him, thanks to some assistance from Rajo Rani.

'Bill's kept his nose clean for most of his life, except for a brief stint in prison as a twenty-five-year-old,' Rajo had told Kaplan over vodka and lime.

Sharp, stylish and strategic, Rajo had no personal grudge against Jia Khan, but their business was a blood sport, and alliances were its currency. And this was before Adam Diaz had sought the Guild's agreement to end the war.

'What's convinced this Bill to help?' Kaplan had asked.

'Love, of course.'

'It's always a woman.'

'This one is his granddaughter,' said Rajo. 'Her boyfriend is one of our button men. She's asked Grandpa for help so she can get married, and he's too soft to say no.'

Bill had been told it would be easy.

'All we need is your business name and import papers. No risk to you,' the young man had reassured him. 'We'll handle the rest.'

Bill, who was as naive as he'd been when he was twenty-five, had agreed.

He had no idea that he was being used as a mule, not just for product but for liability. If it all went south, his would be the name on the bill of lading, the importer on record, the fall guy. That was how the Guild did business.

What none of them realised was that someone had overheard the deal. Someone who cared.

The woman worked with buttercream and sponge. A quiet woman who ran a stall two lanes down from Bill's in the Glasgow fruit market; people spoke freely in front of her. She baked elaborate birthday cakes, pastel-hued biscuits for baby showers and towering floral wedding confections, but most of all, she listened.

'Ms Khan,' she had said, sitting in Jia's office, having taken the train down specially. 'Folk think I don't know much, but I hear stuff, y'know? I hear everythin'.'

Jia offered her tea. 'Tell me what you hear,' she said.

'I've baked cakes for men that wouldnae flinch at tellin' someone to kill. Dealers, traffickers…even some folk you'd call enemies. They dinnae notice me. I'm just the cake woman. But I mind names. Addresses. Birthdays. It's no use to me. But you…you could do somethin' with it.'

Jia nodded slowly. She cut a slice of the pistachio cake the woman had brought. The lime icing cracked beneath the silver blade.

Women like this cake maker were the backbone of the Khan's network. Invisible, underestimated and omnipresent, they were cleaners, caregivers, shop girls, nurses, translators. Women who passed on information and were maligned as 'gossipmongers' to strip them of their power. When men did it, they called it 'intelligence' and used it to bring down nations.

Jia shared the news with Sakina later that day. 'I don't like it,' she said, 'that they use these old men as shields.'

'We can't let it slide,' Sakina replied.

And they didn't.

***

British customs agents, tipped off by an anonymous source, seized ten of the twenty-two banana shipments at Clydeport as they were loaded on to lorries bound for Glasgow. Border Force agents claimed they'd used intercepted EncroChat messages to track the deal.

But that was a lie.

It had been the cake maker's intel that had been vital to helping Jia's tech crew. Embedded in the cartel's infrastructure for months, they had decrypted the plans and fed it to law enforcement like a breadcrumb trail. In exchange, British intelligence services turned a blind eye to some of Jia's operations in Marseille. They kept the beast fed on scraps so it stayed away from the steak.

Of the remaining banana consignments due to be shipped on to other destinations, four were misrouted and eight disappeared entirely.

The authorities took the win. Jia took the cocaine.

Later on, Bill Davidson would be arrested and then released. He would vanish, his escape a gift to the cake maker, who was sweet on him. A year on, word would filter back that he'd resurfaced in Utrecht, living quietly above a florist's shop. His granddaughter was married now and expecting, living in Lisbon with her husband, and the new baby would be an incentive for him to keep his nose clean.

Another debt paid by Khan's code, a philosophy passed down from her father, a set of quiet, ruthless rules hidden behind kind eyes and clean ledgers.

Miles away, Yanick Kaplan was still playing king, but the throne beneath him was cracking.

CHAPTER 18

The air in the private perfume atelier was heavy with jasmine, oud and amber.

Rajo stepped through the carved doorway of Maison Marrakech and into the filtered light of the courtyard. Gold-flecked patterns danced across the marble floor, cast from intricate latticework above. She glanced at her phone. She was in the right place.

Entry to this place came by bloodline, invitation or blackmail. For Yanick Kaplan, it had been all three.

He sat waiting at a cedarwood table, its surface inlaid with mother-of-pearl. Laid out before him like a ritual were antique vials of rare perfume oils: Iranian saffron, Cambodian agarwood, Sumatran benzoin. He inspected each one like a general surveying his troops.

The old perfumer worked in silence behind him, his silk gloves moving over glass vials and instruments. He knew better than to interrupt.

There was no street noise, no shouting from the souk, no traffic. Just the slow drip of an ancient fountain and the sharp click of Kaplan's lighter as he lit a slim cigarillo.

'Money and power,' he said as Rajo entered, 'have their own fragrance. Did you know that?'

She said nothing, lowering herself on to a low ottoman.

'The nouveau riche drown themselves in overpriced colognes. They think cost means class. But you and I, we know better. Real power doesn't announce itself.'

'Is that why you've asked me here?' Rajo asked. 'To buy perfume?'

Kaplan smiled. 'Yes, and also it's a good place to wait on good news.'

Before he could lift another vial, his phone buzzed.

A breathless voice on the line: 'Sir…the Red Line is gone. All the shipments taken.'

Kaplan's eyes narrowed.

'What else?'

'The buyers in Marseille have pulled out. They say the ports aren't secure. The word is she's consolidating.'

'Who is?'

'The Khan.'

The name hit him like a blade.

Kaplan listened as his contact unravelled the details of his defeat. His empire was being publicly dismantled. His supply routes were all gone, his credibility fractured, and any leverage he had no longer existed.

He hung up and rose slowly, adjusting his cuffs, his reflection twisted in the curved perfume bottles before him.

'She's taken the cocaine. All of it,' he said. 'No cocaine, no buyers. No buyers, no leverage. No leverage, no power.'

He was angry, but he knew that his rage would serve no purpose at this point. He turned to Rajo. She dropped a sugar cube into her tea, stirring slowly.

'What will you do?' she asked.

Kaplan's eyes were steady. 'She thinks she can be a ruler and a mother. Ruthless and righteous. That is her flaw.'

He uncorked a vial and inhaled. His head cleared, and it was a moment before he spoke.

'Many of the ingredients in perfumes come from the unlikeliest of places and difficult circumstances,' he said. 'Take, for example, this ambergris,' he said, handing Rajo the vial. 'It comes from the sperm whale. Whales eat squid but they can't digest its beak, and it continues to irritate the intestine, forcing the gut to produce ambergris. People call it "floating gold" because of its rarity, and despite it being rotten at its core, they will pay thousands for it. This is an opportunity for us, Rajo Rani.'

'Go on,' she said.

'She's a woman. A wife. A mother. That's where her strength lies. But a woman's life, as you know, is only an illusion of balance. Jia Khan thinks she can be both ruler and mother, both ruthless and righteous. Let's show her the truth of that lie.'

Rajo leaned forward, hesitant at what she was about hear. 'You want to take out her family? My uncle is unlikely to agree to something like this. It goes against our values, our way of life.'

'Your uncle has lost his appetite for this business. He'd rather be sipping cocoa in retirement while you and I are left to pick up the pieces of a surrender on Jia Khan's terms,' Kaplan replied, swirling the perfume slowly under his nose. 'Anyway, I mean only to exploit her vulnerability. Her husband. Her child. Her peace. To cut her wide open. Not with blood – no, that's far too messy – but with grief. Grief is an acid. It dissolves everything – logic, empire, even the desire for vengeance.'

'Why not just kill her?' said Rajo, watching Kaplan closely, weighing up which side of the intricate situation she would fall on.

A smile crept across Kaplan's face. 'Because death would make her a martyr.' He looked at Rajo closely. 'When I'm done with her, she will be ruined, and all thought of revenge will have fled her mind. What you must decide is whose side you're really on.'

He looked at her, unblinking. 'So choose, Rajo. Whose is it to be?'

CHAPTER 19

Amal sat in the sitting room of the private members' club, leaning back into an oversized armchair.

'Women aren't going to want to come here after a long day's work unless it offers something they're not getting at home,' she'd told her partner at the private equity firm.

'Well, what do you suggest then?'

'I'll send you a list,' she'd said. 'But to start with, a spa. Not the usual Groupon voucher place, but something with travertine tiles, soft lighting and exquisite food. Wealthy women of colour are not going anywhere for cheese and biscuits.'

He'd scanned the list, hesitant at first, but he knew better than to question her instincts. Amal had made the firm more money in a year than they'd made in the previous decade. Her network was as powerful as her net worth. She gave them access into international money in a way that the average white middle-class male – even with a prep school, boarding school and Harvard (thanks to a tennis scholarship) polish – could not.

The club had become everything she had envisioned. It was exclusive, refined and discreet. Judges, barristers, artists and authors, bankers and venture capitalists, IT entrepreneurs and women who kept the homes running all gathered under one roof. What happened at the club stayed at the club.

Before it had opened, there had been months of heated debate about diversity and inclusion, and about bursary memberships.

'If we want to keep our eye on what's going on in the wider world, we have to have a representative group of women,' Amal had said.

'Yes, but these women don't work. They have no power. What's the point of that?'

'Don't be naive Jeffrey. Don't you know that the more educated you are, the more likely you are to quit your job and stay at home to raise your children?'

'What rubbish! Where are you getting this?'

'Silicon Valley. Also, you must be married to someone who earns enough to pay the bills if you're not doing paid work. Notice the word "paid" in this sentence.'

'In that case, their husbands can pay.'

'Do you think it's easy for a woman to ask a man for money? If they know about us, they're smart enough to join the club. These women keep the world turning, they're intelligent, and their value to us in not based on their membership fees. It's based on what they know, who they know and the circles they have access to.'

Now, the club was her sanctuary, and with her children away at boarding school and a husband who, as a neurosurgeon, frequently worked late, she'd often spend evenings here, playing chess and backgammon.

She'd also come to the club to swim and take the edge off the day. Summers were spent stretched out on the outdoor day beds, reading the *Economist* or the latest bestseller recommended by the book club.

Winters brought firelit lounges, steamy jacuzzies and the sleek pool, which stretched from indoor to outdoor, a glass door dividing the two spaces. The pool had been Jia Khan's idea, and Amal was glad she'd listened. They hadn't seen Jia since she'd moved north after her father's death.

Amal had wanted to attend the funeral but hadn't gone. She wasn't sure what she would find, and she didn't know if Akbar Khan had finally told Jia about her. She hadn't wanted to be the one to break the news. Mary, her mother, had come to London, and they had grieved their loss together. That he was her father, that Jia was her half-sister and that she had known for some time, were delicate truths with heavy consequences. They required measuring, and the details of how much and what to tell needed weighing up.

'*Mon coeur*,' her mother had said, stroking her daughter's hair. 'He loved you, and he tried, but men from his world and time had complicated lives. And your father was a complicated man.'

They moved smoothly between English and French, the languages of Mary's homeland in Cameroon. Like many West African women, Mary had only grown more striking with age, seeming to deepen into herself, melanin a gift that kept her skin supple and wrinkle-free.

Years had passed since their father's death, and Jia hadn't been in touch, making Amal doubt that she'd found out. But now it looked likely.

Amal shifted in the chair. Her feelings about her half-sister were complicated. She hadn't expected to like Jia so much, and she'd certainly not expected to have so much in common with a woman raised across the world. She'd grown up in Chicago in the US, and Jia had spent her childhood in the northern part of England, but they shared more than geography would suggest. Maybe it was due to both of them being women of colour, or of faith, or maybe it was encoded in their DNA, and scientists were yet to map it out.

Amal had thought of reaching out before they'd even met, but between raising children and the demands of a high-powered job and a marriage she was constantly questioning, the timing never felt right. That was until fate intervened.

She remembered clearly the day her PA had brought her the invite list for the company's monthly angel investor dinner to glance over. A curated mix of interesting people, including the gauntlet of lawyers, CEOs and medics with money, alongside government offi-cials, artists and writers. The last three were there to make the conversation less dry. Without them, the dinners were as dull as an HMRC tax bill.

'Is this a new addition?' she'd asked her PA, pointing at the list.

'Yes, she's the plus one for Adam Diaz. Jia Khan. She's a highly successful barrister and probably should have been on our radar earlier,' said her PA.

'Seat her next to me,' she said. 'The list looks good. I see you've added names from the diplomatic list. Excellent job,' she'd said, handing back the printed copy – her eyesight couldn't take too much tech.

The dinner had been delightful, and Jia Khan had been more interesting than Amal could have hoped. They'd hired a private room in The Ivy, the wine flowed, the food was divine, and the conversation was thoughtful but not heavy. It was a clear night, and Tower Bridge was beautifully bathed in orange light.

Amal had spent the evening quietly studying Jia, trying to find similarities in their features. Aside from their eyes, she'd found little else.

'I love your blouse,' she'd said, when the political conversation hit a lull.

'Thank you,' Jia had said. Then, leaning forward, she whispered, 'I'm resisting the urge to downplay how much I spent on it.'

Her eyes sparkled, an unspoken invitation to sisterhood. Amal laughed in recognition at that shared instinct to conceal extravagance. It felt intimate, and their friendship had been cemented. Powerful women rarely revealed their vulnerabilities, but when they did, Amal knew bonds were forged quickly and deeply. This, she would later learn, was Jia Khan's superpower.

Jia had principles. Where Amal saw moral lines as negotiable in the pursuit of profit, Jia saw boundaries and held them. Amal found herself admiring her half-sister, wishing she could talk freely about their father and ask questions.

She'd even taken a DNA test under the guise of researching her ancestry. She had hoped to convince Jia to do the same, but she'd been reluctant. Amal hadn't pushed.

But now she'd had an email from the genetic testing company: 'You have a new relative match.'

Sipping her Earl Grey in the comfort of the club, Amal wondered how long it would be until her sister got in touch and what it was she would want from her. She secretly hoped it would be the truth.

CHAPTER 20

Sweat soaked, Jia's pinstriped nightshirt clung to her legs as she scrambled from the bed to the window. She flung it open, taking in the rush of cold, sweet northern air that filled her lungs and the room.

On nights like this, she was glad to be in Yorkshire. No amount of personal wealth could do anything about the pollution outside the Piccadilly apartment where she'd lived for over a decade.

Exhausted, she slipped to the floor, pressing her back against the wall, grateful for solid ground to lean on. She felt Elyas at her side now, his hand on her back, his fingers gently moving strands of hair from her face.

She turned towards him, leaning into his arms. He took her weight easily and helped her to her feet, guiding her back to their bed. Seeing her soaked pillow, he switched it for his, pulling back the duvet and smoothing the crumpled sheets before helping her in.

She leaned against the tall, upholstered headboard and closed her eyes as he left the room to settle Lirian, who had stirred. Elyas switched on the nightlight as he tucked the boy in.

Lirian had begun asking for lights to be left on and doors left open, confessing his fear of the dark.

'Why is he afraid?' Jia had said, worried that his fears were a symptom of something deeper than childish nerves.

'Ahad was the same at his age. He'll grow out of it,' Elyas had said.

Jia had been absent during Ahad's early years and was adamant that Lirian's nightlight be left on whenever he asked for it. Maybe it was guilt, or maybe it was just mothering.

When Elyas returned with a glass of water, she took it with quiet gratitude, sipping slowly.

'You need to slow down,' he said. 'We both do.' This was the fourth night she'd woken like this, the nightmare repeating itself. She was reluctant to speak about it, but she knew that something was off.

Their lives had accelerated at a time when others their age were easing up. She felt like she was in an Aston Martin with the brake lines cut, curves coming faster than she could navigate.

He thought her nightmares were about Zan. She hadn't corrected him. For years after her brother's death, she would wake like this: alone, drenched in sweat, gasping for air. She relived the argument with her father, the sound of the crash, the smell of engine oil, the sight of his twisted body on the tarmac surrounded by glass and crunched-up metal. Even now, the tang of petrol and call of sirens would bring it all back like a crushing weight on her chest.

She had made herself invincible after that, wrapped herself in armour and pulled away from those she loved. She had built herself a life fortified against her pain and that of others. It was her father's death and the return of the son she had long believed dead that had cracked that armour. The birth of her second son had blown it apart completely. Now, she was exposed to life with all its elements, and to her enemies, the people who wished her harm. That was why the nightmares had returned. But this time it wasn't Zan she saw; it was her children.

Jia Khan did not fear death. She had readied herself to meet her maker decades ago, back when she believed her soul clean. Later on, she made peace with the knowledge that no amount of amends would make good on the scales of good and evil. She would be reliant on the mercy of the Creator, because redemption, she believed, was not for the likes of her. She had answered God's most difficult questions as best she could.

Motherhood had carved her open. She feared what the world would do to her children, but more than that, she feared they'd see her for who she truly was. She feared their disappointment.

She knew evil; she'd defended bad men. The perpetrators of unspeakable crimes often looked like ordinary folk. She knew that awful things happened to good people, and when that happened the sky did not crack, the ground was not rent asunder, the sun still rose, the moon still waxed and waned.

Elyas's arms wrapped around her, and she breathed him in. Their lives had formed around each other like wet clay. Separation had chipped at them, but that first imprint had remained. On good days, they slipped back into the old ways, like calloused hands in well-worn gloves.

When Jia finally drifted off, Elyas stayed up, adjusting himself around her, propped against the headboard. He reached for his book and glasses, reading with one hand, glancing down at her now and then.

He believed love was much easier than people realised. Love was watching over his wife as she slept. He had lost her once and borne the heaviness of her parting in his heart. He carried the scars of her absence in his soul. He was too old and tired and in love to run.

Jia stirred in her sleep, mumbling incoherently. Each time, he soothed her back into slumber, tapping all her concerns away the way his mother had done for him, and her mother had done for her, and so on for generations before – a form of somatic therapy that calmed the nervous system.

He gazed upon her olive skin, her dark hair on his shoulder, her body in his arms, and he wondered what stories their children would tell their own sons and daughters about them.

CHAPTER 21

By morning, the nightmares were gone.

Jia woke to a breakfast tray beside her. Elyas pulled back the curtains, and the soft creamy light spilled into the room, reminding her of the many reasons to start over.

'Thank you for sitting up with me,' she said, taking a bite into a slice of hot sourdough toast, butter, like liquid gold, dripping from her fingers. He handed her a napkin, and she took it gratefully, wiping her hands and her lips.

Romantic love, she often thought, was a trick of the mind, a thing created by biology to ensure the survival of the species. What mattered was a love far deeper than that, one that emerged after excavating the darkest parts of life, covered in mud and soil and used to build a life together brick by brick.

There were ties that grew strong due to the seasons that had been spent together, seeds that had been planted and protected, watered with tears and silence, faith and hope. And then there were the bonds of blood. These were formed without choice and they both elevated and submerged the soul.

'I know you don't need me the way some women need men,' he said. 'It's why I love you. But sometimes I want to be needed, and I worry that, one day, we will look up and life will have passed us by.' His voice was wistful, and when his eyes locked with hers, she felt she would catch alight.

'Can I confess something?' he said.

She shifted, making space beside her.

'So, I was teaching yesterday,' he said, slipping into bed. 'And I realised that no one notices me anymore when I walk into a room.' He ran his fingers through his hair, and she noticed the grey.

'What do you mean?' she said.

'I mean, I'm just the old man who gives the lecture.'

'What do you mean?'

'Come on, you know exactly what I mean,' he laughed.

'You're serious?' she said. 'You're bothered by that?'

'You're just trying to embarrass me. Look, I'm not particularly proud of myself for being this shallow but, yeah, I miss being seen.'

'Elyas Ahmad, I did not have you pegged for that guy who bases his self-esteem on how hot women find him,' she said. She sipped her tea slowly, her eyebrows raised over the rim.

'Wait, listen, hear me out,' he said. 'Just because I'm seen as some deep intellectual type doesn't mean that I don't want to be admired too.'

Her laughter rang out again. Most people knew Jia Khan as a serious and determined woman. Elyas felt a quiet privilege in witnessing this version, unguarded, light. He had access to the vulnerable, tired version of her, and that he got to be the one who held the woman who held other people together, made him feel good about himself.

'I'm all ears,' she said, 'about your grey hair and crow's feet.'

'What do you mean *crow's feet*?' He grabbed his phone, checking his reflection. This rarest of days, one beginning with laughter and lightness, made him hopeful for their future.

It was a Sunday morning. Sanam Khan had taken Lirian into her room. There were no scheduled meetings or work-related calls for Jia, only the prospect of a long leisurely lunch, and before that, sitting on the sofa with music and books and the comfort of tea being refilled without asking.

Jia had suffered burnout a year ago, and this had taught her a vital lesson: how to slow down. She had handed over more of the workload to Sakina and Idris, depending on which arm of the business it was. The presence of more women in the Jirga had given the enterprise a different shape. Things were less fraught, the foundations grounded, and the business more communal.

'The power pie is not finite,' she had said told her Jirga, addressing the room but speaking directly to the women. 'Don't let them make you think it is. Men worry because they think the matriarchy will operate on the same principles as their patriarchy has done for hundreds of years. They forget that we are the mothers of sons, the creators of both patriarchy and matriarchy. Nothing is possible without us, and we believe in equality for all.'

The women had nodded. Their power had grown steadily since joining Jia Khan's Jirga. They didn't just listen to her words, they implemented them. Faith, trust and fealty were at the foundation now. Misunderstandings didn't fester. They surfaced and dissolved with dignity. They were trying to end a war, and every one of them knew that the best fighter was never angry.

'Let the straight white women be angry,' Fozia Khan had said. 'We've been angry long enough. Now we have agency, let us alchemise the rage and build something better for our children.'

The arrival of women in the Jirga had brought a kind of peace to Jia's life. She had been unprotected for so long, caught in the crosshairs of a world that centred maleness in all its guises and viewed anyone who questioned the autocracy as the enemy, that it had left her nervous system shattered. The safety of sisterhood, and a brotherhood that didn't need to dominate to feel worthy, was a new phenomenon and one that she was starting to enjoy.

Elyas had noticed. She could tell from the way he looked at her. She was softening, shades of the old Jia Khan returning.

He wanted to put down his armour too, she could see it in his eyes, as if the act of vulnerability itself would heal him. He'd just told her he was afraid of ageing, of becoming invisible and irrelevant to the world. 'Remember what it felt like to be checked out?' he said.

The soft linen bed covers were crumpled around them. He smoothed out the wrinkles of the pillow as he spoke, propping it against the back of the upholstered headboard. The house was silent, the only sound coming from the birds perched in the tree outside the bedroom window.

Jia savoured the rare moment of calm as she considered his words, turning them over. 'No one checked me out,' she said, thinking back to the days of bohemian skirts and floaty blouses, of scouring charity shops for florals and gaudy patterns. Her wardrobe now was couture, elegance and neutrals. 'Maybe I was too uptight or maybe it was a different time for brown women…

'Perhaps we should all go away somewhere,' she said, suddenly changing the subject.

'Can you do that?'

'Sure. It's my company. I have Sakina and Idris. They can handle things.'

'I would love that,' he said.

She wanted to believe she could pause, but she'd been running for so long, she didn't know how. Like so many women, her self-worth was knotty, tied up with work and achievement, alongside motherhood and guilt. 'We've been living in snatched seconds,' she said. 'Somewhere between answering calls and helping one child tie his shoelaces and the other apply for a job or navigate his queer love life.'

'You know it's just "his love life", not "his *queer* love life", right?'

'I do, and am aware I'm still failing at parenthood, thanks.' Her smiled was tired. 'Equally, I'm afraid that if I stop and do nothing but parent and breathe, it will tear me open, and my insides will spill out, and I won't be able to put myself back together the way I was.'

'Maybe that's the point,' he said.

'What is?'

'You're not supposed to be put back the way you were.'

She looked at him, unsure whether the idea frightened or relieved her. 'Maybe you're right,' she said.

There was a moment of silence.

'I checked you out. I still do.' His words caught her off guard, and she laughed despite herself, a genuine sound. The warmth of it sat in the room between them, but then her phone buzzed once more.

She turned it over, fingers already typing as she replied.

'Everything OK?' Elyas said.

She nodded, not quite meeting his eyes. 'Yes.' She set the phone down. 'I feel the same about ageing, by the way. Feminism tells us we're not supposed to care, that there are more important things to worry about than lines and wrinkles, but we all want to be desired.'

'I am no longer what I used to be,' he said, shaking his head comedically.

'Why do you think I'm still here, then?' she said. 'Because it's not for that Jamie Oliver's colonised chicken karahi.'

'You told me you liked that karahi!'

Her phone buzzed again. This time it was persistent, refusing to be silenced. The tone in the room changed.

She picked it up. Her eyes hardened at the message.

'I lied,' she said quietly but clearly. 'It's what I do. Don't ever forget that.'

There was a chill in her voice; the banter was over. Elyas knew that this wasn't about his karahi. Her spine straightened, her face returning to its familiar set.

'Something's come up,' she said. 'I need to call Idris.'

She walked out without looking back.

Elyas, still in bed, sighed as the last traces of their Sunday faded.

CHAPTER 22

Benyamin winked at his nephew. 'Let's eat,' he said. 'We can't talk on an empty stomach.'

Ahad looked so much like Zan that it knotted the complexities of their relationship even more and made his responsibilities all the heavier.

Benyamin had been a small child when his brother had died, and he recalled his mother's grief more than his brother's absence.

He and Maria had been left to fend for themselves for a while after the accident, looked after by Chilli Chacha and the aya who had been brought over from Pakistan to care for them. Sanam Khan's depression had been deep, and she hadn't been able to drag herself out of bed. When she finally did, Jia was gone.

Without guidance, Benyamin had floundered, and school had been a complicated place. He was street-smart and knew himself to be cleverer than most in his class, but the application of that intelligence had never come easy to him. He now realised he had left school at eighteen never having fulfilled his potential. And there was more to it than the trauma and upheaval of Zan's death.

'Do you think you might be dyslexic?' Jia had asked last year, after hearing him talk about his struggles at school, being unable to reconcile how hard he worked with how badly he performed in exams. The system was not made for kids like him, but he had not known that.

'No. Why?'

'Because you always loved stories when you were little, and you're smart. I was surprised when you didn't go to university. There's a disconnect between who you are and what you've achieved academically. Let me make a call?'

He'd pondered her words. 'Sure,' he said.

He'd agreed to the assessment partly because he was intrigued. It had thrown up results to confirm that he was severely dyslexic. His IQ was high, but his profile was spiky, showing empathy and comprehension at higher levels than most.

He'd started to unravel this information in the last few months and had applied to university. 'Zan was interested in astronomy, and physics too,' said Jia when he told her that he wanted to study maths, higher maths and physics.

Akbar Khan had often commented on his son's skills with numbers. The boy was faster at calculations than anyone else in the organisation. Even the accountant had trouble keeping up with him. Now that he had had it confirmed that it wasn't the numbers that were the problem but the reading, he had started looking at his life and himself in a new way.

He hadn't told anyone yet that he wanted out of the family business. He'd met a girl, and he was desperate to move on from the scars of the past without them bleeding into his new life. He also didn't want his nephew to step into his shoes.

'I'm not going to let you do that,' he'd said to Ahad, when the boy asked his advice about it.

'Why?'

'Because there's better stuff for you out there.'

'But I want to work for the family, like you.'

'You really don't.'

They were standing in Briggs, Wallace & Price, the award-winning fish and chip shop, waiting to be served. The queue behind them was getting longer, as this was now the most popular chippy in

Yorkshire thanks to a *Time Out* review and some Tiktokker who'd visited on the way to Haworth.

'Two fish and chips, please, love,' said Benyamin Khan to the woman behind the counter. Her apron was pristine and starched to within an inch of its life. She stretched a smile and tapped the order into the till.

'Owt else, love?'

'Aye,' he said. 'Mushy peas and curry sauce.'

'You get so northern sometimes,' said Ahad.

'I'm no southern ponce, like you. I'm a northern ponce – you'd do well to remember that.' The men laughed like two ordinary blokes buying haddock and chips from their local chippy. Their invisibility in a white world belied the fact that they were part of the most powerful and dangerous bloodline in the country. A family that was headed by a woman who would not hesitate to kill for either one of them.

The server added the items and held out the card machine.

Behind her, a large sign detailed why *Time Out* and the TikTok influencer had come here. The menu was an equality and diversity officer's dream, combining the ethnicities of the two largest groups who inhabited the area.

The 'Yorkshire' menu offered traditional cod, haddock, scallops or saveloy and chips, all cooked in beef dripping – halal beef dripping at that – but there was also the 'British Raj' option, which was the Yorkshire with a Pakistani twist.

'You want 'em spicy, love?' the woman said to Benyamin and Ahad.

'One normal and one Raj butty,' said Benyamin.

The woman adeptly lifted a basket of battered fish out of the hot fat and tipped it on to a tray in the food counter. Watching from the other side of the glass, Ahad's mouth watered at the sight of the glistening golden fish.

Then the server took a pair of stainless-steel tongs and placed one large battered cod on to a square of greaseproof paper on the counter. Her huge diamond ring caught the light as she shovelled chips into paper bags with a scuttle – a sign of the financial success her chippy was experiencing. She added salt, spritzed them with vinegar and wrapped them swiftly in brown paper, placing the parcel to one side.

She then took another box and placed a large teacake inside. It was split and buttered, ready for the huge fish that she slipped into it. 'How spicy? Mild, medium or hot?' she said.

'Medium,' said Benyamin, watching as the woman added chopped spring onions, sliced red chillis and a deep orange dynamite sauce.

'Help yourself to drinks, love.'

Ahad surveyed the cold shelves lined with row upon row of soft drinks – Salaam Cola, X and Irn Bru. Coca Cola was absent from most shops in the county.

'Do you think the city boycotting brands makes a difference?' he asked Benyamin, who shrugged.

'Who knows,' he replied. 'But money is all that anyone really cares about, nephew. Money and power. Once the wealthy start seeing their income decline, they change their beliefs, allegiances and even their religion. Still, whether it makes a difference or not isn't the point for me. I don't want a child's blood in my mouth.'

They took their food and climbed into the Ferrari. They drove a little way, stopping at a local beauty spot. From here they could see the city lights below them. Sitting side by side on a wall, their fish and chips on their laps, they watched over the valley as they ate, knowing the Khan empire was doing business under the cloak of darkness.

Benyamin no longer did the milk round. Jia had insisted that her siblings distance themselves from the dirty work. Benyamin had been reluctant at first, afraid that he was being muscled out, but with time he'd seen his sister's wisdom. He was tired, but he knew who he was. He'd experienced more in his twenties than most men did in a lifetime.

Ahad glanced at his uncle. He was so sure of himself, navigating the city with a confidence and swagger Ahad greatly admired. Benyamin could live anywhere, buy a house in any city in the world. 'Ever think about moving away?' he asked, biting into a chip.

Benyamin considered his nephew's question carefully. 'Why would I do that?'

'I don't know. Just a thought.'

'People know me,' he said. 'It's my city. The air is clean, the land is beautiful, and I don't have to smile like a clown at some gora to make him feel comfortable around me.'

Ahad nodded. He understood too well what his uncle was saying. The discomfort of toeing the line imposed by white society was exhausting. Money and education made things easier, but there were still moments when he was caught off guard.

It was good to be able to live without judgement, without encountering that look that every black and brown person had experienced on walking into a café or restaurant. Sometimes it was a flicker, sometimes a stare, and it always felt like a slap. There was less of that here, and though Ahad missed London, he was not sure he would ever move back there. There was an ease to this city, to the conversation and the community that his grandfather and now his mother had created. He wanted to be a part of that.

'What does your mum say?' said Ben. 'About you getting involved in the business.'

'Not much. You know what she's like. But I don't think she'll stop me.'

'And your dad?'

'Well, he doesn't really know what the family business is.'

'Is that true? I mean, how can he not?'

'I don't know, man. Who knows?'

'You ever asked him?'

Ahad shook his head. He hadn't discussed his mother's work with Elyas because he was afraid of inadvertently revealing too much and of his father's reaction. 'My dad, he's a good guy. I'm not like him – you know what I mean?' He turned to his uncle, and a look passed between them, one that was exchanged between people with complicated lives, the kind rarely understood by ordinary folk.

His father had always been the epitome of integrity, and Ahad was not ready to have him fall off that pedestal.

'You need to ask him, kid,' said Benyamin. 'This life, once you're in it, is hard to get out of.' He paused and stared hard at his nephew. 'I should know,' he said, his voice low, his words solid.

'You seem to be doing fine,' said Ahad, taking in the spread of lights that twinkled across the valley.

Where Ahad saw his mother's territory, Benyamin saw only responsibility. Miles and miles of people who relied on the Khan family business for their day-to-day, for advice, for money, for survival. These were all things he hadn't understood when his father was alive. He wondered what it would be like if his father hadn't been murdered. If Jia had gone back to London, and Benyamin had come to realise that he wanted out of the family business. Would he have run to her and sought sanctuary in her life?

He looked at his nephew, not much older than he'd been when he began his apprenticeship in the business. 'Sometimes,' he said, 'I think about what would have happened if I hadn't gone to the hotel with Mina. If I'd not got her to take Nowak's keys…if he hadn't done what he did.' There were wounds that time could not heal, and they ran deep within Benyamin Khan. 'Maybe Jia jaan would not have stayed, Baba would still be alive, and you, you'd be an ordinary kid on some graduate trainee scheme.'

'And you? What would you be doing?' said Ahad.

Benyamin shrugged. He missed his father, the solidity of life when he had been here, the certainty of what needed to be done, the clarity. But in truth, he knew that manhood would have come upon him even if his father was alive. It may have waited a few years, but it would have arrived in all the colours of the dark and demanded he choose his path.

'Do you think Nano knew about your dad?' said Ahad.

Benyamin Khan took another bite from his fish and chips. 'I don't know, you know. I often wondered if she did, but women, they can hide from these things. Or they could in my mum's day. She worked in the home, raised us, and she didn't have the freedom that women have today. She was an immigrant, and everything was foreign. But with your dad, things are different. Elyas knows the score.'

Ahad knew all of this too well. 'I don't know. Sometimes I think I should leave and pretend this doesn't exist. But then I wonder if that's fair on everyone else.'

'The only one you can save is yourself. If you can do that, that is enough.'

They looked out across the city again. The winding golden street lights shining like a caravan of travellers crossing to the other side of the valley. The air was clear and clean. The world seemed full of possibilities. Somewhere in the distance, they heard fireworks. The pop and whizz of them started filling the air, the colours lighting up the sky in yellows and greens.

Benyamin took Ahad's fish and chip wrapper and threw it in the bin nearby. 'Come on,' he said. 'The shipment is in.'

They were getting back into the Ferrari, when he added, 'You know who buys this stuff, don't you? The same morons that judge us.'

She had been expecting the message from Idris, just as she had the call from the prime minister's office. Jia Khan's power had been growing steadily, and her name was dropped, spoken and whispered in countless boardrooms, both business and philanthropic, and along the corridors of power.

Her old adversary, Henry Paxton, had long-standing links with the Ministry of Defence, and she knew he had put her on the government's radar.

Her ambitions had never been political, that world appearing murkier than her father's business interests. But she had politicians, police and businessmen in her pocket, and had consolidated her power stealthily. She arranged the strings that needed pulling, letting them hang loose and free until the moment they were needed. Then she yanked them like a puppeteer: precise, unapologetic and entirely in control.

She understood loyalty. She understood the desire for power that consumed some men and women. She played both cards well.

'At least we know we're dirty,' she said to Idris when they met up and he raised the Foreign Office call and, now, the PM's request. 'Oliver Blundell pretends to be clean, all the while bending and manipulating the rules to fill his pockets and grow his power.'

'They're clearly very keen for us to help them with a problem,' Idris said, raising an eyebrow.

Jia stifled the steely satisfaction she felt at the thought of the prime minister asking her for a favour.

'You mean, they want us to get our hands dirty instead of them.'

Idris nodded. 'You're enjoying this, aren't you? Keeping them hanging?'

'Not at all,' she said. 'It's just that these stale men look down their long noses at us for years, with their anti-immigration rhetoric and their enforced integration. And then they can't govern without our help.'

It was early morning, and they were deep in the Yorkshire countryside, walking along winding roads, past dry-stone walls. The sun glinted on the frozen fields, and Jia was glad for her good sense in putting on her hiking boots. They'd come here to talk, and walking in the fresh air always clarified things. That, and it was away from all listening devices.

As the family business had grown, so had the need for secrecy.

'Any news on my stalker?' she asked wryly. Jia had first noticed the woman when she'd dropped Lirian at school. Something about her reminded Jia of the Enforcer.

'Not yet,' he said. 'We've pulled another image of her from CCTV, but she's clean. We can't find a thing on her.'

'Keep searching. It's unnerving being watched by a white woman at the school gates. Makes me feel as if I'm wearing last year's fashion.'

Jia had become suspicious after she noticed the same woman in Café de Khan and then later at the gym. To the casual observer, she was just a woman in grey joggers and a T-shirt. Her hair was tied back, her nails short but not painted, and her make-up was minimal. In a city where more was more, she stood out by attempting to disappear.

Sakina had understood when Jia mentioned her for the first time. Idris had been a little more reticent. 'She may have moved here from down south,' he'd said. 'Things are changing. We do have Sweaty Betty and Lululemon here, you know. I see the brands. I know what's happening.'

'Well, I'm glad you have your finger on the pulse of women's attire. But this here is why Sakina has the role she does within the organisation, and why you handle external affairs,' Jia had replied. 'Her eyes see things that yours don't.'

'No one moves here unless they have ulterior motive,' Sakina had said. 'I wish it was different, but it's either family or work, and both of those are trackable. I'll ask around.'

She'd gone to the usual sources, the pimps, the ground-level dealers, the foot soldiers of the organisation. She'd passed a photograph that Jia had surreptitiously taken on her phone on to the people at The Company, the tech arm of the Khan empire. The woman didn't exist on systems, in records, and she had no footprint that could be found. If they couldn't find her, then her profile had been created by someone powerful, someone who could wipe data, wash social media and make someone a ghost.

***

Later that morning, Jia mentioned the woman to Elyas, in case he'd noticed her.

'She sounds like a female version of Michael Knight,' he said. He was on his way to a meeting. He pulled the strap of his brown leather bag over his head and across his body.

'Who is Michael Knight?' Jia said, as he dropped a stash of pens into his bag. He was the second man to make light of her concerns, and it was beginning to grate. 'Do you not understand the gravity of what I'm saying?' she said.

'I do, I just need to get to this meeting.'

He was riffling through papers, as if her words hadn't registered. His disorganised ways annoyed him as much as they did her. She watched him, wondering what it must be like to be a man, to walk through the world as a master of the universe, to say exactly what one felt without measuring and adjusting oneself for the ease of others. What did it feel like to be taken seriously without being patronised?

I could have him killed. The thought flickered across her mind, brief and uninvited, like a firefly blinking in the dark. Of course, she never would. She loved him, in her way. But there were moments, like this one, when his carelessness made her feel exposed. He moved through life so freely, unaware of how closely it brushed danger. She let him, because she still wanted to believe he was safe with her, and perhaps because he was handsome, and their children had inherited the best of him. Sometimes she wondered if not for that, if not for the tether of history and blood, whether she'd have walked away. She could have become like him, hurting him the way he did her with his indifference, his disbelief, his blind spots. But she hadn't. She had chosen to stay and to fight for their marriage.

He found his reading glasses and hung them on the front of his jumper, then turned to look at her, ready for her to say more.

She could tell from the expression on his face that he was compartmentalising, siphoning the personal information from the public, and work from life, and it felt like a needle pushed under a nail bed, she thought.

'Why do you need all those pens?' she said. 'Take the tablet or use your phone.'

'I can't think without a pen in my hand,' he replied.

That's one of the most ridiculous things I've ever heard, she thought, but she held her tongue.

Their son Lirian was playing nearby, ready for school in his red jumper and grey blazer. He came racing in with a Hot Wheels car in his hand.

'Come on, dude, let's go,' Elyas said. He smiled at Jia. 'I'll drop him at school on the way to my meeting. If that helps?'

'Sure,' she said.

He was at the door before he turned and stopped. *'Knight Rider,'* he said.

'Sorry?' she said, looking up from her phone.

'Michael Knight. He was the man who didn't exist. Remember KITT, the talking Trans Am?'

'No, I don't,' she said. 'I was reading Nietzsche when you were watching *Knight Rider*.'

Elyas flinched. He hadn't expected life to turn into a cold war, peppered with silences and unresolved skirmishes, with only the occasional brief truce. She was either working or handling Lirian, or meeting with Idris and Sakina, or seeing the rest of her family, her siblings and cousins.

In the rare moments when they went anywhere alone together, to a restaurant or café, she'd sit silently, watching the world. 'You're not like this with your friends,' he'd say. 'I hear you talking with them, laughing. Why don't you do that with me?'

'I'm tired, Elyas,' she would reply. She'd assumed he was a safe space, someone she didn't have to mask with, or be engaging or in control, but she'd been wrong. There was no safe space, nowhere she could just be herself.

This was their marriage. They were two people held together by vows and blood, death and longing, curiosity and fear.

Some days it worked. On those days, Jia Khan assumed that, despite his intelligence, Elyas was unable to see the truth of who she was and what she was doing. On other days, she considered the possibility that he simply wasn't brave enough to look the truth in the eye, and for that she was grateful.

The reality was, Elyas had seen so much death and devastation while reporting on the destruction of societies, that he had learnt how to compartmentalise and make peace with things that most men could not. He had found a way to be content with what was, without wishing for what could never be. Jia Khan was not the worst of what he had seen.

The therapy he'd had soon after becoming a father had given him the scaffolding he needed. 'I don't feel anything,' he'd said to the counsellor. Doctors told him they couldn't find a medical reason for the numbness in his fingers. His hands had written the things his eyes had seen. They were keeping score, and when they found no outlet, they made the harm known.

Men didn't deal with their emotions in the world he'd seen. They buried them under harsh words and punches thrown at each other and at women and children. He'd witnessed first-hand the war that caused within them, and he had no desire to have his son become a casualty of it.

He'd found a therapist through friends. It had been helpful, but he'd decided it wasn't enough, and so he had set about building walls within himself. Like an endless maze, he sectioned off parts of himself until such a time as he was able to deal with the minotaur within the maze. Survival required that he ignore them.

But in the years that he had been with Jia, he'd found himself compromising his moral code more than he had ever expected. It was getting harder and harder to set apart his wife's work and his career as a truthteller. He'd won awards for investigative journalism, for revealing the crimes of others, and he was sitting on a mine of information. But Jia Khan was the mother of his children; to reveal her was to damage his children. He also remembered the young woman she had once been. Somewhere inside him was the nagging feeling that if only he'd tried a little harder, he would have been able to save her. And maybe he still could.

'I'll be home late,' he said, taking their son by the hand. 'I've got a meeting and then I'm heading to the gym.'

He gripped Lirian's hand a little tighter. Some truths, he decided, were better left buried. For now.

CHAPTER 24

David Black was sitting in Pearls, sipping a latte, when Elyas arrived at the café. The twenty-something fresh-faced reporter was desperate to make his mark in journalism. Someone had neglected to tell him that the world of Fleet Street, liquid lunches and traditional phone tapping was over. He was the kind of man that would have worn a brown mackintosh and a fedora with a press card tucked into the band in the sixties.

That said, he was young enough to know that he didn't have all the answers, and smart enough to know that to get ahead he needed a network. He'd contacted Elyas through a tutor at university after Elyas had come in to give a guest lecture. He was the only man of colour who'd been invited to speak, and David had looked into his background.

He stood to greet him as he arrived.

'So, tell me about your work,' Elyas said once they were settled, the paraphernalia of their profession on the table. Elyas's leather-bound journal was bulging with cuttings and clippings of the things he was working on. He never left home without it. It no longer smelt like leather, but instead carried the scent of his cologne, laundry detergent and all the experiences that made him the man he had become. The Mont Blanc pen he had gifted himself when his first book became a bestseller was slipped into the green elastic holder on the edge of his journal. His phone sat on top of the book.

David Black had none of these things. He had his phone and a tape-recording device.

'I used to have one of those,' said Elyas. 'That Nokia must be twenty years old.'

'I ditched the smartphone after I read about Pegasus,' said David. 'And I like the slow burn of a story. The iPhone was taking over my life, and I was losing time to it.'

The young journalist reeled off a list of his achievements. He spoke at speed, his passion for his profession spilling out into air and infecting Elyas, reminding him of who he used to be.

'They commissioned me to go to Namibia after a couple of viral videos I did, travelling around South Asia.' He spoke of his stories, the things he'd discovered, the injustice he had revealed. 'Can you believe they were getting away with this stuff?' he said.

His large brown eyes shone as he talked. His skin tone probably darkened in the summer to olive and paled in winter, letting him slip between the cracks of race. People in many lands would assume he was one of them if he played quiet and small long enough to find out what he wanted. Elyas understood the advantage of this when travelling in foreign lands.

He found himself leaning in as David spoke. He was smart, idealistic, but balanced. There was a light in him that Elyas realised he'd lost, and despite his youth and inexperience, David had broken stories that more seasoned reporters would have missed.

The café was busy, filled with young men and women on their laptops. The staff were run off their feet. When the waitress finally brought their order, she apologetically placed their plates in front of them. Elyas's was piled high with poached eggs on a bed of verdant green spinach and creamy yellow Hollandaise sauce. David had ordered a stack of silver dollar pancakes. 'Can I get you both another coffee?' she asked.

They nodded. As the waitress turned to leave, the strap of her apron caught the small syrup jug that was sitting on the edge of the table. It fell, landing on the napkin in David's lap, the syrup dripping down his jumper. The waitress, now horrified, moved to help.

'Don't worry,' said David. 'It'll wash off, and the napkin saved my trousers.' He took off his jumper and placed it in his bag, before picking up his fork.

In that moment, Elyas warmed to him and resolved to help him in any way he could.

'I was actually here for a story a while back,' said David. 'Hyphen commissioned me, but I couldn't make any headway.'

'What was it? Maybe I can help.'

'There was a murder here some years back, a man named Akbar Khan. I had a call from a friend who said that there was something odd about the way it went down. It was a gangland killing.' He paused. 'No one wants to talk,' he said. 'I know that happens, but I can usually find something. But not here.'

Elyas's stomach tightened. 'It's a close-knit place,' he said. 'If you're not from here, it can be difficult to understand the dynamics.'

'What are the dynamics?'

'The city has been burned by reporters coming whenever there's some terrorist incident or a grooming ring. They don't trust easily.'

'It's not easy, this job, is it? How have you managed to stay in it without getting jaded or lost?'

Elyas thought of Jia, and what he would do to protect her, to keep his sons safe from the trauma that came with being dragged through the tabloids and seeing their mother's name in breaking-news banners. 'I don't know if I have,' he said.

He tried to imagine a conversation where he told his wife that a journalist was looking into her father's killing, but he kept coming up short. He had never been able to lie to Jia Khan. She always saw straight through him. That was why he skirted so many hard truths, but the more he circled them, the more they whirled like a black vortex, threatening to consume him. They would have to talk about the truth soon, or he would lose his soul.

'No, it's not easy,' he went on. 'Most investigative journalists I know are deeply moral and driven by a desire – almost an *affliction* –

to right wrongs, give voice to the voiceless, shine a light in dark places, and all that stuff. But I suspect others are deeply corrupt, or at least easily corruptible. The same forces and characteristics are in play in both types – their fascination with power, their under-standing of how laws can be bent with impunity, their exposure to violence and suffering, their sense of superiority, et cetera.

'I remember, years ago, a journo friend talking about a brilliant colleague who was famous for his heart-rending coverage of terrible human events but also a complete asshole who cheated on his expenses and his wife, betrayed his friends and privately sneered at the poor people he wrote about. I was so shocked. "Even great journalists can be terrible people," my friend told me. He was right.'

The realisation dawned on Elyas that he'd become a version of that hated colleague. He wasn't cheating on his wife with another woman, but he was cheating on the truth. He had failed to keep her honest to who she had been at the start of their friendship, and in doing so he had let her down.

'Remember this, my son,' Elyas's father had told him when he was a child. 'The only judgement you need to fear is Allah's, and the ultimate sin in Islam is idolatry.' Elyas had come home from school and told him one of his friends had said he wasn't a real Muslim because he didn't pray five times a day, and his mother wore skirts and didn't cover her hair. 'People will tell you all kinds of things about Islam, but Allah forgives all things except shirk. That's all you need to remember. Don't take anything or anyone as your God, not money, not power, not people, and you will be a Muslim.'

It was harder than it sounded, navigating life by the compass of faith in oneself and one's Creator. Elyas saw that he had betrayed his father's advice. That he was losing himself, that he was afraid of losing his family, and that maybe he had made Jia his master.

'Elyas, one of the reasons I wanted to talk to you was because I'm following a lead on a people-smuggling ring in Pakistan,' David said. 'I'm heading out there later this year and want to line up some meetings. It would be good to have someone with your experience involved. I'm going to be out of my depth, and I could use your expertise.'

'Why don't you send me an email about what you're thinking of doing, and what you need, and I'll get back to you,' said Elyas.

CHAPTER 25

As Elyas left the meeting, he couldn't help thinking about his youth, the days when he and Jia thought life was easy and it was people that made it hard. They didn't know then that it takes years to learn to live, to separate what one wants from what life demands, and how it extracts its due from you slowly, painfully, over time.

His wife had seen the world in monochrome. Her passion for defending the innocent had excited him; her hunger for change, her fight for what she believed in, had set his emotions alight. Passions that burn fast burn out, and so he knew that a slower pace of life was for the best. He couldn't help but yearn for those days, though.

He switched on the car and his phone connected to the audio system. The music that he played were the tracks on which the train to impossible places travelled: that place was his past. He was twenty-something years old again, sitting on the sandy bay that was Scarborough Beach with his girl. She was eating hot chips from a newspaper cone, mulling over the kind of pointless things one did when one was free of the dread of responsibility and had time to shoot the breeze.

'There are seven stages of love according to Sufis,' she said. '*Dilkashi, uns, mohabbat, aqeedat, ibadat, junoon* and *maut.*' She popped a chip into her mouth, but it was too hot, and she tried to cool her mouth down by waving her hand vigorously in front of it.

'What do they mean?' he said, laughing and handing her a bottle of water. She gulped the water down.

'Attraction, infatuation, love, faith, worship, madness and death.'

'And where are we on that scale?' he'd asked.

'I'm nowhere near it, but you're clearly on the point of madness. If my dad knew we were here, he'd kill you.' It had been a joke, but one he now knew was closer to the bone than either of them realised back then.

He had been infatuated and had fallen in love, and as he drove through the streets of the city, some twenty years later, he considered that he'd probably passed the first five stages and was circling the last two.

'Of course, this list is about Allah and not about men,' she'd said. 'And worship of anyone other than God is the ultimate sin.'

The words *halal* and *haram* had been bandied about so readily when they were young, but the lines between what was lawful and unlawful blurred with experience and the overstepping of lines.

Elyas had once overheard Jia explaining shirk to Ahad. 'The worship of anyone other than the Creator is a sin because all other worship destroys you, but annihilation in the Lord leads only to light.' Later, she'd told Elyas, 'He asks questions that I once asked of my father, and I find myself giving the same answers and wondering if we're destined to repeat the same mistakes over and over again.'

He thought of his father-in-law, the man of many faces, and a past that split into two families, the daughter he had raised and the daughter he had not.

When Jia had first told Elyas about Amal, he'd been surprised. Akbar Khan had been many things, but he had always been devoted to his wife, Sanam.

That he had a child elsewhere, and that he had known of her and kept the two parts of his life separate, made Elyas wonder who he really had been, and in doing so it forced him to consider what he himself was capable of, what he would have done in such a situation.

'Does your mother know of Akbar Khan's past?' he'd asked Jia.

'You mean, does she know that he had another child? I don't know,' Jia had said. 'I'm not sure if I should tell her, either.'

The secrets that unravelled families seemed to grow with the decades. Only last week, an old friend had called to tell Elyas he was leaving his wife of twenty years for an old flame.

'But why?' he'd asked. His friend had seemed to be living a charmed life – a lovely wife, two children who were about to leave for university, another at home.

'When I'm with her, I remember who I used to be,' his friend had said.

'What does that even mean?' he'd said to Jia later that evening. 'The woman he's having an affair with is someone he split up with after uni, when he went travelling. They both lived separate and full lives, reconnected on LinkedIn, and now he's leaving his wife and kids.'

Jia had looked up from her papers, peering over the top of her glasses. 'Do you believe him? That he's in love?'

'I don't know,' said Elyas. 'I mean, he's leaving his three children, and she's leaving hers.'

'I don't believe it,' she said.

'Well, tell him that, because he's imploded his life.'

'Why do you care so much?' she said.

'I don't know! Maybe because…loyalty!'

'I think we've got our own lives to get on with,' she'd said. He didn't seem happy with her reply, so she tried again. 'They're in love with who they used to be, Elyas. Don't you ever miss your old self? And he's not brave enough to see that person has gone, he will never return, and he's found a way to con himself.'

Elyas considered her words and wondered at their wisdom. She had been his first love and would probably be his last. The time without her had been slow and empty. She was the only habit he hadn't been able to kick. The words rang true because it was how he felt about her.

On days when she was curled up on the sofa, their children close by, he would find himself watching them, wondering at the complexities of fate. She'd look over and catch him, and her smile would remind him that this life of theirs was a slow dance in a burning room, and that at any moment, the roof could cave in.

'Jia,' he'd say.

'Yes?'

'Nothing…I love you.'

'I know,' she'd say. 'I'm sorry about that.'

CHAPTER 26

Jia reached into her back pocket and felt for the playing card with its red thumbprint. She kept it with her, a reminder of her life and the challenges she faced.

Two men always stayed with her now. The security threat was real. She asked them to maintain a distance while she was out with her sons, but she never forgot they were there. They were a constant reminder of the work that she did, and the war that she had started.

'I'm in York for a few days,' she said to Sakina, when her consigliere called to give her the news that she could find nothing on the woman who'd been watching her. She was paying for a colouring book and pressing her card to the machine. 'Bring Idris, and we can talk properly.'

The cathedral city, with its Roman origins, was one of Jia Khan's favourite places. She'd first visited on a school trip to the Jorvik Viking Centre, for the sights and sounds of the past. As a teenager with a freshly minted driver's licence, she'd driven here with her school friends, and they'd walked from Whip-Ma-Whop-Ma Gate by St Crux Church through the city's snickelways and historic streets, passing haunted landmarks on a ghost tour.

She'd returned to the city's narrow streets and alleys as a student with her brother Zan, and these days it was where she escaped to with her sons, Lirian and Ahad.

She'd taken a few days out to spend time with the youngest. They'd booked into a boutique hotel and had been taking in the sights, returning to the Viking Centre that had started Jia's love affair with the city.

She knew Lirian would be grown and gone in a decade and a half. The responsibility she felt raising boys to be men weighed heavily on her, especially when she knew she had other people's sons in her army.

Working with men, most of whom were incapable of speaking their emotions aloud, the importance of a mother in a son's life was at the forefront of her mind. She had observed the way her men responded to the opinions and advice of women and measured the actions she took. She had come to see the importance that men and women played in the edifice of each other's lives, and to understand that both were incomplete without the other. Insight came from seeing the opposite of oneself; understanding of the whole of society was derived from experiencing it through the eyes of someone who saw the world from a different vantage point.

She walked through the Shambles, hand in hand with Lirian, the sun warm on her cheek, his little fingers wrapped around hers. She pointed out the houses to him, how they furled, as if bending to whisper secrets to each other.

'These houses have been here a long time, huh, Mama?' he said. 'They must know a lot of secrets. They can't speak either, so no one will ever know.'

His statements no longer surprised her. He was insightful, and smarter than most children his age. 'Yes,' she said, 'you're right, my love, these buildings will have seen more than most.' She ruffled his hair, and he smiled up at her. She was tired; her feet felt as if they were starting to swell. 'You want some cake?' she said. 'I need some tea. Let's head to Bettys.'

As they walked towards the tea house, she considered the things she'd hidden from the world, and what it was that someone was trying to steal from her. She was being watched, she had been marked for death, and she worked with dangerous men. These three things alone were enough to make her aware of the fragility of life, the importance of family and the fierceness it would take to protect hers.

They sat down by a window that looked out across the square, her security detail at a table by the door. Jia took out the colouring book and a pencil case filled with felt-tip pens and gave them to Lirian. He began colouring in a picture of York Minster in a bright pink, a colour that the building had probably never seen.

The afternoon tea arrived, served on a silver stand that was placed in the centre of the table. There were three tiers, each housing a beautiful plate, one with tiny triangles of bread filled with cucumber, dill and cream cheese or coronation chicken or slivers of smoked salmon. There was also a savoury quiche with sun-dried tomatoes, fragrant basil and mature cheddar cheese – and, of course, there were cakes.

Jia chose her tea and watched as it was poured out. She savoured every sip, Lirian silent as he filled his mouth with sandwiches and cake: summer fruit slice, coconut and lime Battenberg and a chocolate cube filled with mousse, each one more delicious than the next.

Lirian coloured in happily as Jia sipped her tea and gazed out of the window. And then she saw the woman. She was standing by the lamp post, watching her, dressed again in indistinct grey clothing to make her disappear in a crowd. Jia instinctively reached her arm out placed it protectively around her son. He looked up from his pens and smiled. Jia smiled back and then looked out at the woman again. She was walking across the road now, heading towards the tea house. Jia watched her enter the room and come towards her. She looked as though she was going to walk right past, but then she hesitated by Jia's chair, her hand resting on the cream upholstery.

'I understand you've been looking into me,' she said. She was long and lean, and Jia could tell from the way her shirt clung to her upper arms that she was strong. Her hair was tied back and pinned in place. Her boots were black leather and laced.

Jia measured the distance between them with a glance. She looked from the teapot filled with boiling water, to the metal trays that held the cakes and then to the butter knife on the table, weighing up which item she could reach first and what could inflict the most damage. The knife was the obvious choice, but it was messy. The tray would have an impact and leave her paralysed for a short time, but enough for them to get away.

She tightened her arms around Lirian and then released him, letting him sit back in his seat as her security detail approached the table. 'Everything OK, Khan sahiba?' asked the taller of the two men. His name was Hassan, and Jia had been friends with his mother when they were children.

She nodded at him. 'If something happens to my son, kill her,' she said in Pashto. Then she turned to address the lady in English. 'My advisors are concerned about my well-being, and I indulge them.' She leaned back in her chair. 'I apologise if they've offended you.' She noticed the woman's grip on the chair loosen.

Jia moved her hand from Lirian's shoulder and picked him up. She moved his fringe from his eyes. 'Baby, will you go with Hassan and choose a cake from the trolley over there so we can take it home for Nani?' The boy nodded and climbed off his mother's lap, running to the close protection.

Jia relaxed, having put space between her child and the woman who had been watching her for weeks. She was about to say something when she felt Lirian's arms wrap around her. 'I forgot to kiss you!' he said, placing his lips to her cheeks and holding her tight. She pulled him into her hug and then kissed him hard. This could be the last time he was kissed by his mother – a thought that crossed her mind often, fed by her age and her unique circumstances.

She watched him run back to the men who were charged with protecting him, maintaining the balance between safety and invisibility so as not to upset the sensibilities of the tea room clientele. Then she turned to the grey woman again. She was still standing, seamlessly blending into the environment. This was her comfort zone – no one would consider her out of place here, unlike Jia.

'What a darling little boy,' said the woman, pulling the seat out beside Jia. 'May I sit down?'

Jia poured herself some more tea. 'I'd rather you didn't,' she said coldly, putting the hot liquid to her lips.

She remained calm, stoic even, aware that most people in her situation would be flustered, their palms sweating, their instincts screaming at them to leave the building. But Jia Khan refused to be intimidated by anyone. It annoyed her more than frightened her, getting in the way of the work she had to do and the life she wanted to lead.

Life had drilled her in the art of combat and preservation, and martial arts had consolidated the work. 'Be the hunter,' her sifu's voice said in her head. 'Don't choose it, but when the fight is brought to you, lean in.'

'You don't need to dig up my details. I am happy to answer any questions you have about me,' pressed the woman.

'You have crossed a line by coming here,' said Jia, her eyes dark. 'My child is not part of your world, and he is not a pawn in whatever game you are playing. Go back and tell Yanick that.'

'It's not Yanick Kaplan who sent me, although I do know a lot about him that could be useful to you…' She leaned forward as if to reveal what she knew, but a little voice broke in.

'Mama, we should choose the chocolate one!' said Lirian excitedly. He'd raced past old ladies in twin set and pearls, their partners beside them, their faces alight as they watched the sprint and excitement of childhood.

The grey woman leaned back in her chair, the interruption having given her pause to reconsider her plans.

'OK, darling, let's go get it, shall we?' said Jia, kissing her son on the tip of his nose and leading him away from the table. They stood at the counter, choosing fat rascal scones and cakes and tins of tea blends. When they returned with the ribbon-tied boxes and bags, the grey woman was gone.

In her place was a small white card. Jia picked it up and turned it over in her hands. It was heavy, expensive. Embossed in black ink were the words 'The Interior'; a series of letters and numbers and shapes were on the back.

Jia photographed the card and messaged it to Sakina. 'Meet me in York Minster tomorrow. Bring Idris,' she typed and hit send. She bundled up her son and took him back to the hotel by way of the Transport Museum, but her mind was elsewhere.

She slept badly that night, wondering about the danger she'd put her child in, wondering about her choices and if she'd have made different ones if she'd known, back at the beginning, that she was pregnant with Lirian.

Then she remembered that women like her only rarely had choices. The path had presented itself and she'd had no choice but to walk it. To have left after Akbar Khan's death would have resulted in the end of a business that was relied upon by scores of families back then, and hundreds more today. The empire expanded whether one wanted it to or not. That was the thing with money and power: once there was enough of it, it grew like leaven, pulling in what it needed to thrive from the environment.

<h1 style="text-align:center">CHAPTER 27</h1>

The sun came up mean and bright, spilling gold over York Minster's gothic bones. Jia walked towards it with her coat pulled tight and gloves half on. She'd sent Lirian to soft play with one of her security details.

Inside, Sakina and Idris were waiting. The rose window poured fractured light over the stone floor, just as it had done the day the union of the royal houses of York and Lancaster was declared. This was a place of peace-making, but before that there was war.

Grand places of worship like this always felt eerie to Jia, and she wondered what this meant about the presence of God. Maybe He wasn't here at all; maybe He was in back alleys, homeless shelters and soup kitchens with the broken and bleeding. Maybe He hung out in maternity hospitals, where babies were born and where women felt ever so briefly like gods before being plunged into a lifetime of saving souls. Maybe His real work was quiet, invisible and dirty, and places of worship no longer interested Him.

She slid into the pew beside Idris. He took her hand without looking. 'You OK?'

She shrugged. 'Define good,' she said.

'The card she left, it's a cypher,' he said. 'Haines is on it.'

'She said she wasn't connected to Yanick.'

Idris nodded, his eyes on the stained glass and vaults of the minster. 'They say it is easier for a camel to pass through the eye of a needle than for a rich man to enter heaven, but would this place exist without those men?'

'Cathedrals don't build themselves,' said Jia. 'The ones who quote that line usually have enough money to ignore it.' She looked up. 'There was a fire here when I was a child. *Blue Peter* asked for designs for the ceiling rosettes. I didn't think that meant people like me. I used to think it was imposter syndrome, that I doubted my abilities, but the truth is I didn't feel welcome. These places felt white.'

They were sitting in the back row of the nave. Three Muslims, talking crime, power and survival in the ark of salvation, under the stained-glass gaze of saints and martyrs.

'Do you still feel that way?' said Sakina.

'Now, all spaces are my spaces,' Jia replied.

'We need to make sure it stays that way,' said Idris. 'The Guild have gone quiet.'

'Would we go quiet?' said Jia.

Idris shook his head.

'Then neither have they. Silence means planning, and I want to know what for. Tell me what you know about the woman.'

'She is protected and has powerful backers,' said Sakina. 'We still haven't found any digital footprint for her, and that kind of erasure takes money, power and technical skills far beyond ordinary capabilities. Her invisibility makes me think she's linked to an assassination agency or intelligence. The question is, who runs the Interior?'

Since her father's death, Jia had nurtured and tended to the family business. Its roots were strong, fed and watered by the Pashtun family that had sown seeds in the northern city where Akbar and Bazigh Khan had settled after leaving London in the seventies. Its branches had spread into other countries and were now starting to bear fruit.

Jia had made herself known to the men who ran the world's most powerful crime families. She had done the impossible: she had united women. They had come together under her watch and were under her protection.

Their invisibility was not built on firewalls or code. It was rooted in one of the oldest cons, that true power wore a man's face.

A phone buzzed. They all reached for their bags and pockets. Idris put his hand into his overcoat pocket and pulled his out. But before he could speak, an old woman in pearls and disapproval pointed to a 'No mobile phones' sign.

Idris held up a hand in apology, mouthed 'sorry' and then turned back to Jia. 'I'll be back in a moment,' he said.

Jia leaned towards Sakina. 'Did you know that in Islam true believers are described as women, not men?' she said.

'I didn't know that,' said Sakina.

Jia dropped her voice to a whisper. 'You want to know how powerful women are? Look at how hard men work to oppress us. Asiya, the wife of Pharaoh – Bithya to our Jewish cousins – and Mary, mother of Jesus. These women are our standard.'

'You've read more theology than most imams,' said Sakina.

'Why do you think they're afraid of me?' said Jia. 'I fight them with their weapons. If you live in the house of the enemy, you learn his ways, but you also understand his weakness. Asiya must have been quite a woman.'

'And Mary?' said Sakina. 'They present her as meek and mild – how do we relate to her?'

'Imagine finding yourself pregnant and unmarried all those years ago. No one believes you, and you're branded a sinner, then you give birth alone, under a date tree, crying out for God to have taken you before this day came. But He doesn't, and so you raise your son, teach him right from wrong in the face of all the judgement, and then he turns around and takes on the establishment. A mild-mannered, meek woman does not raise the kind of man who turns over the tables in the temple. Then they took her son and crucified him while she watched. Mary was no weak woman. Her only subservience was to God.'

Sakina pondered her words. Jia Khan was a woman of measure and what she said always came with meaning. 'What does that make us?' she said.

Jia pressed her palms, then slowly parted them. 'We live in the house of evil and do what we must to survive,' she said. 'Scripture doesn't speak kindly of women like us, but then no one does, and no one ever will. That is our fate. We set men and women free. That must be enough.'

For a split second, Sakina glimpsed a sadness in Jia Khan's face, but it was gone as fast as it came. They sat in silence for a while. 'You're pregnant, aren't you?' said Sakina.

'Yes,' said Jia.

'But how? I thought –'

'That I was too old? The doctor warned me to make sure the contraception worked. Seems she was right.'

'What will you do?'

'I don't know. I've hidden it well under clothes and coats. Winter is good for that. I've even hidden it from myself.'

'Elyas? How is he?'

'Like all men, more practical than I need right now.'

Idris returned, bringing the conversation to a close. He slipped into the pew beside Jia.

'So, it turns out the Interior is a group of powerful people pulling strings under the guise of an advisory council to the Foreign Office,' he said. 'You can't contact them unless they want you to. Haines cracked the cypher.'

'What does the woman want with us?' said Sakina.

'We have a meeting scheduled with the Foreign Office. So I expect we'll find out soon enough.'

CHAPTER 28

The sky outside the compound was bruised, yellow turning purple and then to black.

In the back of the Bedford truck, the students sat pressed together, a mix of nerves and heat and shallow breath. They were being moved again.

Sami kept her spine straight, her arms around the other girls. Her chador had slipped, but she didn't fix it; she was too tired to worry about modesty.

Their kidnappers didn't like to keep them in one place for long. Through the windscreen of the truck, she could see that the building they were in now was sturdier and less temporary than the last one. The walls were clay-lined and mattresses lay on the floor. There were sinks with taps and electric lights. Someone was preparing for a longer game.

Their kidnappers hadn't said much. Orders came in by radio, passed between the older men in clipped, educated Pashto. These weren't village boys with borrowed guns. These were operators, trained, armed and smart enough to know when to wait.

Sami knew what leverage looked like. And she knew when it was about to be used.

***

Twelve miles east, Captain Rory Hadley stared at the satellite image that had just been uploaded to his tablet.

'Six guards. Two roving. Uncertain number inside. Hostages possibly in this building here,' said the analyst beside him, jabbing the screen with a gloved finger. 'No sign of a tripwire or perimeter alarms.'

'Too clean,' Hadley said.

'You think it's bait?'

He checked his watch. They had less than twenty minutes of moonlight before the drone feed went dark.

'We go,' he said.

****

The breach team moved in two groups. Four through the south wall. Four from the adjacent ridge. Drones overhead. Their orders were clear: no gunfire unless fired upon. Get the girls out.

Hadley's team were ten metres from the building when the lights came on.

Bright, blinding, every floodlight in the compound lit up at once.

They'd walked into a trap.

'Contact! Contact!'

Hadley hit the ground. Static in his earpiece. He could hear shouting in Pashto, English, radio chatter, everything overlapping. It was chaos.

And then, nothing. No shots were fired. There was just movement. Shadow figures stepping from the doors, weapons raised but not firing.

A voice crackled over loudspeakers. 'Captain Hadley. We're aware of your operation. Lay down your weapons. We have no intention of shedding blood tonight. But we will defend ourselves.'

The soldiers froze. That wasn't part of the plan. There weren't supposed to be negotiations. There wasn't even supposed to be a conversation.

'We're holding your men. They're alive. For now.'

Hadley's stomach dropped.

Inside the building, two soldiers knelt, their hands zip-tied, flanked by guards with cloth over their faces. One of them was kicked in the stomach, the other hit across the face with the butt of a Kalashnikov.

They'd been the first to enter through the south door. Their job was to cover a hallway, but they'd vanished before their other team members had even stepped inside.

Hadley's radio clicked once. Command was listening, but they offered no guidance.

He looked towards the building. Amatus Sami was standing in the doorway, framed in light, a pistol to her back. She looked frightened.

'They have your men,' she called. 'You need to leave, or they say they will kill us.'

CHAPTER 29

Jia sat at her desk, looking out of the window. The Jirga had been summoned.

Where her endless shelves had once been on display, now they were behind tambour covers, hiding her books and papers. She found herself becoming overstimulated by sight, sound and, often, conversation. The demands on her time had increased and with it her sensitivity. She'd pared back the room, had pictures removed and lighting adjusted.

She'd often turn away from her desk towards the window, gazing out on the green hills and valleys that were visible from her vantage point to help reset her brain. Pukhtun House was set among landscaped gardens, its manicured lawn stretching far into the distance.

Outside her window, the gardener was mowing the lawn, maintaining the standards that Akbar Khan had set. Cutting back, leaving to rest, planting when the season dictated – Jia pondered the gift of knowledge that every kind of work offered.

Becoming a mother had unravelled her, brought her to the edge of sanity. Ahad was taken from her – she'd believed him dead – and by the time he re-entered her life, he was sixteen, and she was someone else. The arrival of Lirian had threatened to open her up again. It had been both beautiful and brutal, much like her Jirga.

As she waited for the twelve men and women to arrive, she considered how far they had come, and the connectedness of humanity. Women carried their oppressors within their womb; they endured pain to bring them into the world and to raise them, and then more pain at their hands.

Jia's solidarity ran generations back, to the first woman who had wrapped her arms around the woody trunk of an ancient tree and breathed life into this world.

She surveyed her people in silence as they entered, the men and women who helped run her empire. Akbar Khan's Jirga of old men was a lifetime away from Jia Khan's. Now they were young and old, gendered and gender fluid, straight and queer. Their politics was money, community and loyalty.

The adjustment had not been an easy one. Even in changing times, the idea pervaded that to be a real man was to be the opposite of all that was female. It was inevitable, therefore, that with the learning of masculine traits came a hatred of feminine ideals, and without even knowing it, little boys were being taught to hate the women they loved, the ones who raised and protected them, who comforted them, even those who bore their children. The message was also imbibed by women, who learnt to hate themselves, and so went on the never-ending cycle.

Unpicking centuries of patriarchy would take time, but Jia Khan was intent on ensuring that change continued. She used all the methods she had at hand to talk to the men and women in her company. Skilled in theology, she would quote Quranic verses, silencing anyone who might deign to disagree, because to disagree was an act of kaafir. '*We have created you in groups to keep each other in check,*' she said, paraphrasing verses she'd memorised in childhood, both in Arabic and in English.

The imam would reinforce her words during his Friday sermon. But she knew that ultimately it would be the rise in bank balances that would quell disagreements. It was in their financial interest to be diverse. It widened their access to money and power; it allowed them to make more robust decisions.

'It is in our interest to understand each other. We are all business people, and it is no longer just the straight white man's world,' she'd remind them.

'Stuff enough cash in people's mouths and they stop arguing,' she'd once told Idris and Sakina when they had asked how they would handle any fallout from her changes to the Jirga. 'They will murmur and complain at first. As they rub along together, their edges will wear down.'

Afzal Khan had been their main concern. He'd come from Akbar Khan's Jirga and had felt a sense of duty to the old ways. He'd always wanted more than was offered. He'd argued every point, negotiated every penny and was rarely satisfied.

This was why Jia had navigated him out of the chain that allowed their drugs' traffic to safely arrive and be distributed. She'd promoted him with money while decreasing his ability to cause issues. He'd seen dollar and pound signs and pounced at her offering.

He was less of a threat now that he was dead. Jia had been pulling suits from the house of cards and replacing them with bricks and mortar. Change was incremental; evolution, not revolution, was what they had planned for.

'Idris and I have been invited to the Foreign Office,' she told the twelve once they were all sitting around the table in her study.

'To get your visa checked?' said Malik. Like his cousin Nadeem, he was ready to step down from his role in the Jirga and had asked Jia to replace him. But finding someone as trusted as him was difficult, and so he stayed.

'Not quite,' said Idris.

'We don't know what's coming next from the Guild and the Interior,' said Jia. 'We need to prepare.'

'You sound like you have political ambitions,' said Nadeem. 'You need to be careful.'

'He's right,' said Fozia. 'Those political types are part of the same gang, from the same school, the same university, and they play us against each other. But they're the real gangsters. They see the country like a Monopoly board. It won't end well.'

'It will start badly,' said Idris. 'And it will get worse, but it won't end that way. When we're done, we will have control over the country, and we won't stop there. They won't be able to do anything about it.'

'What about other countries? What about Yanick, and all the other heads of families whose cages you rattled?' said Malik. 'We're still handling the repercussions of that, and I still don't know why you did it.'

'They came for Afzal, and we've put five bodies into the ground. Those guys worked for us,' said Nadeem. 'We respect you and trust your plans, but things are getting harder, Jia.'

'I know, brother,' she said, leaning forward in her chair. 'We are united in our grief, but we must not let Yanick Kaplan divide us. Idris?'

'We are working on a solution. We need to lobby members of the Guild individually, alongside Adam Diaz.'

Sakina, who had been listening silently until then, began handing out a folder to each member of the Jirga. 'In here is a list of names. Each one of you has been assigned a Guild member that we want you to approach. The file has their personal details – likes, dislikes, business interests – the usual stuff, and then…' She paused. 'There's also the more intimate details of their lives.'

Jia looked at her Jirga. 'Try diplomacy first,' she said. 'Reason with them, show them why it is in their best interests to work with us. But if that doesn't convince them, do whatever it takes.'

***

Idris closed the door to Jia's study and sat down beside Nadeem, Maria, Benyamin and Malik. The others had gone home, leaving the inner circle, the ones all joined by blood.

'Are you sure about this, Jiji?' said Nadeem.

He hadn't called her that name in a long time, and it awakened an old softness in her. They'd buried so many of her father's men in the last few years due to age and illness, and now war, that she'd forgotten how to feel. But she knew that this was how survival was done. Nadeem worked for the charitable arm of the family business and usually stayed away from Jirga meetings.

'This business of ours,' said Idris. 'It's going to be unwieldy.'

Jia stared out of the window. 'I agree,' she said.

'We always said we'd get out,' said Malik.

'Maybe the Foreign Office meeting will hold the key,' said Jia.

'And the mine?'

'I'm working it.'

'Shall we head to Pasha's tonight? For old time's sake?' said Malik.

'I can't,' said Jia. 'The smell of shisha makes me nauseous.'

'Since when were you bothered by shisha smoke?' said Malik.

Idris looked at her, his eyes concerned. 'Since she was pregnant,' said Idris. 'That's when we stopped going to Pasha's.'

They turned to Jia Khan, looking at her as if she was a unicorn. 'Are you guys kidding me?' she said. 'How have you not noticed?'

'I mean, we did think you should lay off the pies,' said Nadeem.

'And only last week, Maria said, "Jia really should stop wearing belts", but we just figured you were happy.'

'I did not say that,' said Maria. 'I would never comment on a woman's weight. Besides, I knew!'

'Dudes, I am huge,' said Jia, enjoying the release that laughter brought. It reminded her why she was here, why she had stayed so long. These were her people: she loved them, and they loved her. It was complicated, some of it was unresolved, but it was family.

'Yes, but you're *our* huge,' said Nadeem, kissing the top of her head.

'Mubarak! Another boy child?' said Malik.

She shrugged. 'They're what I seem to make,' she said. 'Maria makes the girls in this family, and you too, Nadeem, of course. Maybe Idris could step up and fill that gap.'

The fire in the hearth burned brightly that night, the siblings and cousins catching up like old times. It had not been like this for a while. They laughed and joked and simmered into silence occasionally, then moved to the kitchen, where they found Sanam Khan slicing onions and potatoes for pakorai. Idris flicked on the kettle for tea, and Benyamin grabbed the gram flour to help his mother mix the batter for the pakorai. He poured the fine yellow powder into a bowl and added the vegetables his mother had julienned, along with slices of green chilli and salt.

He placed a wok on the heat and filled it with oil, dropping balls of the mixture into the hot fat until they rose to the top, turning golden as they cooked. The kitchen was filled with the aromas of their childhood, the very smells they had hated and tried to escape for fear of them penetrating their clothes as they headed out to see their friends.

It wasn't long before they were dipping crispy pakorai in ketchup and chutney and drinking hot cups of chai.

'I can fry the shami kebab too,' said Sanam Khan, heading towards the freezer. It was filled to the brim with samosas, chicken patties and kebabs made of minced beef and chana daal.

'I can't eat meat anymore,' said Jia. 'It turns my stomach.'

'You going back to your old ways, Jiji?' said Idris.

She smiled and sank down into the sofa, enjoying the ease of the evening.

Jia looked at her cousins, her community, the ones who came when she needed, and she wished that life could stay this way. But she knew that it wouldn't last.

Something was coming, and its reverberations would be felt throughout their lives.

CHAPTER 30

Sitting in the lobby of the Foreign Office, Jia and Idris Khan looked out of place. It wasn't their skin tone or their manner, it was that they were too well groomed, too impeccably turned out to be civil servants. They looked like the kind of people who should not be made to wait in the lobby of a government office, and yet there they were. She checked her watch. He looked apologetic. The meeting should have started half an hour ago.

'Let's get out of here,' she said. 'I'm losing the will to live.'

Her morning sickness was still strong, her patience thin. He nodded and picked up the leather document case he had with him.

She tucked the Swiss watch under the cuff of her pristine white shirt and stood up to leave just as the security doors parted. The man who had invited them to the government office stumbled through the turnstiles.

He was dishevelled in a 'couldn't care less' kind of way, and Jia Khan exchanged a look with Idris; he knew they would be discussing this on the way home. The man dropped his notebook on the table. It was bound by an elastic band and bulging with papers and Post-it notes, making Jia wonder if he was wise to the privacy risks of digital devices.

'Did you check in alright?' he said. 'Get your passes and everything?'

'We did,' said Idris. 'But we're leaving now.'

'Right, well, let's go through to the meeting room,' he said, ignoring Idris's words.

'We must get home to my son,' said Jia, her politeness in stark contrast to her annoyance. 'London takes more of my time than I'd like.' She looked for a sign that he had human feelings, some semblance of emotion, of empathy, to cross his face, but nothing came.

'You ever notice how these political types never apologise?' Idris had said to Jia on the drive over. He was watching her now, the same thought crossing their minds, her smile patient, revealing nothing, and his lips remaining tight.

'They make no attempt to conceal their activities,' she'd replied in the car. 'They've invited us to the Foreign Office, they will check us in, add our names to their database and pretend it's all above board. Then they'll slip what they really want on to the table.' Outside the car, the Yorkshire landscape had morphed into the Midlands and would shortly change to the M25. Jia often felt as though northern dry wit was shed as they drove down the M1.

'Blundell is a liar and a narcissist,' Idris then added.

'We deal with men and women like that on a daily basis,' Jia replied.

'Yes, but the people we know bend and break the law for survival. These men do it because they can, because they think they're better, and because they are hoarding money and power.'

'Man continues to want until his mouth is filled with soil,' Jia had remarked, but she noted his concerns. 'I'm taking you with me because I'd like to believe that what they will ask of us will pave a way to leaving the old ways behind. I would like to believe that, but until I see it, I won't. Blundell is going to ask us for something, something he can't get through legitimate means. His blatant disregard for the law will play into our hands, and he will later regret it. But we are old hands at playing with men like him, and we can use him to our advantage. I trust you to do what needs to be done.'

'Traffic was a nightmare,' said James Singleton now. It wasn't an apology. 'I wish I'd left that meeting earlier. I won't keep you long, Ms Khan. This way, please.'

The conversation Idris had had with Jia in the car was fresh in his mind as they followed Singleton through the security barrier. They passed into an ordinary-looking office furnished with blue pinboards, grey office chairs and laminate tables.

'So let me get straight to it,' said Singleton when they were seated. 'We need your help Ms Khan. The PM needs your help.'

'Please, speak plainly,' said Jia.

'I've invited you here because I'm a great admirer of your work. What you've done with your city, it is truly impressive. I was hoping we could find a way to work together. Young people need role models. You can help with that. Build infrastructure, create jobs, improve people's lives.'

Jia leaned back in her chair. She had hoped for something a little more imaginative from the prime minister's man. She sat back, allowing the silence to fill the room, letting Singleton soak in discomfort.

She watched as he shuffled in his seat, his grin pressed into his face. He knew who she was, what she was capable of – that was why he had asked her here. So the charade was for the benefit of his ego. She didn't like games, and she didn't like men who tried to sharpen their claws on her.

She was here because she wanted to clear the family money, and political power was the fastest way that gangsters and criminals could make themselves respectable.

She reminded herself of that goal, but she wasn't going to let him get off too easily. 'My cousin Nadeem handles all our corporate social responsibility work,' she said. 'Idris, can you put Mr Singleton in touch with him.' She smiled. 'But that's not why you've invited me here, is it?' she said.

'I was told you were direct,' he said. 'I'm part of the campaign re-election committee, and, well, we need a little nudge with the voters.'

'I'm not sure I understand,' said Jia. She understood perfectly.

'We could do with your influence,' he said. 'If you understand my meaning.' She wouldn't have been surprised if he'd added a wink after the statement. She turned to Idris, knowing full well what he was about to say.

'Are you asking us to bully the voters, Mr Singleton? Because that's not something we can help with,' said Idris.

'Is it because we're of Pakistani heritage that you think we would know something about this kind of thing?' said Jia. She almost felt like a cat playing with a mouse.

'No, no! Of course not!' said Singleton, his discomfort growing, his face turning pink and then red, leaving Jia feeling as if he might burst out of his skin.

'We work in tech,' said Idris. 'We can help with government proposals, AI, advisory groups, but election fraud is out of our remit.'

'No, no! You misunderstand me. The PM is interested in your company's technology. You are the best in the country and fast becoming the best in the world. We need a proposal to, maybe, sway the voters away from the opposition. Something a little like this.'

He took a red folder from his beaten leather bag and pushed it towards Jia, his nails unclipped, their ridges rough and broken. Jia wondered at the audacity of mediocre men as she reached for the folder, her own nails pristine, clean, filed and painted in clear polish. Inside the folder was a single piece of paper. She looked at him and closed the file.

'You're asking a lot,' she said. 'What do we get in return?'

James Singleton smiled, his thin lips parting to reveal plaque-covered teeth. 'The PM's unending gratitude,' he said.

'Most of London is now owned by Arabs and Asians, soft power dressed in jilbabs and hijabs,' said Idris. 'We have access to the power that comes with Chinese money and Malaysian manners. You're offering us access to a crumbling empire. Why would we want that?'

They were set to reign over a new world order made up of people who came from the same continent as their ancestors. 'We speak multiple languages, understand the nuances of multiple cultures, and we're adept at navigating worlds other than yours,' said Idris. 'We are the bridge between East and West. We understand the importance of community in Asia and the power of individualism in the West.'

Jia Khan knew that capitalism was king, and that James Singleton was on a losing side. She smiled patiently at him. 'As much as I'd like to, we can't monetise your gratitude, Mr Singleton…James,' she said.

He nodded. 'No, no, of course not, but there must be a way that we can help each other.' He cocked his head to one side, trying to be charming but failing. The room fell silent again and stayed that way for an age.

Then he tried a different tack. 'Is that a Greubel Forsey? May I?' he asked, leaning forward, his tiny eyes squinting at the timepiece. Jia brought her wrist close to his face, letting him smell what real wealth looked like.

The watch, like the woman, was a rare mix of precision, complexity and elegance. Meticulously crafted, through masterful engineering in the case of the watch, and intellect, wit and experience in the case of Jia, their value and depth weren't always recognised by the untrained eye.

Like the Greubel Forsey, Jia Khan operated on multiple levels: just when you thought you'd figured her out, she revealed another fascinating layer, and you doubted you'd ever really known her at all. Idris knew this about his cousin, and he knew it well. His work was to be beside her and step up when she needed him. He knew where he stood in the hierarchy of the family business.

Singleton was also a man who believed in hierarchy, but he had misunderstood the pecking order. Jia Khan was a woman wearing a watch worth more than the average British home, and he was a man who could only dream of such things. And yet he'd tried to make her feel small by keeping her waiting and pretending she was there for reasons other than what he required.

'James, our interests are not aligned,' she said. He leaned back in his chair. There were few who said no to the prime minister. 'I came here because Oliver's wife asked.'

'I see,' said Singleton.

Oliver Blundell's wife, Anita, was a wound in Singleton's side, one that refused to heal. It was widely known that she held the true power in her marriage, and she had scuppered many of Singleton's best laid plans.

'Understood, understood,' he said. He was seething now. He hated how this brown woman from some poor northern city had come here in her fancy shoes and watch and said no to him. Who did she think she was?

Even though James Singleton had female friends and espoused the idea of equality, he was an increasingly angry man, one who could not bring himself to name his pain.

Diversity was a wonderful part of his home city of London: he loved the rising aroma of Brazilian grills, helping himself to perfect-shaped golden falafel, the spring rolls by the Chinese vendor and, of course, the Indian restaurants and their nihari, haleem and biryanis. But if they all got the top jobs, where would that leave him?

'It's all the Indian parents who hot-housed their children! That's why Marcus didn't get a place at Sycamore Gray,' his wife had said when their son missed out on a place at their local grammar school.

He was pissed off, and wokism meant he wasn't allowed to express it.

Jia knew this because she'd seen the emails detailing his feelings. Her techies had extracted them, along with several indecent images of him shagging various men and women, from his devices.

The truth was he'd have to admit to himself that he was a racist, and that he'd benefitted from the absence of competition. When he'd won the bursary to Eton, when he'd landed a place at Cambridge, he'd been the best, hadn't he? Now they were saying there were all these other people who had been held back – so what did that say about his qualifications? He was not going to let these fuckers make him feel like he was less.

'This other folder contains a list of your, shall we say, enterprises,' he said. 'It is in neither of our interests for this to get out. You have done a lot of good work for the community, and we want it to continue.' He put the folder back in his bag. 'We know you want to go clean. That's in both our interests.'

Jia had been in two minds about her next steps. She was hoping not to have to go there. But she didn't like being blackmailed, especially by a bedraggled man with poor hygiene. She looked at Idris and nodded.

He opened his case and pulled out a green folder, handing it to Jia. She, in turn, pushed the folder across the desk to Singleton, her perfectly manicured nails meeting his crooked ones.

'The thing is, James Marlon Singleton – that is your middle name, isn't it? – I'd say a few of the items in this dossier are in the grey, and even without scrutiny the rest are illegal activities. I know you won't want the vultures picking over them.' She paused. 'Take your time. We'll leave it here for you to look at. I have a digital copy if you need, and I can share it with you, and others.'

She lingered on the final word, her eyes locked and loaded.

***

They stepped out of the Foreign Office and into brisk, cold air and then the warmth of the waiting car. Jia Khan tucked her hair behind her ear and took her place in the back seat of the Bentley. 'What a motherfucker,' she said and then laughed.

It occurred to Idris that to those who didn't know her, Jia appeared soft, fragile, a delicate Pakistani woman. In truth, she was possessed with unshakable determination. She took care of herself and everyone around her, and that required a collected exterior. Underneath, Jia Khan was a volcano of emotions, but there were few that knew this about her.

'It makes you feel good about yourself that you can read her, doesn't it?' Sakina once said to him.

'Does it bother you?' he'd replied.

She'd shaken her head. 'Of course not. She's Jia Khan.'

Outside the Foreign Office, Jia had just put her head back on the headrest and closed her eyes when there was a rap on the window. She opened her eyes and saw the woman in grey standing on the other side of the glass.

Jia turned to Idris. 'This is why we're at the Foreign Office and not the Home Office. Her.' She nodded to the woman outside the window. 'This is the meeting we're actually here for.'

'What do you want me to do?' he said.

'Let her in. Let's hear what this has really been about.'

CHAPTER 31

'Would you mind stepping outside,' the woman in grey said to Idris as he opened the Bentley door. He turned to Jia for confirmation.

'Give us a moment, please, Idris,' she said.

He climbed out of the car and the woman took his place. 'I'll be close by,' he said.

Jia nodded, and he closed the door, leaving the women to their conversation. The woman glanced at the driver. 'St James's Park is close by,' she said to Jia. 'Shall we take a stroll there?'

***

They walked west on King Charles Street, past the Churchill War Rooms and towards Clive Steps, Idris a safe distance behind, keeping Jia in his eyeline.

'He's protective, isn't he?' said the woman.

Jia didn't answer.

They turned left on to Horse Guard Road and crossed over to the park, and Jia wondered what they were doing here.

'This is the most royal of all London's parks,' said the woman as they entered. She sounded like a tour guide pointing out the highlights of the city. 'Shaped by monarchs and bordered by palaces, home to ceremonial events, weddings, jubilees, parades and parties, this is the park where history is made.'

Jia had remained silent the entire six minutes it had taken to walk from the Foreign Office to the park. Eventually, the woman turned to the matter at hand. 'I owe you an apology,' she said. 'For the other day in the café. Our intel was that you were alone.'

Jia's interest was piqued. 'Go on,' she said. 'I'm listening. But no more tourist chat. I assume you're not here to sell me the city.'

The woman shook her head. 'We need your help. A few months ago, six female students were kidnapped from a college in Peshawar.'

'Yes, and you were going to help bring them home,' said Jia. 'That was widely reported.'

'It was, but what wasn't reported was that we launched a rescue operation. It failed, and two of our men have now disappeared. We don't know where they are.'

Jia stopped walking and turned to look at the woman. 'I need to sit down,' she said. 'These shoes weren't meant for pregnancy.' They sat by Duck Island, looking out at the nature reserve. To the casual observer they appeared to be two women on a lunch break. 'Did you know that there are seventeen species of birds in this park?' said Jia. 'Including mute swans and pelicans.'

'I did not,' said the woman.

Jia nodded. 'I used to live around here. That's why your tourist information narrative, lifted straight from royalparks.org.uk is wasted on me. I'm used to being underestimated, but when someone who has been watching me does it, it can be especially tiresome.'

They sat in silence as a duck dived into the pond, its tail feathers visible and up in the air as it searched for something beneath the surface of the water. Men and women, young and old, walked along the path, enjoying the greenery of the nature reserve, holding hands, laughing and chatting.

'So, you sent a group of white men to rescue six brown women, and now you want me to help rescue the white men.'

'We effed up. And we don't know how to fix it. We have the resources but not the knowledge.'

'And you can't publicly admit that, because it would make everyone see you for the shit show you are.'

'Exactly. Also, there's another complication. It has to do with a project that you're interested in.'

Jia paused a moment. 'The Reko mine,' she said, piecing things together. 'You're not interested in the welfare of the women, you're interested in just one woman, because her father makes the decision about the mine.'

The woman nodded. 'We want that mine under the control of a British company, but with all the decolonisation rhetoric that is currently going on, we can't make the overt overtures that we used to. We know you want the contract, and we know we can work with you.'

She looked at Jia, scrutinising her face, searching for a sense of what to say next to bring her on side. 'Look, Jia – may I call you Jia?'

Jia shook her head. She did not wish to be on first name terms; fake closeness would muddy the waters of her work.

'Ms Khan then. It has been a boys' club for a long time, and although women have been coming in and making changes, we keep coming up against the usual structural bullshit.'

'Then dismantle it,' said Jia.

'That's easier said than done.'

'The truth is, you don't want to dismantle the old ways. They serve you as much as they do the men. You get to choose which part you play and when you want to take a back seat, raise your children and let the men protect you.'

'Maybe you're right, but what good does that do the six women in Peshawar right now? They're caught up in something that's not their fault, and we have made it worse with our colonial clown feet. I know you're familiar with that part of the world and have contacts and inroads that we do not. We were hoping that you'd have some ideas of how to help. In exchange, we will make sure that you win the contract for the mine.'

'How do you know the hostages are alive?'

'One of the students got a note to her family, likely smuggled out by one of the kidnappers.'

'One of the kidnappers?'

'Yes. We think it may be someone who knows her or her family.'

'And she managed to convince him to help her?'

'This kind of power is why men don't want women to be free.'

Jia didn't need thinking time. 'I'll do what I can because I can't say no to bringing the women home. But you will have to find another way to repay me. I don't work for free, and I don't like working for people who have me followed.'

'I was under orders, and while I wasn't in agreement, I needed to work with what we have. Look, I know that you're moving your interests towards things considered legitimate by the masses, and I can help with that. There's change coming and we need women like you at the forefront.'

'But the mine contract is not yours to give and I don't need your help to get it.'

'You don't, but your plan to clean up the family business can be greatly helped if certain people with influence are in your corner. The Interior is a powerful entity, embedded within government structures but independent and free from scrutiny, making decisions that determine who runs the world. I'll send you the information you need – it will be encrypted, but I know that you have the means to access it. You managed to crack the code I left. That was the final test the Interior asks for.'

Jia was asleep before they hit the M25. She was bone tired, wanting to sleep all the time. She made a mental note to get a blood test.

She drifted in and out of slumber, the sounds of Noor Jehan and Mehdi Hassan peppered with eighties' pop making her lose track of when and where she was. What a strange thing time was. It had passed so slowly when she was responsible only for herself, and now she was perpetually running out of it, trying to hold on to the smiling moments with her children while wishing away the complications that she knew she would one day miss.

She woke to Harry Styles welcoming her to 'the final show'. The lyrics felt particularly apt.

'Why don't these men know how to dress?' she said to Idris.

'Which men?'

'Singleton.'

'They've inherited positions and place, but not style. That is for people like us,' he said.

'It's disrespectful. Don't ever turn up to a meeting looking like him,' she said, pulling the cuff of her white sleeve through her black blazer, encouraging it to sit perfectly. She brushed a piece of lint from her jeans and looked at her cousin.

'When have you ever seen me look like a tramp?' he said.

'I'm just saying, don't start. Just because these rich white men think they can get away with it, doesn't mean we can. I blame Zuckerberg.'

'You know how much Mark Zuckerberg spends on one of his white T-shirts, don't you. Six hundred pounds. Brunello Cucinelli.'

'Exactly.' Jia closed her eyes again and folded her arms.

'What are we going to do about the Peshawar debacle and getting the hostages out?' said Idris.

'We'll figure it out,' Jia replied. 'But right now, I need to sleep. It has been a long day.'

She slept all the way home, her head full of work and life. There was a baby coming and she didn't want this one born into the life her other sons had been born into. If she could do what the Interior wanted, maybe they could get out from under the yoke of crime.

CHAPTER 33

Spring was beginning and the village was waking after a long and sleepy winter. They walked along the beach, Lirian running ahead with his cousins, picking up seashells from the sand and shingle. His jeans rolled up, his feet bare, he ran back to his mother, handing them to her for safekeeping. She would find them in her pockets and bag days from now, along with little pebbles, Hot Wheels cars and Lego pieces.

Rest had been added to the agenda on the insistence of Elyas, and so the Khan family had driven ninety miles to the coastal village.

'Remember when we used to come on these outings with Baba?' Jia said to her mother. The women were walking a little way behind the others. Maria was walking arm in arm with her husband, watching the children.

'I do,' said Sanam Khan. 'In those days I would pack kebab and naan and Afghani pilau, and we'd sit together on the beach. All the families together. Bazigh lala, your father, Sher Khan and sometimes the others.'

'I miss those days,' said Jia.

'Me too,' said Sanam Khan. She was walking slower now, and her hearing was not what it used to be. It was why she stayed back from the crowd. 'I miss holding hands with someone,' she said. 'Now that I need someone to steady me, your father is gone and I am a widow. May Allah grant him a high place in heaven.'

Jia took her mother's arm. 'You loved him a lot,' she said. 'I remember.'

'I did,' said Sanam Khan.

Seasonal attractions were starting to reopen, and temperatures were rising, but only a little. Sanam Khan pulled her coat around herself. 'Let's go inside,' she said to her daughter, pointing to a café on the other side of the beach. 'The others can run ahead – my bones are feeling the cold. Come, I want to talk to you about some things.'

Jia helped her mother cross the beach. She settled her at a table inside the café, before coming back with a latte, a croissant and a pot of tea. She placed the coffee in front of her mother.

Sanam Khan seemed lost in thought, as she had been for the last few months.

'What did you want to talk about, Mama?' said Jia, after she'd removed the layers she'd been wearing, placing her overcoat on the back of her chair.

'I want you to forgive me,' she said, taking Jia by surprise.

'For what?'

'For this life that you are living. I sometimes think that it is my fault.'

Jia hadn't spoken to Sanam Khan about the work she had inherited from her father, and the responsibility she had taken on. She'd always assumed her mother was blind to Akbar Khan's activities and to his past. There were days when she'd wondered what this said about her.

'When I was a girl,' Sanam Khan said, 'I wanted to marry a boy who lived across from us.'

Jia looked at her mother, as if seeing her for the first time. Sanam Khan had never spoken of these things before, and Jia realised she hadn't considered her life outside of the realms of Akbar Khan and her siblings.

'I can tell you're surprised,' she went on. 'When I married your father, I buried so much of my past. It wasn't to do with your father, it was to do with wider, deeper loves, like family, and leaving the land where I was raised. When I met Akbar Khan, I told him about the boy, and he understood. You see, he had been married before…'

'You knew?' said Jia.

'Your father and I had no secrets,' said Sanam Khan. 'Despite all your talk of feminism, you still see me within the confines of the kitchen, and you think this makes me less intelligent, less knowledgeable about the world.'

Jia wanted to protest, but she couldn't. He mother had pulled back the curtain to Jia's inner workings.

'It's alright,' said Sanam Khan. 'This is what men have done for hundreds of years, set us on stone steps in the auditorium of life, above and below each other. And then they have stoned those of us they feel most threatened by.'

'Mama, I am sorry,' said Jia, taking her mother's hand in hers.

'I have done as much as one caged bird can to set another free. It is why I took you to the library when you were little, made you study, tried to keep your honour blemish-free so no man would force you to choose between the devil and the sea.' She looked out at the ocean from the window of the café.

'At least with the sea, there is hope,' said Jia. 'With the devil, there is none.'

'Jia Khan, I know you,' said her mother. 'I know the inside and outside of you. I know you think I don't like you, but I do. I have been afraid, that is all. You see how your little one goes out in the world and picks up sticks and stones, and you worry, and then the older one says he is queer, and you worry what the world will do to him? Let them live their lives. Let them be free. Remind them that Allah loves them always.' Jia listened to her mother, incredulous at what she was hearing. Sanam Khan was a woman of few words, who had been a very conservative mother, and yet here she was, telling Jia to let her sons live their lives far from the rules she herself had considered sacred for decades.

Out of the window, Jia could see her husband, children, siblings, nephews and nieces laughing and having fun. They looked like any normal family, and yet Jia knew that they weren't.

Her mother sensed her melancholy. 'Your father and I would come to places like this, remember? You and your siblings would run, and we would sit in the car and sip chai. He was often subdued away from the house and his Jirga.'

Jia was again surprised. 'I'm sorry,' she said. 'I should have known that you were aware.'

'There is nothing that happens in a woman's house that she is unaware of,' said Sanam Khan. 'She may close her eyes and her ears, but she knows. Your father shared his life with me. He had been used to that with Mary…'

By now Jia understood that she had spent decades underestimating her mother's mind and had never really taken the time to get to know her.

'I overheard you speaking to Elyas about Mary one day, and I was relieved.'

Jia watched Lirian running across the beach, heading towards the café.

'He never meant for you to be a seawall for us,' said Sanam Khan. 'He wanted you to be free.'

Jia heard the bell of the door jingle, and saw the little boy heading towards them, beaming with joy, his father close behind.

'The others want to go for fish and chips,' said Elyas.

'Tell her to call Amal,' said Sanam Khan, standing to leave. 'Maybe together they can find a way to save us and your family from this legacy.'

'Place them in a crisscross pattern,' said Elyas as he handed Benyamin Khan the kindling.

'I can't believe we booked a place without central heating,' said Ben, placing the sticks across the base of the wood burner, two on the bottom and two above them. 'It looks like the balsa wood we used in woodwork.'

'I always think that too. I'm surprised they had woodwork when you were at school,' said Elyas.

They'd been about to leave the coastal town when they hit trouble. Elyas had jumped in the car with Ben, but it had broken down close to Robin Hood's Bay. Realising that the AA would not put two men on their priority list, Elyas had swiftly found them an Airbnb close by.

'I'm glad Jia agreed to take Ahad and Lirian home,' he said to Ben. 'It would have been a nightmare with all of them here.'

They'd arrived at the small cottage to find that the only source of heat was a log burner and an open fireplace in each bedroom. Elyas had found a stack of firewood, kindling and old newspapers to the side of the house.

'Where did you learn how to do this?' Benyamin said, as Elyas demonstrated how to set up the fire.

'YouTube,' said Elyas. 'We have a burner at the London house. So, look, you need to leave space for the air to flow. Then light the firelighter or paper that you've put under the grate. It's going to look impressive, and you'll think you've nailed it, but unless you add the logs, it will burn out and you'll be left with nothing but ash and sad, cold, charred kindling.'

'It's a lot like life,' said Benyamin Khan. 'It starts out burning fast, and then if you don't keep adding bigger and bigger logs, it burns out.'

'Or you learn to use other kinds of fuel that last longer, need less work,' said Elyas.

He'd been watching Ahad and Benyamin grow close. They'd been spending a lot more time together, playing football, watching movies and shooting the breeze. Benyamin seemed more like an older brother than an uncle, and it had occurred to Elyas that he didn't really know his brother-in-law as well as he should. Benyamin had been a kid when Elyas and Jia had got together.

Benyamin, for his part, had become quieter, more contemplative. He'd even come to Elyas for advice a couple of times, which had surprised Elyas, because he'd always assumed Idris was the one he'd turn to. He wondered if Idris's relationship with Sakina had changed that.

The fire was roaring now, and the men turned their attention to their stomachs. 'Do you think there's a restaurant close by? Some Uber Eats type thing?' said Benyamin. He was looking through the welcome basket of eggs, bread, cheese and milk that had been left on the kitchen counter. Beside it was a pile of takeaway menus. Benyamin flicked through them until he found a pizzeria.

The food arrived thirty minutes later, and by that time it had started to rain. Benyamin took the red, white and green pizza box – standard issue no matter where in the country you were – from the delivery man. His hood was pulled up, his jacket smattered with rain. The wind was biting, and Benyamin was glad that Elyas had convinced him to stay over rather than wait for the AA man by the side of a cold, wet road.

'Thanks, mate,' he said, tipping the man and closing the door, grateful for the fire, food and dry lodgings.

He placed the box on the dining table and flipped it open, turning on the TV in the background.

They were ravenous by now, their silence a testament to this and the deliciousness of the large slices of stone-baked sourdough they were holding. 'You can't go wrong with a Margherita,' said Elyas. 'It's the safest bet when buying from somewhere you don't know.'

'You ever been to this place?' said Benyamin, gesturing to the reporter on the screen in a flak jacket and hard hat.

Elyas nodded.

'You've pretty much travelled all over the world, haven't you?'

'Pretty much. There are still places I'd like to see,' he said. 'Maybe when Lirian is older. Ahad and I used to travel together a lot when he was a kid, but it feels more difficult now.'

'How so?'

'Single fatherhood is hard, but when you're the only one deciding, you can just get up and go, make all the calls, no one to stop you. You don't have to clear anything with anyone.'

'That must feel good,' said Benyamin, 'to be able to just get up and leave.'

He seemed weighed down by thought as he stared out of the window, where the rain was coming down harder now.

Elyas saw a flicker of something pass over him and recognised it: it was the face of a man who needed to talk but didn't know how.

There were things Benyamin needed to say, that needed to leave his mind and body. To speak was to exorcise demons, but there were few safe spaces for men. Women were encouraged to converse, to share their emotions, to sit in each other's company and say what had happened to make them the way they were, to shape them. It was as if their conversations warmed them, lit them from inside, and they left their pain behind like the ash left in a fireplace.

Men were encouraged to share ideas and problems, and measure their self-worth on the football pitch, the tennis court, the shopfloor, the boardroom. But there were things that needed to be said, done and passed over to loved ones to handle. Without this, men could not fortify themselves.

There were widening cracks in Benyamin's armour, and Elyas could see them now, because he was older, wiser and had raised a boy to manhood. He had acquired this understanding from the women he had worked with, those who had shaped him through their friendship and those he loved.

He considered how to make Benyamin feel safe enough to speak. Asking him outright would spook him, that much he knew, and not asking him was not an option – there was a brotherhood that needed to be created if his sons were to live differently from the way men had in the past. 'You know,' he said. 'I've reported from war zones and visited places after natural disasters and terrorist attacks. One of the things I've seen over and over is how different countries handle the aftermath.'

Benyamin looked up at him, wondering where he was going with the conversation.

'They start rebuilding,' said Elyas, 'creating employment, and consider ways to make sure they're ready for the next time disaster hits. And they also focus on mental health. But you know, in Pakistan they have less than three hundred psychiatrists. Three hundred for a population of two hundred and forty million people.'

'Mate, that's such a white man's way of looking at things. These people don't have enough to eat. And you think they want to sit around and talk about their feelings?' Benyamin wondered about his brother-in-law's intelligence sometimes. The man had won awards, but his view of the world was skewed by education, privilege and the industry he worked in.

Benyamin Khan's life had been shaped by the rules of the street, that you had to be ruthless to survive or people died, that there was no room for sentimentality, and no one cared how you felt when it came to making money, and money was king, queen and every other chess piece on the board. Without it, children died, women sold their bodies, and men bartered their souls.

'I know you think differently,' said Elyas, 'but it's not enough to survive, and yes, it is a privilege, but it is one that everyone deserves. The mental well-being of a community is part of what makes it strong. Listen, after the earthquake in Pakistan, there was nowhere for men to say how they felt, no place where they could be weak.'

'Crying is not part of any society that you and I belong to,' said Benyamin Khan.

'You sound just like Jia,' said Elyas, the words tumbling out of his mouth. Without meaning to, he'd spoken a truth that he had been avoiding.

'You ever seen her cry?' said Benyamin. 'I have. A long time ago.' He took the pizza box into the kitchen and came back with a bottle of whisky.

'Where did you find that?' said Elyas.

'It was in the welcome basket,' said Benyamin.

'You're kidding, right?'

'Of course, I am. It was in the cabinet. I'm sure they won't mind,' he said as he poured himself a drink.

'I didn't know you drank.'

'I don't really,' he said. 'But I think today counts as "medicinal purposes". You want one?'

'No, I'm good,' said Elyas, holding up his hand.

'You ever drink?'

'Not really,' said Elyas. 'It's never appealed to me. I tried it maybe once or twice, and I wasn't into it. Media used to be very boozy, and I found it a huge turn-off.'

'What about my sister?'

'Not that I know of,' said Elyas. 'We've never spoken about it.'

The room felt chilly now, and Elyas moved towards the fireplace. The once roaring fire had dwindled to a listless glow. He picked up the poker and began to stir the embers. Nothing happened. It seemed to have burned itself out, even before it had consumed all the firewood.

'Maybe it's given all it can,' said Benyamin, sipping his drink. 'You should give up on it.'

Elyas was not one to be deterred; he had a history of doing things others said could not be done. The challenge of restoring the fire's vibrancy loomed large. He carefully blew on the embers and then added more kindling, strategically placing it to ignite and revive the flames. He added another kiln-dried log and continued to poke and prod gently. The charred wood glowed red hot and shades of orange as he turned it over and over, embers flying as the iron poker cut through them, then fading away, it seemed. And then, just as suddenly, they weren't. They began to flicker, and the fire, once on the brink of collapse, was alive. He watched as the flames started licking the length of the wood, before breaking into a larger blaze.

The crackling broke the silence, as if this was the sign of redemption that he'd been searching for.

'You don't give up easy,' said Benyamin. 'You like hope, don't you?'

Elyas didn't answer. He knew the conversation was no longer about the things they'd been talking about at the start. It was about Jia Khan, and Elyas, and all the things no one spoke about with him. This was the day Benyamin Khan had chosen to bring it all crashing down.

Elyas had long been aware of his wife's armour, the way she withdrew from society and the ones she loved, her silence never judgement but often misconstrued by those who didn't know her. She was enchanting and infuriating, but ultimately she was governed by love and loyalty. Jia inspired him, and he admired her.

Jia Khan did not lash out, despite the arsenal of words and information at her disposal. She understood well the damage she could inflict, but she had been on the other side of pain for long enough to protect others from it.

Her husband knew that her armour was never about war, that beneath it was the soft underbelly of a wounded woman.

'Jia is aware of her wounds,' he said. 'We both know that. She has her ways. But the women I spoke to in Pakistan – the ones who had been happily married until the earthquake struck – they did not have her independence or her mind. A natural disaster made them victims of the tragedy, but more than that, in the aftermath, many of their men became violent. The psychiatrists I spoke to said it was a known phenomenon. No man can handle that much pressure alone without a brotherhood. They fell prey to extremists, those who would make them believe that others were the reason for their problems.'

Benyamin contemplated what Elyas had said. 'Isn't it the same everywhere? Fascists marching through our streets here and in Europe blame us. We blame them.' He paused. 'What about you, Elyas?' he said.

'What do you mean?' said Elyas.

'You know what I mean.'

'Tell me.'

'You should leave.' His face was dark now. 'Take Ahad and Lirian and get away from here.'

'Why would I take them away from their mother?'

'Because who would choose this life? She and I were born into it, we have no out. Even though our dad didn't want this for us, he couldn't prevent it from happening. You, though – you've chosen to be here. What I've never been able to figure out is how you keep lying to yourself. I know you love my sister, but how are you blind to everything around her?'

Elyas had no way to explain to Benyamin that he *hadn't* chosen this life; it had chosen him. Like quantum entanglement, he was entwined with Jia Khan, so much so that, despite time and distance, his feelings for her had not dimmed. There were moments when she would look at him, and everything else would fade away – the responsibility, the change in his physicality, the fact that he couldn't run after Lirian the way he had with Ahad. There was nothing more beautiful than her mind, her eyes, and he lived for those moments alone together. For then it was as if no time had passed since they first met; they were young again, caught in an infinite time loop.

But he couldn't say any of this to his brother-in-law. Instead, he picked up his things. 'I'll see you in the morning,' he said, and headed to his room, where he closed the door and, sitting on his bed, thought about all the things he avoided thinking about.

Benyamin watched him leave and then picked up the plates. He washed and dried each one, put them away in the cupboard and then took his glass and sat back down beside the fire.

He could feel the heaviness descending on his chest the way it did every evening, blurring the edges of his thoughts. The cottage was eerily quiet, being distant from the main road and away from passing traffic.

He sipped his whisky and leaned back into the chair. His phone was on the other side of the room, and so he looked out of the window. The moon was round and fat, judging him for the drink in his hand, but kinder and more inviting than the thoughts in his head. As the night wore on, he sunk deeper into the armchair; his eyelids became heavy, leaving the complexities of life and the intricacies of family on the other side, in the waking world.

CHAPTER 35

Ahad watched London from the back seat of the warm Bentley, considering how different this trip was from the ones he'd made with his dad, navigating grimy tubes and homeless people holding out paper cups and cardboard signs with requests for coffee and cash.

The car passed through Berkeley Square, and he watched a security man locking the gate at one end of the park in the centre, trying to get people to leave as it started to get dark. Ahad looked at the guard, wondering what came next in his life. Was he eager to get home to a dog and a family and dinner in front of the TV? He was going round, locking gates at each side of the park and encouraging stragglers to head to the bottom entrance.

Ahad had visited this area with his father many times, usually at Christmas, when it was their tradition to head into central London to see the lights and drink hot chocolate as they strolled from here through Burlington Arcade and past the luxury hotels with their bauble arches and fairy lights.

'You wanna get out and have a wander?' said Benyamin.

Ahad shook his head. It was rush hour and every inch of the pavement from here to Piccadilly and Green Park would be taken up with shoes and boots, the main roads snarled up with black cabs and red buses. He knew the smell of pollution, of public transport and of polyester suits and acrylic jumpers. He wanted no more of it.

The Bentley slipped through the back streets, pausing at lights to let pedestrians pass. Little children held on tight to their parents' hands as the throngs crossed. The car pulled up outside a townhouse in the Mayfair Conservation Area. Heavy velvet curtains in deep red were draped on either side of the large window. The clients who came here were the same people in the ivory towers of London's private clubs.

This was one of the city's oldest sartorial institutions. A business associate of Jia Khan had made the introduction, because services were offered by invitation only. There was no signage, no way for influencers and wannabes to turn up and knock on the door. There was no mention on Reddit, no thread or rabbit hole to follow. Tailoring required discretion; stealth wealth conveyed power. It's what sent people scrambling to sites like HEWI, Vinted and Nearly New Cashmere to find brands like Lanvin.

The Khan family had no need to search the internet for such things. They went straight to the source and ordered what they needed. For beyond these brands was another level of wear for those who didn't need to ask how much something would cost.

Benyamin and Ahad stepped out of the car and Benyamin pressed the discreet white bell to the side of the black door. They were greeted by a woman in a tailored navy skirt suit, her shirt so white and crisp that it made Ahad wonder if she just stood to the side of the wall all day, trying not to move until it was time to go home and put on lounge pants.

'It's gonna be fine,' Benyamin said to his nephew. 'They'll sort you right out.' He was in black trainers and a blazer, and he handed his overcoat to the woman. He looked a lot like his sister, and Ahad noted that he had started dressing like her. The family business seemed to have a uniform that only the very few could afford.

The tailoring shop was imbued with the smell of sophistication and wealth. The seamstress led them into her office. The walls were a rich ochre, and in an average-sized London townhouse, the dark colour could have felt oppressive, but this was not a place for the ordinary. The white ceiling was as brilliant as the tailor's shirt, the moulding intricately formed.

Benyamin and Ahad took a seat on the soft leather Chesterfield. Above them, a golden chandelier bathed the room in soft light. They were offered tea, and as Ahad took a sip of the Royal Blend, with its soft raspberry aroma, it reinforced how much he liked the life his mother had given him.

'You want something sharp, sophisticated and dapper, but not like a mafioso,' Benyamin had told him. 'I'll come with you. We can make a weekend of it.' That was why they were here.

CHAPTER 36

Ahad slipped into his new suit, removing a speck of dust from the shoulder, fastening and unfastening the buttons as he checked himself in the mirror.

He was attending an event with his mother and uncle, and he wanted to make a good impression. She rarely allowed him near her work, and he wanted to know more.

Jia had been keeping her son at a distance from the family business since his kidnapping by Meera Shah. And yet, while she didn't want him to be part of it, she could talk openly with him about work in a way that she couldn't with his father.

Ahad understood things that Elyas could not, even though his father had brought him up single-handed. It left Jia wondering if his bloodline controlled his destiny – if, at a cellular level, Ahad never stood a chance of holding on to an ordinary life.

'I don't want to hand on a legacy to you that I have avoided, without you at least trying to fit into wider society. The price you will pay for being part of the family business is heavy. Once your hands are dirty, you can't wash them clean.'

Ahad had listened to his mother, grateful for her honesty. She treated him like an adult and always had. But he had lived an ordinary life, and he had no desire to go back to taking the bus when he had the option of Bentleys, Aston Martins and modified Range Rovers.

He wondered what life would have been like if Jia Khan had raised him, how protective she'd have been, and if she'd have been so open with him about the family business. She had only met him when he was sixteen.

As their sleek black Bentley approached the grand façade of the luxury hotel, the city's frantic energy seemed to dissipate and was replaced by an aura of elegance.

The hotel, a Grade II listed building, was a symbol of high society and stood proudly against the backdrop of the bustling metropolis. Its exterior had little trace of English architecture, being heavily inspired by a Parisian style that spoke of sophistication.

Tall arched windows adorned with intricate iron grilles hinted at the impressive interiors, while elegant balconies draped with vibrant flowers brought natural beauty into the urban landscape. A stone staircase led up to the stately entrance, flanked by two marble pillars that guarded the heavy black doors like sentinels of a bygone era. The hotel was known for its impressive service, and as the car pulled up, a uniformed valet stepped forward, opening the car door with a white-gloved hand.

Jia stepped on to the crimson carpet. Soft and pristine, it stretched to the doorway, welcoming her, her son and her brother into a world of unparalleled luxury and indulgence. Ahad offered his mother his arm and led her up the steps. The hotel, a testament to a day when opulence was an art form, was a place where money talked, and Jia Khan had enough of it to be courted by some of the wealthiest and most powerful people in the land.

They were there for a political event put on for the British Asian Trust.

'The PM will be here,' Jia said, 'but unofficially – as his wife's plus one.'

'I'm guessing there's no press here tonight?' Benyamin said.

Jia nodded. 'It's a closed affair,' she replied. 'It's how these high officials get their money. They network with us but don't want to be caught on camera with our kind.'

Dressed in a black chiffon sari, her hair in a chignon, Ahad was always proud to be seen with his mother. She'd never been the kind of parent to make him jam sandwiches with the crusts cut off, but she was the kind he could call on, even if he'd committed a crime.

He knew her loyalty to him was unconditional. She had proven herself to him over and over again. He was, in turn, more loyal to her than he would ever be to anyone else.

He wanted to be like her in so many ways.

At the top of the steps, she let go of his arm and reached out her hand to him as if he were a small child. But he took it. There were only two people in the world who Jia Khan would do this for: the other was his little brother. She'd brought him here because she was proud of him. Her reaction to his being queer had hurt him, but he understood better now. She loved him, and she wanted to keep him safe.

She led him into the lobby, where someone was waiting to receive them. It was a man in an emerald green suit that matched his eyes.

'How do they know who we are?' Ahad whispered to his mother as they followed him. 'We could be anyone.'

'With events at this level, they pre-clear you. People don't like being asked for ID and made to feel like criminals. So how about this guy? Is he your type?'

'Mum! Stop it!'

'That was out of line, I know. I'm sorry.'

Jia Khan thought of the ease with which she expressed regret to her son. 'Sorry' was a word her parents had rarely used. Asian parents didn't apologise, and 'I love you' was reserved for end of life.

'Their expressions of love were different,' she'd told Ahad. 'It was a different world they grew up in. You'll know my mother and I have argued when she brings me a bowl of yakhni and then later uses what's left of the bone broth to make mutton pilau.'

'Oh, is that why we had so much of that last year?' her son had replied.

Jia had laughed. 'I often wonder if things would have been different if my father had been able to say sorry. If we could have crossed the bridge to each other and sat together, holding hands and crying tears of love and regret.'

But it hadn't happened, and she carried within her the seed of regret that she hadn't had the tools to reach Akbar Khan while he was still alive. Maybe if she had tried harder.

They were talking by the window in the hotel's opulent reception room, when Jia noticed Oliver Blundell and his wife making their way through the crowd.

She turned to her son and leaned in. 'Here's what I want you to know before the PM comes over. Democracies don't run the world. Remember that. The world is run by violence – it always has been. When the British colonised India, it was not by the rule of law, it was not because they were smarter. It was because their methods in organised oppression were better, and we wrongly assumed they shared our ideals of community. They were ruthless, cold and calculated. Some of the men and women in this room are the descendants of people who did not hesitate to murder, rape and mutilate to take what was ours. Never forget that. No matter how wide their smiles, how dainty their china cups and how refined their manners. They are cold-blooded killers. The only difference between the dance then and now is that we've been trained in their arts by them, and we know their every move.'

Ahad looked up just in time to see the prime minister approaching.

'Jia Khan, it's a pleasure to meet you. I've heard so much about you from my wife and from my colleague James.'

'Prime Minister,' she said. 'I have a great deal of respect for your wife.'

'She would be very flattered to hear that,' said Blundell, casting a look across the room to where his wife was chatting with other guests. That Jia Khan's respect was for her and not him, needled him, but he masked it well. 'The feeling is mutual.'

'I don't feel the same about your man James, though,' said Jia, her voice almost a whisper.

'Yes, quite. But there are good reasons to keep a bulldog, as I'm sure you understand. I hope he conveyed how much we would value your advice on the re-election campaign as well as other pressing matters.'

'I understand your numbers are down quite considerably,' she said, holding his gaze. 'I'd suggest not sending people to countries that have recently been ravaged by war and genocide as a way to appease voters, even if, in today's climate, many are likely to cheer you on. And yet, even with such measures you are still far behind in the polls. What does that tell you about how the country feels about you, Prime Minister?'

It was unlike her to be so direct. Like most women, she had learnt to adjust herself to her surroundings, to appear to be accommodating, since experience had taught her that that was the way to get the best response from a situation. But recently she'd grown tired of the gameplay between the world of men and women. The truth was that she'd spent enough time in the company of men to know herself and her worth, and she had found that their estimation of themselves and their place in society was far from accurate. She needed no man's acceptance, and her army was greater than theirs, because she had managed to unite a sisterhood.

She understood why men like Blundell strutted into rooms, but she also knew that they were a part of an empire on its knees. The sun was setting on patriarchy. And so, when she spoke to the prime minister, a man she knew needed her help to stand any chance of winning the next election, she did so as an equal. Jia Khan now owned technology that could overthrow governments.

'I know what they cheer for, Ms Khan, and so I care little for the boos of the cheap seats. You and I know that there are people who have no idea what is good for them. A leader's role is to teach them that.'

'It sounds like you know better than everyone else what needs to be done. My whole life I've watched boys chase power to finally feel like men. But you know what I've learnt? Popularity and power are not the same. Real men know that true strength doesn't need an audience. Invisibility, to be known by the select few, that is the game of the puppet master and that is true power,' she said.

'Ms Khan, you understand how politics works. We do what we must do to maintain power. I know a little about your business too.'

'My reputation precedes me,' she said. 'I do what my people need, not what suits me.' She put her arm around Ahad. 'But, Prime Minister, let me introduce you to my son. Ahad, meet Oliver Blundell.'

The prime minister smiled and shook his hand, then made his excuses and moved away, taking a handkerchief from his pocket to wipe his brow as he did so. His conversation with Jia had riled him, leaving Ahad impressed. Jia Khan cared little about the feelings of the country's leader, and this was why he wanted to work for the family business.

Later, at the bar, Ahad watched his mother across the room, his glass in his hand, the hum of the party a distant murmur in his ears. She stood by the window, her black chiffon sari catching the light as she conversed quietly with a few of the guests. There was an ease in her presence, yet something about her made even the boldest voices in the room hesitate before speaking. He knew that look – the way people deferred to her without even realising they were doing it.

'She's something else, isn't she?' Ahad said to Benyamin, who had joined him at the bar. He took a sip of the iced drink in his hand, not taking his eyes off Jia.

'She's something, alright,' he said. 'I didn't understand why people were afraid of her until I started working with her.'

'How do you mean?' said Ahad.

Benyamin's glance moved from Jia to Ahad and back again. 'She was never loud or aggressive, but people just fell into line around her, grown men, even the ones who hated on women. Then I figured it out.'

'Figured what out? '

'My sister doesn't need to be loud or even assertive, because she watches, notices, remembers. She sees the deeper layers of things that others don't.'

Ahad was intrigued. He put his glass down on the bar. 'What does that have to do with fear?' he said.

'People don't like being seen for who they really are, Ahad,' Benyamin said. 'And Jia sees straight through them. She can expose a weakness, hidden insecurities, motivations, all without saying a word. She's not cruel about it. She just knows stuff. Even in the early days, before The Company was able to access data, she knew everything. We used to call her "the Oracle". She could read a room like nothing I've ever seen. That kind of knowledge unsettles people, makes them feel vulnerable. It is pure power.'

Ahad considered this for a moment, his eyes moving back to Jia. She was speaking to a man in his mid sixties, his pristine white shirt collar crisp, the high-count weave of his pale grey suit betraying his wealth and his stylist's eye for elegance. Jia stood tall, her eyes soft, her gaze respectful. The man seemed nervous, and even from a distance deferential. Benyamin's words had given Ahad's observations new clarity. It was as if the lenses of his glasses had been smudged and were now crystal clear, and through them he saw the way people leaned in and listened to his mother, hanging on her words, fear mingled with respect.

'People can be vulnerable without her even saying anything,' Ahad said.

Benyamin nodded. 'Our father was the same. He didn't need to say anything. He radiated presence. I would be telling him a lie, a half-truth, or a complete story, and the whole time he would be listening, having already unravelled it in his mind. It's the same with Jia. People sense what people like my father and sister know. It's like some ancient exchange of information, downloading from the mainframe of the universe. Our nervous system senses danger like an anti-virus alert. It's why people hesitate around her. They fear she will see through them, expose what they don't want exposed, see them for the frauds that they are.'

'And what about you?'

'I don't have anything to hide from her.'

Ahad's gaze remained on Jia. The room was getting warm and he pulled at his tie, wishing he didn't have to wear it. He unbuttoned the collar of his shirt. 'I always thought it was her intelligence that people feared.'

'No one was ever scared of Stephen Hawking or Einstein or… the Persian guy who invented algebra and algorithms.'

'Muhammad ibn Musa al-Khwarizmi.'

'Yeah, him. The only people afraid of him are twelve-year-olds worried about failing exams. Look, your mother is smarter than every man she's ever met, but she doesn't wield it without reason. She's beautiful, and she has our father's charm, but yes, she sees through the bullshit.' Benyamin watched his sister as she walked towards them. 'That's what makes her dangerous. Jia's power is in her silence, her ability to look at someone and know them better than they know themselves. It's fucking terrifying.'

Ahad looked at his mother, who was always so stoic, her eyes so private, her words measured but never false-flattering or disingenuous. 'They can't escape what she sees,' he said.

Benyamin smiled, respect in his eyes as he watched his sister stop to talk to someone. 'Ruthless men can be handled, but how do you handle a woman who can't be fooled? Men are made of deception. We have no power over her.'

Something shifted inside Ahad, a slow realisation dawning. He looked at his uncle. 'You think I'm like her, don't you?'

Benyamin's face spoke volumes that Ahad had tried for years to hide from.

Ahad turned back to Jia, watching her effortlessly command the attention of the room, and for the first time, he understood the weight of the quiet power she held.

'Yeah,' he said. 'I think I am too.'

He watched powerful men and women navigate the room, his eyes on his mother. She was a masterclass.

CHAPTER 37

Across the room, Jia could see Amal watching everyone and everything. Where most would have been on their phone, she seemed comfortable to just sit. Finally, her eyes met Jia's.

'If you'll excuse me,' Jia said to the man she'd been chatting with, and she started to make her way through the sea of suits, saris, black dresses and bejewelled slippers. Jia had waited a long time for this moment. She could count on one hand the people whose views she cared about, and Amal was one of them. She had made Jia who she was today, introducing her to luxury perfumeries, encouraging her to exchange false nails for a French manicure, teaching her the art of dressing like the people she wanted to be in rooms with. She had advised her where to eat, who to meet in order to get ahead, and how to navigate the world. Little did Jia Khan know then that Amal was doing what all older sisters do to help their younger sisters get ahead. This was generational wealth.

Amal had told her she came from old Cameroonian money, and Jia had never questioned that. She made everything look easy and everything make sense.

It had been some years since Jia had seen her, and she hadn't changed. Her lips were still rouged in pillar box red, her cheekbones were sharp, and as she stood to embrace her, Jia noted that she still liked expensive scent.

'My darling,' said Amal.

'My sister,' said Jia. The word that had remained unspoken for so long lingered between them. 'I wish you had told me.'

'It was not my secret to tell,' said Amal.

'It was our father's,' said Jia.

Amal nodded. She took Jia's hand in hers, searching her face for hints of her own.

When Jia Khan had discovered Akbar Khan's letters to Amal's mother, Mary, in a box in the attic, she had folded them and taken her time to consider her next move.

That her father had loved someone other than Sanam Khan was hard enough, but that he had had a daughter before her, one that he had known about who lived in London, had complicated her feelings further.

She had pieced together the information in the letters and sat with them for some time before revealing them to anyone. It was Elyas she'd chosen to confide in. She'd hoped he had enough distance from the family to be unemotional about the news, but he hadn't reacted in quite the way she'd expected.

'Well, Akbar Khan, you old dawg!' he'd said.

'I was looking for emotional support, not a salacious response,' Jia said.

'Yes, of course. I apologise. That was rude of me,' he said. 'What are you going to do? Do you know who it is?'

That had been the other thing. Jia did have suspicions about who her half-sister was, and it was a woman she greatly respected. That Amal had known all along and hidden their true relationship from her, stung Jia. She had spoken openly with Amal about her father, the rift between them, and Zan. Amal had been one of the first people Jia met when she moved to London. Had that meeting been contrived? Had Amal been spying on Jia and relaying information back to Akbar Khan?

So many questions remained unanswered, and Jia still felt wounded by her father and her best friend's deception.

She'd called Amal a week after the results of the DNA test. She'd been hesitant about the call. There wasn't much that made Jia Khan nervous – she had faced down her demons and slayed most of her monsters, but the emotional baggage of family was still unhandled. She'd lost her brother Zan when she was in her early twenties, and since then she'd got used to being the older sister.

When Amal had eventually picked up, the conversation had been stilted. Neither woman knew what to do. Both were skilled negotiators, but neither had been here before.

'When I first met you, I was simply curious. I had no intention of liking you, of being your friend, but then we hit it off, and you were alone. I could relate to that. My mother had taken me away from Akbar Khan – he did not abandon me, but by the time she told him, he had married Sanam Khan.'

Amal had waited, holding the silence, and when Jia didn't speak, she'd continued. 'I worked through my issues, and seeing you caught up in yours made me want to help. I thought I could get to know you, the life I could have had, the sister I'd always wanted. I am sorry if that was the wrong thing.'

Jia was taken aback by the apology. Amal had always been so forthright, so boundaried, that Jia had never heard her express regret. She had expected some kind of comeback, a retort, an argument, but not this. Of course there wasn't an argument. That wasn't who Amal was. She solved strife, handled problems; she never created them. She was Mary and Akbar Khan's daughter, and that made her balanced, and self-possessed, smart and skilled at life. She was the best of both, and she was everything Jia Khan would have wanted in a sister, if only she had known.

So it was with sincerity that she now approached her half-sister.

'And now you know, will things change between us?' said Amal.

'I honestly don't know,' said Jia.

'You always have a plan of action. You say you don't know, but that brain of yours is a lethal weapon. Am I the enemy now, or are we friends?'

'I've not decided. I'd like to say many deeply emotional things and make promises of blood and sisterhood, but I will not force ties I cannot keep. And as yet, I am still unsure.'

'I can respect that,' said Amal.

Like Jia, Amal had been raised in money. There was nothing she needed or had wanted for, but the absence of her father had left its mark, and she had channelled that into productivity. She had been made partner in an international investment firm at a young age, had met and married an equally ambitious man while at Harvard, and together they were raising beautiful and high-achieving children. To the casual observer, Amal's life was perfect, but it wasn't. She had questions that would never be answered, and she was trying to find them with Jia Khan, the daughter her father had raised and adored.

After discovering the existence of a half-sister, Jia had started sieving through her memories to see what mention Amal had ever made about her mother, Mary.

She knew from her father's papers that they had met in the mid seventies, when Akbar Khan had newly arrived in London. From photographs, Jia knew he'd been a dapper young man, and from her letters, she could tell that Mary had been an accomplished woman who was in London to complete her studies.

It was a diamond heist that had come between them. He'd stolen the precious stone to raise himself in the eyes of Mary's father but instead he dropped in her estimation, and she left him.

'I found the letters that my father and your mother exchanged,' Jia had told Amal on the phone after the DNA test. 'I don't know what I had hoped to find, maybe something sordid and tawdry so that I could hate him.' She'd paused briefly, the phone to her ear, her lips dry. 'But it turned out they shared a deep respect for each other and mutual feelings of admiration. My father had found something rare – two clever and accomplished women to share his life with.'

That phone conversation had been the beginning of a dialogue that continued for weeks, as Jia and Amal tentatively began to get to know each other anew.

Today was the first time they'd met in person since learning of their familial bond.

'My mother would like to meet you,' said Amal.

'I'd like that very much,' said Jia. 'Maybe we can arrange something in a few months' time, when the weather is warmer.'

'She's actually coming to England next week, and I thought it would be good for you both to catch up.'

Suddenly Jia wished that Akbar Khan was with her, that she could leave him to sort out his mess. Her father had left so many secrets in so many places, she was growing tired of keeping track. She thought back to her life before all this happened, the existence of single-serve pasta, empty evenings, returning to a beautiful home but without the sound of children.

If Akbar Khan were here, if Benyamin had not been taken by Andrej Nowak, she would not be running the Jirga, she would not benefit from Elyas's wisdom, she would not be party to Ahad's wit, and Lirian's kisses and warm hugs would not exist. Life gave and it took, and there was always a price to pay.

'What did you learn?' Jia asked Ahad in the car on the way home.

'That power doesn't speak,' he said, staring out of the window. 'It silently screams.'

CHAPTER 38

The people from Bentley arrived early, bringing the lorry up the driveway and depositing the new car in the grounds of Pukhtun House.

It was waiting there when Ishy arrived for work. She wanted to take it for a test drive before Jia came out with Lirian for the school run.

Ishy swept the inside of the car for devices. It was clean. She wiped the car down and then checked it for any marks or paint issues. Since the five families of the Guild had been stoked, Jia had told everyone who drove for her to check every car before setting off. Security was tighter than it had been in years.

Ishy opened the bonnet and made sure everything was in order. Then she looked under the car.

She climbed into the driver's seat, clicking the key to start the ignition. The car didn't start. She pressed the key fob again, harder this time, and it purred into action. The car smelt strange. Ishy couldn't quite put her finger on what it was, but something wasn't right, and she leaned forward to see if she could find where it was coming from. Then she heard it, a tiny click. She'd imagined that life passing before her eyes would mean running all the conversations she wanted to have through her mind, all the kisses, all the smiles, all the beautiful places she wanted to go. But in the end, it was nothing, just silence and blinding light.

Elyas had been getting Lirian dressed when the explosion echoed around the building. Jia had been in the kitchen, Benyamin, Ahad and Sanam Khan asleep.

They ran to find each other, Jia by the front door before any of them. The family stepped outside to see the Bentley aflame, the Khan's security men surrounding it like insects. 'Spread out and search the grounds,' she told them. 'Ben, call Idris and message Sakina.'

Elyas asked Ahad to go back inside and reassure Lirian, who was under instructions to stay upstairs in his room. Jia wanted Lirian away from here and in school, but she needed the fleet of cars checked before anyone got in them. She wouldn't take any chances.

She watched as the car burned, the shock that it was meant for her soaking in as the petrol fed the flames licking the metalwork. She'd bought it as a gift for herself. After years of driving black cars, she'd finally opted for racing green, knowing that they upgraded their vehicle so often that she could afford to change the colour if she tired of it. Jia had always been careful with money, aware of her privilege and keen not to make others aware of their lack of it. But her role as Khan came with introductions to people who understood hierarchy and worshipped power. Walking into a room with her place already established in the world order greased the wheels of life.

Ishy had not had that privilege. She had been Jia's driver, and a trusted one at that, and now she was dead. Working for the Khan came with risk, and Ishy had paid the price.

Jia watched as Benyamin ran towards the car with the fire extin-guisher they kept in the kitchen in his hand. His mum called his name, urging him to be careful as he pushed the nozzle and foam poured out of it. It was too late. Ishy had died on impact.

The police sirens and emergency services became louder as they approached Pukhtun House. She knew how this would go down; she'd been here before.

She watched the burning car. Elyas tried to take her inside, but she couldn't turn her face from the flames. She had blood on her hands. She'd started the war and now it had claimed Ishy. Her people had trusted her to lead them. But how could she lead them now?

'Let's go inside,' said Elyas gently. 'There's nothing you can do here.'

'I'm staying,' she said. 'I'm not leaving her.' She remained there until the fire crews had put out the flames. Someone laid a blanket around her shoulders, someone else brought a chair, but she refused it. They cut Ishy from the car, and she allowed herself to lean into Elyas's arms.

'I've got you,' he said.

She waited until she'd seen Ishy's blackened remains laid on the gurney and zipped into the body bag, then carried into the ambulance. The doors closed and the vehicle drove away.

It was only then that she felt her insides quake. The adrenaline left her body. Elyas felt her full weight on him as her knees buckled.

CHAPTER 39

Jia sat down at her desk, her head in her hands, her insides still shaking, watched over by a photograph of her father that hung on the wall across from her. She wanted to tell him to go fuck himself, to ask him why he'd not tried harder to stick to the straight and narrow, why he'd built the great web of drugs and guns, prostitution and racketeering, and then used it to feed families, like dripping blood into the mouths of babes.

She'd just got back from seeing Ishy's parents, and they had turned her away. The baby inside her moved, its tiny innocent foot catching under her rib. Its movements felt like a butterfly flapping its wings against the inside of her belly, but she knew the kicks would get more painful. She placed her hand on her stomach and wondered what destiny had been etched into the palms of her child at the sound of the grieving mother's screams.

The door to the study opened slowly and Idris came in, a tray in his hand. He placed it on the desk beside Jia. 'Your mum said you'd not eaten when I called. So I stopped off for a parmo.' She looked at the tray, the cup of tea, the chicken parmesan sandwich in the seeded brioche roll, the black pepper crisps, and she almost cried at the thought of how well her cousin knew her. She smiled at him, and he saw that she looked tired. He moved the plate closer to her, and she took a bite of the sandwich.

'It was in her phone,' said Idris. He wanted to rub her shoulders, to take her pregnant feet in his hands and ease her pain, but the line between men and women was more rigid than that between women, and so he simply sat. He'd not seen her like this before. She was always so composed, her emotions contained. To see her frayed edges concerned him, and he measured his words. 'There's no way we could have known,' he said. 'The technology is moving so fast that by the time you decipher one thing, it's already moved on to something new.'

Jia listened carefully to his words. The sandwich filled her stomach, but the emptiness inside her remained.

'It was a download, Jiji,' he said, letting the words sink in. 'There was a code inside that triggered an explosive device in the car when it was turned on.'

Jia looked at her phone, registering what that meant. If Ishy's phone had been targeted, then all of their devices had been.

'And the car?' she said.

'Our contacts at the police forensics team say that a device was probably planted when the car was taken in for its service. The phone being in proximity to it was the trigger. Until then it appeared innocuous to our checks.'

'Who has technology like this?' said Jia.

'We do, and so do the Guild. What do we do, Jia?' He looked at her expectantly, as if she held the answers, knew the game plan, had a vision for the way forward. The idea that she didn't know any more than he did, that she was afraid and tired, weak and ready to crumble like the bricks in a once beautiful building that had been left to rot and ruin, did not even cross his mind. She was Jia Khan, the head of their organisation. She had steered them through difficult times before and had brought them into safe harbour.

They were each walking around with the trigger to a bomb in their pocket. The red thumbprint was a message to them all. Anyone who got in a car with her child, held his hand or picked him up was a potential weapon, because every one of them carried a phone.

Jia thought of Ishy's mother, of the way she had looked at her, the despair in her eyes, the silent screaming wishes that it was Jia

Khan in the coffin and not her daughter. She felt the world closing in around her, her chest tightening, her once strong biceps shaking under all that she carried and the crushing truth that if she didn't show up, no one else would. She was the candle that burned at both ends to light the way for others, but she was spent.

She wanted to stop, to be a normal person, to give birth, to take maternity leave, to push a buggy in the park, to not have to worry about bombs or men who had no honour or wish to make peace because they had not been taught how to do it.

But such thoughts were for privileged souls, men and women who walked in skins other than hers, who had structures and systems that protected them. She looked at the photograph of her father, and she mentally wedged a stick in the walls that were closing in. She straightened her spine and finished the tea that Idris had brought her, placing the cup back on the saucer. She'd allowed herself to wallow in self-pity, but the careful planning of the attack meant she had to shake such indulgence off her shoulders. She turned to her cousin. 'Find out whatever you can,' she said.

It was not courage that drove her on, it was necessity. She was the only one who could lead them out of this situation. A life skirting the law was a different proposition in her father's time. Enemies came at you with warrants, guns, knives and fists. In today's world there was nowhere to hide and still live a normal life without dropping off the grid. Everyone who loved her, lived with her and worked for her was a potential target. Ishy's life had been claimed this way.

'How were Ishy's parents?' said Idris.

Jia shook her head.

'I don't know if it was the right thing to do, but I went,' she said.

When Jia had arrived at the house, she'd pushed the front door gently; it had been left open to allow the steady stream of mourners to arrive and leave without issue. As she'd stepped inside, the words of salaam had come out of her mouth without choice or decision, the quiet greeting of peace to the house, for those who still lived within these four walls and for those who would never again step over the threshold.

The starched white sheets that ran the length of the hallway, the rows of shoes placed perfectly at the entrance, were a sign of what visitors needed to do to pay their respects. Catching sight of Ishy's brightly coloured trainers, Jia's heart had ached. She steeled herself for the family; this was their grief, their loss before hers, and her tears would count for nothing at this time.

She'd removed her black Blahnik pumps and placed them next to the trainers, sandals and slip-ons. Black and brown, blues and greys, people had chosen muted colours despite there being no uniform for Muslim mourning. The blending of cultures was evident to those who had eyes to see.

Then she'd walked to the living room and joined the women in prayer. They were sitting on the ground, their legs crossed, the white sheets covering every inch of carpet. Mourners read from the Quran, others prayed in silence, some clutching the pearls of the tasbeeh, moving along each bead with every completed prayer.

'Sister, let me bring you a chair,' a woman said, seeing Jia's condition. She declined the help, knowing that seating her above everyone else could be construed by the family as disrespect.

Photographs of Ishy were everywhere, on the walls, on shelves – a sign of a daughter loved and celebrated. There were more in a glass display cabinet, the kind you would see in a boutique clothing shop. A multicoloured Fisher Price toy phone sat on the middle shelf.

Jia's eyes fell on an overcoat draped over the back of a dining chair. It was Ishy's, waiting as if she would walk in and throw it on. On the other side of the room, Ishy's mother was telling everyone who would listen: 'I used to tell her off for not hanging it up. Every day she would leave it there. Every day we would argue.' She began sobbing into her soft dupatta, the women around her embracing her. Helpless to ease her pain, every now and then someone would reach over and knead her folded knees or her shoulders, as if pressing sympathy into them, as if that was how grief was removed.

Jia noticed Sakina sitting quietly at the side of the room, her back against the wall, her face stoic. She met Jia's gaze, and her eyes spoke of the pain she was carrying. Jia could read Sakina better than anyone else, even Idris. They were both women whose lives had fallen short of their expectations, who had been unprotected, and who had sacrificed themselves for people who could not do the same for them.

This was the first woman they had lost. They both knew that the time was coming when their losses would mount. They'd been preparing for it. That it would come this fast and be so close had hit them harder than expected. They were strong women, used to struggle, but Ishy's death carved into them, forcing them to look at what was inside.

The death had sent reverberations of shock through the family and the company, and the news had spread across the country. Jia trusted her people but understood the nature of power, that fair-weather friends ran at their first taste of blood and fear.

She would have to send out a message that the organisation was robust and able to take care of its own. The thing that set her apart from other leaders was that she was acutely aware that she also needed to wipe the tears of a woman who had lost her only child.

Ishy's mother hadn't noticed Jia until she stood to leave.

The sight of her was too much to bear, and she had lunged at Jia, arms outstretched, her hands ready to wrap around the Khan's neck, to squeeze every last breath from her body.

Seeing her speed, Sakina was faster, placing herself between the two women. She gently moved Ishy's mother away.

'Let her grieve,' Jia said. 'She has a right to be angry. I have let her down.'

Jia Khan was intimately acquainted with grief and all its monsters. She knew that this was not the time to defend herself, to explain that she had put every plan possible in place to keep her people safe, but that things were moving faster than at any time in history.

She could have said that she had no idea how a bomb had been placed in her car, that there was no way she could have done more, that maybe it was Ishy who had slipped up, but Ishy's mother would not have understood, and Jia Khan did not make excuses. Any defence would be akin to holding an incendiary device above a barrel of oil; it would have been explosive and no good would have come of it.

Understanding this, and her Khan's wishes, Sakina had stepped aside then.

Ishy's mother lashed out, and Jia took it. She knew that anger and grief were two clasped hands, pulling and dragging each other in turn. Life shifted between one and the other; that was the game.

When eventually Ishy's mother stopped, exhausted, spent, she collapsed in Jia's arms.

Jia took her hands in hers and looked into her eyes. She wanted to take on her sorrow, to convey the understanding that she knew what losing a child felt like. There was a time that Jia had thought her own infant child dead.

She'd been led to believe that for years by her father, and she had borne the deep scars alone. She was well acquainted with the howl that came from deep within a woman's womb when her child died.

'The womb is connected to the jaw of a woman,' a womb healer had once told her when she'd visited for painful periods, the agony pushing her to try anything. 'The silencing of women by the world, by their fathers, husbands, brothers and then their own offspring, those from whom we came and those who come from us – all that tension is held in our jaw.'

Jia understood the importance of letting the woman speak, and the witness that must be borne to her words.

'She was our first child, our only child,' Ishy's mother had said to her, her voice threadbare, barely a whisper. 'We gave her everything we had. When she was one, her father saw a little toy phone, with a dial and a bell, in the window of Rackhams. He rushed back to buy it the next day. He spent so much.'

Her eyes had held a faraway look as she remembered that distant time, and for a moment she seemed at peace. She was twenty-one, thirty-six and fifty all at once. The new mother nursing her baby, the mother of a teenager and the broken woman about to bury the love of her life.

Her heart must have hardened again at the thought. 'You should have been in that car,' she said to Jia. 'It was you they were after. You came to this city and ruined everything. I told Ishy not to work for you, that we would find another way, but she didn't listen. I want you out of my house!' Her voice had grown strong by then; she'd found her rage once more, and it ravaged her like fire through kindling. Her husband had come running.

'Please, let us grieve,' he said. 'My wife doesn't understand, please forgive her.' There was a strange look in his eyes. It was fear, and it hurt Jia Khan more than his wife's words had. 'I will call you when we have buried our little girl. Ishy explained everything to me. We are not ungrateful to you. Now, please.'

Then Jia had moved towards the door, Sakina close behind, Ishy's mother calling out after them: 'You have no idea what it feels like to lose a child. I curse you! You will know my pain.'

Sakina had quickened her pace, ferrying Jia out, as if speed would help them outrun the curse.

They came from a supernatural culture, one of nazar and curses that took the form of prayers calling for calamities. They were smart, educated women who had their own thoughts on the idea of the evil eye and curses, but they had also seen enough of life to know that not everything could be explained. The colonised mindset considered western religion to be better, its way of life more scientific, and that was why the white man had conquered so much of the world. But, as Jia had explained to Ahad, the unravelling of colonialist ideologies and the unpicking of the fabric in which it was cloaked had revealed that it was their implementation of organised violence that had been superior, that was all.

Later that night, Jia Khan knelt by her sons' beds and whispered the Quls, the prayers she'd been taught to protect herself and those she loved, over their sleeping faces.

And afterwards, kneeling on her prayer mat, away from the gaze of the world, she thought of Ishy and her mother. She wept silent tears at what more was to come, asking her Maker for strength as she tried to understand their lives, and to balance the equations of good and evil.

The situation was dangerous, and she had no idea how to handle it. The pregnancy hormones were flooding her brain, making simple decisions feel overwhelming. But this was not something she could speak to the men of her Jirga about.

She needed to leave, go somewhere she could think, regroup and rest. She thought of her family home in Karachi, where her mother had spent the summer she was pregnant with Benyamin. Maybe there was something in that.

Elyas came in to find her sitting on the prayer mat, her chador wrapped around her head and shoulders, her eyes red.

'How are you doing?' he said softly.

'I'm tired,' she said. 'I need a break, and I'm not sure if I'm in the best mental state to be running the company.'

'Yes, you are. Even your fifty per cent is more than everyone else's hundred per cent. You're doubting yourself because so much has happened.'

She looked at her husband, wishing that, just for once, he'd tell her she wasn't good enough to do something. She was tired and she was looking for an out, some crack of light that would allow her to quit. She sighed and began folding up her prayer mat.

'Get the passports,' she said. 'Take my credit card – I left it on my dressing table. Book tickets to Karachi for us all. It will be a chance to rest and reset. You can help that young journalist and I can attend to some business I've been handling remotely. I wanted to avoid flying but I can manage a seven-hour flight.'

She unwrapped her chador, her hair falling loose around her face. Her exhaustion was written across it, her eyes empty, her cheeks hollow.

'How long will we stay?' Elyas said, his eyes falling to his wife's swollen belly.

'I don't know. But if it means having the baby out there, so be it.'

Elyas tarried a moment, considering what she was suggesting. He'd been investigating the story David Black had spoken to him about, but had been putting off a trip to Pakistan due to the complications and responsibilities that came with fatherhood. Now, all the things that could go wrong while travelling with family rose to the forefront of his mind, and he realised he'd lost the wanderlust he'd once had.

But more than that, he was afraid of the things his wife was hiding. He wanted to ask if there was anything he should know, what it was that had prompted her decision to leave at such speed, what or who it was they were running from – but he was frightened of what she might reveal.

The car bomb had shaken him; its reverberations ran through the foundations of his family. He'd often played with the idea of taking the boys away from the life that his wife had built, but he couldn't quite seem to manage it. At times he felt himself a coward, a man afraid of confronting his wife's actions in case she left him, taking their children with her. He was used to holding others to account, investigating the darkness, bringing it out into the light, telling himself that the truth needed to be told even if it destroyed lives, and yet he was unable to hold himself to that standard.

He toyed with the idea that his wife could not possibly have done the things he knew her to be capable of, that he had misheard, misread and misunderstood. He gaslit himself in moments when the truth dared to raise its head, saying it wasn't possible for the mother of his children to be a cold-blooded killer and the head of a criminal organisation that profited from a trade in drugs, data and other illicit activities. She'd taken over her father's company and was wiping the stain of sin from it: that was the truth he chose to believe most days.

But in the end, it was the mundanity of life that held him captive. There was always a child to be collected, a deadline to be met, a nose to be wiped and a head to be kissed. The complicated, knotty things fell second to the ordinariness of life that men and women navigated in their day to day.

Now here they were, about to fly to Pakistan.

CHAPTER 40

Ahad held his little brother tightly as they passed through immigration. The boy had slept some of the way and spent the rest on his iPad.

Their parents were bleary-eyed, while his brother remained well rested. They had managed to gather all their cases and pass through the various checks without incident.

Beside them walked Jahanzeb, the man Idris had arranged to smooth their way. 'This country, like every other, is one where networks and money ease the path,' said Jahanzeb. He was tall and striking, a typical Pathan, who reminded Jia of Imran Khan in the 1980s, before he married Jemima Khan.

Idris had flown out a few days earlier and had greased palms while making plans. His father, Bazigh Khan, had been living between his homeland and England since his brother's passing – he found the winters in Karachi milder than in Yorkshire. Now that his niece and son were running the organisation, he considered himself semi-retired. But he had used their family money to fortify their influence here. Expanding their operations was important, and Jahanzeb was their man in Pakistan.

'The guys here are in pink and holding hands. I thought you said this was still a homophobic country,' said Ahad to Jahanzeb as they entered the arrivals lounge. Men in loose-fitting shalwar kameez ranging from pink to blue, black to white, and shades of cream and biscuit, were standing by the gates, waiting for family and fares.

'These things are colonialist constructs, chotai sahib,' said Jahanzeb. His polished English carried the hint of an accent. 'Pakistan is a complicated and strange place. Sexuality here is a private matter. No one "comes out". When you don't have enough to eat, your priority isn't telling your parents who you love. These things are for the elite and the likes of foreigners.'

Jia placed her arm protectively around her son. She was torn. She wanted him to be his authentic self, but in a country like Pakistan, his openness was dangerous.

'I'm not telling you to hide anything,' she'd said to him as they'd packed. 'I'm asking you to be careful about who you tell.'

'That sounds likes you're telling me to pretend I'm not queer.'

She had looked at Elyas, exasperated by their eldest child and his need to be honest.

'Jaan,' Elyas had said to his son, 'you can be authentic and not reveal everything to everyone. I try to be authentic, but my authenticity differs between work and home.'

'That sounds like a cop-out,' Ahad had replied.

'It's not a cop-out,' said Elyas. 'It's life.'

Ahad had rolled his eyes and left the room.

'I'll send him a research paper I read about authenticity,' Jia said to Elyas.

'Because sending your son a research paper has been working for parents since the start of time!'

'I blame you and your principles,' she replied. 'He's going to get himself killed.'

Elyas had thought she was joking, but her eyes told him otherwise, and her words cut.

'I'd leave him at home, but right now it feels safer to keep him with us,' she'd added. She also hoped that seeing his ancestors' homeland with his own eyes would shock him out of his entitlement. Pakistan was a whole new experience to someone who had grown up in London and Yorkshire.

Jia stood beside her husband and their two children, her hand on the luggage trolley, and wondered what had happened to her life. There was a time when she had been far from domesticated, her evenings full of legal briefs, dinners with clients and holidays in child-free resorts.

As they waited for Idris to come, she watched the hustle and bustle around her, people arriving to greet loved ones, hurrying to take their bags, and remembered that the life that centred on family time was a worthy life too, and in some ways more fulfilling. Her clients did not enquire after her health, hug her the way Lirian was doing now, and they would not be thinking of her when she was old and infirm. She hoped that Lirian might, though, and she had tried to make amends with Ahad, piecing together a new relationship, free of the mistakes of the past.

She watched as weary travellers appeared relieved to be taken into the heart and embrace of family and friends. A young woman dressed in white shalwar kameez adjusted her dupatta, her eyes searching the crowd for someone. Jia wondered who she was waiting for with such keen eyes. She was too young to have a husband and unlikely to be meeting a lover in a public place. A fiancé perhaps? A man in his twenties came and stood beside her, his eyes surveying the crowd too. 'Any sign of him, bhai?' Jia heard her say to him.

'There he is!' the brother said, pointing as a man in a tweed blazer and dark trousers appeared out of the double doors of customs. The girl ran towards him, her face shining, her eyes filled with an innocence Jia knew she no longer possessed.

The girl flung her arms around the man. '*Abba! Itna intezar karaya!*' she said, gently scolding her father. As he put his arms around his daughter, Jia felt a tug at her heart and would have given her entire life to be sixteen again, caught up in Akbar Khan's bear hug. What would life have been like if he had not had to leave his country to build something new, if he had met and married Sanam Khan here, the two of them having children and raising them among people they would not have to explain themselves to?

Then she realised that it would have erased the parts of herself she liked the best: her resilience, her ability to cross cultures, her sense of empowerment at belonging to many worlds and having the option to leave places that did not value her. And, of course, there was the sister she now knew she had. She thought of Amal, of their conversations, and how glad she had been to be able to speak to someone who loved her father.

She remembered being at this airport as a little girl herself, having arrived weeks before Akbar Khan, waiting for him to appear through the double doors.

'Your thoughts are distracted,' she heard her father whisper now. 'But I'm always with you.' She straightened up as much as her tired feet and pregnant belly would allow as she saw her cousin. He was heading towards them.

She could have spotted Idris in a crowd here with ease. It wasn't just his attire, although his threads were always sharp, his hair always in place; it was the way he walked.

Body language was the thing that marked a foreigner from a local, even when skin tone was matched, and local languages were spoken. It was in one's gait, the way one nodded, a flicker of a facial expression. Whether they liked it or not, Jia and Idris were Britishers here. Their Englishness was accentuated the moment they stepped off the flight. Ahad's need for authenticity was a sign of the safety he'd been raised in.

Jia was strangely more invisible in Britain than in the land of her ancestors.

'Are you alright?' asked Idris.

'I think airline food doesn't agree with me.'

'Either that or you're pregnant,' he said, looking at her pregnant belly and putting his arm around her.

'What time is our meeting?'

'Not until this evening. Things start late here. We can go home, freshen up, and maybe that will help you feel better.'

'It feels strange being here without Baba,' said Jia. Trips to Pakistan had always been made with their elders; she'd always been along for the ride. But this time was different. To her husband, she had couched it as much-needed downtime, but really Jia was here for business – and in a land where patriarchy was more visible and stronger than most, it wasn't going to be easy.

The dusty roads, the sounds of the autorickshaws as they passed them on the highway, the cool air con of the car, all reminded her of simpler days. Days she now knew had been far from simple for her father and her uncle. She watched as Ahad and Lirian pressed their faces against the window, staring out at adverts for biscuits and mattresses, air conditioners and lipsticks.

The streets were wide, the pavements raised slightly, separated from the road by tiny black and white stripes. The car wove through bustling bazaars, past minarets and decaying buildings that had once been architectural gems and that, in countries where survival was not the first thought, would have been adopted by a conservation trust, named as listed, protected by laws and regulations.

'It's a travesty that these places are left to ruin,' said Ahad.

'We are a land that was divided, ruled and ruined by the country that you were born in,' said Jahanzeb. 'The life you get to live was built on the backs of our beloved lands. Don't judge us by your experiences.'

'Excuse my son,' said Jia. 'I indulge him, and there are some truths he has never known.'

They headed past the bazaars and dusty streets and turned on to a beautiful black tarmac road. Either side of it ran one palatial house after another, each set back from the street behind high walls, with guards sitting out front.

As the car pulled up to one of these houses, two men who had been resting under the shade of a great peepal tree stood to attention. Swinging their AK-47s over their shoulders, they ran to pull open the great metal gates behind which stood the Khan family home. They stood aside, one hand on their chests, their eyes lowered as the car passed into the grounds of the villa.

'It's like a mansion!' said Ahad.

'Did you think we'd built a mud hut?' asked his mother.

'No,' he said, taking in the gleaming white pillars, terraces and wrought-iron balconies. The architecture of the building had silenced him.

The pillars stood sentry in front of the house, which overlooked a pristine green lawn, its colour so sharp that Jia wondered what the gardener was feeding it. Large terracotta pots ran the length and breadth of the low wall that surrounded the house, each filled with plants of varying hues, their textures sharp, smooth, their leaves a mix of large and wide, long and narrow.

Climbing quickly out of the car, Ahad chased Lirian around the perimeter of the house, surveying the trees and lawn at the back.

Jia stepped out and looked up at the immense family home rising in front of her. Her father and Bazigh Khan had dreamt of building houses in every major city in Pakistan, and they had done it. The intense heat and the act of looking up left her dizzy, and she placed her hand on the car to steady herself.

A young boy arrived, carrying a tray of mango juice in cut-glass tumblers. The sight of him reminded her of the last time she'd been here with her parents, long before Zan's death.

Jahanzeb pushed open the huge carved wooden door that led into the house and whispered a prayer of safe entry. They left the blistering heat outside and stepped into their home, Jia speaking the words 'Assalamualaikum' into the vast empty space – the pristine marble and newly whitewashed walls as cooling on the eyes as the air con was on their bodies.

'Why do you do that whenever you come home? It's like you're greeting the house,' said Ahad.

'I am, in a way,' she said. 'My father used to do it, and it stayed with me. He said our homes protect us and deserve peace. Equally, I don't know who or what dwells here, seen or unseen. It's best to make one's intention of peace clear. No one benefits from war.'

A look passed between her and Idris. They were here for many reasons, safety being the first of them, but equally they needed to find a way out of the complex situations that they now found themselves in.

Oliver Blundell and his request to cook the election could wait, but the Interior and the help they wanted with bringing home the kidnapped women needed to be handled if they were to move forward with plans to take over the Reko mine. And in the background lurked the Guild.

Jia breathed in the house, nostalgic memories rushing back to her. She was a child of two worlds. Britain was her birthplace, the place she called home, but Pakistan was where her bloodline began. She had spent countless summers here with her cousins, a completely different existence from their life back home. Surrounded by drivers and servants, cut off from the outside world, time punctuated by the comings and goings of the maali to water the lawn and tend to the plants, or the dhobi, carrying the huge bundle of washed, starched and ironed clothes on the back of his bicycle.

'We didn't know what we had,' she said to Idris. Zan's death had ended their trips, bringing with it the responsibilities of life and the longing for that childhood. 'What would we have done differently if we'd known what was to come?' she said.

'I don't know if we could have done things differently,' said Idris. 'We were tight knit because we needed each other, and our parents needed to keep the fire in their hearts alive. We're lucky that we found our way back to each other, and ourselves. I was lost for a while back there, but I guess most people are in their twenties.'

'But for what reason, and at what cost?' she said. The flight, the planning and the pregnancy was taking its toll on her, and she suddenly felt the need to vomit.

'Are you alright? You don't look well,' said Idris.

She pushed him aside and dashed to the closest washroom, threw up in the pristine porcelain toilet bowl.

'Maybe you should lie down,' said Elyas, helping her up and wiping her face.

'Yes,' she said. 'I'll see everyone later.'

Elyas took her to their room, removed her slippers and helped her manoeuvre into the unusually high bed. He pulled the covers up and kissed her forehead. The work and world didn't seem to stop. She felt as if she were on a travelator, being jostled forward by all her responsibilities, her feet aching, her body bone-tired. She could not help but wonder how different things would be for a man in her position. Leaders were not allowed weakness.

She dreamt of strange and complicated things, finding herself in a bathroom, looking down as a red insect scuttled around the white tiled floor. She watched it move this way and that, hemmed in with nowhere to go, its desperation evident, no way out. She lifted her foot and crushed it, putting it out of its misery. When she stepped back, she saw its small, lifeless body lying on the cold, hard floor, flattened, unmoving, stuck to the tile like dried blood. Then another appeared, and another, and another.

They began swarming, crawling on top of each other, over her feet and up her leg. She tried to scream, but the sound seemed stuck in her throat.

She felt Lirian's arms wrap around her legs, desperately pressing his little face into her as he tried to escape the scuttling red bugs. 'Mama!' he shrieked. 'I'm scared! Help me, Mama! Help me!'

The adrenaline surged inside her, her heart rate rising, the boy's presence disallowing any sign of weakness. 'Open the door, darling,' she said, her calm voice masking her own anxiety; she had years of practice. 'We're going to get out of here, but I need you to be strong.'

'I'm scared, Mama,' he said again. 'They're going to get me.'

He was holding her tightly, the room so small that she couldn't turn around, the walls closing in on them. She called out a name: it echoed through countless halls beyond, bouncing off the walls, getting weaker as it travelled further away from her. There was no turning back, nowhere to go, and no one was coming to rescue them.

Then she heard it, a single voice in the distance, getting louder and louder, until someone grabbed her arm and pulled her out of the nightmare. It was Elyas; he was beside her, his hand on her arm.

'You sounded like you were drowning,' he said, his concern written across his face.

'I had the most awful dream,' she said, then paused. 'I think I'm homesick.' She closed her eyes.

He put his arms around her and stayed there until she fell back asleep. Pregnancy made Jia Khan slip her skin and reveal her soft underbelly. It was rare, as was her confiding in him. It made him feel good about himself. He also understood that what his wife was homesick for was those halcyon days, and they would never return, not for either of them.

She slept deeply after that, waking to the azaan, the sweet sound of the call to prayer making her feel for a moment the way she did as a child, when the world had not defined her, and when she had not made the choices that she now called her life.

She'd dreamt of her sister Amal, of their last conversation, one in which they had both tried to make amends. It was a deep, layered dream, the kind that lingered on the fringes of wakefulness.

'My intentions were good,' she'd told Amal.

'I know, my love,' had been her sister's reply. 'They always were, just as your hopes were always high, but we don't get to choose what life makes of us. We simply go with what is offered.'

Amal's gentle wisdom was what was missing from Jia's life. Her people were battle-ready, willing to follow her every directive without question. What she needed was someone who was unafraid to tell her the truth and could help regulate her mind.

'I'd like you to come and stay with us when I return,' Jia had said. 'I could do with an older sister.'

CHAPTER 41

She heard a gentle knock at her door, and the sound of the maid telling her breakfast was ready. She reached out a hand and realised the space beside her was empty – Elyas must have woken earlier and taken Lirian down already. She pushed back the sheets and climbed out of bed, her feet hitting the cold marble floor, a stark contrast to the deep pile carpet of her bedroom in Yorkshire. She felt for her slippers.

In the wet room she washed her face. As she dried herself with the soft black towel, she realised she'd been too tired to notice the renovations that had been carried out in her absence. The large pink tiles that had been here since her father bought the house had been replaced with tiny white mosaic ones. They glistened in the light, and she wondered how many men it had taken to tile the wet room.

Generations came and left, each one placing their mark on the land of their ancestors. Her family was now spread between lands, and at some point the connection with this place would be permanently severed; it was the way of the world and of life. She wondered what it was that remained of her own life, and what it was that she was fighting to hold on to.

Her father had left Asia and created a new life in Europe, but he had also left his mark in Africa. There too was a woman who loved him, with a daughter and grandchildren whose heritage was grounded in that great continent. Now he was gone, and there was no protector, and they had to navigate the things he'd done. She needed to call Amal, but she couldn't deal with that now.

She put the matter aside and pulled on her dressing gown and headed down the sweeping staircase to the dining room. The eighteen-place table was filled with white china and silverware that Sanam Khan had brought with her on various visits from England. Jia made a mental note to call her mother as she took a slice of sweet apple from the fruit platter and placed it in her mouth. The fruit was paler in colour than the apples in supermarkets back home, but so much more fragrant and flavoursome. The bowls of bright red pomegranate seeds, the bananas and juicy oranges were her father's favourite. He would cover segments of oranges in black salt and feed them to his wife and children.

'Chai, bibiji?' the maid asked, appearing at her elbow. Jia nodded, and the young woman placed a strainer on the cup and poured the tea. The fragrance of it took her back to childhood. She put the cup to her lips, relishing the creaminess of it as the sweet aroma rose to meet her.

The unpasteurised milk was boiled every morning after the milkman delivered it in plastic bags tied with tiny rubber bands. Jia remembered seeing great silver pots bubbling away on the hob as a child, at her mother's home.

She leaned back in her chair and wondered what she would have been if she had been planted and grown here. But, of course, her mother's family's fortune had dwindled, and her father's had been made in a foreign land.

'Bibiji,' said the maid, interrupting her thoughts. 'There are some women here to see you.'

'Where is Idris sahib?' said Jia.

'They're in purdah, bibiji, and say they will speak only to you. Sahib has said they work for you, but he has gone to the shop close by. They have been waiting since Fajr, bibiji. I tried to send them away, but they said they would stay until you woke.'

'Please show them on to the veranda,' said Jia. 'Take them some chai. I'll be with them shortly.'

She wrapped herself in her chador, drawing it over her dressing gown, and walked across the hall to the veranda. Rays of sunlight washed the mosaic tiles of the floor as they spilled in through the windows, casting shadows of the curved grilles outside.

The women were sitting under the arches of the terrace, waiting for her. They stood to greet her. 'Salaam, Khan sahiba,' said the eldest of them, Amina, moving her shawl to reveal her face. She took Jia's hand and kissed it, before moving back to take her seat on the ground in front of the bamboo seat where Jia was about to sit.

'Please,' said Jia. 'Sit beside me, here.' She gestured to the milky white cushions of the garden furniture, and the woman hesitated, taking in her dusty clothes and worrying about the marks she might leave.

'Don't worry about the cushions,' said Jia, noticing her concern. 'They are replaceable, but I get the sense that you may be irreplaceable to my organisation. Now tell me, what has brought you here? I understand you would not see my cousin Idris.'

'I know he is your cousin and he is also betrothed to our cousin, Sakina, but in this country, we are wary of the intentions of men,' said the young woman.

'In my country, too,' said Jia, understanding now who these women were, and what their purpose here was. 'We women live complicated lives.'

The woman nodded, her eyes softening. 'We work only for women, and then only by recommendation,' she said. 'My sisters and I wanted to thank you for the work your family has brought us. We make mithai and deliver it to weddings and parties. Sakina helped us set up, and she sent us money, as did her father before her. He paid for our education – that is why we are fluent in English – and we were graduating from university when he died. Sakina took over and helped, but it wasn't enough. We hoped to find work in Dubai, but it seemed that was not to be. Still, the mithai business is thriving, and we now want to focus on other opportunities here in our own country.'

She handed Jia a large cardboard box covered in red and white paper and nudged her to look inside. It was filled with pieces of barfi, a sweetmeat made of cream and sugar, milk, nuts and saffron. The woman's eyes remained on Jia. 'There is more underneath,' she said.

Jia removed the top layer of white, pistachio green and saffron yellow squares, and discovered the box had a false bottom. She looked at the woman and then removed the base of the box. Underneath was filled with wads of cash. 'They're American dollars,' said the woman. 'That is the only currency we take, also bitcoin if it is online.'

Jia closed the box. 'What was it you studied?' she asked.

'We're coders,' said the woman. 'All of us.'

'Do you have contacts in other parts of Pakistan?'

'A woman is nothing without her network, bibiji.'

Jia smiled. 'That's good. I may need your help soon.'

'*Hukum karain,*' said the woman in Urdu, seeking instruction.

Jia hoped she would not have to call upon them.

CHAPTER 42

Jia would think of the women for many days afterwards, especially when she learnt the truth about Oliver Blundell, that he had been tracking her every move since she left England, and that even here, his eyes were on her.

Jahanzeb steered through the streets of Karachi, Idris and Jia deep in conversation in the back seat. They were on their way to the British Deputy High Commission to confront the person who had been sent to spy on them.

'You are too hard on yourself,' Idris said to Jia, when she mentioned her guilt about being away from her children so much. 'I lost my mother young. Having her here, even busy, would have been enough.'

'You miss her still,' said Jia. She glanced at him, thinking of all the ways her people buried their feelings.

'Pashtun men don't grieve the way women do,' he said. 'Maybe if we did, our lives would be different.'

'Even women don't get to grieve in our world,' said Jia, looking out of the window as the car stopped at a red light. 'Did you arrange the security measures back home?'

Outside, a group of hijras laughed raucously beside the traffic lights. They were unashamedly themselves; life had left them no other option. Like the brightly coloured saris in defiant shades of red and pink that were wrapped around their hips, they announced their self-proclaimed identity. The shadow along their jawlines, the jut of their Adam's apples, revealed that they had once been male, now women or, in some cases, neither or both.

Idris rolled down the window and handed one of them a dark blue note bearing the image of the founding father of Pakistan.

'Idris sahib, don't give them money,' said Jahanzeb. 'Or more beggars will come.'

'What's the point of all this money if we can't share it and make people's lives easier?' said Idris.

Jia caught his eye, proud of his generosity, though she said nothing. She recognised his wounds, the ones that made him eager to bring change. They matched her own. Life had cut them open, and they used their blood to cleanse others.

'You ever wonder why God made us in so many forms?' Idris said, watching the hijra walk back to their tribe.

Jia gave a short laugh. 'All the time,' she said. 'In between handling the Guild, laundering our business and raising children, I sit and ponder these things. Doesn't everyone?'

Jahanzeb pressed the accelerator as the lights turned green. The car purred through the traffic as, all around it, horns beeped and rickshaws spluttered alongside clip-clopping horses pulling carriages.

Jia's lightness surprised Idris, and for a moment the weight lifted.

'*O humanity! Indeed, we created you from a male and a female and made you into peoples and tribes so that you may know one another,*' he said, quoting the Quran.

Out of the window, the houses of the elite turned to the shacks of the poor and then the decaying architectural gems of the past. Jia realised she didn't want to think anymore; she wanted to put down the burdens of work and life, to be an ordinary woman with mundane days and mundane problems. No more rescuing others. She needed someone to rescue her.

But they wouldn't, and so she did the only thing she could do: she reassured everyone else.

'I don't want to know any more about the world, thank you,' she said. 'We have seen enough. We wait to pass on to the grave, where we will sleep. Until then, we have no choice but to keep walking through the fire with buckets of water for everyone else, consigliere.'

'Jia Khan, you could convince anyone of anything except that I am your consigliere,' Idris said. He wasn't sure if Jia still needed his advice, or if she indulged him because he was her cousin. Since Sakina had taken over his old duties, he'd seen less of Jia in a day-to-day business capacity.

'She does trust you,' Sakina had told him. 'Would you feel the same way if she was a man?' She had touched a nerve. Idris had called her earlier, on Jia's orders, to confirm security arrangements in Yorkshire. They needed to make sure their operations on home soil were watertight, and that the tech company was impenetrable. The Guild's next move could be cyber or physical; they had to prepare for both. Sakina had stationed foot soldiers in company buildings and had reinforced entry and exit points. She had had Maria's family moved to a safe house and had put Pukhtun House in lockdown mode. No one entered without prior clearance.

'Are you worried about my loyalty, Jia?' Idris said quietly, as the Deputy High Commission gates loomed.

Ahead, guards with rifles slung over their shoulders stood on either side of the black iron gates. Beyond them rose the bricks and mortar of the former colonialist power that had helped cleave the country from Mother India.

The car slowed, tyres crunching over gravel. A guard knocked on the window and Jahanzeb handed over the documents as they waited for clearance, sniffer dogs circling the car.

Jia turned to her cousin, irritation tightening her jaw. How many times must she soothe the bruised egos of men before battle. 'You're my cousin, my blood, you know where all the bodies are buried. Trust me, brother. I do not doubt you.' She held his gaze. 'But remember this – in these circles, your word is more respected than mine only because you're a man, not because you're smarter or better. If you forget that, you are of no use to me. You are here to put people at ease while I do the real work.'

The Union flag snapped overhead as security waved them through.

'Since when do we put anyone at ease?' he said.

'Since it keeps us alive,' said Jia as the security guards opened the car door. 'We don't tell them anything,' she added, straightening her shawl.

CHAPTER 43

A week before the embassy meeting, she'd wandered through the bazaar like a tourist, pausing at stalls with Elyas, Lirian and Ahad, admiring rugs and handicrafts. Jahanzeb had been nearby.

A shopkeeper unfurled a roll of deep red silk, tossing it so it fanned out across the shop floor, pooling on the raised dais where he sat. Around him were piles of fabrics of every hue and texture. Raw, katan and chiffon silk, different kinds of cottons, lawns and sheer organza filled the shelves, and the shops of the Shiraz Centre bustled.

Women gestured at stacks of folded cloth, the vendors endlessly opening and refolding fabric, presenting piece after piece.

'They sometimes look at twenty pieces and move on without buying a thing,' said Ahad.

'It's the way the bazaar works here,' said Elyas. 'Customers walk away, knowing they will be called back with a better price. It's the rhythm of trade. You must have spent a lot of time here, Jia?'

She nodded, thinking of the long, hot summers she'd spent weaving in and out of the market with her mother, sipping on bottles of ice-cold drink through a straw as Sanam Khan chose fabrics and designed outfits for her and her sister.

'Nothing changes,' she said, as vendors shouted 'Thanda!' to apprentice boys stationed by the doorways. The boys, dusty-footed and in shalwar kameez, raced to retrieve bottles of icy cola, bright green Pakola and orange Mirinda, just as they did when she was young. Jia watched them now, their skin darkened and their hair lightened by the hot sun, thumbing mobile phones while they waited for orders. Everything had changed.

'We used to visit the tailor afterwards,' she said, her eyes combing the side streets. 'I think he was down one of these alleys. He had worked for the family for decades, and his father before him, and his father before him. I loved it because they would bring us chaat. They'd be balancing steel plates filled with chickpeas and potatoes, covered in creamy yoghurt, spices and sweet tamarind sauce.' As she spoke, she could almost taste the crispy, crunchy papri.

The bazaar pulsed with life. Ceiling fans stirred heavy air, offering no real relief. Women in vibrant shalwar kameez browsed beside women in black and white burqas. Neither choice of dress reflected wealth or piety. Jia knew that there was never one reason for what women wore. Religion, modesty, fashion, rebellion – it was all of it and none.

And if evidence was ever needed that chadors or burqa offered no protection from uninvited glances or hands, the bazaar was it.

Jia noticed a woman, pregnant and young, collecting rubbish from the street. Her feet were dusty, her clothes sun-faded, her face deeply tanned brown. She couldn't have been more than twenty, but her body told a different story. Jia felt the weight of accident, of being born on one side of the tracks rather than the other. She peeled off several blue notes and handed them over, wondering how many women she could help in a lifetime. It never felt like enough.

Ahad and Lirian had wandered to a sports shop with Elyas. Ahad was hunting for a cricket bat, and Lirian a football. Jia, too tired to keep going, headed back to the car.

From a distance, she noticed a crowd begin to gather around a woman in a black burqa. The woman was shouting at a man. The crowd grew, men and women pushing closer. The man didn't answer. His head was down, his arms raised in shame or defence – he knew what he'd done. The woman pulled off her slipper and began striking him.

'*Ghar mai ma bhehan nahin hai?*' she screamed, as if having a mother or sister at home should have taught him decency. She kept hitting him until her fury ebbed, and someone finally led him away. She adjusted her burqa and walked off as if nothing had happened.

As she passed Jia, she paused.

'He pinched me!' she said in crisp and unmistakeable received pronunciation, her eyes flashing with indignation. 'Can you believe it? The nerve of the man! Do I look like I'm inviting such behaviour? And Imran Khan tells us we should cover up to stop this kind of thing. What more am I supposed to cover?'

Jia looked at her suspiciously, then sensing Jahanzeb at her side, she said: 'You're English?'

The woman nodded. 'This part of the city is full of ex-pats, as I'm sure your driver will confirm. What are you doing in this dusty place and not in the air-con mall and designer boutiques?'

'I could ask you the same thing,' said Jia, her eyes flitting to the sports shop, searching for her children. Something about the arrival of the stranger worried her. Anything out of the ordinary put her on alert.

'I'm a designer,' said the woman. 'The best tradespeople are here, and the women who were taught skills by their mothers still live here. My husband, Salim, keeps advising me to set up our own workshop, but I like the old ways, coming here…'

'Running into abusive men,' said Jia.

'Indeed,' said the woman. 'Here, let me give you my number. My name is Marina.' She handed Jia a thick cream-coloured business card. 'Message me if you're looking for clothes and need a designer. I'm at The Pakistani most days – it's my husband's restaurant.' She started to move away, calling over her shoulder, 'Drop by tomorrow if you like.'

Jia relaxed as she saw Elyas, Lirian and Ahad walking towards her.

'Who was that?' asked Elyas when they reached her.

'I don't know, but she sounded like she was from London.'

'Strange to run into her here,' he said.

In the time it took for Marina to get to her car and climb in, Jia's eyes never left her.

'Let's go home,' she said.

The restaurant was tucked away in the old part of town. It was early evening by the time Jia arrived; the sun was beginning to fade and the trees cast long shadows.

From the road, it was all too easy to overlook the colonial period bungalow. Hidden behind a thick wall of foliage, sheltering it from prying eyes, it was the kind of place only those in the know visited.

As the gates opened, the car rolled on to a tiled courtyard shaded by ancient trees that seemed to hold the wisdom of the ages. Jahanzeb helped Jia step out, before joining the other drivers by the servant quarters.

The building was pale yellow, an architectural beauty that whispered of a time of vanished glamour. Thick plaster columns, a balcony and art deco windows, sun-dappled and soaked in bird song, protected visitors from the bustle and clamour outside.

'Salim's mother was an Italian aristocrat,' said Marina, greeting her. In the privacy of her own home, her face and long hair were uncovered, and Jia felt there was something familiar about her. 'She came to Pakistan in the seventies, married a photographer and never left.' She led Jia through, weaving stories of old parties, fading film stars, politicians and icons of days gone by. 'It's a young country, and the days of the idealist writers and poets are not far behind us.'

The courtyard had been converted into a restaurant. A group of women dined beneath the shuttered windows. One pulled a bottle of red wine from her Birkin; another followed with white. They poured into tumblers and sipped, their designer bags hooked neatly beneath the table.

'I'm sure it's a very different country to the one you remember,' said Marina, following Jia's gaze.

'It is,' said Jia. 'That was the world of PTV, and dramas where women covered their heads, and everything seemed simpler. But then, maybe I was naïve and blind to the truth.'

'This country was a dream for the dreamers who cleaved it from Mother India,' said Marina, filling Jia's glass with water. 'The founding fathers dreamt of social welfare, democracy and progress, all the virtues ordinary Muslims believed in. But those dreams didn't survive reality.'

Jia knew that truth well. The machinery of wealth, power and connection functioned no better here than in the West. 'It's never in the interest of the rich to dismantle the systems that keep the poor in place,' said Jia.

'And the poor?' said Marina. 'Hooked on religion or drugs, kept compliant, fighting among themselves. They deserve all that they get.'

In that moment, Jia realised that she and Marina could never be friends. But maybe she could prove useful. 'You must see a lot of interesting people pass through here,' she said. 'Do you know anyone from the mining company? The one that has the contract to mine in Balochistan?'

'I do. The offices are close by,' said Marina. 'The executives often come for meetings here. Salim will know more. He knows everyone. The corruption around contracts is unlike anything I've ever seen. Pakistan is a mess. Things are much cleaner in London.'

Jia didn't answer. She thought of all the ways she'd seen the law manipulated in the United Kingdom, all the ways it served those who had wealth and titles. Bribes disguised in Fortnum and Mason carrier bags from a Saudi prince to a king could buy you many things, even in England.

She'd watched pretend fairness run through the judicial system, and it had changed her. She knew that judges passed sentences on a whim, making judgements based on skin tone, gender or education, but she said none of this aloud. There was no point disarming a woman who wore her privilege like armour and benefitted from living in a country where she had staff who referred to her as 'memsahib'.

The next day, sitting in the garden with Ahad, she said, 'I've seen enough to know that rot runs deep everywhere. Take this cake, for instance. It's the same as the one you're eating.' She pointed to Ahad's slice. 'The only difference is that the frosting on mine is on the top, whereas yours has it hidden inside. Cut the West open and you find the same frosting that covers society here. They are masquerading. The politicians, police and judges, they're all worse than us because they pretend to be honest.'

'They will never accept us,' said Ahad, 'no matter how clean we are. It's not the colour of our passport that matters, it's the colour of our skin. Why bother?'

'They don't have to accept us. They just have to fear us and not be able to get to us with their twisted laws.'

'What about the woman from the Interior? Didn't she say she would help us win the government contract?'

'She did, but I don't trust her.'

'If we're going to go a hundred per cent legit, we have to trust someone.'

Jia closed her eyes. Her unease at Ahad's interest in the family business had not faded, and it was growing. She was beginning to wonder what she would have to do to make it stop.

CHAPTER 45

The evening pulsed with energy, the air thick with the hum of anticipation as the highbrow of the city filled Frere Hall.

Elyas could sense Jia's deep affection for the city. Its history was layered, its people resilient. This was a place built by those who had fled Partition, seeking safety in the seaport that became their second chance.

'We used to drive past here as kids,' Jia said, gesturing at the pointed arches and ribbed vaults of the building, which had originally been a town hall. 'My father always said that it was like us, a blend of British and local architecture.'

Elyas followed her gaze, admiring the limestone structure, the symmetrically shaped quatrefoils and flying buttresses.

'See the decorative white stone?' said Jia. 'It's oolite from Bholari. And the red and grey sandstone used to highlight the gothic features comes from a Sindhi town called Jungshahi.'

'How do you know so much about the place?' he said.

'There wasn't much to do when we were kids, so I read a lot and drove my dad mad with lots of questions.'

She felt him take her hand. 'I'm sure he loved it,' he said.

They strolled towards what had been called the 'Queen's Lawn' and was now known as 'Bagh-e-Jinnah', after the father of the country.

The atmosphere was one of quiet elegance. Silks and satins rustled as men in neatly pressed Nehru jackets mingled with women in delicately embroidered kurta pyjamas, their dupattas draped on their shoulders or modestly over their heads.

The refined murmur of guests softened as they took their seats. The stage was set with tablas and harmoniums, soft bolsters and large floor cushions. They had gathered to witness the much-anticipated Qawwali concert, sung by one of the country's finest female performers. She sat cross-legged at the centre of the stage, her hair as dark as her eyes, her kameez that deep pink that was the navy blue of India.

Jia sat across from her, in the front row, her posture composed, her eyes scanning the room with quiet precision. Elyas reached for her hand. 'OK?' he said.

'Just tired,' she whispered. She'd been hesitant about leaving Lirian and Ahad at home, and her mind kept wandering to them.

The velvet seat beneath her was soft, but it did little to soothe her aching back. Her feet would swell from too much sitting, but compression socks were not an option at a gig like this. Her belly was a subtle curve under a sleek, dark emerald-green kurta, the material shifting as she tried to get comfortable.

'*Yaar ko hamne ja-ba-ja dekha. Kahin zaahir kahin chhupa dekha,*' the portly woman sang. Her voice was rich, restrained and as deep as the ocean that cradled the city. Her song spoke of a beloved who was in all things, seen and unseen.

Elyas smiled at his wife, recalling a time when he'd misunderstood the nuances of Urdu poetry, when he had thought all love songs were romantic.

It had been Jia who had introduced deeper meaning to the poetry and his life. 'Politics, homelands, the divine — there are more important things than you and me,' she'd once told him, pulling out cassettes, vinyl and then CDs that covered all the sounds of their heritage and history.

He'd continued listening to those tracks long after they'd separated. On lonely nights, with the rain battering his windowpane, the wind rising after he'd put their son to bed, he would play them, trying to understand her, searching for fragments of Jia Khan in all the things she'd loved and spoken to him about.

Now, seated beside her once again in such elegance, he still hadn't solved the puzzle of who she was.

Jia, meanwhile, was elsewhere. Her mind circled constantly around her family's safety, trying to figure out what the Guild's next move would be and considering how she could sew up the wounds that she'd opened and inflicted.

She glanced at the people around her and wondered if their education and refinement had brought them empathy that extended beyond themselves, or if it had insulated them from compassion.

She was inclined towards the latter. Jia Khan trusted no one.

Humans, she thought, were dangerous.

When animals killed, they did so out of need, to satiate their hunger, to protect their young. But human beings conspired in concert halls; they plotted in political arenas and schemed in salons, searching for ways to take from each other. They were insatiable; no amount of money, power or possessions was enough.

She had been meeting with people her father had once known – men whom Bazigh Khan had introduced her to – and women who now ran parts of the city, thanks to her backing and reach. They'd started with micro-grants, and help had been extended to schooling, health and emancipation.

The Jirga paid off the fattened imams, men who had fed on the fears of ordinary folk, convincing them of sin and taking their alms in exchange for a ticket to heaven. Jia had stuffed rupee after rupee into their mouths until the self-proclaimed men of God had declared themselves full. Happy with their stipends, they now left communities alone, allowing them to access the services provided by the Khan and her Jirga.

'What happens when they trace where the money comes from?' Idris had said.

'Our aim is to be obsolete,' Jia had said. 'We build a new system and then exit.'

'How British of us,' Idris had said.

The charities and non-governmental organisations they had partnered with welcomed their help. One such director found Jia during the concert's interlude. Elyas had gone in search of cold drinks.

'Thank you so much for helping us regulate the madrassas,' the woman said, handing her a beautifully wrapped gift. 'I've brought you a small gesture of our appreciation. I heard that you had a penchant for shawls, and we have some of the best in the world.'

Jia unfolded a powder blue shawl, its borders delicately stitched with a line of Kashmiri embroidery. It was light as air, and clearly expensive.

'It's exquisite,' said Jia. 'I could never have known where to find something so delicate. Thank you so much, for this and for your insight.' Jia wrapped the shawl around her shoulders. The night had brought cooler air. A chill was setting in.

'The old ways are dying,' said the woman sadly. 'And with them we are losing traditional crafts and skills. Things are expensive. When sugar costs the same as it does in London but the salaries are a fraction of that, people have no choice but to leave these things behind.'

'We are aware that we are outsiders,' said Jia. 'And that our ways are not necessarily the best ways, but I'd like to help develop this part of your work – if you'd allow me?'

The woman nodded. 'It is easier to deal with someone who shares at least some of our background,' she said. 'There is less to explain, fewer prejudices and more respect.'

'Women's concerns are universal,' said Jia. 'We see the world differently to men. It is in both our interests to develop your city. It is the land of my father, and my children may feel its pull one day. If I can give back, then all the better.'

'Our hope is that our children and young people are exposed to a variety of outlooks and opinions, allowing the free thinking that the country's founding fathers intended. Working with returnees from foreign lands is a good way to build bridges. Also, the rugmakers and sweetmeat vendors that you work with are thriving. They speak highly of your work.'

From the corner of her eye, Jia spotted Marina charming a crowd of people round her. It was the third time that week that she'd seen her. The woman followed her gaze.

'Ah, you know Marina?' she said.

'A little, yes.'

'All you Britishers know each other. And, of course, it must be helpful to know the senior people at the Deputy High Commission.'

The words brought undeniable clarity, confirming what Jia had feared. Marina had failed to mention her embassy connections, and her omission spoke volumes.

Jia controlled Karachi's black markets in drugs and guns, as well as running computer hacking operations in and beyond the city. Though no one could trace her precise role, those who worked in the shadows whispered her name in both awe and fear. That was how power worked, how it was built, consolidated and legitimised. Marina had to know who she was.

Jia moved through the mingling crowds, past waiters bearing trays of canapes: crispy spheres of puri filled with chickpeas, tamarind chutney and spiced water. Her pregnant belly warned her off the spice bombs. The growing baby had pushed her organs up, and they were crowded, making even small meals burdensome without heartburn. She knew their light appearance to be deceptive, like everything else at this event.

The garden lights flickered, and the *taap taap* of the tabla matched her steps. As the music soared, the baby inside her kicked hard. Jia pressed her hand to her belly.

This child and its siblings would inherit the empire she had built. A world where power was everything, where loyalty was forged in blood and fear, and where deceit lingered in every smile. Clean or dirty, all business was built on the back of this.

She glanced ahead, towards Marina.

Why had she lied? And why, despite everything she knew, was Jia still crossing the garden and walking into the fire?

CHAPTER 46

Marina greeted them at the entrance to the Deputy High Commission. She was dressed in a tailored beige trouser suit that stopped just above her ankles. In the daylight, Jia could see more clearly the features that hinted at her mixed heritage.

They stepped out of the oppressive heat and into the embassy's cool interior, where ceiling fans whirred overhead at speed. Spanning the full length of the hall, they traced wide arcs through the lobby's stillness.

'You lied to me,' said Jia once they were seated opposite each other in a side room.

A uniformed attendant arrived with chilled glass bottles filled with Pakola, straws in each, and placed them in front of Idris and Jia.

'Maybe a little?' said Marina. 'I withheld information more than lied.' She leaned back in her seat, her posture relaxed. 'I *am* married to Salim, and he does own the restaurant where we met, and I do design my own clothes. The rest is unimportant at this point.'

'You understand it makes you seem untrustworthy?'

'I wanted to get to know you and to find out why you're here.'

'That's not the only reason.'

'The truth?' said Marina, her voice lowering a little. 'I was intrigued. You see, I know your sister, and she asked me to keep an eye on you.'

'Maria?' said Idris.

But Jia already knew who Marina was talking about; it wasn't Maria. She knew all her little sister's friends, and Maria had never mentioned a connection in Pakistan. Amal, on the other hand, had been a ghost in more ways than one.

The atmosphere tightened as no one immediately responded. Jia realised that the situation was way beyond anything that she had considered. She felt a shift in Idris as he sat straighter beside her, his jaw clenched, understanding that he was missing critical pieces of the puzzle. She saw him press his lips together, swallowing his disapproval.

Marina also sensed the change in him.

'Ah, Idris,' she said. 'You weren't aware of Amal? Akbar Khan's eldest child. She and I are old friends.'

In that moment, Jia finally understood why Marina had struck her as looking familiar when she'd seen her at her husband's restaurant. They had met before. It was an investment event, the same one where she had first encountered Amal. Marina had been seated across from them.

'I know that you came here because Yanick Kaplan killed one of your women,' said Marina. 'You needed time to regroup. That intelligence did not come from Amal, by the way. We have other sources.'

Jia straightened, the weight of her sister's betrayal sitting heavy in her chest. She was angry, but it wasn't just at Amal. She had allowed emotion to cloud her judgement, chasing connection where there was none. She had been naive.

The silence in the room swelled. The low hum of the ceiling fan and the sound of a koel outside broke the stillness. Jia thought of her father, of the chaos he had left behind that she'd been cleaning up since his death. She felt the sinews in her neck tighten and twist as the cuckoo continued its irreverent call, oblivious to the storm within her.

She managed her life with precision, yet her family kept throwing curveballs, like a cat bringing dead mice to its owner's doorstep. It was exhausting. She was tired of the surprises, tired of Akbar Khan and of the daughter he'd fathered and failed to tell her about.

His carelessness had made them vulnerable, and now that weakness was being exploited.

'Marina,' she said slowly. 'I'm not a puppet to be pulled by strings of half-truths, and I am not inclined to do business with people who lie to me.'

'I see that I've upset you,' said Marina, brushing a speck of lint from her trouser leg. 'That was not my intention.'

'I'm not upset,' said Jia. 'The pregnancy makes me uncomfortable, and I've never been much good at hiding it. Now, we really must go.'

'Of course,' said Marina. 'But before you do, I'd like to discuss a certain proposition with you.'

Jia's phone rang in her bag. It was Elyas. 'If you will excuse me,' she said to Marina. 'It's my husband and I really must take this.'

Without waiting for a reply, she rose and glanced at Idris, who got up and followed her.

They exited the Deputy High Commission and stepped back into the car. Idris turned to her as soon as they were safely inside, his expression tight; he was braced for answers.

'Jiji…what did Akbar Khan do?' he said.

She dropped her head into her hands. 'What did that man not do,' she said. 'I want out of this mess. I have a feeling there is much more that we still don't know about, and that if we don't get out fast, it will bury us.'

'Then we need to bring those girls home fast and close that mine deal,' said Idris. 'But first, Jiji, you have to tell me everything.'

CHAPTER 47

They had been working on the plan to rescue the women for a while. Jia hadn't expected to be involved in the mechanics of it, but since she was here, it would have felt negligent not to meet the women who were risking their lives for her cause. She'd flown from Karachi to Peshawar to see them.

When she arrived at the building, the air was thick with the scent of wool and dye. Strands of threads in soft pinks, pale blues, creams and greens littered the floor.

The workshop was alive with the chatter of the women, and the steady rhythm of needles passing through the warp as they rewove and repaired old rugs together. This was a cottage industry started by a micro-grant from the Khan Foundation.

In one corner, a dozen women sat cross-legged beside frames, rugs from Iran, Pakistan and Afghanistan stretched taut over them. Their hands moved with swift precision, their faces softly illuminated by the afternoon sunlight filtering through the windows.

'Each rug is unique,' said a woman seated to the side. Her hair was silver, her face pillowy soft. 'The rugmakers' choice of pattern and colour reveals its country of origin.' She reclined on a charpoy, a frame strung with tapes, giving instructions to the younger women as they worked. Her voice was gentle, threaded with 'mashallah's, 'alhamdulillah's and 'subhanallah's. *Mashallah meri jaan,* she murmured to every woman who showed her a piece of work.

The women worked carefully, their fingers mending hundreds of tiny knots, restoring the intricate stories held within each rug.

'Fatima, careful there,' the elder woman said, as a young woman began trimming the tassels of a large Isfahan rug to repair its damaged border. 'Pull gently or you will ruin the pattern. Every rug tells a story, one that we must preserve as we bring it back to life.'

Fatima had learned much under her grandmother's guidance, but the responsibility of working on such a delicate piece weighed heavily on her shoulders. She ran her fingers over the worn edges, then selected a shade of cornflower blue to match the original weave.

Jia looked around the workshop. She had grown up admiring her mother's tapestries and rugs, but this was her first time witnessing their making and mending. The rugs in her childhood home had been finely woven masterpieces, their patterns sharp and vivid, held together by thousands of knots per inch.

Around her the women worked in harmony, each bent over her own spread of colour and wool, slowly coaxing the fibres back to life.

'We must trust our hands,' the old woman said to Jia. 'These rugs have passed through the hands of generations of men and women, through war and peace, hands calloused and kind. They hold our heritage, our patience and our skill.'

Jia watched the women with quiet reverence, their hands flowing with the rhythm of the craft.

'Sabr is in our blood,' said the woman. 'Woven into our lineage like the threads of a Bokhara rug. We bide our time and build lives from the scraps that the men throw at us. We carry this tradition with dignity.'

The women worked to preserve a piece of their culture, their history, the fabric of their shared past.

'It's beautiful,' said Jia.

'It is beautiful because we have worked on it together,' said the rugmaker. 'The men and the women. We weave the work together. But now, come with me for the real reason you are here.'

She led Jia to the back of the workshop, through rooms filled with roll upon roll of rugs, some piled up in the corner, some hanging on the walls.

'Take a look at this one. It is my favourite.' She took Jia by the hand and placed her palm on the weave of a large Tabriz that hung on one of the whitewashed walls.

'Come, you've never seen a carpet like this.'

As she lifted the rug to show the underside, Jia felt a draft. She moved forward and looked at the old woman, who smiled. The rug was hiding the entrance to another room.

The old woman held the rug and Jia stepped through.

On the other side, stacked neatly, were rows of metal boxes painted in green and black.

'What is this?' said Jia.

'Insurance,' the woman said, moving forward and picking up a crowbar. She walked slowly towards Jia, the cold, heavy metal glinting in her hand.

For a breathless second, Jia froze. Her fingers moved instinctively to her belly, shielding it. She felt the baby shift beneath her palm.

The woman's eyes flicked down, just briefly, as she stepped past Jia without a word and stopped in front of a large box that was placed against the wall. There was a string of serial numbers printed in white on the outside of the crate, together with the word 'NATO'.

With a grunt, she wedged the crowbar under the lid of a crate and prised it open. It was full of small arms and ammunition. She picked up a grenade and held it out to Jia.

'Where did you source them?' said Jia, taking the grenade and turning it over slowly.

'A woman can get her hands on anything in this city if she's willing to pay the price,' said the rugmaker. 'Of course, working for you means the price is no longer as steep as it was. They take our cash now instead of our bodies.' She smiled at Jia, grateful for the change in circumstance. 'We knew this day would come,' she said. 'And we decided you would prefer our plans to our empty words.'

Jia leaned back against one of the boxes. The baby kicked again, and she wondered if it was cheering.

She felt the adrenaline drain from her body and the tiredness return. This was what it felt like to no longer need to work at twice the level of everyone else, to know that her business was in safe hands, that her workforce was loyal. She no longer needed to explain every part of the plan to ensure that the outcome was exactly what it needed to be. This was why she had hired women for the job, and not men.

'We know where they're being held. We've arranged a delivery nearby, returning rugs that were brought to us for repair work. Within them we will hide the ammunition we need and our best assassins. You do what you have to do. Leave the rest to us.'

<h1 style="text-align:center">CHAPTER 48</h1>

The sunlight lingered over Peshawar, casting long shadows through narrow alleyways. The air was thick with the aroma of chapli kebab and charcoal, and the banter of traders echoed between the ancient walls of the city.

In a cramped, forgotten alley, a battered van pulled to a stop. Inside, thick rugs lay tightly rolled. They had once graced the marble floors of proud homes; now, they were a disguise. Hidden within them were four women, armed and waiting.

Zara, the eldest among them, had been wrapped with practised precision. Cocooned in wool and darkness, her breath was shallow as she listened to the faint sounds of footsteps outside. Her heart pounded in her chest, as did the heart of Noor, a younger woman with cold blue eyes, who lay beside her. Further back, Safia and Fariha were curled in silence, weighed down by the gravity of the situation. They'd volunteered for this. They knew what was at stake.

Outside, voices could be heard, low and deep, the sound of men in conversation. The doors to the van creaked open, feet shuffled, and the rugs were inspected, but not closely.

'Watch out, they're heavy,' said the driver. 'They're made of twice the knots and twice the size. Don't worry about it.' He'd been paid for his silence and support. The men did as they were asked; they always did.

Hiding in the thick woollen folds, the women waited. They knew the drill.

Zara felt the shift as her rug was hoisted, two men grunting as they carried her inside. She pressed her arms against her ribs, bracing. Their heavy boots clattered on the hard dirt floor. The women had planned for this, and several rugs were above her in the van, ensuring a soft landing. The men dropped the rug on top of the others with a thud, not hard, not soft, just enough to jar her bones.

She closed her eyes and whispered a prayer to the Almighty, reminding herself of Allah's greatness, phrases she had known since childhood. The words anchored her. She was a woman, and so she knew how to blend into her surroundings, and how to fade from the world when necessary. It was what her kind did to survive.

The rugs were carried in one by one, including an even heavier one, lined with guns and grenades. No one suspected a thing, the men exchanging banter as they unloaded, unaware that their fragile existence was one step away from being torn apart if the women so willed.

The room was windowless and quiet. The men's footsteps echoed briefly, then faded. The women waited.

Somewhere the azaan began, the muezzin calling the men to prayer. The silence stretched. They would be gone for at least half an hour.

Zara's heart quickened. This was their moment. She nudged the edge of her rug, fingers gripping the woven edge. The air that met her face was sharp and cool, a stark contrast to the stifling heat inside the rug; it felt like freedom.

One by one, she helped the others out. They rose like shadows reborn.

They inhaled deeply, then moved with precision, unwrapping the arsenal they had brought with them. They slung Kalashnikovs over their shoulders as they filled bags with bullets and grenades, tucking pistols into the waistband of their shalwars and into their bra straps.

No words were exchanged. They knew the plan.

They moved silently down the hallway, slipping through an outer door into a narrow alley, guided by their memory and their mission.

They'd been raised in these streets; they knew every bend and turn. They knew how to make themselves invisible in this 'City of Men'.

Their destination was an old passageway hidden beneath a crumbling water fountain, a place where old walls still whispered secrets of resistance. The passageway led into the basement of the house where they knew, thanks to their network of informants, the captive students were being held.

The city around them was unaware of what was unfolding.

As the men knelt before God, the women took matters into their own hands. They had been carrying the weight of their families and their dignity for generations, and they were tired of waiting for Allah to raise His believers into better men. They were warriors and emancipators, they had agency, and they had justice on their side.

They slipped into the secret passageway. Inside the tunnel, the air thickened. Zara led the way, one hand brushing the cool stone walls towards the basement room where the captive scholars were being kept. She paused, listening, waiting. Faint sounds, snatches of conversation.

Zara's hand gently gripped the worn handle of the iron door, its bitingly cold surface sending a shiver through her. The handle refused to turn. Noor shone her torchlight while Zara pulled a small red leather package from inside the fold of her kameez and took out a tension wrench and a thin pick. She slipped them into the lock. She tilted her head, listening for the grammar of clicks that held the door shut. Each movement measured, each moment achingly long, she felt the tension sigh in the lock, and then she twisted the handle again. This time there was no resistance, and the door creaked open.

The room was dark, the air thick and stale. Inside were the students, their frightened but hopeful faces gathered about the door, shrinking now from the torchlight, squinting as their eyes became accustomed to it. Then flickers of joy bloomed on their faces as they saw the women.

'After the soldiers came and were captured, we stopped hoping,' one of the students whispered.

'Where are they?' Zara's voice was soft but urgent. 'The ones they sent to rescue you?'

'Across the way,' whispered one of the women, pointing to another door. 'We heard them bring them in. They are in bad shape.'

Zara nodded, checking the time. She moved towards the door and listened for a few moments, before setting to work on the lock. This one was easier to pick. She stole a glance out into the hallway, her eyes sharp, breath held. It was empty.

She slipped into the passageway, reaching for the opposite door handle, once again pulling out the small red leather roll containing her tools.

Within a minute of inserting them into the lock, she felt it click under her hand, the handle twist, its mechanism soft as butter. She slowly pushed the door open.

The stench of men's sweat and blood hit first. The room was dark, the only light coming from an overhead bulb that flickered, a moth dancing around it.

Inside, two British soldiers lay shackled, broken and bruised on the cold stone floor. Their uniforms were dirty, their faces gaunt from weeks of captivity. A look of relief flooded their faces as they saw the women approach.

'Help us,' one of the soldiers said, his voice hoarse from thirst. His nose was broken, his eyes bloodied.

'Don't speak,' said Zara as she knelt beside him. She soundlessly unshackled his wrists. 'The men are at prayers but may have left someone to keep watch.'

Noor knelt beside the other soldier, quickly cutting the ropes that bound him. 'We need to move fast.'

With the hostages in tow, the women hurriedly retraced their steps towards the underground passageway. Zara entered first, with Noor at the rear, while the other two took the soldiers' weight as they made their way, with the students, towards the exit behind the fountain.

Outside, the city had shifted. Friday prayers were over and men began to go back about their work.

Zara motioned for the group to hurry. 'Stay close,' she said, ducking into a quiet alleyway. But they weren't in the clear yet.

They rounded the corner at the end of the alley, and the small, unmarked door of the safe house came into sight. It had taken months to arrange, to make sure that they had a place away from prying eyes with the means to escape when the time came. This was their final step; it would swallow them to safety.

But then shouts, loud and urgent, reached their ears, followed swiftly by the pounding of boots in the surrounding alleyways. The men had returned to find the rooms empty and the secret passageway open.

Noor thought fast, gripping the grenade in her pocket. 'Go,' she shouted. 'I'll buy us some time.'

Zara grabbed her arm. 'No!' she said.

'Go! I'll be right behind you! Trust me.'

The boots were closer now, their sound sharp, steady and unforgiving.

Zara didn't flinch; there was no more time to think. She shoved the students and soldiers towards the door, urgency in her voice.

The men rounded the corner just as Noor stepped out of the shadows, cool as death. The grenade left her hand in a clean arc. Then came the bark of her gun, sharp and fast, and hell broke loose.

The explosion ripped through the alley, flinging the men back in a storm of dust and fury.

Without missing a beat, Zara drove the others inside the house and through the rooms, teeth clenched, every step a gamble.

Noor staggered but remained standing. Soot-streaked and breathless, she emerged from the smoke like a ghost of vengeance and followed them.

On the other side, the front door yawned open, and one by one, the women and hostages slipped out of the safe house into the sun, their faces beaded with sweat, their eyes sharp and alert.

Waiting for them, two black vans, engines purring.

They didn't look back as they climbed in, and the vans sped away.

CHAPTER 49

'Thank you for sorting the contract.'

'It's in hand,' said the woman. 'You have my word.'

Jia ended the call as their car pulled up to the shrine.

She had planned to feed as many of the city's hungry as she could that day, to give sadqa for the safe return of the students. This was the place to do it.

Outside the shrine, the road was lined with the langar: giant cooking pots, large enough for a small child to climb inside, bubbling over with barley, wheat and meat, slow-cooked with spices and tempered with fried onions and hot oil. Worshippers funded a few pots each and then shared the rich stew among the poor who gathered there morning, noon and night.

Jia stepped out of the car with her husband and children. Idris had gone to the jeweller to buy Sakina a gift and would join them later.

The hot sun bore down hard on them. Jia took Lirian by the hand, feeling more reluctant than she had expected to let him out into the world. Her own fear startled her.

Inside, the white marble floors of the shrine felt cool under her bare feet. She covered her head and walked towards the saint's mazar. Hundreds of people sat in silent meditation; some read the Quran; others, like Jia, simply watched.

The tomb was draped in green and gold fabric, gifted by worshippers. Some placed sheets of woven fresh flowers over it, whispering prayers as they asked the saint to intercede on their behalf.

Jia understood the need for hope. She'd seen how people flailed, searching for something to latch on to when life became hard, but she didn't believe that anyone stood between her and her Creator.

The music of the qawwali pulsed through the corridors. Incense curled into the air, mixing with the scent of rose petals and the murmur of prayers, creating an air of serenity. Devotees from all walks of life gathered together.

Jia was clasping Lirian's hand tightly when she felt a tap on her shoulder. She turned.

'What a lovely surprise,' said Marina.

Jia didn't believe that for a moment, but she kept her feelings to herself. 'We are here to donate to the langar,' she said. 'We had some good news.'

'I heard,' said Marina. 'You've been awarded the Reko mine contract. That's huge news. It will change everything for you and for your children.' She smiled at Lirian. The little boy hid behind his mother's chador.

'Thank you,' said Jia. 'We hope it will.'

Her instinct and investigations had told her that Marina was not trustworthy. *Not everything you know is worth revealing,* her father's voice echoed in the back of her mind. Something about the way Marina looked at Lirian made her uneasy. She would remember this moment, long after the evidence of her truth emerged, chastising herself, wondering if there was something she could have done.

Jia turned to look for Ahad and Elyas, but a crowd was heading towards her, pouring into the mausoleum, obstructing her view. She caught a glimpse of them on the other side of the tomb, but the mourners filled the room like water through a breach, forcing her and Lirian back against the wall.

She shouted for Elyas, but the qawwali was loud now.

He spotted the panic on her face, just as Lirian's tiny hand slipped from hers. She pushed men and women aside, trying to make them move so she could reach her child. He saw her scramble to grab him again, but it was too late, and the child was carried along with the crowd until it swallowed him up.

Wrestling his way between the men and women, furious, frantic, frightened, Elyas headed towards Jia, Ahad at his heels.

'Elyas! He's gone!' she cried, casting her eyes desperately around as the wave of mourners swept past her.

Something caught her eye on the marble floor at her feet, and she knelt down to pick it up. It was a playing card. Fear tore through her with such force she couldn't breathe, she couldn't think. Her body felt weighed down like a sack of sand.

The world dimmed. She knew it to be a cold and dark place, but the places her mind went in that moment were deeper and darker than anything she had ever experienced or imagined. She screamed, her heart splitting in two, her chest cracking wide open.

And then she began searching the mausoleum again, frantic at the thought of her missing child. The crowds began to disperse like scurrying insects as she pushed through them, grasping the arms of anyone who would listen, her eyes wild, her voice trembling.

'He's wearing an orange T-shirt and blue shorts. His name is Lirian,' she said, repeating the words over and over as she grabbed every man, woman and child she could reach. The world was beginning to spin faster and faster, acid rising in her mouth, nausea in her stomach. The baby kicking inside her.

Thoughts of all the things she'd done began to crush her. All the blood she'd spilled, all the lines she'd crossed, every shred of pain she'd inflicted, every fingernail she'd had extracted from those who'd crossed her. Was this the price?

She saw her child's face, his soft brown eyes, the way he brushed his hair from his cheeks. What if they hurt him? What if they took his innocence? Her small and perfect boy. She cried out in agony as Elyas reached her.

She wanted to scream, to shriek off all the weight she was carrying. She wanted to protest that she had been misunderstood, maligned, misrepresented, when really she had changed and saved lives. Ishy's mum blamed her for her daughter's death, but she didn't know that Jia had found the girl about to sell herself to an old man with a fast car. That Sakina had brought her in, held her hand as she'd cried, and that together they had worked to end the cycle of trauma in which Ishy found herself trapped.

'I thought I could make it better,' said Jia, clinging on to Elyas, her eyes red, her face raw. 'But I couldn't do it, and it's not my fault.'

'I know, my love, I know,' he said, his eyes on Ahad as he frantically searched.

Jia's face was hidden in Elyas's shirt. 'I gave up years of my life. Of our lives,' she said. 'I'm so sorry. I'm so sorry. I just want him back.' She was bereft.

Elyas held on to her, helpless. He had never seen Jia like this. He felt the blood rush to his head, roaring in his ears, his senses heightened, leaving him overwhelmed.

Jia had always been the one who stepped up, brought order to the chaos of their lives, but now she was paralysed by loss, unable to function.

He thought of all the times he'd questioned her abilities as a mother, as a wife. The times he'd thought of taking the boys and leaving her, the doubts he'd had about their life, her actions, her choices.

He had judged her from his ivory tower of cis manhood. She handled everything, the responsibilities of her life, the business and her father's legacy, alongside the complexities of womanhood and motherhood. The world thought she'd been handed aces, but Jia Khan had been playing the game with the only cards she had: a pack of jokers.

Rain began to fall, the water coming down, heavy and relentless, leaving the marble slick. The drainage system was not built for rainfall like this, meaning the streets would flood soon.

He heard Jia whispering something over and over again. 'I did what I had to do, to save us, to save everyone. I don't know what else I could have done.'

She never spoke like this. He watched her coming undone before his eyes, raw, honest and afraid. She began telling him things, truths he already knew, about her father and his death, and he wanted her to stop. She was laying open her wounds, and he could see his part in her pain.

He had been a passenger in their marriage, letting her shovel coal while he judged her from first class. He never asked where the money really came from and didn't talk about her father's death. He loved her, and he wanted to be with her, and somewhere along the line, he'd ignored anything that got in the way of that.

He was a gold digger, and he was complicit. He was as much to blame as she was for the taking of their son.

He remembered the girl she'd once been, the one who believed in justice. There were nights he dreamt about her, standing in her father's garden, sunlight on her face, a bright young thing in a white shalwar kurta, her chiffon dupatta draped over her head. Akbar Khan beside her, his hand on her head.

Now, she was beautiful scar tissue, forged by fire, stronger than him, stronger than most. She didn't pretend to be something she wasn't.

She slumped in his arms. He had to act so she could do what needed to be done. She was the only one who could.

She was Jia Khan, daughter of Akbar Khan, mother of Ahad and Lirian, and the Khan of strong men and brave women. But she was also a human being, and like all humans she was light and shadow, strength and fracture, and she needed piecing back together. He thought of Lirian, somewhere with strangers, and he knew that it was only the Khan and her army that could bring him back.

'Jia, listen to me,' he said, steadying her. 'We'll find him. But you have to hold it together. I understand now, and I'm sorry. I know I've not always been here for you. I'm here now, and I'm not going anywhere.'

She could hear Elyas somewhere in the distance, calling her name. She could feel her father stroking her hair. 'You have to get up,' he said. 'They can't do this without you.'

She'd lost her son. Maybe Ishy's mother's curse had taken hold. She wanted to tell her father she was sorry, tell Zan that she'd failed him; she wanted to set Elyas free and tell him to take Lirian away from her, but it was too late. He was gone, and she couldn't bear to carry on.

She searched the recesses of her mind, looking for something to help piece herself back together. She tried to speak, but the words dissolved on her tongue. She had held so much together, had tried to shape fates for the better, and in the end, everyone had let her down.

Pieces of her had died so that those she loved might live, and now her son could be dead. The thought struck like a powerful bolt of electricity, sharp and searing, and it pulled her back into her body.

A hand touched on her cheek. It was familiar, steady. She heard Ahad's voice. He was saying something, something that mattered. His tone was calm, unwavering.

He was everything she wasn't, everything she had hoped he would become.

'I've scoured the place,' he said. 'One of the cooks outside saw a boy matching Lirian's description getting into car with a woman in a black burqa,' he said. 'I've called Idris.'

Jia felt a shiver run down her spine. The thumbprint on the playing card had thrown her, but her gut was screaming the answer. 'Marina,' she said slowly. 'It was Marina.'

She didn't need any more proof. Her instinct had been whispering it all along, and now it roared.

Elyas was watching her, and she could feel the weight of his gaze.

He had once believed the world was simple, had told her so many times: 'Life is easy. It's people who make it hard.'

He had meant it. And she had let him believe it. But now he saw what she had always known: the world was ruthless, and it demanded things of women like her that it never would of men like him. He'd had choices. She'd had survival. And still she had built something good out of the wreckage.

She stood there, pregnant, frayed, held together by will alone, and yet she had not fallen.

'If anyone can bring him back, it's you,' Elyas said, stepping towards her. 'Jia, do whatever it is you have to do. Bring our son home.'

His words steadied her then. She took a long, deep breath to clear her mind.

Her phone began to ring.

'Answer it,' said Ahad. His face was unreadable, his eyes cold like steel. She recognised that look. She'd seen it in her father. He'd worn it like armour, and so had she, and for the first time, it frightened her.

Ahad belonged to the Khans. It didn't matter who'd raised him. His destiny had been written long before this day.

Time seemed to unravel, laying bare what she had refused to believe. She had not made him; she had simply delivered him.

And he would survive. Whatever came next, he would endure.

She was no longer alone in the fight.

Her phone buzzed again. She looked down at it, then up at Ahad.

'It's her,' she said.

CHAPTER 50

Jia felt Elyas and Ahad's eyes on her as they huddled together in a quiet corner outside in the rain. Time slowed to a crawl as she held the phone close to her face and put the call on speaker.

'He's safe, Jia. I have him,' said the voice.

The best fighter is never angry, her father's voice echoed in her mind. *The people who anger you, control you.*

Anger had cost her too much; she'd lost her brother and father. She couldn't afford to lose control now. She needed to remain calm, to find out where her son was being held, and what they wanted.

She nodded once at Ahad and pulled him closer, grounding herself as she spoke.

'What do you want, Marina? Give me back my son and you have my word I'll give you what you want. A Pashtun's word is her honour.'

'The election,' she said. 'I need you to fix it.'

Jia blinked, confused. 'Which election? Here in Pakistan?'

'Oliver Blundell,' said Marina. 'You've been blowing him off for long enough. He needs to win. Do you understand?'

'Who exactly do you work for?' said Jia. 'Why help him win?'

'It doesn't matter who I work for. Do what I've asked, and Lirian will be returned to you. You have my word.'

Jia's mind was already racing. 'The election is the day after tomorrow. What do you expect me to do in two days?'

'Everything,' said Marina. 'You run the world's most powerful underground technology company. Use the power you've built.

That's what it's there for. The British government, the Guild, the Interior – all of them know who you are and what you can do. But things can't always be on your terms.'

Jia froze.

'I want to see him,' she said. 'I don't trust you.'

'Well, you're going to have to,' said Marina. 'If you really want to see him again.'

Jia felt Elyas's eyes on her, intense and full of questions. The weight of responsibility bore down on her as she calculated her next move. Ahad stood in front of her, meeting her eyes with that steely look again.

'He will be with me the entire time,' said Marina. 'Lirian, your mama wants to have a word. Can you do that for me?' Marina's voice calling Lirian's name made the knot in Jia's stomach tighten.

She felt Elyas's hand on her shoulder, Ahad's unwavering presence before her. 'Hi, baby boy,' she said.

'Mama?'

'Yes, darling, it's me. Are you OK?'

'Where are you, Mama? Are you upset with me?'

'No, baby, I'm not upset with you. You're going to stay with Auntie Marina for a couple of days, OK?'

'Mama,' he said, 'we're going to get ice cream and then you can come and get me?'

'Mama is going to come and get you very soon. I love you. I'll be there soon.'

As the line fell quiet, Jia's mind spun, trying to figure out her next move. An idea began to form at the periphery of her mind. It was distant, blurry, but it was there. She looked at Ahad, and she closed her eyes.

'I'll do it,' she said. 'I'll do what you need, but you have to do something for me first.'

'What is it?'

Jia paused, then looked at Ahad. 'You have to take my other son too,' she said, her voice stone cold.

'Done,' said Marina. 'But not before I'm satisfied you're fulfilling your end of the bargain. I will send instructions.'

The line went dead. Jia felt her breath catch. Her heart stopped, the silence swelled, only to be interrupted by Elyas.

'Jia!' he said, his jaw dropped into speechlessness.

Ahad was staring at his mother, a myriad of emotions running across his face. 'Why would you do that?' he said.

She turned and began to head away from the shrine. He followed her, Elyas keeping pace.

'Where are you going?' Ahad said, calling after her. 'Talk to me!'

'I have my reasons,' she said, already stepping into the back of the car. 'Get in.'

Her body felt too large, too visible. Everyone here looked at her like she was sacred, the halo effect of the baby she carried inside her. For a brief moment she had forgotten that she was not of the light. She was a cold-blooded killer. Like the goddess Kali, she lived in dark and desolate places and the warm hearts of her devotees. It was her children who kept dragging her into the sun. She did not belong there and she could endure it no more.

Elyas sat in the front passenger seat, Ahad beside his mother.

The car rolled through the city, weaving past small children in dusty sandals who tapped on the windows with garlands, combs and empty hands, selling their days to fill their bellies and those of their siblings.

They drove through the raucous streets without speaking, except for the cacophony in their heads.

Elyas broke the silence. 'What are you doing?' he said, turning round to face her. Jia refused to look at him. Her mind was calculating, but her energy reserves were low. She needed to bring her boy home, and she did not need emotional outbursts from her husband.

'What I need to do to bring Lirian home.'

'You're sending Ahad into the arms of death.'

'Don't be so melodramatic,' she said, her voice calm, her eyes on the passing streets. 'You told me to do whatever it takes, and now that I am, you're back to questioning me.'

'This is because he refuses to pretend he's straight, isn't it?'

'Don't be stupid, Elyas. This isn't about that. Now calm down and let me do what I have to do.'

Elyas looked at Ahad. His voice cracked. 'It's what she does. She makes people love her and then, when she needs to, she uses them. What's wrong with her?'

Ahad sat frozen. He watched his parents, his father's emotional outburst and concern, his mother's face stark and set, and he squared the facts of all that he knew about them and who he was as a result.

His father's love was unconditional, washing over him like an ocean; he knew that there was nothing he could do to stem its tide. His mother's love was the same, but experience had taught her to build sea walls to protect those around her. He understood her in ways his father could not.

The gates of the house opened soundlessly, and the car pulled up to the front entrance. The driver stepped out to open the door for Jia.

'Nothing's wrong with her,' Ahad said to Elyas, drawing himself up and going to stand beside his mother. 'I'll go,' he told her.

Jia closed her eyes, just for a brief moment. 'I need to change,' she said quietly. 'Find Idris and set up the war room.'

CHAPTER 51

She closed the bathroom door behind her and caught sight of Lirian's pyjama top. Pressing the soft muslin fabric to her face, she breathed it in. It had been hanging there since his morning shower and his scent lingered on it.

Still holding the shirt, she stepped into the shower fully clothed. Slowly, she slid down the tiled wall, letting it take her weight, until she found herself on the ground. Her belly felt impossibly heavy. The water poured over her, washing away the sorrow and crippling fear, the exhaustion and the longing for an easier life.

For the first time in years, she wanted to cry. To weep for the woman she once was, for the man Zan would have become, and for the man her father should have been, a young man with dreams of legitimacy.

She wanted to sob for the life she and Elyas were meant to live. For every man, woman and child who suffered, held back not just by systems, but by other men, women and children.

If she let herself cry, her sobs would be hard. She had bottled them up since the shrine, knowing that her cries would be ugly, her muffled screams crawling along the mausoleum floor and into the grave of the dead saint that had not protected her son.

But women like her were not allowed grief. They were the glue that held men together. If they cried, who would clean up the mess that humanity had made?

After an eternity, she found the strength to rise. She slowly peeled off her soaked clothes and dried herself.

She stood naked before the mirror, staring at her reflection, wondering where the young woman had gone. Her body had stretched and grown large, the child inside her taking what it needed, demanding space, displacing her organs and putting itself at the centre of the universe.

And still she saw power. Even stripped of wealth and influence, she would be formidable. Life had entered the world through her twice, and it was about to do so again for a third time.

She was hollowed out, and she was tired, but she was not broken. Not by any stretch.

She dressed deliberately, choosing the soft cotton angrakha that hung on the back of the door. She tied the strings of the shirt to the side, brushed her hair and moisturised her face. Then she looked up.

She steeled herself for the side of the Khan that neither her son nor her husband had seen and that she was about to unleash.

'Where is Idris?' she said.

Her hair was tied back, her eyes clear.

'He's in the study, setting things up,' said Elyas. His eyes were hardened. She could see the fire in them. 'Jia, about Ahad –'

She cut him off and walked out.

She needed to speak to her son. Ahad was in the living room, his head in his hands. He was caught between saving his brother and sacrificing himself, but he trusted his mother.

'I don't want to ask questions, but…'

Jia sat down and took his hands in hers. 'Ahad,' she said. 'This is the life you have been born into. I can't fight it for you, but I will stay with you, and I will not let you down. You can ask the question.'

He looked so small as he sat beside her. 'I know you're worried about Lirian,' he said. 'I am too. But this…? How does this make any sense?'

Elyas had followed her into the room and stood nearby, listening. He was afraid; she could see it in his eyes. That is what decency did: it brought fear.

She realised that he needed something to do, something that made him feel useful, that kept him out of her way.

'That journalist you've been helping, David Black,' she said. 'Hasn't he been investigating people going missing? Find him. Tell him our son's been taken and that we need any help he can give us. No one knows we're connected to him, and he can access things without drawing attention.'

'He'll ask about the police.'

'No police. Say whatever you have to. Just get information. Go now!'

She watched him leave, the urgency in his step reassuring. He would come back with something, she knew it. He could be trusted that way.

'Get me some water, please,' said Jia to her son, knowing that it might be the last thing she ever asked of him. 'And then I will explain.'

Her head was spinning. The nausea was overwhelming. She had been consumed by the question of how she would raise three children, and now the very real possibility loomed that she would not have to. She pushed the thought aside.

She considered her options again.

She ran a multimillion-pound empire, navigated the world of powerful men and women, and sidestepped the law. She could order hard men to do brutal things, inspire women into rebellion. She could dismantle systems and pull apart structures that pinned down the oppressed. She could rain revolution down on the heads and hearts of men. But motherhood? That was something else entirely.

It wasn't power, it was vulnerability. It had caught her mid-sprint through life, and now it felt like she was crawling through mud and mire, over glass shards and through tunnels darker than night.

The fear of failure was suffocating. It was why she had nightmares and why she woke drenched in sweat. The devil had a shotgun pointed straight between her eyes.

CHAPTER 53

Marina worked for Oliver Blundell. He was a politician who masquer-aded as a man who knew his own mind, a man of the people, complete with brown wife and ideals to make the country sovereign. But it was a lie. Behind his every move was the hand of the Interior, gently guiding his decisions and rewarding his compliance. And because the Venn diagrams of power were always interlocked, the Guild circled nearby, benefitting from the same currents and decisions. The stakes were high, which meant Oliver Blundell was ruthless. He would do anything to win an election, even take Jia's son.

That was the difference between the West and the countries they so readily condemned. They called it 'covert operations'; they believed their religion purer, their way of life more advanced, their ideals more righteous, but their true expertise was in organised violence.

So was Jia Khan's.

By the time Jia was ready, Idris had already set up the war room. Sakina and the rest of the Jirga were online, some clustered in one location, others scattered across the country.

Jia had found ways to expand the legitimate part of the business. The money from the mine would need clean investment channels. The old businesses were tainted and becoming obsolete. They had to be cleaned, closed or, in some cases, handed over.

All the key players were present. Men and women, their top tech consultants, waiting.

'They want us to win them the election,' Jia said.

'But that's not possible,' said Haines. The young tech wizard was the granddaughter of Chilli Chacha, one of the Khan family's oldest and most loyal employees. She had risen quickly through the ranks under Jia's leadership.

'Don't tell me that,' said Jia. 'Tell me what you can do.'

'If we cave to this, they'll have leverage over us and be able to hold us to anything,' said Nadeem.

'I've thought of that,' said Jia. 'Right now, the priority is getting Lirian back. The rest we'll deal with later.'

'But, Jia —'

Something in Nadeem's tone needled her. 'Just do what I tell you, brother,' she said, her words curt and clipped. She was nine months pregnant, her son had been kidnapped, and she was in a foreign land. She'd gone above and beyond self-control. She didn't need a chorus of doubts; she needed action. 'They've taken my boy. Now do your job, and I will do mine.'

'It is our job to advise you,' said Nadeem. 'That's all we're doing.'

She heard him out but couldn't help wondering why, in this moment of crisis, he felt compelled to list obstacles she already knew. Was it the sight of her pregnancy that had made him forget who she was? Did the sight of her swollen belly make him think she needed a reminder of limitations?

'We can flood the socials with compromising footage of the opposition,' said Sakina. 'We can use some of the graduates from the training programme to push it through. TikTok, Insta, Snapchat, Reddit, all of it. We manipulate the algorithms. We control the narrative.'

'We'll use the AI agents we've been refining,' added Haines. 'Get that right-wing fascist tech bro to blast our data drops. That ought to create enough havoc. We've got dormant accounts waiting for this kind of thing. Chaos is a tap away.'

'Do it,' said Jia. 'No one sleeps until after this election. And I want boots on the ground at every count site. We can't take any chances. If the vote turns against us, we resort to more old-school methods. You know what that means.'

One of the women looked at her, her face resolute. 'We've got you, Jia Khan. You take care of yourself and bring your son home. We'll hold the line here.'

She felt a twinge in her lower back and knew she didn't have long. The baby wanted to make itself known.

Once, women gathered to celebrate the impending birth of babies, to nourish, heal and help new mothers. They brought panjeeri in silver trays, semolina roasted in ghee, with almonds, pistachios and other nutritious nuts and seeds to encourage breast milk to feed the new arrival and heal the mother.

Jia's Jirga was a version of that, standing beside her as she birthed not just a child, but a new world order.

CHAPTER 54

Elyas was waiting by the gate when David arrived.

David was holding a brown envelope.

'Have you got something?' said Elyas.

'The trafficking ring I've been investigating goes very high up. I don't know if it has anything to do with your son's disappearance, but I'm prepared to share my notes with you in case it does.'

'My wife thinks the Deputy High Commission is directly involved.'

'Interesting,' said David. His eyes narrowed. 'You sound doubtful, though.'

Elyas wiped the sweat from his brow. 'They've taken my son. You're suggesting it could be connected to a trafficking ring while my wife says the embassy. I don't want to believe either of you, but certainly not both of you.'

'Because the British government is the last bastion of honesty?' David said dryly. 'You know better than that. This Marina woman you told me about, she has no scruples. No moral code. She was recruited at eighteen when she was at Cambridge and she's been in and out of the secret service since then.'

'How did you find all this out?'

'Sometimes white men aren't mediocre,' said David. 'I know how to make use of my privilege, the network, the open doors, the patriarchy. I started at the front of the race, so if I lose, it's on me.'

His honesty caught Elyas off guard. 'I appreciate it. Thank you.'

'Just get your son back,' said David. He hesitated, still holding on to the envelope, then added, 'There's something else, the other reason I came to find you back in England. You've not really talked about your wife before this happened. I know she is Akbar Khan's daughter – I've known for a while. So…I couldn't help wondering whether you were involved in her affairs.'

Elyas had had a suspicion that David was on his case. He was a good journalist, so to expect otherwise would have been foolish. What he didn't know was what David would do with any information he had.

Jia Khan had killed her father, a man who ran a criminal empire, and instead of dismantling it, she had claimed it. Proving it would be a difficult task but a juicy prospect to an ambitious reporter. He watched David, hoping for a flicker of revelation, something that would hint at his intentions, but nothing came.

David looked him in the eye, his demeanour cool, his breath steady. 'It's OK,' he said. 'Conflict of interest. I get it. I'm asking you to put public interest ahead of your own.'

'No,' said Elyas. 'You don't get it.'

'OK…so does that mean you're willing to talk?'

Elyas inhaled and waited, weighing up his options, the tension between the two men palpable. On the one hand there was his need for truth and openness, to confront the life he was living with Jia Khan, the mother of his children, the queenpin to rival all kingpins. He could tell David everything, bring him the diaries he kept, the list of things he knew, hand them over as evidence, a trail of breadcrumbs that would lead to the demise of the Khan. It was the right thing to do, the thing he had encouraged countless others to do.

Then he thought of his son.

'Get out of here, kid,' he said. 'Get out while you can. You're way out of your depth. I've got bigger problems than you and your conscience right now.'

'My conscience is clean, Elyas. It's yours that isn't. Don't patronise me. I've seen enough shit go down to know what's what.'

'The hell you have. You fly into war zones, take photos of dead children, then go home to scones and pubs and sipping wine at dull fucking weddings in some quaint village. You score some coke, shag some women, and that makes you know what darkness is? You don't have a fucking clue. You're a ghoul.'

'If I'm a ghoul, then what are you? You didn't win those awards for hosting garden parties.'

'When I went into those places,' said Elyas, his voice low, 'those people looked like me. Same blood, same faith, our names flagged up in airports and getting us trapped in security for a grilling. The boys I saw buried under rubble, the ones you photographed, they looked like my son. What I saw changed me. You think I could just switch that off? I have sons to raise. I had to survive, I had to act like a normal person. Yeah, I'm a ghoul. But at least I know who I am. You only wonder how I can be with Jia Khan because of this mask I wear. I love her. I understand her. I don't judge her. Because if I did, I'd have to judge myself.'

'Elyas, you don't understand,' said David.

Elyas understood perfectly, but he didn't have time to explain. He needed to find his boy.

'I understand that I need to find my little boy. Now, are you going to give me those notes or are you going to stay on your high horse and shit everywhere?'

CHAPTER 55

Marina's instructions finally came through as election day dawned in the UK. Ahad was dropped off at the gates of the Deputy High Commission, where he was searched by security before Marina was called. She came to collect him herself and led him inside, through dim offices and long, winding corridors, the air heavy with the scent of dusty tomes and bureaucracy.

The hallways were made of marble chips, covered in well-worn rugs. Faded photographs of past diplomats hung on the walls.

Finally, they stopped outside a plain wooden door. Marina wordlessly opened it.

Inside the room was quiet. On the floor, surrounded by crayons and paper, sat Lirian. He was gazing out of the window.

'Bhai!' he shouted, scrambling to his feet.

Ahad dropped to his knees and threw his arms around him, relieved to find him safe and in one piece.

'Bhai, can we go home now?' said Lirian.

'Soon, little brother,' said Ahad. 'Are you OK?' He pulled back, gently turning the boy's face in his hands, checking for bruises, signs of fear. 'Did anyone hurt you?' he said.

Lirian shook his head. 'No, but I'm hungry.'

Ahad opened his bag and pulled out a box. Inside was a sandwich and pieces of fruit that Jia had made the kitchen staff prepare and pack. 'Here, let's eat this together,' he said.

Then, turning to Marina, his eyes narrowed. 'How long has he been left him here alone?'

He didn't wait for an answer. He already understood why his mother had sent him. Because, in the end, he was the only one she trusted to protect her son, and he knew she had been right.

CHAPTER 56

As Elyas had followed leads and Jia had waited on news, her tech team had worked around the clock, manufacturing fake news and funnelling into every corner of the digital world.

They had uploaded, shared and clicked their way into the billions. The traditional media had caught on, cautiously navigating the landmines to report what they could.

Nothing had been off limits, from the obscene to the mundane, pornographic to racist. Phones buzzed, emails pinged, and the polls had begun to swing in favour of Oliver Blundell.

Jia paced the cool marble floor of the family estate. She imagined Ahad wrapping his arms around his little brother, shielding him from the worst of the world. She worked while silently praying for their safety.

Bazigh Khan sat quietly on the sofa, watching his brother's daughter commanding forces and navigating a new world that neither he nor his brother could ever have envisioned.

He had lost his wife to this life and knew its cost all too well. He had built his empire around family, and now in his old age he longed to retire, to pass the mantle to his sons, to sit with his granddaughter and rest. But that kind of peace felt like a fantasy.

'You are right to do this,' said Bazigh Khan. 'But do you trust that woman to return your son?' he said.

Jia shook her head. Marina knew more about Jia's business than an ordinary civil servant should. She was a mercenary and could never be trusted, and that was why Jia had other plans to bring her son home.

CHAPTER 57

The kitchen was alive with the hum of activity, the scent of sweet syrup thick in the air. Laughter and chatter mingled with the soft clinking of utensils and the gentle sizzle of oil heating in a large cast-iron pan. Four women stood side by side, each with their own role in the small but bustling kitchen that had been transformed into the heart of their growing micro-business.

Amina, the eldest of the group, stood at the counter, carefully measuring the flour and powdered milk for the dough. Her fingers moved with familiarity; she had spent years perfecting the art of making the golden, syrup-soaked gulab jamun, which had become the most famous in the city.

She looked up from her work to see Jia walking around the room, her presence warming but a firm reminder of what was at stake.

'Don't rush, Fatima,' Amina said to her sister, eyeing her rolling technique as she shaped the dough into small balls with quick, practised movements. 'If they're too big, they won't cook all the way through.'

Fatima frowned. This batch had to be perfect. Taste might not be critical to the plan, but her standards wouldn't allow for shortcuts.

Nearby, her sister Zainab stirred the syrup pot in careful, deliberate circles, making sure the sugar dissolved evenly.

'Careful not to let it boil,' Amina told her. Then she turned to Jia Khan. 'We will bring your boys home,' she said. 'Leave that part to us.'

Samina, the youngest member of the team, stood watch over the oil. She dipped a small piece of dough into it to test the temperature, watching as it floated up to the surface with a soft sizzle.

'It's ready,' she called to the others.

'I'd like to come with you,' said Jia.

Amina nodded, wiping her hands on her apron. 'I understand, but if you're seen, the risk is too high.'

The women moved around the kitchen with precision, their movements dance-like as they gently dropped the balls of dough into the hot oil. The gulab jamun began to puff up, their surfaces turning golden brown, the kitchen filling with the comforting smell of frying dough.

Amina looked up from her work and said to Jia, 'The way to a man's heart is through his stomach. That is why we started this business.'

'Yes,' Jia replied, 'but the fastest way is in through the upper left abdomen, around the oesophagus and in between the small intestine. That is the other reason.'

Amina smiled. 'Bazigh Lala said you were a good woman, and you have changed our lives.'

'What is it they say about the difference between giving a woman a gulab jamun and teaching her to make gulab jamun?'

The women laughed.

This was a very different war room from the one that was cooking an election, but it was no less important.

'And now we use the change from charity to empowerment to build our lives,' said Amina. 'We have customers everywhere, from rich to poor, and we deliver the mithai with whatever else is ordered.'

She took one of the empty boxes that the sweetmeats were delivered in and flipped it, revealing a false bottom.

Jia placed a pistol inside. 'Give this to my eldest son. He will know what to do.' She checked the time. 'May Allah be your guide,' she said, leaving the women to their work.

Her belly tightened. It wouldn't be long now.

CHAPTER 58

The sun dipped low, casting a deep orange hue over the city. The sky was awash in reds and purples as the van bumped along the dusty road. In the back were red and green cardboard boxes filled with sweetmeats and concealed weapons.

Amina drove, her grip steady, her eyes fixed on the horizon. Silence filled the van; this was no ordinary delivery.

Fatima glanced nervously at the rear-view mirror. 'Are we sure this will work?' she said.

'It has to,' said Amina. 'We owe that mother more than we can repay.'

Zainab whispered quiet duas to protect them. 'We have the best chance now. Sakina says everyone will be distracted by the election.'

'They'll check the boxes,' Samina said.

'They'll see only what they expect to see,' Amina replied, her voice firm. Her knuckles paled as she gripped the steering wheel.

As they neared the checkpoint of the Deputy High Commission, their nerves coiled tight. Heavily armed paramilitary guards stood before a gate of metal and concrete. Amina eased the van to a crawl, her hands steady on the wheel, her face composed. She leaned forward, eyes fixed on the guards as they motioned them through the gates.

As they passed through, a young guard held up his hand for them to stop. He stepped towards the van, rifle slung on his shoulder, eyes sweeping over the vehicle. He paused at the driver's window, his gaze lingering on the boxes stacked in the back, then turned to Amina, his face expressionless.

'What is your business?' he asked, his voice flat.

'Just delivering sweets for the election party,' she said. 'Ordered by the deputy high commissioner's wife.'

The soldier raised an eyebrow, his gaze still on the boxes, his eyes narrowing. 'I'll have to check,' he said, leaning on the driver's door and peering in.

Amina smiled. 'Please do, bhai,' she said softly, using the word 'brother' to convince him of her honest intentions. 'But please hurry. We're running late and don't want to upset the commissioner sahiba.'

The guard stared at the vehicle and at the women, studying their faces for information. The women held their breath, wondering what would happen if they were found out, the moment pregnant with problematic potential.

Just as they were losing hope, the guard pulled his hand back.

'Fine,' he said, nodding at the van. 'Move along, then.'

Amina didn't wait. She pressed the pedal, and the van lurched forward, inside heavy with silence.

In the rear-view mirror, they could see the guard's eyes tracking them, still watching, still suspicious. Only when the checkpoint was a blur behind them did anyone breathe.

The women exhaled in unison, the van filled with cries of 'Alhamdulillah!' and choked-back relief.

They had passed through these gates before, but never like this. Never with this kind of hidden cargo. It wasn't the first time they had delivered sweetmeats, but it was the first time they had come armed for a rescue operation as well.

They didn't speak. They just drove, the familiar path guiding them towards the house they knew and the kitchen staff who were waiting not just for sweets, but for orders.

When they arrived, they handed over the boxes, and with them, the next step in the plan.

CHAPTER 59

The pain hit sharper this time, low and tight like a vice around her spine. Jia pressed a hand to the table, steadying herself as the activity in the room continued without pause, screens flickering, data streams flowing, strategy being forged in real time.

'Are you OK?' Idris asked, his eyes lifting from a screen.

Another wave surged, deeper now, pulling at her breath. Her hand moved instinctively to her belly. The baby had dropped. It was happening.

She straightened. 'I need a secure room,' she said.

'Now?' said Idris, raising his eyebrows.

'Yes. Now.'

She walked out of the war room without waiting for confirmation, her tread steady but her breathing sharp. Every step took more effort than the one before, but she didn't stop. She wouldn't let anyone see her falter.

In another life, she might have had her mother by her side. But her mother was not here, neither were the women who had raised her, aunts and cousins, female friends, women who told birth stories as tales of battle and described labour as initiation. She hadn't believed them then. She did now.

Idris caught up with her just as she reached the entrance hall. 'I'll take you to the room,' he said, and he led her through the corridors of the family home to a door.

Jia stepped inside. The room was simply furnished but cosy. A bed. A chair. Clean towels stacked neatly. The nurse was already there, tying back her hair and rolling up her sleeves.

'Elyas has had it ready since we got here,' said Idris.

It was in moments like this that Jia knew why she stayed with Elyas. 'Where is he?'

'He said he was going to see the journalist again.'

Another contraction hit Jia, and she doubled over in pain, grabbing for Idris's hand.

'You waited too long,' said the nurse, seeing her condition.

'There were things to do,' said Jia dryly.

'There are always things to do. You're having a baby.'

'Tell me something I don't know,' said Jia.

Idris raised his eyebrows. 'Maybe not a good idea to be sarcastic to the nurse,' he said.

'She understands,' said Jia. 'We women always understand.'

She moved towards the bed slowly, letting the next contraction move through her without resistance.

'You'll be better standing,' said the nurse. 'The gravity will help,' she added, wiping Jia's brow.

The contractions came hard and fast, without build up, like a torrent of pain. And then her waters broke, and time ceased to exist.

There were only the waves, cresting and crashing, and the fire in her hips that split her open from the inside. She felt the burn of it, the cleaving of worlds.

'You're close,' the nurse whispered. 'One more push.'

There was only breath and silence, water and pain. Just doors away, an election was being stolen, a future being made. Here in this room, without epidurals or machines, flesh and heat and will were carving another kind of future.

Jia clenched Idris's hand tight, her nails digging into his palm.

He remained stoic, watching as she finally screamed. It was louder and fiercer than anything he had ever heard. It was not fear, not weakness, but a war cry and a prayer. It was anguish and command, as her body arched, clenched and bore down, the baby inside her forcing its way into the world, no care for the woman who had created and carried it for nine months.

The scream was followed by exhaustion and a deafening silence.

'Why is there no sound?' said Jia, desperate now. The nurse had caught the child, wrapping it in a blanket, and was rubbing its chest and working its lungs.

Jia caught sight of Idris, the concern written large across his face, and she remembered how weak men were. Then she watched as a sudden cry, thin and furious and alive, made him light up, and she remembered why womankind continued to love men, despite their flaws.

The nurse handed the baby to Jia.

She looked down at a red face, a shock of black hair, and tiny and defiant fists ready to join the fight.

'Welcome,' Jia whispered, 'to a broken world. But we're going to make it whole, you and I.'

She let her eyes close and breathed in the scent of new life, raw, bloody, miraculous.

Then her phone buzzed.

She didn't reach for it. Not yet.

CHAPTER 60

Ahad was sitting beside his little brother, who was asleep on the sofa, when the maid entered with a tray of tea and a red box of mithai. The door was unlocked, the security cameras he'd seen and the guards at the gates enough to deter any thoughts of simply walking out of there.

'It is a big day in the land of the Britishers,' said the maid. 'This box is for you. Make sure to check the bottom,' she whispered. Her English was broken and mixed with Urdu, but Ahad understood enough. He moved fast, opening the box and feeling beneath the sweets. He could be disturbed at any moment.

His trembling fingers found the loose panel and closed around the pistol. It was heavier than he expected, its cold metal handle fitting snugly into his palm. As he lifted it, the weight settled into his hand and the power felt familiar, like a returning memory.

Adrenaline coursed through his veins, spreading through his body, like coolant.

'Let's go,' said the maid, her voice low and urgent. 'If they stop us, you need to take me hostage. That is the only way you get out of here alive.'

Ahad swallowed hard and nodded. He hid the gun and turned to Lirian, gently shaking him awake. 'We're going home,' he whispered, 'but you need to stay quiet.' He'd protected his brother, and he hoped their luck would last.

The maid scanned the hallway. Finding it empty, she beckoned to Ahad. His breathing shallow, his nerves stretched thin, he walked towards her, the pistol tucked in his jacket, his hand gripping Lirian's tightly.

The ceiling fans hummed overhead, stirring the thick, humid air. The only other sound was the evening chorus of the birds outside the windows and, nearby, the clatter of dishes and laughter from the kitchen as preparations were made for the party that would start late in the night as election results began to trickle in. The maid moved towards it. Just a few more steps and they'd be through. Beyond that kitchen door was safety.

Then… 'Ahad.'

He froze as the voice sliced clean through the moment. Instinctively, his fingers went to the pistol and tightened around the grip as he turned to see who had called his name.

Marina stood in the hallway, her arms folded like a schoolmistress, stern and controlled. 'I was hoping your mother would storm the embassy and we'd have a shoot-out,' she said, stepping towards him. 'But this seems a little dull.'

Ahad's mind was sharp now, as clear and as cold as ice. He knew what he had to do, understood why his mother had sent him. 'She's done what you wanted. It's time for us to leave,' he said.

'I know, and I would have handed you over if you'd respected my rules and not tried to run. But this little escape? Sort of ruins the ending.'

'I'll stay,' said Ahad. He could feel his brother press against his leg, small and shaking. 'But my brother leaves,' he said. He raised the pistol, steady, and pointed it at her forehead. 'Now.'

She didn't flinch. Just regarded him, amused. But Ahad didn't look away. He nudged Lirian towards the maid. 'Get him out.'

Still holding Marina in his line of sight, he waited while the maid scooped up his brother and opened the kitchen door.

Amina and her sisters were at the ready. They took the boy, wrapping him in blankets to hide him, and hurried him out of the back door. They were almost at the van when it happened.

Marina lunged. Instinct took over and Ahad fired. One, two, three times, the shots hitting her in between the eyes, the silencer on the gun muffling the sound. His body jerked back but he kept on firing. He watched as she collapsed like a puppet with its strings cut.

He stood there, the gun still warm in his hand, his chest heaving. The white marble floor beneath her was slick with blood, and it hit him then: he wasn't made for this. He'd once thought he could be a gangster, part of the family's shadow trade. But this wasn't ambition. It was a reckoning.

In the garden, Amina and the maid held the boy tight. He was still trembling as they lifted him into the van and covered him with a blanket, the pops of muffled gunfire making them move faster. Lirian said nothing, but his face revealed his fear, his silence a sign that he knew he was in danger.

'Start the van,' Amina said to Zainab. 'If Ahad isn't already dead, he will be soon, and the rest us too if we don't leave now.'

Zainab nodded.

'Get in,' Amina urged the maid, slamming the back door of the van shut behind her.

Before the engine could turn over, Ahad burst through the side door of the embassy, blood spattered across his collar. 'Open the door!' he said, sprinting towards them.

They flung it open and yanked him inside, bundling him with his brother and covering them with blankets. Samina stacked mithai boxes around them.

There were shouts from inside the building. Perhaps someone had discovered Marina's body. The alarm would come next.

The van set off, Zainab trying to drive calmly, without drawing attention.

'The checkpoint,' she said as they rolled towards the gate. 'They're not going to let us through.'

The same guard from earlier stepped into view.

Zainab's heart slammed against her ribs. Her hands trembled on the wheel. The van crawled forward.

The guard approached. He peered inside, eyes flicking from face to face – Amina, Samina, Zainab, Fatima, and then the maid.

'Bibiji,' he said, recognising her. 'Is everything OK?'

'No,' said the maid. 'There's been a shooting inside, and I'm worried that if I don't leave now, the police will keep me here all night. And a woman who stays out all night is ruined.'

He nodded in understanding, the tension in the van palpable as the maid made her excuses. Zainab's mind was in overdrive. They weren't going to make it out.

Lirian wriggled under the blanket and Amina put her hand on top of him, praying that he would not speak.

Time stretched thin, but after what felt like an eternity, the guard stepped back.

'Give Bibi Khan my salaam,' he said quietly, touching his hand to his chest and bowing his head. In that moment, Zainab understood that Jia Khan's reach had infiltrated the embassy.

The van passed through the checkpoint. They didn't speak until they were far from the gates.

'We're taking you home, beta,' Amina said to Lirian when they were clear. 'Just hold on a little longer.'

***

Jia's phone buzzed beside her.

The child was calm now, swaddled in Idris's arms as Jia closed her eyes, waiting for news and for Elyas to return.

The nurse moved about the room with quiet efficiency, cleaning up, whispering prayers under her breath.

Another buzz.

'Take the call,' Jia said. 'Put it on speaker.'

The nurse answered.

'It's Ahad,' came the voice. He sounded tired but strong. 'I have Lirian. He's safe. We'll be home soon.'

Jia exhaled. Her shoulders dropped.

'I love you,' she said.

'I know,' said Ahad. 'You don't have to say it again.'

She put the phone down and turned to Idris, who was looking down at the baby. 'You want one of them? They're a lot of trouble and they make you feel more fear than you could imagine.'

'I know. But who else are we doing all this for?' he said.

'Good,' she said. Her body ached, but her mind had never been clearer. 'Then it's time we go on the offensive.'

She looked down at her daughter, sleeping against her chest.

'One child out. Two children home. Now let's finish this.'

CHAPTER 61

Steam spiralled from Jia's teacup, disappearing into the soft golden light of the club. Her eyes were on the door. The low hum of conversation, the weight of the velvet chairs, the portraits of women in quiet defiance adorning the dark-panelled walls: this place was a contained battleground in a velvet glove.

The fragrance of cedar mixed with lemon balm conveyed money and restraint. The fire was lit and the scene set when Amal arrived, her trench coat damp from the rain outside.

She handed the coat to the concierge as he directed her to her sister. Something in the brief glance she cast across the room betrayed her nerves. It was rare to see Amal unsettled.

She wordlessly took a seat opposite Jia, eyes skimming the menu as if it could shield her from what lay ahead. The silence stretched between them, heavy and deliberate, like the years without explanation or apology.

Finally, she spoke. 'Are we going to talk about it?' she said. 'I know neither of us want to.'

Jia's gaze didn't waver. 'I want to talk about Marina,' she said. 'But I don't know where to start.'

Amal stiffened, just slightly. Her teacup hovered mid-air before she set it down with care.

'You're friends with her,' said Jia.

'I've known Marina professionally for years,' said Amal, voice clipped. 'She's a strategic consultant. Occasionally, she's useful. But not anymore.'

'She kidnapped Lirian,' Jia said. 'Did you know that?'

Around them, women laughed, forks scraped on porcelain, deals were being closed with smiles and handshakes, but Jia and Amal were in a colder and sharper climate than the rest.

'I didn't know,' said Amal. Her eyes conveying her honesty.

'She was acting under orders. To win an election,' said Jia. 'You must have known, or suspected, at least?'

Her words pinched, and Amal's eyes flickered with something unreadable. She'd hoped for kindness, a coming together, but this was the other kind of familial. 'You've always been righteous, Jia,' she said. 'Lines and rules. I used to think that was admirable. Now I think it's dangerous.'

'Dangerous is turning a blind eye to power that crushes people. It is forgetting family.'

Amal didn't flinch. 'Family?' she said. 'You say that word with such ease. I never had that. And I don't have the luxury of idealism in my world. The men I deal with wear civility like cologne. They'd eat me alive if I brought feelings into the room.'

'She abducted a child.'

'Yes, you said. So that a government could win an election. And yes, I've kept quiet about things in the past, but not this. And you think I haven't paid for my mistakes in my own way?'

Jia sat back, disappointed but not surprised. 'What did she offer you?'

'She didn't offer me anything. We move in the same circles. I knew what she was. That's why I never left her alone with my children.'

'That's not good enough.'

Amal's laugh was bitter. 'You think you're outside this machine? You think justice works in clean lines? We're both inside it, Jia.'

Jia's expression was hard. 'I want everything you have on her. Names, dates, links to Blundell. Everything.'

Amal exhaled, eyes narrowing. 'You're not asking. You're demanding.'

'I'm giving you the chance to do the right thing before I take Blundell down.'

'Do you even care what it will mean for me if people find out I have shared confidential information?' Amal asked. 'My firm, my standing, my children?'

'I care about family,' Jia said, her voice suddenly breaking through its even register. 'And I care about every mother who doesn't have the money or connections to pull their child back from the dark. You know I would not let anything happen to my father's children.'

There was silence again, deeper now. The kind of silence that grows roots. The question was, would this tree blossom and bear fruit, or had the rot set in?

Amal turned her head slightly, staring out towards the frosted glass doors that led to the pool. Beyond them, the surface of the water shimmered, cool and blue, dividing two worlds.

'You know,' Amal said quietly, 'when I saw your name on that guest list all that time ago, I was afraid you'd hate me.'

'I don't hate you,' Jia said. 'I need an older sister, but I have to be able to trust her. There are enough shadows in my work, I can't have them in my personal life.'

Amal looked at her, and for a moment her composure cracked, not out of panic or guilt, but something older. It was grief and lone-liness. For women like her, life was lonely. She was envied for her wealth and success, but few scratched the surface to see what was beneath the veneer. Jia had been the only one.

'I'll send you what I have,' she said.

Jia studied her. There was a sincerity there she hadn't expected. A crack in the armour. Then she nodded. As she stood to leave, Amal reached out and took her arm.

'Jia,' she said. 'I'm sorry. I didn't know. I honestly didn't. I want us to be friends like we used to be.'

'What we were was based on a lie,' said Jia.

'Not for me, it wasn't. I always knew who you were, what we were. You and I are alike, and we need each other. I can tell. I'm as much Akbar Khan's daughter as you are. I believe in loyalty and in family. Let me prove it to you.'

Jia smiled gently. 'Let's see,' she said, then turned and walked away, her heels echoing against the marble floor.

Behind her, Amal watched, eyes filled with regret and the fear of losing the only person who truly understood who she was.

CHAPTER 62

In Geneva, in the depths of a decommissioned private bank, retro-fitted with mirrored walls, biometric locks and soundproof vaults, members of the Guild sat around a circular black glass table with some of their most valued associates. Outside, by the Quai du Mont-Blanc, the lake shimmered beneath the moonlight, serene and cold.

The atmosphere in the underground room, however, was anything but peaceful.

Yanick Kaplan stood at one end, flanked by guards, tension rippling through every nerve. He wasn't bound, but the unspoken threat hung in the air. This was an unofficial board of the world's most powerful illicit strategists, and tonight he was being called to account.

'Jia Khan is the nicest woman you'll ever meet. Until she's not,' Yanick said, spitting the words like venom. 'Then she's a sociopath.'

He faced the table of silent judges.

'You've failed,' said Odile Moreau, head of the Marseille traf-ficking corridor. She wore dark sunglasses despite the underground lighting. They made her sleek, surgical and unreadable.

Yanick didn't flinch. 'I tried everything. Surveillance, disinforma-tion, strategic leaks. I even opened backchannel lines with the British government when Marina approached me.' He let that sit for a moment. 'I thought I could use the Blundell operation to collapse Jia from the inside. Instead, she exposed them. Marina is dead.

Blundell's inner circle is in tatters. I lost four assets in two weeks – it was like she erased them from the grid.

'She's not just smart,' he added. 'She's relentless. I've worked black ops in nineteen countries. She's colder than any of them. And she hides it behind silk blouses and Birkin bags.'

Arjun Singh, old and sharp, sat across the table, arms folded. 'And you thought you could outmanoeuvre her,' he said. 'You made an alliance with Marina without consulting us.'

'She was useful,' Yanick countered. 'Isn't that what we do? Make inroads into the powers of state?'

Arjun's voice was hard, like steel on stone. 'She crossed a line, Yanick. She abducted a child. I told you I was done. And now we find our fates tied to your own stupidity, like rocks to a sinking ship.'

'I never sanctioned the abduction,' said Yanick, standing his ground. 'That was Marina's call. I distanced myself the moment it escalated.'

'You didn't distance yourself,' said Odile coldly. 'You underestimated Jia Khan, and now Marina's dead, thanks to her eldest son, and Blundell is exposed, and Jia Khan is not going to rest until every single person connected to her child's kidnapping is dead.'

Silence fell.

Odile leaned forward. 'She's calculating and strategic. She is principled only when it serves her long game. You think she's playing defence, but when the moment comes, she'll strike. It is our unanimous decision that you are no longer under our protection, Yanick Kaplan,' she said.

Yanick protested, but it was too late. Arjun Singh and his colleagues had made up their minds. Behind Arjun stood Rajo Rani, poised and silent, dressed in charcoal grey, her arms folded. The last year had been her training ground, and she had absorbed more in that time than most heirs did in a decade. She said nothing during the meeting, but later, in private, she turned to her uncle.

'What do you make of this woman, Jia Khan?' she asked.

Arjun poured himself a drink, his voice reflective.

'She can be like the Indus, if we let her, connecting Peshawar and Punjab. Where the river flows, bounty grows.'

Rajo tilted her head. 'And if we don't let her?'

'Then she becomes a flood,' he said. 'And floods drown kingdoms.'

CHAPTER 63

Jia had also had enough of the chaos Yanick had brought to her life, and she was exhausted by the many demands on her. Survival forced her to strip life back to the essentials.

She left the baby sleeping in her crib, her husband dozing in the rocking chair and the freezer full of breast milk. She boarded the British Airways flight to New York, with only hand luggage. When her seat reclined into a bed, she pulled the cotton duvet over her shoulders and slept.

Childbirth and the sleepless nights took their toll on a woman's body, but for Jia Khan they had come with additional complications – the kidnapping of her son, the closing of a billion dollar deal that would sever her family's ties to organised crime, and entanglements in political intrigue. The work of a mother was never done, and neither was that of a criminal queenpin.

The adverts for baby formula, wipes and nappies lied. So did the people who said motherhood came naturally. Childbirth marked not just the beginning of child's life, but the death of a woman's old one: the end of being the most important person in her own world.

Jia Khan had an army to help raise and protect her children, but even then it was exhausting, and she had nearly lost both her sons. The responsibility of the men and women who relied on her also lay heavy on her shoulders.

She had suffered enough.

It was time to sew up old wounds and start life anew.

Wearing a baseball cap, dark glasses, black track pants and a hoodie that hid a multitude of sins, Jia walked out of JFK airport and on to American soil, where Adam Diaz was waiting for her in a pale grey Bentley. He took her to one of the brownstones she'd quietly bought over the last twelve months.

He watched her pad barefoot around the kitchen, her hair pulled into a ponytail, her face makeup-free, as she made tea.

'This tastes like dishwater,' she said, pulling a face and pouring it down the sink.

'That's why we drink coffee here,' he said. 'Think you could get used to it?'

She shook her head.

'What are you going to do?' he said.

'Finish what I started,' said Jia.

He didn't press further. He knew that she wouldn't tell him even if he asked. He took her in his arms and held her tight.

'I know it's hard, but you're doing the right thing,' he said.

'I just wish I had done this years ago,' she said.

'Will you stay afterwards?' he said, his voice hopeful.

She couldn't bring herself to meet his gaze. She thought of all the unlived life between them, what could have been, what would have been if she'd been braver and less loyal to her father and family.

'Thank you for being here,' she said eventually. She kissed his eyes; it was all she would allow herself. The smell of his cologne reminded her how much she could have loved him if only life had panned out that way. Then she stepped back. 'He'll be alone?' she said.

Adam nodded. 'It's arranged. He's ready to talk and call a truce. The rest of the Guild, you already know about.'

The chaos inflicted by the Guild had been her fault; she had rattled Yanick Kaplan's cage. The deaths that followed had scarred her. She thought of Ishy, of the dreams she'd spoken of, of her boyfriend and her parents. She thought of Afzal Khan and his wife and children. Despite his lack of loyalty, he had been her cousin, a member of her father's Jirga.

She had been their leader, and she had to take responsibility for their deaths, and to finish the unfinished business of the criminal fraternity.

The empire she had mothered was on the verge of independence – and wasn't that what parenthood was all about? There was a path ahead that was new and freshly paved by her.

She put on her white trainers and tied the laces, thinking about how far she had come. The diner that Adam had chosen was walking distance. 'I'll be here when you get back,' he said.

She knew he would be.

She walked slowly, purposefully, the sleep having left her refreshed. Dark, threatening clouds hung overhead, and she clutched the umbrella Adam had handed her as she left, holding it like a weapon, one that she hoped she wouldn't have to wield.

The diner was newly painted in dark green, a sign on the window announcing the freshly baked bagels and breakfast rolls whose scent greeted her as she stepped through the door.

A little girl was sitting in the corner of the eatery with her father. Her long brown hair plaited in a way that made Jia think of her life. She had been braiding the strands of countless responsibilities with faith, patience and love. Now, there was only a little more to do, and then hopefully she could rest.

Yanick Kaplan was waiting for her. He looked up from his menu and smiled, standing to welcome her like an old friend. She shook his hand and slipped into the booth across from him.

'Should we set the pleasantries aside?' he said.

'I'm in no hurry,' said Jia, picking up the menu and glancing through the list. The waitress came over with coffee, but Jia already knew what else she wanted. 'I'll have the special with poached eggs, and a stack of silver dollar pancakes with syrup, please. Can you switch the corned beef for something else?'

'You don't eat meat?' Kaplan asked.

'I've lost my taste for it,' she said.

'That's quite a large order for a woman,' said Kaplan.

'I'm breastfeeding,' she said, her tone sharper now, a flash of red in her eyes.

He realised his mistake. 'I apologise,' he said, placing a hand on his heart. His words sounded sincere. 'I have spoken out of turn,' he said, taking a sip of the black coffee the waitress had topped up earlier. 'My wife was exhausted when our children were very little. How are you doing?'

She thought a little before answering. 'I'm good,' she said, surprised at the realisation that she was doing well, and that she felt happy to say so to him.

'Winning the contract for the mine would do that, I imagine. Congratulations,' he said. 'I was hoping it would come to me, but it seems your contacts were far better.'

'Yes, I suppose they were, and thank you for saying so,' she said. 'For the first time in years, I am hopeful that things will turn out well.'

It was unlike her to be so relaxed and talkative, but she felt herself turning over a new leaf, as she stretched her legs out.

'You worked in the legal profession, I hear,' said Kaplan, as the waitress arrived with Jia's order and placed the food in front of her. 'Enjoy,' he added.

Jia picked up a fork and began slicing through the stack of syrup-soaked pancakes. They were as good as she had hoped. Maybe that was because this was the first meal in a long time that she'd eaten in a restaurant without the worry of a small child, or maybe this tiny café really did make the best buttermilk pancakes in New York.

'Yes, I used to be a barrister,' she said, swallowing her bite.

Kaplan studied her, enjoying her levity. This wasn't how his meetings went. They were usually in offices or swanky restaurants, and almost always with men. Jia Khan had been described to him as similar, so this was a revelation.

'And now?' he said.

Across the diner, a chair made a scraping sound as the little girl with the plait stood up. Her father helped her into her raincoat, paid the bill and took her by the hand. She waved at Jia, who had been smiling at her, enjoying the magic of youth and remembering her own breakfasts with Akbar Khan. The tiny bell in the doorway tinkled as they left.

The waitress picked up plates and wiped tables as the breakfast rush came to an end and the last of the customers left.

'Now,' said Jia, slicing through the poached eggs, the golden yellow spilling out on to the plate, 'I am a judge and jury.'

She leaned forward in her chair.

'And executioner?' he said.

She shook her head. 'In the past, maybe, but not now.'

'What changed?' he said.

'Life, motherhood, love.'

The freedom that came with honesty felt good. She hadn't felt this way since childhood, but there was no reason to hide anything from Yanick Kaplan anymore. She had financial power, political clout and no more use for old codes of honour. She didn't care for him and his ways, and he would not be a problem much longer.

'Your husband, the journalist, he understands?'

Jia glanced out of the window at the mention of Elyas. It was starting to rain outside, the drops slowly turning to sheets that came down in torrents. The diner darkened under the weight of it.

'Some days he does,' said Jia. 'Some days he doesn't. But, you know, there is more to life than a man's opinion. So many more important things to concern myself with.'

Yanick Kaplan roared with laughter. She sat upright, surprised.

'I'm glad my wife is not like you,' he said. 'You know, you're not what I expected. I had heard that you were a woman of few words, but you've got plenty to say.'

'You'd be surprised,' she said, her face unreadable, 'at what your wife is really like.'

His smile faltered. He put down his cup and tilted his head a little, the slow realisation that she was deadly serious now, the lightness having left her voice. She knew something he did not.

'No, I know my wife,' he said, shaking his head. 'She takes care of me and of herself. Women are different where I come from. Sarauniya would never dress in things like this black tracksuit that you're wearing.'

'Why would you say that?' said Jia. 'And here I was, just starting to like you.'

Kaplan became aware that the diner was empty. Among the casual conversation, he'd dropped his guard and forgotten who he was talking to.

'Men like you never understand the real value of something,' said Jia. 'But then, diamonds are only recognised by experts, as my father once told me. Most men are like little boys who have been coddled and pandered to. It's sad, because I considered, for a moment, giving you what you wanted. It was just after your wife called.'

Kaplan scanned the room. One of the waitresses was watching them. She looked vaguely familiar. He couldn't place her. He scoured his mind.

The waitress turned the sign to 'Closed' and locked the door, and it dawned on him who she was. His heart was racing now, but Jia was still talking.

'But then you started interfering in my plans to take the Reko mine, and all I wanted to do was to leave quietly, but you couldn't let me, could you? Why don't men let women do what they want?'

Jia placed her cutlery down on the plate and looked at Yanick. He shifted uncomfortably in his seat, sensing the change in temperature. He felt the hairs on his neck stand on end.

'Maybe your wife asks herself that same question,' she went on before he could speak. 'Remember how she told you to come here? That I'd be amenable to your plans, and that I was ready to make peace.'

Yanick's skin prickled with sweat. His wife had led him into a trap. The woman he slept beside, whose lifestyle he paid for, whose children he had fathered, she had handed him over.

'As I said, I am not an executioner anymore, but I want you to know that your wife and children will be looked after.'

He flinched as she stood up. The air felt oppressive. Something about her demeanour made him afraid. The look in her eyes, her grip on the umbrella, the way she leaned in, all signs that she was always the hunter and never the hunted. One wrong move, and she would skewer him.

He resigned himself to his fate. She had taken the mine, and his wife, and there was nothing without those two things.

'See you next time?' he said dryly.

'I'm afraid not,' said Jia, as she turned to leave.

'That is a shame, just when we were becoming friends.' He didn't need to turn around to know that the soft footsteps coming towards him were bringing his demise. He had killed enough men to know how this went down. Also, without his wife and children, he may as well be dead.

She was by the door when she heard the three shots, they were muted and followed by the guttural sound of his body slumping on to the table.

'Thank you, Rajo,' she said to the waitress, who gave a silent nod. 'I'll see you soon.' The tinkle of the bell was the only sign that she'd left the building.

She walked out into the cold light of day and back towards the brownstone, safe in the knowledge that her team were manipulating cameras in the city, wiping her image from them and adding AI-generated agents to cover her tracks.

Witnesses, if there were any, would say many things, but without technology to corroborate their stories, nothing would be done.

Yanick Kaplan was dead and no one would ever pin it on her. That was how powerful she was.

CHAPTER 64

Jia Khan knelt on the prayer mat in the brownstone, her hands moving from her knees to the floor as she prostrated herself before her God.

There was so much she wanted to say. She had done what she considered best for her family, both blood and chosen. She had taken on her father's work, and through it, countless families were able to live, eat and thrive. There were so many young people who had found purpose, so much potential that would have been squandered if it wasn't for her sacrifice.

But after Ahad was taken by Meera Shah a couple of years ago, and then Lirian by Marina, she had wondered whether she had done the right thing.

It wasn't her soul she worried about, or her life, it was those of her children. Her work had put her sons in danger, and it would continue to do so unless something changed.

She needed to get the people she loved out.

It was no longer about good and evil, the morality of ordinary men or saving others' livelihoods. It was about the violence that went hand in hand with the life she and the Jirga lived. Their choices were their own, but they should not define the lives of those who came after.

The old codes had meant children and women were out of bounds, but the bringing of women into the business had blurred that line. Villainy was not the sole domain of men, and women too had exploited the thing they knew to be her greatest weakness.

She prayed to her God, 'Oh Allah, You know my every action. No sin is hidden from You. I ask You to take care of the innocents. They are caught in the battle between heaven and hell, but they deserve better. Set us free from this destiny.'

No answer came from on high. She was no longer naïve enough to expect her God would make time for her. Redemption was not for Jia Khan, but maybe the young could break away.

ONE YEAR LATER

CHAPTER 65

Jia Khan stalked the corridors of power, her fingers trailing along the polished wooden panelling of the walls as she reflected on the men and women who had walked these halls.

Ahead of her, Sakina moved with quiet command. Dressed in a sharply cut Italian suit, her hair pinned back into a chignon, she looked as if she had always belonged in these rooms.

As if she'd been born for this life.

In some ways, she had, but it wasn't lineage that placed her here. Her journey from prostitute to politician had been made possible by the Khan's money and influence. Sakina had the intellect to thrive in this world, but she knew that without Jia Khan she would still have been walking the streets of the northern city where she was born, blowing punters for cold, hard cash.

The truth was rarely far from her mind, and today it was closer than ever. As Sakina pushed open the door to the chamber, standing aside to let her mentor walk through, she reflected on how far they had come. That was what women did in this new world. Where men had climbed ladders and pulled them up behind them, women opened doors and held them open for others to follow. It was a brave new world, one which Jia Khan and her people were building brick by brick.

Jia Khan stepped on to the deep carpet of the chamber and smiled coolly at the twelve men there. The chairman glanced at his colleagues seated beside him around the oval table. Their expressions mirrored his displeasure. They had not expected the interruption and did not return her smile.

'You shouldn't have come here, Ms Khan,' said a man in a blue pinstripe suit, his face much older than his years.

'Someone needs to put him back into his grave,' Jia said to Sakina.

'Our business has been concluded,' said the man, 'and you have been remunerated for your trouble.'

'I'm afraid that wasn't our deal. If you check with Mr Sackville, he will explain,' said Jia. 'But you are well aware of that, as are your associates.'

A shadow fell across the man's face, his discomfort evident. 'Well, this is most unacceptable,' he said, turning to one of his colleagues in the hope of support. 'This is not how things are done here.'

Jia walked to the far side of the room, lifted a lone chair, and placed it squarely between the twelve men, dividing the dozen into six. Then she sat down at the table.

'Well then, why don't we start by you telling me how things are done, and we'll finish with me telling you how it's going to be done from here on in,' she said.

For a moment, there was silence, heavy and calculated. The soft hum of central heating and the muted tick of a grandfather clock punctuated the tension. A few of the men exchanged glances: flickers of unease beneath tailored restraint.

Sakina stood silent. Her presence alone was a message of security, loyalty, leverage.

'You're trespassing,' said the man in the pinstripe suit, voice low and clipped. 'This room is not for theatrics.'

'No,' Jia said, 'it's for decisions made behind closed doors. For gentlemen's agreements, public denials and plausible deniability. I understand perfectly.'

She leaned forward slightly, just close enough to remind them she wasn't afraid. 'You've brokered power among yourselves for decades. Ministers, mandarins, media barons. But the arrangement has frayed. The public has changed. And you've all lost your touch.'

Another man, older, with a ruddy face and a discreet parliamentary pin on his lapel, shifted uncomfortably. 'We've indulged your ambitions, Ms Khan. But this, this is beyond the pale.'

Jia didn't blink. 'You haven't indulged anything. You've tolerated me because you thought you could use me. Now you're realising I've come not to sit at your table, but to replace it.'

A younger man to her right scoffed quietly but said nothing. The others didn't look at him.

She sat back in her chair. 'You can resist, leak stories, call in favours and whisper to the press, but make no mistake, this isn't a bid. It's a transition, from your order to mine.'

Across the table, one of the men exhaled through his nose and picked up a pen, his eyes on the notepad in front of him.

Jia's voice softened. 'The empire you built is crumbling. I'm offering you a chance to stay relevant while it's rebuilt. Under my guidance.'

She let the silence sit again, and this time, it was hers.

CHAPTER 66

By the time the remainder of the Guild had arrived, a truce was already in place.

Sakina had been assigned to the task, and she had attended to it in the same way she had her wedding, with ruthless precision and pride.

They were meeting in the Naanery, one of several business ventures backed by Jia Khan. She had provided a legal business loan, contacts, and was mentoring the owner as part of the excruciatingly slow plan to go clean, plans that kept being derailed. The Naanery served the bread of their ancestors, alongside Nutella, cheese and even carpaccio. In the old days, they would have mixed the flour deliveries with cocaine, but these days they were trying to keep the lines clean.

The Khan family now owned every mill in the county that once stood empty, tending to them the way children tend to their ageing parents. Money was a part of their mission – without it nothing else was possible – but the small plans in their home city, the ones that focused on love and soft power, were equally important.

They'd turned the mills into homes, art galleries, boutique businesses, and of course the tech company that connected multiple aspects of their business. They'd started out as the Ocado of drugs and the Deliveroo of sex services, and these enterprises continued, but they now had interests across the globe. Jia's newly found political clout offered them the kind of protection that had not been possible before. The contract for the Reko mine gushed money like a geyser, bringing more wealth than the illegal business had ever brought in, but she now understood that the bodies trapped under the rubble of the past needed to be extricated slowly, or they would not survive. It was possible that the legacy of her father's business would only end with her death, but that did not stop her desire to go clean.

'If we let them go, they'll be taken over by someone who isn't as careful and generous as we are,' Jia had said to her Jirga earlier, echoing the words she'd once heard her father say. 'People will always want the substances society tells them they shouldn't have. If we shut up shop, they'll flood the streets with cheap and dangerous products. I have a plan to make sure this doesn't happen.'

She had other sources of power now, ones that she intended to use. But the old trade still bothered her.

'We're leaving the business my father started,' Jia Khan announced to the members of the Guild gathered in the Naanery.

She had watched as they had filled their plates with Afghani pilau, covered in slivers of butter-softened carrot and sweet sultanas, over-sized chapli kebab and, of course, naan. They were less likely to argue if they were well fed.

'There have been losses on both sides,' she said to them. 'The last few years have been difficult, and I take responsibility for that, and I know that no one wins in war.'

The Guild members nodded in agreement, knowing that whatever she offered would be an improvement on the current state of affairs. Jia Khan was known for her generosity, and for her foresight. Since Yanick's death, Arjun Singh had been offering counsel, and there was a steadiness to his hand.

'We do not want war,' he said to her now. 'The pendulum is swinging to peace time, but still, we must have assurances of what is to come. Removing yourself from the family business will leave a void, and that could result in a turf war.'

Jia nodded. 'You are right,' she said. 'But you will not be without my vision. I am handing over my interests to Rajo Rani. In exchange, we will live our lives without fear. I will offer her my loyalty, support and any guidance that she needs in a legal capacity.'

Later that evening, Jia sat at her desk, the amber desk lamp casting a soft halo over the paperwork that formalised the break with the past. The room was quiet but for the scratch of her pen and the slow tick of the clock on the wall. Idris stood by her side, not saying much, just watching as she signed the last of the documents.

'It's been a long road,' he said quietly.

She leaned back in the chair, the leather creaking beneath her. Her fingers rested on the paper.

She didn't look at him when she replied, 'I wonder what my father would say.'

'That you did the right thing.'

'He would've said I was naïve. That the world doesn't change. Only the hands holding the blade.'

A pause hung between them, the silence weighty and full of memory. Then came the small, urgent and undeniable cry from the floor above. A soft wail that cut through the air like a call to the here and now.

Jia stood slowly, handing the final contract to her cousin.

'I've done what needed doing,' she said, more to herself than to him. 'The war is over. We don't need blood to hold power anymore.'

And with that, she left the room. No more talk of empires or legacies. No more ghosts of fathers and brothers. Just the soft footfalls of a mother walking towards her child, leaving behind the life that had made her, and nearly unmade her.

Downstairs, Idris remained at the desk, looking over the contracts. The ink was still drying. And for the first time in decades, the family business was truly closed.

CHAPTER 67

It was the heavy scent of oud that made Jia think of her father: Akbar Khan, standing in the warehouse office, watching through the one-way glass as crates of textiles were unloaded by hand. Outside, it looked like any other legitimate mill, but the goods inside were just the window dressing. The real trade – cash, secrets and protection – flowed in silence.

In this memory, a young Jia sat in a corner of the room, legs swinging beneath the leather chair, a book on her lap, pretending to read. Meanwhile Akbar Khan's Jirga was in session, Bazigh Khan beside him.

'You see that boy down there? The one lifting boxes?' Akbar Khan said. 'He was going through the bins outside The Karachi on Ruler Lane when I found him. Came here without papers. Now he eats twice a day, his visa is being processed, and he sends money to his amma in Lahore.'

The men nodded as he spoke, respect for Akbar Khan written across their faces. In just ten years he had built a northern business empire to be reckoned with. Now, he was offering them the same.

His voice was calm. 'This world doesn't care about people like us. We don't get offered power, we take it.'

'But what you're asking of us, is it legal?' one of the men had asked.

Akbar stepped closer. 'Legal is a word that men in parliament invented to keep people like us in our place. Morality is what the weak use to excuse their failures. I don't deal in either. I deal in loyalty, and whatever keeps our people safe and our children fed. You want a better world? Build it from the top. Own the banks, the streets, the judges. But first, you must own the men who think they own you. That's the rule. That's the price. Never let anyone tell you different.'

He'd straightened his jacket then and walked to his daughter's side, ruffling her hair.

'Respect the family,' Jia remembered him saying. 'Always. And if blood must be spilled to protect it, then you spill it cleanly, and you never look back.'

Shaken out of this daydream by the sound of Elyas talking to their newborn, Jia made her way to the nursery. She stood at the nursery door, watching her husband rock the baby back to sleep, his face full of contentment.

Her fingers rested on the frame, her wedding ring glinting in the lamplight. Akbar Khan's voice echoed faintly in her mind.

Respect the family. Always.

'Yes, Baba,' she murmured. 'But not like that. Not anymore.'

CHAPTER 68

'You ever make bread?' Jia said to Benyamin.

'A couple of times,' he replied. 'But always with yeast. I mostly make sweet things.'

Outside, snow had begun to fall, softening the afternoon light into an amber haze. The garden beyond the doors shimmered in the fading glow, the manicured lawn holding memories of snow angels, laughter and steaming hot mugs of tea in their parents' hands.

Inside, the youngest child slept, curled in Elyas's arms, watched over by the rest of the family. Sakina and Idris's wedding, only days away, gave Jia a kind of hope that she had not felt in years.

Amal was there too, sitting with Sanam Khan, but her mind was elsewhere, caught in the memory of that night in the rain, when she'd stood outside Pukhtun House. It wasn't long after Jia had confronted her in the club about Marina.

They had been able to move on since then. But only after Amal had arrived late one night, unannounced. The rain had been falling hard and she'd stood at the gates. Jia had watched on the security camera as her sister slowly became drenched. Nothing fell harder than northern rain on a sinner who had come to make amends.

Jia had sent for Idris. He'd parked up and stood beside Amal. 'She won't forgive me, Idris,' said Amal.

Idris opened an umbrella and held it over his newly found cousin. 'You know who I am?'

'I do. I know everything about her. She is my sister. It is a bond stronger than men can ever understand.'

'Then why did you do it?'

'I didn't. It was an honest mistake. I didn't know what Marina was involved in, and I didn't know she was putting information together to hurt Jia. I would have cut her out if I'd known.'

Idris had looked at his smartwatch. A message from Jia. 'She'll forgive you,' he said. 'She already knows it wasn't your fault. If it was, you wouldn't have been allowed this close to the house. Come on.'

He'd ushered her into his car, and that was night the gates of Pukhtun House opened on Akbar Khan's first born for the first time.

Amal was family, and this was the season when even those responsible for causing great harm were allowed back into the fold.

Jia flicked her phone to a music app, connecting it to the kitchen's speaker. The year's Spotify Wrapped playlist filled the air, eclectic and spanning decades, languages and continents.

As Jia and Benyamin baked, the sound of children's and cousins' laughter filled the house.

Lirian wandered into the kitchen, in search of orange squash, trailed by Maria's daughter. They were in their pyjamas, half supervised by Nadeem's daughter.

Idris followed behind. 'Come on, kids. The juice is on the table. The film's about to start,' he said, ushering them out.

It was Christmas Eve. The fire was lit, the projector screen was up, and popcorn and pretzel-filled bowls were waiting, alongside mithai and namak parai.

'It was all so quiet after you left,' Benyamin reminisced. 'We stopped celebrating everything.' He looked older somehow, his cheekbones sharper. 'I wish Dad could have seen us like this.'

Jia opened the larder and ran her fingers over the labels of the flour bins, from bread to chapati, self-raising to plain, wholemeal to white. The shelves were lined with glass jars filled with lentils, red through to yellow and green, pulses and grains for the soups and haleems that Chilli Chacha made.

Her hand hovered over the jars, and for a brief moment she imagined her father hiding narcotics there, a thought so absurd it made her glad her children would never inherit such suspicions. Behind her, Benyamin's voice pulled her back to the kitchen, and she took the flour to the kitchen counter.

'How are you finding motherhood third time around?' he asked.

'Exhausting,' she said. 'And beautiful. Pregnancy was harder than anything else I'd ever done.'

'That is saying a lot for someone with your life,' he said.

She laughed at his words.

'Why are you laughing?' he asked.

'The absurdity of it all,' she said. 'Us, here, baking bread like a pair of middle-class white people, not the drug dealers that we are.'

'The drug dealers that we *were*,' he corrected. 'And what are we supposed to do? Sit in a drug den in sad clothes and bad hair?'

'And then there's that bloody great Christmas tree,' she said, pointing at the huge tree in the corner of the room that Elyas had insisted on buying.

'Tradition! I love Christmas,' said Benyamin. 'My friends never understood why we had a tree and decorations. I never asked Baba, did you?'

'It was Zan. Baba found him crying after school one day, and he asked if we were on the naughty list and that's why Father Christmas hadn't brought us any presents. The next year we had a tree and decorations and a small present. You know what Baba was like.'

'Yes,' said Benyamin. 'Family first, before anything else.'

Jia took the sourdough starter from the jar and showed Benyamin. 'You see the tiny bubbles? That's a sign it is ready.'

'My friends think it's wrong that we have a tree and buy the kids presents.'

Jia took a glass from the tall cupboard and poured water into it, then added a spoonful from the top of the starter. 'See, it floats, which means it is ready to make bread. When we learn to swim, we learn to float, to trust our bodies, to let go of every bit of tension, and so it is with this. Pass me the jug,' she said.

She weighed and measured and taught him what to do, and when she'd finished, she ran her hands under the tap.

'I don't think any of this is easy,' she said. 'We belong to two worlds. We're Muslim, working within all the lines that come with it, but we also live in a country that is Christian. We need something in these dark days. If it means we come together and stop working, there's nothing wrong with that.'

'I love joining the white people celebrating the birth of a brown man,' said Benyamin.

She smiled at how far they had come, the two of them together.

'Make me some tea, will you?' she said as she sat down at the table. She watched him take mugs from the cupboard, all neatly lined up, their handles tucked in beside each other, like supplicants standing in prayer.

Jia leaned back in the chair and untied her hair, letting it fall around her face. She seemed softer in the evenings. The weight of the world dropped from her shoulders as she stripped herself of the accoutrements of business and put on the garments of ordinary womanhood.

If someone had asked, she would have told them that this was the most extraordinary part of her day, but no one did.

Benyamin placed the tea in front of her. He watched her with a kind of wonder she rarely noticed. His youth had taught him that life was fragile. His mistakes had shown him that the only dependable people in the world were the women of his family. They came when no one else did, even when he whispered for them from dangerous places.

Jia Khan was carved from the same unyielding ore as their father, a formidable presence that bent the world around her. It was easy to forget that she was human, fragile and in need of the same small graces that everyone else was.

'Jia,' he said, taking a seat beside her. 'I'm leaving.'

She didn't speak right away, just sat straighter and sipped her tea.

'I don't want to work for the family anymore. I know we're changing but I want to start afresh.' His eyes stayed fixed on his cup. 'I'm sorry, but I want to be able to walk down the street and not feel like a shadow. I never questioned it, this life. I stepped into the emptiness that Zan left behind, I wanted to be a good son, but you showed me there's another way.

'I've spoken to Adam Diaz. I'm thinking of leaving England. I don't want you to talk me out of it,' he continued. 'I just don't want to be included in what comes next. I'm sorry for letting you down, Jiji. I…just…'

He turned to look at her, desperation seeping out of him. He'd been hiding for months, and he couldn't bear the secret-keeping anymore.

'What will you do?' she said.

'I don't know yet. I want to figure it out. Maybe open a restaurant. I've been looking at courses.'

She leaned across and took his hands in hers. 'OK, brother,' she said. 'If that's what you want. Now, can you go check on the boys?'

After he left, she stayed in the chair for some time, sensing her father standing beside her, his hand on her shoulder. She'd done well. She'd set one of Akbar Khan's children free.

CHAPTER 69

Idris and Sakina's wedding had been spectacular, full of hope and possibility. Benyamin wished his girlfriend had been by his side, but she'd had a shift at the hospital. That's where he was racing to now.

The night was black, the tarmac slick with rain and engine oil that reflected the neon signs from chicken shops, cafés and ice-cream parlours. People clustered under awnings and umbrellas, waiting for tables, drawn in by the aroma of charcoal-grilled meats.

Benyamin gripped the steering wheel of the Vengeance Volante, knuckles pale against the black leather. Tension ran through his neck and shoulders, a sliver of pain that he couldn't shift.

The engine roared beneath him, the vehicle struggling to keep pace with his mind. He took the bend and curves of the streets at speed, but of all the laws he'd broken, he cared the least about this one. He wanted to lose himself, to outrun his mind.

He'd seen Jia and Elyas sitting in a quiet corner of the stately home, watching the wedding frivolities. His arm was around her waist, her head on his shoulder. She'd looked happy: finally, things were going back to how they should always have been.

Benyamin had promised Sanam Khan he'd help with the children while Jia and Elyas escaped for a mini-break. They'd left the party early to catch their flight and were probably miles ahead of him, somewhere on the country roads. They would be back from their trip before he departed for his culinary tour of Asia, where he planned to hone his skills.

'So this is what it feels like to be happy?' he'd said to his sisters and cousins as they'd gathered to send the bride and groom on their way.

'It would seem so,' said Jia.

She'd laughed and he had seen her eyes light up like never before.

'We did it,' she said. 'We got out.'

'WE GOT OUT!' said Nadeem.

'Can I get a takbir?' Idris said.

'*Allahu Akbar!*' they cried in unison.

He deserved this life, full of legitimacy and hope. That he'd never expected it, made it sweeter. His father's legacy, the violence, the shadows – they had shaped him, but they did not have to define him. He would start afresh, away from his past, the way Sakina had.

His playlist throbbed in time with his pulse. He pumped the accelerator and the Volante shot forward, tyres hissing on wet tarmac. The speedometer climbed until the street lamps blurred into streaks of light and shadow, orange and green.

Some days he was consumed by the choices he had made in life, and the ones that had been forced upon him, the kidnapping, the drugs, his father's murder. The dam of emotions he had built inside himself was cracking, and he knew that it wouldn't be long before the flood, but it was the only way to set himself free. His girlfriend had taught him that.

That Jia had rescued him from that life, taken him to a place of clean living and legal activities, where dreams were possible and the police were not to be feared, still took him by surprise. His skin, race, the family name, had robbed him of all this before he was even born, and he was ready to reclaim it.

For the first time in years, he felt content.

The street lamps disappeared as the city streets turned into narrow country roads flanked by dark fields. He slammed his foot harder on the gas, the tyres skidding a little as he veered around the bends, curve after curve. The speedometer climbed from sixty to seventy and beyond.

He should have slowed down, but he knew the roads well, and the car's power made him feel invincible. The world could go fuck itself. He was young, and beautiful, and life was good.

The tail lights came out of nowhere as he took a sharp turn, and his gut lurched. He should have slowed down sooner. His foot slammed on the brake and he threw an arm up instinctively to shield himself from impact as the tyres screeched, gripping the wet asphalt for a moment before losing traction.

The world turned white as the Volante slammed into the back of the vehicle ahead at full speed.

The sound of metal grinding against metal, the shrieking of the crumpled chassis as the car rebounded into a drystone wall. The impact was violent, bone-jarring, crushing. The airbags deployed, but it was too late.

Ben's head snapped violently against the side window. When he next opened his eyes, the world was a blur of flashing lights. There was the sharp scent of petrol, and the faint, distant wail of sirens.

The car was totalled, mangled beyond recognition, but it was the sound of his thumping heartbeat that told him it wasn't over yet.

He struggled against the seatbelt, his body heavy, limbs sluggish. His breath came in shallow gasps. Blood. He could taste it, bitter and warm.

He muttered through clenched teeth, forcing himself to reach for his phone, which had fallen from the dash on to the passenger seat. His vision blurred again. He couldn't focus. His hands were trembling, slick with blood, the screen of the phone cracked, the numbers unreadable. He pulled himself out of the car, into the road.

His body drained of blood as his vision cleared, and he saw what he'd hit.

'Jia...' he screamed.

They pulled her body from the wreckage and lay her on the ground. She was broken. Her hair matted with blood, her eyes closed, her sari leaving her blouse uncovered. Paramedics surrounded her, lifting her on to the trolley wheeling her towards the waiting ambulance, over the crushed glass, the glare of the lights harsh against the cold, black night.

He looked down at his hands, covered in his blood.

The sirens turned to an eerie silence; everything seemed to slow down as his thoughts swam in a haze, images of the past, memories of their childhood, of the choices they had made, of the bond they once shared.

A paramedic came towards him, wrapping a blanket around his shoulders, leading him towards the ambulance. 'Sir, you're bleeding,' he said.

But Benyamin barely heard. His mind was elsewhere. They had walked away. They had tried to escape the legacy they'd been trapped in, and now this. He felt his chest tighten, his legs buckle, as he glanced at the oil-covered road, the mangled cars, the weight of his own body too much to bear. He struggled to keep his eyes open. He looked at his hand, pulling it away from the gash on his chest.

'Jia,' he said, the name barely a whisper on his lips.

CHAPTER 70

The waiting room of the hospital was bright. It seemed too clean, too sterile for something so raw and real as this.

Maria Khan was the first to arrive, her face filled with fear, her eyes wide. She'd left her children with her mother.

Sakina and Idris came next, still in their wedding clothes, hands clutching one another. The rest of the family filtered in, Amal wiping mascara streaks from her cheeks.

Elyas emerged, covered in blood that wasn't his, and he met their eyes.

'They're trying,' he said. 'They had to perform CPR on her twice on the way in. They brought her back both times.'

The silence that followed was cavernous; to breathe was to invite death, to speak was to hurry it along.

'Sabr, brother. She's strong,' Idris said to Elyas. 'The strongest of all of us.'

But patience was hard to come by, and as Elyas slipped into the hospital chair, the blood on his shirt drying in stiff patches, he stared down at his shaking hands.

'I was talking about moving south yesterday. I told her it was time.' He crumpled into his hands.

Idris placed a hand on his shoulder. 'Don't let your mind go there, brother,' he said.

'She agreed it was best for Ahad,' he said, then stopped. 'Does he know?'

'He's home with Lirian and Sanam Khan,' said Sakina. 'He can come tomorrow when she's better.'

But hours passed and doctors came and went, saying things like 'internal bleeding', 'complications' and 'too soon to say'. Words that hung in the air like suspended grief.

When they finally let Elyas see her, he walked as if approaching a shrine, reverent, slow.

Jia lay under thin hospital sheets, her skin grey, a breathing tube down her throat, machines keeping her tethered to life.

And still she looked like herself. Even here, even now, she was the Khan.

'Can she hear me?' he asked the nurse.

'She's in a coma, but yes, she can hear you,' she said.

'The things you do to get away from me,' he whispered as he kissed her cheek, the tears welling in his eyes.

Outside the hospital, Benyamin stood in the car park, a blanket over his shoulders, fresh stitches in his brow and a bandage on his chest. His girlfriend had been shocked to see him brought in at the end of her shift.

She placed her arms around him as he sat down on the pavement, refusing to go back in.

He couldn't bring himself to sit in the waiting room. He had stared at enough hospital walls, waiting for news as his heart twisted inside his chest.

He could still see her car, still hear the sound of metal folding inward, still feel the guilt clawing through his veins.

He had wanted to start over, and instead, they were dragged back here.

'Jia…' he whispered, choking on her name again. 'I'm sorry.'

The storm broke overhead. He looked down at the dried blood on his hands and wondered how much more vengeance God would demand before He let Jia Khan go.

CHAPTER 71

Elyas's hands were wrapped in bandages. He had crawled from the twisted passenger side of their car, over crushed glass, oblivious to his pain, to get to her.

'Jia,' he whispered, standing beside the bed now as machines beeped around him. Her face was pale. Her hands, which had once gripped power, held their babies and caressed his face, now lay limp and mottled with bruises.

'Please don't leave me,' he said, his voice pleading.

He watched the nurse move around her. 'Please don't let her die, not now,' he said, cupping Jia's hand, his words more to God than the nurse.

He brushed a curl of damp hair from his wife's forehead. He thought of how she'd looked earlier that day, wrapped in red. Her smile, at last, had seemed unburdened. They had danced, and they had laughed. She had leaned into him and whispered, 'What do you want to do next?'

But the weight of all she carried – the family, the city, the legacy – had returned with interest, crushing her bones beneath it. He had known that something awful would happen if she stayed; he'd begged her to consider moving away with him, but she'd refused to hear it.

He pressed her fingers to his lips. 'Wake up and argue with me again,' he whispered. 'Tell me why I'm wrong, like you always do. I'll even let you win this one. Maybe.' His voice cracked as he said the words.

That's when he felt her fingers move beneath his palm.

He looked up, breath caught in his chest, as Jia Khan opened her eyes.

ACKNOWLEDGEMENTS

The first draft of this book was written sitting by a pool in Italy, thanks to a writing retreat organised by Writers Mosaic. I was there with a group of highly talented global majority writers, and evenings were spent talking about writing and shooting the breeze. The novel has benefited from being steeped in the kind of shared understanding that comes from conversations with people who make art, face the same struggles, and make you feel safe. To Colin, Gabriel, Clementine, Ishy, Amanda, Katy, Peter, Fiona, and Jo, thank you. Without you, this book would not have been what is. You are all incredibly talented and some of the smartest thinkers I've met. You made me braver.

Writers need space, time, and financial support to do what they love. Raj Khaira gave me that by showing me what sisterhood in action looks like. As a writer and creative, especially of colour, having someone talk money and finance, and open doors is rare. Raj, you are a gift from above. I love you.

My fabulous agent, Abi Fellows, you are always there with support, authentic advice and guidance. You are a rare breed. I am so grateful for your counsel.

Khola, thank you for reminding me I'm not crazy, it's everyone else that is. I would not make it without you.

Kokyee Ng, I cannot thank you enough for dragging me to fight club, and for making me laugh, as we wield knives. The fight scenes are better for it.

Poppy Mardall, you are the wisest woman and the safest space. I love you.

To my Chief of Staff, Saara for all the admin support and gentle nudging, for understanding my love of all things outside of the realms of logic and reason, for the homeopathy, and all the wuwu.

To the women of Brown Lady Brunch. You are the keepers of secrets, the holders of safe spaces, and two of the cleverest people I know. I always leave your company wanting to stay longer.

To Chris Ransom, thank you for all the excellent suggestions over Christmas dinner. You'll find none of them in this book!

Thank you to Zoe Cunningham for the title suggestion. More board games to come!

To Jenny Parrot who kicked off the trilogy, and for Wayne who brought it to a close. I am eternally grateful to you for making this possible. Thank you to Margot for always holding my hand at events, and for organising them.

To Nikesh Shukla, without whom the world may not have met Jia Khan, and to Arzu, my first editor.

To the bakers at Cut the Mustard, I ate way too many pastries whilst writing this book, but every mouthful was worth it.

To the principal at the Oxford College that told me I should be more like KFC. How do you like this chicken?

Thank you to everyone who has bought and read about Jia Khan over the last few years. She lives because you love her.

And to Adnan, if any of the sane ones had wanted to come home with me, we would not be here today. Put the kettle on love, you've pulled.

© Anna Crossley

Saima Mir has written for *The Times, Guardian* and *Independent*. Her essay for *It's Not About the Burqa* (Picador) appeared in *Guardian Weekend* and received over 250,000 hits online in two days. She has also contributed to the anthology *The Best, Most Awful Job: Twenty Writers Talk Honestly About Motherhood*. Saima grew up in Bradford and now lives in London.